One of the world's bestselling science fiction writers, Anne McCaffrey has won both the Hugo and Nebula awards. Brought up in the US and now living in Ireland, she is the creator and bestselling author of the unique Dragon series.

The Dragon Books of Anne McCaffrey can be read individually or as a series. However, for greatest enjoyment the following sequence is recommended:

Anne McCaffrey
All the Weyrs of Pern

CORGI BOOKS

ALL THE WEYRS OF PERN
A CORGI BOOK 0 552 13729 4

Originally published in Great Britain by Bantam Press,
a division of Transworld Publishers Ltd

PRINTING HISTORY
Bantam Press edition published 1991
Corgi edition published 1992 (twice)

This book was set in Palatino by
Falcon Typographic Art Ltd, Edinburgh

Corgi Books are published by Transworld Publishers Ltd,
61–63 Uxbridge Road, London W5 5SA, in Australia by
Transworld Publishers (Australia) Pty Ltd, 15–23 Helles Avenue,
Moorebank, NSW 2170, and in New Zealand by Transworld
Publishers (NZ) Ltd, 3 William Pickering Drive,
Albany, Auckland.

Printed and bound in Great Britain by
Cox & Wyman Ltd, Reading, Berks.

THIS BOOK IS MOST RESPECTFULLY DEDICATED TO

DRS JACK AND JUDY COHEN

who have enriched my life so much

Acknowledgements

The author gives full credit to Dr Jack Cohen once again for making fact out of my fiction and rationalizing the whimsies of my imagination.

The author would also thank Elizabeth Moon for her kind permission to use her poem in Chapter Fifteen which is credited to Journeywoman Harper Elimona.

The author and Dr Jack Cohen are fully aware that some of the procedures, and the development of new manufacturing techniques suggested in these pages would probably take many more months, years, to produce and effect than is here suggested. However, there are certain licences that an author, and her adviser, may take to produce a novel. Then, too, the Pernese had AIVAS to help them, didn't they?

Prologue

The Aivas felt its sensors responding to a renewal of power from the solar panels on the roof above it. The wind must have become strong enough to blow the clogging dust and volcanic ash away from the panels. There had been enough of these incidents over the past twenty-five hundred and twenty-five years so that Aivas had been able to maintain function, even if only at a very low maintenance level.

Running through the main operating circuits, Aivas found no malfunctions. Exterior optics were still obstructed but, once again, the Aivas was aware of some activity in its vicinity.

Was it possible that humans had returned to the Landing facility?

It had not as yet completed its priority assignment: to discover a means to destroy the organism that had been termed 'Thread' by the Captains. It had received no significant input to allow it to complete that task but the priority had not been cancelled.

Perhaps, with the return of humans, that assignment could be completed to their satisfaction.

Power began to swell its resources as the panels were uncovered: not as wind and weather would by a few layers. This removal was consistent with a workmanlike activity. As more of the panels were uncovered, solar energy recharged the long unused power collectors. The Aivas responded by distributing the revitalizing energy through its systems, running rapid function checks through circuits long unused.

Aivas had been efficiently designed and, as power continued to be available, it found itself in full running order by the time the exterior sensors had also been uncovered.

Humans had returned to Landing! Many of them! Once again Humankind had triumphed over tremendous odds. Aivas duly noticed through its adjustable optical elements that they were still accompanied by the creatures called firedragons. Noise, too, was now filtering through the audio channels: human voices speaking in unusual word patterns. A lingual shift? In twenty-five hundred and twenty-five years, that was entirely likely. Aivas listened and interpreted, measuring the altered vowels and slurred consonants against the speech patterns which had been programmed into it. It organized the new sounds into groups and checked them with its semantics program.

Within its vision now came an immense white creature. The descendant of the bio-engineer's first production? Aivas did a rapid extrapolation from the bio-lab's files and reached the inescapable conclusion that the so-called dragons had also matured and prospered. It searched for, but did not find 'white', in the parameters of the engineered species.

Not only had humankind survived the incursion of Thread for twenty-five hundred and twenty-five years of Threadfall but it had flourished. The species had the tenacity to survive where others succumbed.

If they had been able to return from the Northern continent, had they also managed to destroy the organism? That would be well done. What must Aivas then do if its priority was superseded?

Humankind, with its insatiable curiosity and restlessness, would undoubtedly have new tasks which an artificial intelligence voice address system could undertake. It was not, Aivas knew from its memory banks, a complacent species. Soon those who worked to clear the debris of centuries would uncover the entire building and reach its position. It must, of course, react as its programs ordained.

The Aivas waited.

Chapter One

B y the time the AIVAS had finished its recital of the first nine years of the colonization of Pern, the sun Rukbat had set with an unusually fine display. Not that many of the reverent listeners of the history which the Artificial Intelligence Voice Address System narrated were aware of such externals.

During the hours that the Aivas' resonant tones had filled the chamber and penetrated to the hallway beyond, more people had crowded in to hear what it said, and jostled each other to get an occasional look at the incredible moving pictures with which Aivas illustrated his narrative. Those Lords Holder and Craftmasters hastily summoned by fire-lizard messengers willingly crowded into the stuffy inner room.

Lord Jaxom of Ruatha had asked his white dragon, Ruth, to summon the Benden Weyrleaders so they were the first to join the Masterharper Robinton and Mastersmith Fandarel. Lessa and F'lar slid on to the stools which Jaxom and the Journeyman Harper Piemur vacated for them. Piemur frowned at his mate Journeywoman Jancis, when she started to get down and gestured to Breide, standing a-gawk in the doorway, to bring more seating. When F'nor, the Benden wingleader, came, he sat on the floor where he had to crane his neck to see the screen, becoming too engrossed in the history to notice discomfort.

The small chamber was crowded but room was made for the Lords Holder, Groghe of Fort, Asgenar of Lemos and Larad of Telgar. By then, Jaxom had been pushed back to the doorway and there he politely, but firmly, refused entry to anyone else.

Subtly the Aivas increased its volume so that the tale was audible to all those in the corridor. No-one seemed to mind the stifling closeness of room and corridor though matters improved when someone considerately passed around water and redfruit juice, and later meatrolls. Someone also had the foresight to open as many of the windows in the building as possible, thus circulating some air down the corridor, though little enough reached the Aivas chamber.

'The final message received by this facility from Captain Keroon was to confirm that Fort Hold was operational. This message was logged in at 1700, fourth day of the tenth month, eleventh year after Landing.'

When the Aivas ceased speaking, there was a profound and awed silence, finally broken by small scufflings as people shifted, almost apologetically, from long-held positions. A few polite coughs were quickly muffled.

Feeling it incumbent on him to make some response to these historic and unexpected revelations, the Masterharper cleared his throat.

'We are deeply indebted to you, Aivas, for this amazing tale,' Robinton spoke with deep humility and respect. A murmur of gratitude circulated room and corridor. 'We have lost so much of our early history: it's been reduced to myth and legend in many cases. You have clarified much that puzzled us. But why does it end so abruptly?'

'There was no further input from the authorized operators.'

'Why not?'

'No explanation was given. Failing prior instructions, this facility continued observations until the solar panels became clogged and power was reduced to the minimum needed to retain core integrity.'

'Those panels are the source of your power?' asked Fandarel, his bass voice rumbling with eagerness.

'Yes.'

'Those pictures? How did you do that?' Fandarel's usual reserved manner was discarded in his excitement.

'You no longer have recording devices?'

'No,' Fandarel shook his head in disgust, 'among many of the other marvels you mentioned in passing. Can you teach us what we have forgotten?' And Fandarel's eyes glowed in anticipation.

'The memory banks contain Planetary Engineering and Colonizing data and the multi-cultural and historical files considered relevant by the Colony Administrators.' Although Aivas delivered that answer in a discreetly muted voice, Master Robinton was not the only one to glance over his shoulder to see if those in the hall had heard that statement.

The others within the room also reacted warily but those beyond the doorway and down the corridor were involved in low-voiced private conversations and minor arguments.

Before Fandarel could organize another question, F'lar held up one hand.

'With respect, Master Fandarel, we all have questions to ask Aivas.' He turned around to signal Master Esselin and the ubiquitous Breide to come to the door. 'I want this corridor cleared, Master Esselin. This room is not to be entered without express permission from one of us present now. Do I make myself plain?' He looked sternly from one to the other.

'Indeed, Weyrleader, perfectly plain,' Breide said, his manner as obsequious as ever but he was clearly dazed by what Aivas had said and shown.

'Of course, Weyrleader, certainly, Weyrleader,' Master Esselin said, bowing with each use of F'lar's title.

'Breide, make sure you report today's event to Lord Toric,' F'lar added, knowing perfectly well that Breide would do just that without permission. 'Esselin, bring enough glowbaskets to light the hall and the adjacent rooms. Bring a few cots or pallets, as well, and blankets. Some food.'

'And wine. Don't forget wine, F'lar,' called Robinton, raising his voice above the hubbub caused by Esselin's officious manner of implementing F'lar's instructions.

11

'Benden wine, if you please, Esselin, and make that two wineskins. This could be very thirsty work,' he added in a conversational tone, grinning at Lessa.

'Well, you're not going to drink up two skinsful, Robinton,' Lessa said at her sternest, 'talking yourself hoarse with Aivas. Which I can see is what you have in mind. I'd say you already had quite enough excitement for one day. It's certainly more than I can believe in one day.'

'Be assured, Madam Lessa,' Aivas said in a placatory voice, 'that every word you have heard is factual.'

Lessa turned towards the screen which had displayed marvels to her, images of people she knew were dust centuries ago and objects totally foreign to her eyes. 'I don't doubt you, Aivas. I doubt my ability to absorb half the wonders you have described and shown us.'

'Be assured that you have achieved wonders of your own,' Aivas replied, 'to survive the menace that nearly overwhelmed the settlers. Are those immense and magnificent creatures ranged on the slopes outside the descendants of the dragons which Madam Kitti Ping Yung created?'

'Yes, they are,' Lessa replied with proprietary pride. 'The golden queen is Ramoth . . .'

'The largest dragon on all Pern,' the Masterharper said in a sly tone, his eyes twinkling.

Lessa started to glare at him but burst out laughing instead. 'Well, she is.'

'The bronze who is probably resting beside her is Mnementh and I am his rider,' F'lar said, grinning at his mate's discomfort.

'How do you know what is outside?' Fandarel blurted out.

'The exterior sensors of this facility are now operational.'

'Exterior sensors . . .' and Fandarel subsided into silent amazement.

'And the white one?' Aivas went on, 'it . . .'

'*He*,' said Jaxom firmly, but without rancour, 'is Ruth and I am his rider.'

'Remarkable. The bio-engineering report indicated that there were to be five variations, imitating the genetic material of the fire-dragons.'

'Ruth is a sport,' Jaxom replied. He had long since stopped being defensive about his dragon. Ruth had his own special abilities.

'A part of *our* history,' Robinton said soothingly.

'Which,' Lessa said with another stern glare at the Harper, 'will wait until some of us have rested.'

'My curiosity will be contained, Madam.'

Lessa darted a suspicious look at the dim screen panel. 'You have curiosity? And what is this "madam"?'

'Gathering information is not restricted to the curious. Madam is a title of respect.'

'Lessa's respectful title is Weyrwoman, Aivas,' F'lar said with another grin. 'Or Ramoth's rider.'

'And yours, sir?'

'Weyrleader or Mnementh's rider. You have already met Masterharper Robinton, Harper Journeyman Piemur, Journeywoman Jancis, and Lord Jaxom of Ruatha Hold but let me make known to you the Mastersmith Fandarel, Lord Groghe of Fort Hold which we have always known was the first to be founded—' F'lar hid a grin at Lord Groghe's suddenly modest demeanour. '—though certainly not why. Lord of Telgar, Larad, and Lord of Lemos, Asgenar.'

'Lemos? Indeed,' and, before the listeners could react to the mild surprise in Aivas's tone, he continued: 'It is good to know that the name Telgar survived.'

'We have lost the knowledge of the naming,' Larad murmured. 'And are prouder to know that the sacrifices of Sallah and Tarvi are remembered so lastingly.'

'Aivas,' F'lar said, standing himself square with the screen, 'you said that you were attempting to discover where Thread came from and how to exterminate it. Did you come to any conclusion?'

'Several. The organism known as Thread is somehow attracted to the eccentric planet which, at aphelion, pierces the Oort Cloud; as it approaches perihelion, it drags matter with it into this sector of space. This trailing cloud disgorged a little of its burden into the skies of this planet. Calculations indicated that this would continue for approximately fifty years at which time the material in Pern's orbit would be exhausted. Calculations also indicated that there would be

13

recurrences of the phenomenon at intervals of two hundred and fifty years, give or take a decade either way.'

F'lar glanced about him to see if anyone had understood what the Aivas was saying.

'With due respect, Aivas, we do not understand your explanation,' the Harper said in a wry tone. 'A great deal of time has passed since Admiral Benden and Governor Boll led the settlers north. We are currently in the twentieth Turn – what you call a year, I think – of the Ninth Pass of the Red Star.'

'Noted.'

'It has always been *assumed*,' and F'lar emphasized that word, 'that Thread came from the Red Star.'

'It is not a star: the most reasonable explanation is that it is a stray planet, probably drawn out of its native system by some odd event, travelling through space until it was attracted by Rukbat's gravitational pull and became trapped in this system. The matter you call Thread does not come from its surface. It originates in the Oort Cloud of this system.'

'And just what is an Oort Cloud?' Master Fandarel asked in the most ingenuous manner.

'According to the Dutch astronomer Jan Oort, the eponymous cloud is composed of material orbiting a sun far beyond the orbit of its outermost planet. Cometary material leaks from the Cloud into the inner part of the system. In the particular case of Rukbat, some of the material is hard-shelled ovoids which change in a peculiar manner, losing their outer layers and attenuating on contact with the upper atmosphere, falling to the surface in what has been termed "Thread"; this resembles a voracious organism that devours carbon-based organic material.'

Fandarel blinked in his attempt to digest that gout of information.

'Well, you did ask, Master Fandarel,' Piemur remarked with a mischievous expression.

'Your explanations only confuse us, Aivas, for none of us have the learning to understand them,' F'lar said, lifting a hand to indicate he was not to be interrupted. 'But if you knew, and presumably our ancestors knew, what Thread

14

was and where it came from, why didn't they destroy its source?'

'By the time this facility reached those conclusions, Weyrleader, your ancestors had removed to the northern continent and did not return to receive the report.'

Silence, a depressed and defeated silence, prevailed over the room.

'But we are here now,' Robinton said, straightening up on his stool. 'And we can receive your report.'

'If we can understand it,' F'lar added drolly.

'This facility has educational programmes which can supply remedial teaching in all branches of science. The prime directive given this unit by Captains Keroon and Tillek as well as Admiral Benden and Governor Boll was to gather information and formulate a course of action that would end the threat posed by these incursions.'

'Then it is possible to remove the threat of Thread?' F'lar asked, carefully schooling his expression to reveal none of the hope that he was feeling.

'The possibility exists, Weyrleader.'

'WHAT?' was the incredulous response of everyone in the room.

'The possibility exists, Weyrleader, but will require tremendous effort from you and quite likely the majority of your population. First, you must be able to understand scientific language and learn to work with advanced technology. In addition, access to the main banks of the *Yokohama* must be obtained to add to relevant data on asteroid positions. Then a course of action can be initiated that could probably result in the cessation of these incursions.'

'Possibility? Probably result. But the possibility exists?' F'lar strode to the screen and put a hand on each side of its subtly glowing blankness. 'I would do anything – ANYTHING – to rid Pern of Thread.'

'If you are prepared to relearn lost skills and perfect them, the possibility does exist.'

'And you *would* help us?'

'You would require assistance from this facility but the end of these incursions remains the major priority.'

'Not half as much as it is of ours!' F'lar replied. F'nor fervently seconded him.

The Lords Holder exchanged quick glances, hope warring with surprise. The destruction of all Thread was what F'lar had promised them nineteen Turns ago when he had become leader of Pern's then single Weyr. Benden's brave wings of dragons and riders had been all that stood between the certain reduction of mankind on Pern to hunters and gatherers by the totally unexpected resumption of Threadfall after a lapse of four hundred Turns. In their extremity, the Lords Holder had promised support of all his emergency measures. Struggling with the exigencies of the Pass, they had quite forgotten his vow. But all three were quick to perceive the advantages to *them* – if they could also see the disadvantages to the dragonriders – to be quit of their ancient responsibilities. Of them all Jaxom, as both rider and Holder, regarded F'lar with consternation. Yet there was no doubt the Benden Weyrleader meant exactly what he said. That he would do all he could to rid Pern of Thread for ever.

'Then there is much to be done,' Aivas said in a brisk tone. Almost, Master Robinton thought, as if the thing was relieved to have employment after so long a recess. 'Your Records, Masters Robinton and Fandarel, would be of immense value in assessing your history and potential, and what knowledge of science you currently possess. Certainly a synopsis of your own history would assist such an evaluation of the educational programmes required to achieve your goal.'

'The Harper Hall has assiduously kept accounts,' the Harper said eagerly, allowing the Mastersmith time to ponder Aivas's explanation about the origin of Thread, 'though the oldest of them have become illegible over the hundreds of Turns which have passed. I think the more recent Records of the twenty Turns of this current Pass would inform you adequately. Jaxom, could you and Ruth possibly go to the Harper Hall and collect them?' The young Lord Holder immediately rose. 'If you wouldn't mind, bring Sebell and Menolly', and Robinton glanced at F'lar who nodded emphatically, 'back with you?'

'The Records of my Crafthall,' Fandarel began, inching forward on his stool, wringing his huge hands together in an uncharacteristic gesture of tension, 'are missing so many words and explanations: perhaps even one about this Oort Cloud. Generally what's missing is just where we cannot possibly figure out what was meant from the context. If you were able to tell us what words were missing or corrupted, you would be granting us the most valuable assistance to our efforts at self improvement.'

He was about to continue when Robinton's hand on his shoulder stopped him. They all heard Master Esselin come bustling down the corridor, directing those who carried food, cups and wineskins to hand them over to Jancis and Piemur. He peremptorily gestured those carrying pallets and blankets into the smaller adjacent rooms. At a nod from F'lar, he hurried back down the corridor, out of earshot.

'A moment, dear friend,' Robinton said when Fandarel was about to continue his request for help. 'Aivas, you may have all the information the Colonists considered relevant, but I don't really think we should dispense it without due consideration.'

'Exactly what I was about to say,' F'lar added.

'Discretion is a built-in feature of this Aivas model, Masterharper, Weyrleader. You should discuss among you who is to have access to this facility and in exactly what ways it may be of use to you.'

The Masterharper groaned, holding his head in both hands and was immediately surrounded by Lessa, Piemur and Jaxom.

'I'm all right, I'm all right,' he said testily, waving them off. 'Have you all realized just what this source of knowledge can mean to us?' he asked, his voice rough with emotion. 'I've only now begun to absorb how profoundly this discovery could change our lives.'

'I've been struggling to absorb that myself,' F'lar said with a grim smile. 'If this Aivas knows something about Thread and the Red Star that would help us . . .' F'lar halted with a wry smile and held up his hand. 'First, I believe it is extremely important to decide the question of who should be permitted into this room. As

17

you pointed out, Robinton, Aivas cannot be accessible to everyone.'

'Definitely,' Master Robinton said and took a long swig of the wine he had poured for himself. 'Definitely. Considering that crowd in the hall, there's no way we can censor the discovery of Aivas nor,' and he held up his hand at the protests, 'do I think we should. However,' and he grinned, 'we can't just have anyone who wants to popping up here and monopolizing . . . this . . .'

'Facility,' Piemur put in, his expression genuinely thoughtful. 'When word of Aivas gets about, there'll be any number of people who'll want to talk to Aivas just to say that they had, because they don't grasp its significance.'

'For once I agree with you, Piemur,' Lessa said. She looked around her. 'I think there're enough in this room right now with a real need to talk to Aivas and the common sense and courtesy to know when to stop,' and she paused to cast a stern eye on Master Robinton who grinned back amiably. 'Certainly we are representative of the planet – Weyrleaders, Masters and Lords Holder so no-one can say Aivas is being monopolized by one group. Or is that too many, Aivas?'

'No,' and for some reason this easy acceptance made the Masterharper grin. 'The authority may be expanded or contracted as may be deemed necessary. To recapitulate, it is permitted for you,' and all those in the room were named in the pleasant baritone tones.

'And Jaxom,' Piemur added quickly since Jaxom had gone on Robinton's errand and someone needed to speak up for the third party to this discovery.

'And Lord Jaxom of Ruatha Hold, to command my services. Is that correct? Very good. The necessary voice prints have been registered and this facility will respond to no others, or in the presence of others, until further notice.'

'As an added precaution,' Master Robinton said, 'to change that roster, there must be one of the Weyrleaders, one Master and one Lord present in this room.' He glanced about to see if this precaution was acceptable.

Just then, Esselin bustled down the corridor to ask if there were any further orders for the night.

'Yes, Esselin, assign the most responsible and least curious of your men to guard the building's entrance. Only Lord Jaxom and those who accompany him are to be permitted to enter the building tonight.'

By the time Esselin had assured F'lar of his total cooperation, a rather tense discussion had started between Fandarel and Larad as to which Crafthalls should have precedence in learning from Aivas.

'If I may interject a suggestion,' Aivas startled them by saying with a volume sufficient to interrupt all ongoing conversations, 'it is a relatively simple matter to expand this facility to accommodate many requirements.' When the silence lengthened, Aivas added in a milder, almost apologetic tone, 'that is, if the contents of the Catherine Caves are still intact and undamaged?' The voice lifted at the end of the sentence.

'Do you mean the caves at the southern side of the grid?' Piemur asked.

'Those would be the ones and these are the objects required to supply additional stations.' The screen displayed a variety of items to the bewilderment of the watchers.

'Your beaded panels, Piemur,' Jancis said, clutching at his sleeve with one hand and pointing excitedly with the other.

'You're right,' said Piemur. 'What are they, Aivas? We seem to have boxes and boxes of them, all different sorts.'

'Those are computer cards,' and somehow the ring in Aivas's measured tone betrayed a discreet excitement. 'Were there also any of these objects?' And boxes were displayed with screens that now were seen as smaller replicas of the screen facing them and rectangles resembling what Aivas had identified as a touch panel.

'Yes,' Master Robinton said with surprise. 'I couldn't think what they might be when I saw them, swathed in that thick film.'

'If there are sufficient parts in good working order, then there need be no contention for access to this facility. These were the remainder of the ordinary teaching processors. All other voice activated units were packaged for

19

shipment to the north, but these elementary models will admirably suit the current need. With sufficient power, up to twelve stations can be accommodated without affecting response time.'

Once again the audience lapsed into numb silence.

'Do I understand you correctly?' Fandarel began, after clearing his throat, 'that you can *divide* yourself into twelve segments?'

'That is correct.'

'How can you do that?' Fandarel demanded, spreading his arms as wide as he could in disbelief.

'Surely, Mastersmith, you do not limit yourself to one hearth, or anvil or forge, one hammer, one fire?'

'Of course not, but I have many men . . .'

'This facility is not a single hearth or fire or hammer, but many and each can work as diligently as the other.'

'This I find very hard to understand,' Fandarel admitted, scratching his balding pate and shaking his head.

'Before you is a machine, Mastersmith, which can be segmented and each discrete part can function as a separate tool.'

'I don't begin to understand how you can do that, Aivas, but if you can, it would certainly solve the problems of priorities,' Master Robinton said, grinning from ear to ear. Oh, the questions of past paradoxes which could now be answered by this marvellous creature! He took a large pull of his wine.

'To create these separate tools,' Aivas went on, 'will, in itself, provide the first of many lessons that must be understood before you will be ready to attack your primary objective, the annihilation of Thread.'

'By all means, let us begin then,' F'lar said, rubbing his hands together, infused with the first stirrings of real hope he had felt during the last few gruelling Turns of the current Pass.

'There isn't enough space in here for a dozen of us all talking with a dozen of you, Aivas,' Lord Larad of Telgar said reasonably.

'There are other rooms in this building which can be utilized. Indeed, it would be wise to have separate offices and perhaps one larger room where many could observe and learn. It is best to begin at the beginning,' Aivas said and suddenly sheets began to roll out of a slot to one side of the main screen, 'and these are the items that will be needed in the morning, the tools that will be required to construct the additional stations, and a diagram of how to redesign this building to accommodate them.'

Being nearest, Piemur caught the sheets as they were spewed out. Jancis came to his aid.

'More material will soon be needed for the printer,' Aivas went on. 'Rolls should be stored in the Catherine Caves with the other supplies. Paper would be an acceptable substitute.'

'Paper?' Larad exclaimed. 'Wood pulp paper?'

'If nothing else is available, that will do.'

'It would seem, Asgenar,' F'lar said with a chuckle, 'that the skills of Master Bendarek were not developed a Turn too soon.'

'You have lost the skill of extruding plastic from silicates?' Aivas asked and Master Robinton thought he heard a note of surprise in its voice.

'Silicates?' Master Fandarel asked.

'But one of the many skills we have lost,' Robinton said ruefully. 'We will make diligent pupils.'

The flow of sheets stopped and, as Piemur and Jancis sorted them, they realized that there were six copies of each page. When they had assembled the sheets, they looked around at those in the room expectantly.

'Not tonight,' said Lessa firmly. 'You'd break your necks stumbling about those caves in the dark. We've waited this long, we can wait until morning. And I think that we all should,' and now she swung around to pinion the Masterharper with a stern eye, 'either seek a bed for the night or go back where we belong.'

'My dear Weyrwoman,' Robinton began, pulling himself erect, 'nothing, absolutely nothing, including your direst threat would compel me . . .' And suddenly he seemed to wilt and fold in on himself. Piemur caught the cup before it fell from the Harper's hand. As he supported his Master's limp body, he had a smug smile on his face.

'Except of course the fellis juice I put in his last cup of wine,' Piemur said by way of explanation. 'So let's get him to bed.' F'lar and Larad immediately started forward when Fandarel held up one huge hand. Picking up the long Harper in his arms, he nodded to Jancis to show him where to bed the sleeping Robinton.

'Piemur, you haven't changed, have you?' Lessa said, with a mock scowl which turned to a grin for his deception. Then, because she wondered at what this machine would think of what it saw, she added, 'Aivas, Masterharper Robinton often lets his enthusiasm get the better of his well-being.'

'This facility is able to monitor for physical stress,' Aivas said. 'The Masterharper emanated considerable excitement but nothing harmful.'

'You are a Healer as well?' F'lar exclaimed.

'No, Weyrleader, but this facility is equipped to monitor the vital signs of those in this room. However, the medical information stored in files was updated to state-of-the-art at the time the expedition departed for this system. Your medics may wish to avail themselves of this information.'

F'lar's groan was audible. 'Master Oldive must come here as soon as possible.'

'Half the planet must come as soon as possible,' Lessa said tartly and gave a gusty sigh. 'I doubt twelve of Aivas will be half enough.'

'Then let us organize ourselves,' Fandarel said, returning from his errand. 'We must contain our excitement and direct our energies in the most efficient way . . .' There were chuckles at the Mastersmith's use of his favourite word. 'You may laugh but you know it is only sensible, and time-saving, to work efficiently and we are each going in several directions at once tonight. We cannot but be stimulated by this sudden gift from our ancestors but we should do nothing hasty. I will go back to Telgar Crafthold now, if F'nor and Canth will be so kind. I shall make suitable arrangements and draft the services of those who can help us delve into the caves to find the required materials; and to find people to understand the diagrams Aivas has printed for us. But tomorrow is soon enough.

F'nor?' And, raising his hairy eyebrows at the brown rider, Fandarel nodded to one and all, and bowing courteously to the screen, took his leave.

'A moment, F'nor,' Larad said, 'for I should return to Telgar. Asgenar, do you join us?'

Asgenar looked about him and smiled ruefully. 'I think I'd better leave now. My mind is seething with questions to put to Aivas yet I don't think I could actually come out with a sensible query. I'll bring Bendarek with me in the morning.'

Lord Groghe, who had said very little but looked exceedingly thoughtful, asked N'ton to return him to Fort Hold.

'Jancis and I will stay here in case Master Robinton wakes,' Piemur told Lessa and F'lar. Then his mischievous grin surfaced, 'and I won't ask my eight thousand five hundred and thirty-two burning questions all in one breath either.'

'Then I think we all bid you good night now, Aivas,' F'lar said, turning toward the dark screen.

'Good night,' was the response and the lights of the room dimmed to a faint glow and the one pulsing green light on the bottom left-hand corner.

With Ruth festooned with sacks, Jaxom arrived two hours later with both Masterharpers, Sebell and Menolly. By considerably reducing the level of *klah* in the beakers Esselin had provided, Piemur had managed to stay awake while Jancis got a nap.

'One of us has to be alert tomorrow,' she told the young journeyman, 'and organize people. I'm better at that than you are, love,' she'd added, with a kiss to sweeten the comment.

Piemur had no quarrel with that, for a variety of personal reasons, and settled her with a mock paternal kiss on a pallet in the room beyond Master Robinton.

Despite his joke about not asking questions, when Piemur returned to the Aivas room, he found that he couldn't immediately formulate a single intelligent query. Instead, with cup in hand and the beaker beside him, Piemur sat, bereft of words, in the semi-gloom of the chamber.

'Aivas?' he began tentatively.

'Yes, Journeyman Piemur?' The room brightened enough for Piemur to see clearly.

'How do you do that?' Piemur asked, startled.

'The panels which you and Mastersmith Jancis exposed yesterday are capable of drawing energy from the sun: it is called solar power. When all the panels are exposed, an hour's bright illumination will power this unit for twelve hours.'

'You're not going to have ordinary usage from now on,' Piemur said with a snort.

'A query: you apparently utilize the luminescent organism in handlights but do you not have some sort of power generation, perhaps hydro-electric power?'

'Hydro-electric?' Piemur's quick ear allowed him to repeat the unfamiliar words accurately.

'The production of electric current by the energy of moving water.'

'Master Fandarel uses water wheels in Telgar Smithcrafthold to drive the big hammers and the forge bellows, but electric is an unfamiliar word. Unless that's what Fandarel does with those acid tanks of his.'

'Acid tanks? Batteries?'

Piemur shrugged. 'I don't know what he calls them. I'm a harper. Electrics out of water power? So long as it is efficient, Master Fandarel will love it.'

'Would Master Fandarel's equipment resemble this structure?' The screen suddenly lit up with a diagram of a water wheel.

'That's it. How did you know?'

'This is the most frequent primitive application. Have you explored the Landing site, Journeyman Piemur?'

'I don't need my title all the time, Aivas: Piemur is enough.'

'No disrespect would be construed?'

'Not from me, Aivas. Some of the Lords Holder get a bit touchy but Jaxom doesn't, nor Larad and Asgenar. Lessa can be sticky but not F'lar, or F'nor or N'ton. And yes, I've explored the Landing site. What should I be looking for?'

The screen displayed a complex mechanism, set at the base of the river hill.

'Nothing there now like that,' Piemur said, shaking his head.

'As Mastersmith Fandarel already uses water wheels, a new installation can be erected so that this facility is not dependent on the solar panels which will be inadequate for the projected demands just discussed.'

'They didn't store away any of your panels in the caves?'

'No.'

'How can you be sure?' Piemur found such didacticism irritating. It would be totally unfair if this . . . this intelligence was always right.

'The list of items in the Catherine Caves is available data and does not include spare panels.'

'It must be nice to know everything,' he said.

'Accuracy is required of an Aivas system and a very large data base – what you call "Knowledge". But you must not believe that the data base can contain "everything". But sufficient to realize the priorities.'

'A harper has to be accurate, too,' Piemur said in a sour tone. Master Fandarel's search for efficiency had always had, for Piemur, its humorous side. He wasn't sure if Aivas's rectitude would be received with the same tolerance.

'A harper – one who plays a harp, an instrument?' Aivas asked.

'I do that, too,' Piemur replied, his capricious humour revived as he realized that Aivas did not know very much at all about present day Pern. 'The primary function of the Harper Hall is, however, to teach, to communicate and, at need, to arbitrate.'

'Not to entertain?'

'We do that, too – it's a good way to teach something as well – and there are many who only do that, but the more skilled of us have multiple duties. It would be presumptuous of me to usurp Master Robinton's right to enlighten you on that account. Although, in actual fact, he is no longer *the* Masterharper of Pern. Sebell is, because

25

Master Robinton had a nearly fatal heart attack and was made to retire from active service to the Harper Hall. Not that he *has* retired, despite being in Cove Hold now, because of all that has happened since Jaxom discovered Landing and the Ship Meadow, and then the caves.' Piemur halted, realizing that he was rattling on. Just like him to want to impress Aivas with his own knowledge but Piemur was experiencing an intense need to anchor his personal values in the presence of this superior intelligence.

'Sebell, who is now Masterharper of all Pern, is on his way with the Records,' he went on. 'And Menolly. They may look young to you but they are the most important people in the Harper Hall.' Then he added deferentially. 'But you should know that Master Robinton is the most honoured and respected man on Pern. The dragons kept him from dying. That's how important he is.'

'The dragons then have been a successful experiment?' Aivas asked.

'Experiment?' Piemur was indignant and then subsided with a rueful chuckle. 'I wouldn't let the Weyrleaders hear you calling their dragons "experiments".'

'The advice is appreciated.'

Piemur eyed the screen for a moment. 'You mean that, don't you?'

'Yes. The culture and societies of your present day Pern have evolved and altered considerably from the early days of the colony. It is incumbent on this facility to learn the new protocol and thus avoid giving unnecessary offence. The dragons have, therefore, become important above and beyond their initial role in the aerial defence of the planet?'

'They are the most important creatures on the planet. We couldn't survive without them.' Piemur's voice rang with pride and gratitude.

'Without intending any offence, is it currently acceptable to maintain the sports of the breed?'

Piemur snorted. 'You mean Ruth? He and Jaxom are exceptions – to a lot of rules. He's a Lord Holder and shouldn't ever have Impressed a dragon. But he did, and because they thought Ruth wouldn't survive long, he was allowed to be raised.'

'That is contradictory.'

'I know, but Ruth's special. He always knows *when* he is in time.'

The resultant pause did much to assuage Piemur's feelings of inferiority. He had stumped the Aivas.

'Your remark is unclear.'

'You did know that dragons can move instantaneously *between* one place and another?'

'That was a basic ability of the fire-dragons from whose genetic material the dragons were originally bio-engineered. It was similar to teleportation we found in some species on several other planets.'

'Well, dragons can also move *between* one time and another. Lessa did, and Jaxom,' and Piemur grinned, being one of the few people to know exactly when and why Jaxom had moved *between* one time and another.

'But it's an exceedingly dangerous ability and severely discouraged. Very few dragons have Ruth's sense of time and space. So, if a dragonrider times it without his Weyrleader's express permission, he gets royally reamed! If he hasn't come to grief messing around with timing, that is.'

'Would you be good enough to explain in what circumstances timing is permissible?'

Piemur had already berated himself for mentioning Jaxom's little excursion. He should have kept it to Lessa's adventure which was already part of the fabric of recent history. So Piemur switched to a less sensitive subject and told Aivas in detail the tale of Lessa's heroic ride on Ramoth: how she had brought the five lost Weyrs of Pern forward in time to save those in the Present Pass from annihilation. Even if he said so himself, Piemur thought he recited it with considerable flair. Though Aivas made no comment throughout, Piemur sensed that this unusual audience heard, and remembered, every word.

'A spectacularly brave and daring exploit, clearly of epic proportions despite the considerable risk she ran in losing both herself and the queen Ramoth. The results clearly justified the journey,' was Aivas's opinion which was more praise than Piemur had expected. He grinned with satisfaction that he had managed to impress the thing. 'You mentioned that the Long Interval caused the decline of the Weyrs' authority and its prominence in your society. Do you know how many times the cycle has been similarly altered?'

'The cycle?'

'Yes, how many times has the orbit of what you call the Red Star, failed to bring Thread to Pern?'

'Oh, you mean how many Long Intervals? There have been two recorded in our history. We were told that long intervals would occur, but I don't know who knew that. That's why so many people were so certain, right up till the time we had our first Fall of this Pass, that Thread had actually disappeared for ever.'

From her favourite spot, wrapped loosely about Piemur's neck, his golden fire-lizard roused and gave a warning cheep.

'Sensors register that the lump on your shoulder is actually a creature clinging to you.'

'Oh, that's only Farli, my queen fire-lizard.'

'The creatures have remained in contact with you?'

'Yes and no.' Piemur did not think there'd be time to give Aivas the recent history of fire-lizards. 'She just told me that Ruth and Jaxom have returned with the records and Sebell and Menolly.' Piemur stood up, draining the last of the *klah* from his cup. 'Then you'll know all that's happened this Pass. Which hasn't been dull at all but you – you sort of cap it.'

Piemur could hear the exchange of low-voiced conversation down the hallway and he started to the entrance in case Esselin's guards were being officious. He had taken no more than a few steps when the three, Jaxom, Sebell and Menolly, bowed under the weight of the sacks they were carrying, came striding down the hall. Piemur held up a hand for them to lower their voices, unnaturally loud in the night quiet. Menolly, her dark hair still tangled from her flying cap, reached Piemur first.

'Where's Master Robinton?' Menolly asked, looking about her, her narrow, elegant features reflecting her perpetual anxiety for her mentor.

28

'In there, Menolly,' Piemur said, pointing. 'As if we'd risk him.'

She thrust her heavy sack at him and ducked into the room to reassure herself, while Piemur smiled tolerantly.

'And they left you to mind Aivas all on your own?' Jaxom asked in a whisper. 'Learned all the secrets of the universe yet?'

Piemur gave a snort. 'As it turned out, I answered his – its – questions. But it was interesting all the same,' Piemur said. 'And gave him – it – a few tips to the wise.' He laid his finger along his nose, grinning. 'Which is a harper function.'

Sebell, looking browner than ever in the dimly lit corridor, gave Piemur the slow smile which added considerable charm to the handsome intelligent face of the tall Masterharper.

'According to Jaxom, this Aivas of yours is a tale spinner to shame the best of us, with knowledge of all that we were, and what we can be.'

'Well, I suspect Aivas might well create more problems than he solves,' Piemur said, 'but I guarantee you it'll be exciting.' He helped Jaxom remove the Records, carefully, from the sacks. 'Aivas is right interested in you and Ruth, too.'

'What have you been telling him?' Jaxom asked in what Piemur privately called his Lord Holder attitude.

'Me? Nothing you'd object to, friend,' Piemur hastily reassured him. Jaxom could still be touchy about other people discussing Ruth. 'I spent more time reciting Lessa's ride which he said was of epic proportions.' Piemur grinned broadly.

As Piemur talked, Sebell had been taking in the details of the room, his eyes resting on the strange wall furnishings. Sebell rarely rushed in the way he, Piemur, did.

'And this Aivas has preserved itself from our first days on Pern?' Sebell let out a long soft whistle. He tapped one of the clear panels and looked around the room. 'Where does it store its records? Jaxom said it displayed amazing pictures of our past as well.'

'Aivas, speak for yourself,' Piemur suggested cockily,

wanting to see how Sebell handled the entity. Or Menolly who entered just then. 'Aivas?' he prompted, 'this is Sebell Masterharper of Pern, Master Robinton's successor, and Master Menolly, Pern's ablest composer.' When there was still no response from Aivas, Piemur felt his irritation rising. 'They've brought the records for you to read.'

Aivas remained silent.

'Maybe it's used up the power stored in the sun panels,' he said, forcing himself to keep his tone light as he wondered how the Aivas could be forced into answering. He scowled at the unresponsive screen, at the green pulse winking in the corner. The feckless thing was awake so it had to be listening. 'I don't understand,' he said to the others, disgusted by the inactivity. 'He was talking up a storm to me just before you came . . . Oh, shards!' And Piemur dramatically slapped his forehead with one palm. 'Neither you nor Menolly are on his list yet.'

'His list?' Jaxom asked, the frown on his face indicating that he suffered the same irritation that Piemur did in Aivas's silence.

'Yes, his list,' Piemur said, sighing wearily and sagging on to the nearest stool. 'The people he is authorized to speak to. Master Robinton and the others decided to limit those who have access to Aivas.'

'But *I* was here,' Jaxom exclaimed.

'Oh, he'll probably talk to you once Sebell and Menolly leave. It got set up so that it takes a Weyrleader, a Lord and a Masterharper for Aivas to add someone to the privileged list.'

'Well, I'm Lord Holder of Ruatha,' Jaxom began, frowning at this check.

'Piemur's not a Master yet and there are no Weyrleaders present,' Menolly said with a little laugh. 'Aivas is doing as he was told which is more than you always do, Piemur.' She grinned at him to take away any hint of censure.

'Yes, but now would be the best time for Aivas to catch up on our history while there's peace and quiet. And before Fandarel returns to monopolize him,' Piemur said, scrubbing at his face. The effects of a very exciting day were catching up with him.

'I'm on the list though, am I not?' Jaxom asked, a touch of asperity in his voice.

'Yes, you, me, Jancis, Master Robinton, all of us who were in the room when Aivas woke up.'

'And he talked to you when you were alone,' Jaxom said. 'Maybe, if Sebell and Menolly leave – sorry about that – he'll talk to me and I can feed the records to him.'

'Our feelings won't be hurt,' Menolly said, glancing up at Sebell to see him nod in agreement. Sebell might be Masterharper of Pern and an important person but his good sense and equable nature were two of the many reasons she loved and respected him. 'There're other empty pallets, Piemur; you look to be out on your feet. You and Sebell go sleep in with Master Robinton and I'll join Jancis. If this Aivas has waited – how many Turns did you say, Jaxom? Twenty-five hundred,' and she gave a little shudder for such a long span, 'we can wait until tomorrow.'

'I shouldn't leave it all to Jaxom . . .' Piemur said, definitely tempted by the thought of lying horizontal for a while. That last cup of *klah* had made no dent in his fatigue.

Menolly took him by the hand. 'I'll even tuck you in, the way I would Robse,' and she grinned at his disgusted snort. 'You're no better than Master Robinton in taking care of yourself. Come, get some sleep now. You, too, Sebell. Tomorrow – no, it's already today here, isn't it – well, I suspect everyone is going to rush about like headless wherries. So it'll behove us to stay cool and calm.'

When the doors had closed quietly behind them, Jaxom turned to Aivas.

'There's just me here now, Aivas.'

'That is obvious.'

'You were obeying your orders, then, weren't you?'

'That is my function.'

'All right, then it is my function to show you the Records of our history, as Master Robinton wanted.'

'Please place the record face down on the lighted plate.'

Carefully, with full regard that Master Arnor, the head archivist at Harper Hall, would have his guts for garters if he damaged a single one of the precious pages in this process, Jaxom opened the first Record, Present Pass One and laid it on the green glowing panel.

'Next!'

'What? I barely had time to place it,' Jaxom exclaimed.

'Scanning is instantaneous, Lord Jaxom.'

'This is going to be a long night,' Jaxom remarked and obediently opened the Record to a new page.

'Journeyman Piemur said your white dragon is an exceptional beast,' Aivas said, 'with many unusual qualities.'

'Compensation for him being small, white and uninterested in mating.' Jaxom wondered what Piemur had said about Ruth, even though he knew the journeyman was devoted to both him and the white dragon.

'Was the journeyman correct in saying that Ruth always knows *when* he is, and that he has travelled in time?'

'All the dragons can travel in time, at least backwards,' Jaxom said, a trifle absently for he was concentrating on turning the pages carefully as well as quickly.

'Timing is also prohibited?'

'Timing is dangerous.'

'Why?'

Jaxom shrugged as he changed pages. 'A dragon has to know exactly the time *when* he is going to or he can come out of *between* at the same spot he's inhabiting at that earlier time. Too close and it is thought that both dragon and rider will die. Equally, it's unwise to go any place you haven't already been, so you shouldn't go forward, because you wouldn't know if you were there or not.' Jaxom paused, smoothed pages to make them lie flat as the binding was tight on the inner octavos. 'Lessa made a particularly spectacular flight.'

'So Journeyman Piemur told me. A brave feat but apparently not without debilitating consequences. The method of teleporting was never fully explained but, judging by the journeyman's account, an abnormally long period spent in such travel causes sensory deprivations. You and your white dragon have also timed it?'

'That is the term,' Jaxom said in a flat tone that he hoped would discourage further questions. But Aivas was not a

32

human and might not perceive his reluctance from tone or words. 'The episode is not common knowledge.'

'Understood,' Aivas replied to Jaxom's surprise. 'Would you object, Lord Jaxom, to a discussion of the duties of the various social groups which have been mentioned in the Records so far? For instance, what are the responsibilities and privileges of a Lord Holder? Of a Weyrleader? A Craftmaster? Some terms are so well understood by the scribes that they are not defined. It is necessary to have a firm grasp of such terms to understand the current political and social structures.'

Jaxom gave a little chuckle for the subtlety of the Aivas. 'You'd do better to ask one of the more experienced Lords Holder: Groghe, for instance, or even Larad and Asgenar.'

'You are here, Lord Jaxom.'

'Yes, am I not!' The quickness of the Aivas amused Jaxom. So, as talking would certainly relieve the tedium of turning pages, Jaxom complied. And found it very easy indeed to talk to Aivas through the long night. He would later realize how skilfully he had been questioned. Only much later would he realize how valuable his explanations would prove to be.

Jaxom had worked his way through five Turns of the Present Pass when the muscles in his shoulders began to tense. So when he heard someone stirring, he called out softly.

'Who's up?'

'Jancis. You came back . . . oh,' and as Jancis entered the chamber, she grinned. 'Shall I take over? You look exhausted. Why didn't Sebell or Menolly do this?'

'Because Aivas will have nothing to do with them until they've been formally introduced to him. By a Lord Holder, a Masterharper and a Weyrleader.'

Jancis' expression was ruefully apologetic. 'Sometimes we outsmart ourselves. Here I'll take over, Jaxom. Get yourself some *klah*. It should still be good and hot.' And taking the Record from his hands, she spread the pages on the panel. 'Master Robinton, and the others here then, quite rightly decided it was wiser to limit who could talk to Aivas.'

'Hmm, yes, there's no telling what people will think to ask Aivas,' Jaxom said, remembering how he had rattled on and on although Aivas had done all the asking.

By the time he had finished the *klah* which was not as hot as he liked it but did stimulate him, Jancis had finished that volume. She started on another.

How soon, Jaxom wondered, could he get his Lady, Sharra, admitted to the roster? She had been so excited about the medical knowledge Aivas said it possessed. She had two cotholders suffering intense pains which she was unable to alleviate with fellis. They were slowly wasting away. Master Oldive whose advice had been sought was also baffled by their declines. Then Jaxom reminded himself that Master Oldive would have precedence with Aivas, being Masterhealer. Jaxom was careful about using his privilege as Lord Holder and yet, in a case of life or death, could he not make exception?

'That will be all for now, Journeywoman Jancis,' he heard Aivas saying in a muted voice. 'The energy supplies are nearly exhausted. An hour of good sunlight will be needed to restore power. If the remaining panels could be cleared, there would be more power available in the future.'

'Did I do something wrong?' Jancis asked, appealing to Jaxom in her confusion.

'No,' Jaxom said, chuckling. 'It gets its power from those panels you and Piemur uncovered on the roof. Sun power. Sun's been down for hours now.' He yawned hugely. 'It's late. We should both get some sleep.'

Jancis considered this and then reached for the nearly empty *klah* beaker. 'No, I'm awake now. I'll brew more *klah*. We'll need plenty of that when people start arriving.' And she bustled off.

Jaxom liked Jancis: not long ago, they'd shared lessons at the Mastersmithcraft. She'd worked a lot harder than he had – and she was very able too! – She deserved Master's status, and rumour said she'd walk the tables soon. He'd been a bit surprised when she and Piemur came to an understanding though Sharra had heartily approved. Wandering all up and down the southern coastline had turned Piemur strange there for a time. What he'd needed to set him right was a sound relationship. And certainly the impudent young harper would see that Jancis would develop some needed assertiveness. And maybe lose some of the inhibitions caused by her awesome grandfather, Fandarel. Jaxom knew just how capable she was in her area of Smithcrafting.

Tired but unwilling to settle down for sleep, Jaxom wandered to the entrance, nodding to the two bored guards as he walked out into the cool night air, up the ramp of excavated dirt to stand on its summit. Ruth rumbled affectionately at him from the next hillock. Jaxom sent him a caressing thought.

Though Jaxom hadn't even mentioned it to Sharra, he felt oddly proprietorial about this plateau which he and Ruth had originally discovered, and in particular this Aivas entity which they had dug out. Having heard Aivas list the names of the first colonists, Jaxom wondered who had been his ancestors. He had never been comfortable having Fax as his sire, the best reason why he so rarely made use of many of a Lord Holder's traditional privileges. But wasn't it the *whole* of the contributions of the original colonists that were important, rather than an individual's achievements? Larad of Telgar was not a prideful man but he must feel immensely proud of his heritage after hearing of his forebears, Sallah Telgar Andiyar and Tarvi Andiyar. Groghe was a sensible man but to know that his original sire had been a universal hero would make the Fort Lord Holder inordinately proud. But why was Benden Hold in the east? Why hadn't Fort Hold been named after the valiant Admiral? And why hadn't Aivas known more about the dragons? Fascinating. There would be more revelations.

I listened, Ruth said, gliding from his perch to the mound on which Jaxom stood, *to what this Aivas creature said. Is it true that we were an experiment?* Ruth moved forward until he was close enough to touch Jaxom and then he leaned his head against his weyrmate. *What is an experiment?*

Jaxom heard the indignation in Ruth's tone and stifled a chuckle at his friend's reaction.

'A most felicitous happening, dear friend, not that it matters a lead mark how you and the other dragons came to be,' Jaxom said stoutly. 'Besides you've always known –

35

better than anyone else on Pern – that dragons are cousins to the fire-lizards. So why should it bother you how you were created?'

I don't know, Ruth replied in a strangely subdued, uncertain tone. *Is this Aivas thing good?*

'I believe it is,' Jaxom answered, briefly considering his reply. 'I think it will depend on us, the use to which we put the information the Aivas can give us. If it rids Pern of Thread . . .'

If it can, that means dragons won't be needed any more, doesn't it?

'Nonsense,' and Jaxom spoke more sharply than he intended. He threw his arm around his dragon's neck in quick reassurance, caressing Ruth's cheek and leaning into his shoulder. 'Pern will always need dragons. You could do a lot more useful and much less dangerous things than sear Thread out of the skies, believe you me! Don't you fret for a single moment about our future, my friend!'

Jaxom wondered if F'lar, Lessa and F'nor had heard on that score from their dragons. That was not the important issue anyway. The dragonriders were committed to ridding Pern of Thread. Everyone knew that F'lar had set that as his life's task.

'No, Ruth, don't you worry your heart out over that. Threadless skies are, I fear, a long way off in Pern's future! Aivas may know a great deal more than we do about Oort Clouds and planets and things but it is only a machine that speaks. Talk's cheap.'

Still soothing Ruth's cheek, Jaxom looked out over the settlement that his ancestors had once inhabited. There were unsightly mounds in every direction where buildings had been greedily excavated, only to prove disappointingly empty. How ironic that the real treasure should be nearly the last thing to be uncovered. Incredible that the treasure should prove to be the agency that unlocked the truth to their past. Would it be the key to their future? Despite his reassurances, Jaxom harboured some of the same doubts that made Ruth fretful.

Maybe it was wrong for F'lar to wish an end to Thread, if it inevitably meant an end to usefulness for dragons. And yet, to see the last of Thread, in his own lifetime . . . More important to be able to improve life on Pern with the vast store of knowledge Aivas said it had. Surely that was for the good of all?

Just then he saw lights coming up in some of the buildings which the excavation teams used as dormitories. It was not even dawn but obviously there were many who had slept little this night, restless with all the history and incredible moving images churning in their minds as it did in his.

And Aivas's promise of help? It? He? It seemed impolite to refer to this . . . this entity as an 'it'. The voice was so rich and lively. Yet Aivas called it/himself a machine, the product of an advanced technological culture and, for all its knowledge, was an inanimate device. Jaxom would prefer to think of Aivas as real, as real as his own flesh and blood self.

It was then that Jaxom realized he was going to have to revise many concepts. That could be hard to do. The familiar was so comfortable. But the challenge – the excitement gripped Jaxom again – the incredible excitement of a future he could not have imagined just two days before when he and Ruth helped Piemur and Jancis excavate this one building out of the hundreds here. He didn't feel tired – he felt exhilarated.

'It's going to be exciting, Ruth. Think of it that way, as an exciting challenge.' He rubbed Ruth's eyeridge with his knuckles. 'We could both use a challenge, something new. Life's been getting dull.'

You'd better not say that to Sharra, Ruth advised.

Jaxom grinned. 'She'll be challenged, too, if I know my mate.'

Ramoth, Mnementh, Canth, Lioth, Golanth and Monarth are coming, Ruth said, his tone brightening.

'Reinforcements, huh?' Jaxom gave the eyeridge one more stiff drubbing. 'Company for you, certainly.'

Ramoth is grumpy, Ruth said, his tone suddenly wary. *Canth said that lights were burning all night in Lessa's weyr and Ramoth had long conversations with all the other queens.* He sounded anxious.

'Don't worry, Ruth, please. It's going to work out. This is just a new beginning, just as our Impression was! But nothing could ever be better than THAT day was for me!'

Ruth raised his head, his eyes altering from a murky shade to a happier blue-green.

The incoming dragons were circling, their faceted eyes vivid green and blue points against the dawn grey light. As they backwinged, their hindlegs poised to take the impact of landing, Jaxom was just able to discern that each dragon carried passengers.

Some of the dragons waited only long enough to let the extra riders dismount before they launched themselves again, disappearing *between* when they had sufficient height.

Jaxom sighed and gave Ruth an affectionate farewell slap before slipping down the dusty slope to the admin building and Aivas.

When F'lar, Lessa, Master Fandarel with his Woodsmith, Master Bendarek, reached him in the doorway, Jaxom informed them that Aivas was 'resting'.

'Resting?' Lessa demanded and she halted so abruptly midstride that F'lar had to sidestep so as not to barge into his slender weyrmate.

'The solar panels ran out of power,' Jaxom replied.

Master Fandarel looked both aggrieved and incredulous. 'But . . . but Aivas said that he could provide twelve different stations.'

'Lower your voice, please, Master Fandarel. Master Robinton's still asleep.' Jaxom kept his voice low as a hint to the others. 'I brought Sebell and Menolly and the Records Master Robinton wanted Aivas to see. Jancis and I got as far as the sixth Turn before Aivas turned off. He says he'll be all right again after a few hours of sunlight.'

'So we get here in the middle of the night and it isn't working?' Lessa said, disgusted.

'Now, there is much we can do,' Fandarel said soothingly, 'while we await his revival.'

'What?' Lessa demanded. 'I don't want people bungling about in the dark caves, you know. And it's scarcely the time to start reassembling this facility. F'lar and I have

38

questions for Aivas. It's one thing to be *promised* a miracle, quite another to produce it. In courtesy, we should allow the other Weyrleaders to see and hear this Aivas for themselves, for I assure you,' she added at her drollest, 'they didn't believe what had happened here. And if they come and there's nothing to see . . .' Her voice trailed off ominously.

'I hardly believe it myself,' F'lar remarked with a wry grin at Jaxom, 'so I can't fault others.'

'There are more than enough glowbaskets to illuminate the caves,' Master Fandarel said in his approximation of a whisper, 'and the dawn is not far away now. My craftsmen can begin to assemble the items Aivas said it needs. Where are those sheets Aivas made? Bendarek is fascinated by my description of printed sheets emerging from a wall. He's just coming up the hill now.' It was clear that Master Fandarel entertained no reservations about accepting the Aivas's offer to restore his records to legibility.

'Where are Sebell and Menolly?' Lessa asked, peering down the corridor towards the Aivas chamber.

Jaxom chuckled. 'They're getting some rest. Aivas wouldn't even talk in front of them.'

'Why not?' Lessa asked, surprised. 'We told him they were coming.'

'But while I'm a Lord Holder, and Piemur's a harper, we had no Weyrleader present.'

Lessa frowned.

'That's exactly what we stipulated, Lessa,' F'lar said. 'I can trust someone that is scrupulous about obeying orders. Particularly something as potent as this Aivas.'

A bass rumble startled those in the corridor and it took a moment to realize that the noise was Fandarel's chuckle. 'It is the function of a machine to do what it is designed to do. I approve.'

'You approve of anything that's efficient,' Lessa said. 'Even if that isn't always sensible.'

'We've lived too long with dragons,' F'lar said, grinning down at his diminutive weyrmate, 'who understand what we mean, even when we haven't said it.'

'Hmmm,' Lessa replied in a testy mumble as she gave him a sour glance.

'We all will have new things to learn, I think,' Fandarel said. 'And it is time. I'll need those sheets Aivas made, Jaxom?'

Obediently, Jaxom collected them from the flat worktop where Piemur and Jancis had left them. 'Jancis went to make fresh *klah*,' he told Lessa. 'She should be back any time now.'

'Then off you all go,' Lessa said, flipping her hands at them in dismissal. 'Jaxom, take Fandarel on Ruth, will you? That way he won't break his neck stumbling about in the dark. I'll wait for Jancis, and Aivas.'

Chapter Two

B y the time the sun had risen, many had come to view – for those who had heard of Aivas had spread the tale as fast as Thread burrows. Curiosity and disbelief are mighty movers, so there were men and women available from every Hall, Hold and Weyr. To the disgust of some, it wasn't what Aivas could teach them that prompted such fervour, but a chance to glimpse the miraculous moving pictures which this marvel was purported to produce.

Fandarel, supervising the acquisition of the material on Aivas's list, was busy in the Catherine Caves. Breide, overwhelmed with helpers, was making great strides in carefully clearing the ash and dirt from the roof to expose the remaining solar panels so that, by midday, the entire admin building was cleared. Master Esselin was poring over Aivas's redesign plans, though he railed that Breide's men were not working fast enough for him to begin his job. Breide retorted that he hadn't even dismantled the building roofs that were to provide the material for the extensions so what was Esselin bleating about?

Lessa, hearing the argument, told them to stop behaving like apprentices and go about their duties. Then she, with Menolly and Jancis, found willing helpers among the women to do the drudge work of washing down the walls of long disused rooms. The dirty ash that had seeped in around windows and doors had to be shovelled out. The largest room, which the women decided must have originally been intended for conferences, was prepared for that purpose again. Remembering what she had seen stored in the caves, Lessa sent for enough furnishings to make the rooms useful: tables, desks, and as many chairs as could be easily reached without getting in Fandarel's way. All these were washed down, their bright colours cheerful in the otherwise bare rooms. They also turned the room furthest from activity into a private retreat for the Masterharper, complete with a comfortable bed, a well-cushioned chair and a table.

'The only problem will be in getting him to use it,' Lessa said, giving the table a final wipe with her cleaning cloth. She had smuts on her cheeks, across her fine-bridged nose and on her strong chin. Her long black hair was coming loose from its braids. Menolly and Jancis exchanged glances to decide who would tell her that her face was very dirty. In Jancis' private opinion, the Weyrwoman's disarray, as well as her energetic cleaning, made her suddenly more accessible. The young Smithjourneywoman had always been awed by her grandfather, Fandarel, but she was scared of the Weyrwoman.

'Somehow I never thought that I'd see the Weyrwoman of Pern working like a drudge,' Jancis murmured to Menolly. 'She does it with a vengeance.'

'She had practice,' Menolly said with a wry chuckle, 'hiding herself away from Fax in Ruatha Hold before Impressing Ramoth.'

'But she looks as if she is enjoying this,' Jancis added in faint surprise. Actually, she was, too. It gave one a sense of achievement to return a dirty room to cleanliness and order. It was done now, except for the charts which Lessa had requisitioned from Esselin's archive.

These arrived and Lessa had the girls hold them up on the various walls to decide the best position.

'Is it really right to put such precious artefacts to such a . . .' Jancis struggled to find the appropriate word.

'Mundane?' Menolly asked with a grin.

'Exactly.'

'They were initially used in this way,' Lessa said, quirk-ing her lips and shrugging her shoulders. 'So why not put them back up?'

Applying herself to this task had restored her equilib-rium: the discovery of Aivas and its promise to help F'lar achieve his deepest ambition had shaken her. She desper-ately wanted what was promised, almost as much as F'lar did, but she was fearful of the consequences. The morning's scrubbing attack had allowed her to expend some of her anxiety. Now she felt herself peculiarly restored.

'Since the maps haven't deteriorated – amazing material the settlers used,' she went on briskly, 'I see no reason why we shouldn't use them for the purpose they were designed for.' She'd also decided that 'settlers' was a less intimidating word than 'ancestors'. 'The southern continent certainly does spread out, doesn't it?' And she smiled, half to herself. 'Lift your corner a trifle, Jancis. There! Now it's straight!'

She smoothed the map of the southern continent against the wall. Then, with considerable satisfaction, she sited a tack and hammered it in with a rectangular lump of rock she'd found. Esselin had dithered so much about giving them two baskets and a shovel that she hadn't bothered to ask for a hammer. The rock did as well.

She stood back with the girls to survey her handiwork. The lettering on the maps still took her moments to de-cipher. The same and yet different, and certainly larger. She wondered how Aivas had fared reading the crabbed tight script that Master Arnor used in writing up the Records. Poor Master Arnor.

Not to mention poor Robinton who had been so mortified to learn that there had been language shifts despite all the hard work that the Harper Hall had put into keeping it 'pure'. Old Arnor's mind was notoriously inflexible and the old fellow might have spasms when he heard that. Which was yet another aspect of this discovery: its knowledge and its obvious intelligence put Aivas into the role of a Master of Masters in all disciplines – except perhaps the dragons. She might have been reading things into his tone, but had there been a note of excitement in that otherwise level voice when he mentioned the dragons?

'Yes, the maps are appropriate here, aren't they? Not merely decorative?' And she smiled at Jancis and Menolly. This morning's opportunity to work with Piemur's young woman had reassured her that the journeyman was well matched with Fandarel's granddaughter. Lessa had been dubious about including Jancis on Aivas's roster but she had lost her reservations this morning. Jancis had earned a place, and not simply because she had been instrumental in finding the room and was a willing worker. She had the right attitude towards Aivas and the future.

Jancis' eyes glowed as she studied the map. 'They produced so many wonderful things. Things that could last for centuries: materials impervious to Thread. Things that will enrich our lives, too.'

'True enough, but how am I going to reduce this,' Menolly asked at her drollest, waving an arm in Aivas's direction, 'into a ballad that will explain these events to people?'

Lessa chuckled. 'A change from your usual subjects, isn't it. You'll manage, Menolly dear. You always do and splendidly. And don't bother to explain – I doubt even Master Robinton could "explain" a phenomenon like Aivas. Present him as a challenge, to shake us all out of our mid-Pass doldrums.' She pulled out a chair, absently giving it a flick of her rag, before she sat down with a loud sigh. Then she cocked her head at the other two. 'I don't know about you two, but I could certainly use a nice hot cup of *klah*.'

Jancis sprang to her feet. 'And fruit and meatrolls. The cook was up before dawn, complaining about hordes to feed on short notice – but he was making enough food to feed a Gather. I'll be right back.'

Menolly turned to Lessa then, her expression serious. 'Lessa, is Aivas going to be a good challenge? Jaxom told us such incredible things. Some people are simply not going to accept them, or even try to.' She thought of her hidebound parents and others of similarly rigid minds whom she had met in her Turns as a harper.

Lessa gave a resigned flick of one hand. 'It's been found. I don't want to deny it, even if its discovery means some painful reassessments. I found it fascinating to hear how the settlers got here – the pictures they had of Pern in the black heavens are truly awesome. I'd no idea it could look like that! And it was thrilling to hear how bravely our ancestors struggled to destroy Thread. We've been used to it – even if *some* thought we'd had our last Pass four hundred Turns ago,' and her lips curled with remembered malice for those doubters. 'But what a terrible shock it must have been for them.' With an apologetic expression, she lightly touched Menolly's hand. 'You are one of those who truly deserved to hear that history, Menolly, but we'd no idea what had been discovered when we were sent for. Maybe Aivas wouldn't mind repeating it for you, and the other Harper Masters, because that is something the Hall should circulate. It should be compulsory for children to learn our true origins. We'll need new Teaching Ballads. But that is for Sebell to decide, isn't it?' Then her expression altered again to one of awe which became a grimace. 'I can tell you that I had trouble believing my eyes and ears when Aivas said that the settlers actually – "bi-o-eng-in-eered" – his word – created our dragons.' Her grin was tinged now with malice. 'I'm almost relieved that there are so few Oldtimers left alive. They'd have found *that* very hard indeed to accept.'

'Do you find it hard to accept that dragons were engineered from fire-lizards?' Menolly asked, teasingly. Lessa had made her dislike of the small draconic cousins very plain over the Turns and Menolly kept hers out of the Weyrwoman's way.

Lessa made another face, more reflective than angry. 'They *are* dreadful nuisances at times, Menolly. Did you leave yours behind in the Harper Hall today?'

'No,' and Menolly's sideways glance challenged Lessa. 'Only Beauty, Rocky and Diver came along this morning. They're keeping Ruth company. They've always adored him.'

Lessa looked thoughtful. 'Aivas commented on Ruth but he appeared to be quite surprised by Ramoth, Mnementh and Canth. I must ask him why when I get the chance. Well, at least we have something we can explain to Aivas.' She let out a gusty sigh. 'And if he can help us end Thread forever. I only hope that he can!'

To Menolly's fine-tuned harper's ear, she thought that there was an undertone of desperation in Lessa's voice.

The Weyrwoman caught her expression and nodded slowly, her eyes sad. 'At this point in a Pass, Menolly, we do very much need a hope that there could be a way to clear our skies of Thread. And get on with the sort of life the settlers had hoped to lead here.'

'Jaxom told us that Aivas had said that there was a *possibility*.'

'At least Jaxom repeats things accurately,' Lessa said at her driest. 'You should have heard some of the rumours in the Weyr this morning. The Weyr harper is going to see that those are suppressed and accurate information circulated. Hope is all very well but it must be realistic.'

'But Aivas did say it was possible?'

Lessa nodded. 'Possible! But we'll have to work hard to achieve it. We'll have to learn a lot of new things.'

'Even that could improve morale.' Then Menolly added more briskly. 'The wonder is that our ancestors managed to survive each new Pass losing so little of our culture.'

'They had to, as we have had to. But we know now that so much of our culture *was* lost. If that threat were removed, oh what a wonderful future we could contemplate!'

Menolly caught Lessa's eye in a significant stare. 'Wonderful for the dragons and the Weyrs, too?'

'Yes!' Lessa's explosive reply surprised the Harper Hall Master. 'Yes, it will be even better for dragons and Weyrs.' She took a deep breath and exhaled, jabbing her finger at the map. 'We'll have a new world to explore again.' She learned forward, peering at the map. 'I wonder what "Honshu" was.'

Just then Jancis returned, carrying a basket with a *klah* pitcher, cups and food. She was also full of news.

'You should see what they've done while we've been cleaning,' she said, a broad grin on her face. 'You should also see the mob wanting to gawk at Aivas.' When Lessa sprang to her feet, Jancis waved her back down. 'F'lar, Sebell and Master Robinton are in control. We'll be the better for something to eat. Here, Lessa, fresh redfruit and nice hot rolls. If you'd pour the *klah*, Menolly,' she said, passing around the fruit and rolls.

'You're as efficient as your grandsire,' Lessa remarked approvingly, settling back into her chair. The smell of warm bread and meat reminded her that it had been a long time since that hurried early morning porridge at Benden Weyr. 'Menolly, as soon as you've eaten, I want you on Aivas' roster.' She turned to Jancis. 'How long has Aivas been . . .' and she searched for the appropriate word, 'available?'

Jancis grinned over the rim of her cup. 'Long enough to approve or discard what Grandfather brought out of the caves for inspection. Masters Wansor and Terry are attempting to follow a diagram on how to assemble the . . . the components,' and she hesitated briefly over the unfamiliar word. 'They've sent for Masterglassman Norist because two of the screens were cracked. Aivas wants to discover if we have the skill – only he said technology – to duplicate the material. He's very diplomatic but he's certainly putting everyone on their mettle. He . . . it,' and Jancis shook her head, then appealed to Lessa. 'What DO we call the thing. Aivas says he/it is a machine but with that beautiful voice, he sounds very human.'

'Beautiful voice?' Menolly asked through a mouthful of redfruit, hastily stemming the juice from dripping down her chin.

Lessa chuckled. 'Yes,' and she grinned at Menolly's reaction, 'a beautiful voice. Almost as good as Master Robinton's.'

'Really?' Menolly's thick eyebrows rose at that comparison to her beloved Master. 'How clever of our ancestors,' she added, not rising to Lessa's bait.

Lessa grinned more broadly. 'Yes, it's only fair to warn you. The thing is rather awesome.'

Menolly grinned back. 'Too kind of you. I wonder if he knows anything about ancestral music forms?'

Lessa laughed. 'I could hear that question coming.'

'He said,' put in Jancis, keeping her expression bland, 'he had the Planetary Engineering and Colonial Kit in his memory banks as well as what cultural and historical records were deemed relevant by the colonists. Surely music would be considered a cultural necessity?'

Lessa hid a smile, delighted by Jancis' subtle tease.

'If it isn't, it should be. It will be my first question of this Aivas,' Menolly replied equably and took a firm bite out of her meatroll.

'Aivas is a clever enough affair but it's only got the one voice, however mellifluous,' Lessa went on. 'Only one voice to sing with even if it does have ancient music in those formidable memory banks.'

F'lar appeared in the doorway, looking harassed as he pushed a wayward lock off his forehead. 'There you are, Lessa. Menolly, Robinton wants you and Lessa, and we have got to discuss the length of that sharding roster. *Everyone* has questions that require answers from Aivas. Piemur has the right of it though. Most of them don't believe what they've been hearing.' He perched on the table and broke off a piece of meatroll. 'They probably won't believe even after they've seen Aivas.'

'How can we fault them on that score?' Lessa asked. 'But it's a waste of Aivas's valuable time to humour sceptics. And ours. We must have a conference.'

Jancis jumped up, aware that her presence might be superfluous.

'No, child, don't disappear. A conference is not that imminent,' and Lessa gave a droll snort, 'not with everyone rushing around every which way this morning. But do get more cups, *klah* and food. F'lar, eat something.'

F'lar made a dismissive gesture. 'I don't have time right now. There's too much to be done.' But he crammed another bite of meatroll into his mouth.

'When did you intend to stop for food?' Lessa asked tartly and, rising, pulled F'lar off the table and pushed him by the shoulders into the nearest chair. She put the rest of the meatroll in front of him and refilled her own cup for him, adding the amount of sweetener he preferred with his *klah*. 'You didn't sleep last night and if you don't eat, you'll be useless just when you're most needed. Now, who's importuning you? Do we have enough

Lords Holder, Craftmasters and Weyrleaders to constitute a majority?'

'Every single Lord Holder we didn't cram in yesterday is here and every Mastercraftsman,' F'lar flung up both hands in an extravagant gesture of impatience.

'Surely you've explained . . .'

'We've all been explaining,' F'lar said irritably. 'I know we've got touchy prides among our ranking personalities but you'd think each one had been personally insulted by not being summoned yesterday.' He bit into the meatroll, washing it down with a gulp of *klah*. He scowled as he swallowed. 'The worst complainers are those who haven't paid much attention to what's being done here at Landing. Different tune right now, I can tell you.'

Lessa regarded him with astonishment. 'How'd they all find out?'

F'lar flashed an ironic grin at Menolly. 'Guess?' The harper groaned and hid her face in her arms.

'Those dratted fire-lizards again,' and Lessa's scowl was fierce. She shook her head. 'And I suppose they came a-dragonback.'

F'lar grimaced as he pushed hair from his forehead again. 'I should never have given Hall and Hold resident dragonriders. They've taken to using the courtesy as if dragons were runnerbeasts.'

'Oh, well, we have to take the bad with the good and the courtesy certainly improved relations with Hold and Hall. It's just awkward at the moment. Nevertheless, it is essential that the Lords and Craftmasters experience Aivas for themselves. There'll be some hide-bounds who will deny the evidence of their eyes and ears anyway. So, if they're here, they might well have a chance at Aivas.'

'Oh, they're here,' F'lar said airily, waving his second meatroll. 'Sebell lets them in a few at a time and interrupts the session whenever Aivas is needed for the ongoing work. Most of them go away, shaking their heads and trying not to look bewildered. Very few of them have understood the significance of Aivas.' He brought his fist down on the table. 'When I think of what we once had, once were! What we can be again with Aivas's help!'

Lessa smiled at his intensity. 'According to Aivas even Landing wasn't built in one day.' She began to knead the taut muscles about his neck and shoulders. 'Eat, love. We've handled the sceptics before: we'll do it again in our own inimitable fashion.' She leaned down and kissed his cheek.

F'lar gave her a rueful grin. 'And you're handling me as you usually do, aren't you?'

Lessa gave him a look of mild indignation as she slipped back into her chair and picked up her half-eaten roll. 'Reassuring you, dear heart.'

From Mnementh, Lessa heard an incredulous mental snort. *Don't spoil the effect*, she told the bronze dragon.

Not likely, Mnementh replied sleepily. *The sun is exceedingly warm here in this Landing place.*

Ramoth agreed.

Sebell appeared in the doorway then, nodding at the two Weyrleaders as he beckoned to Menolly.

'Master Robinton wants to have Menolly added to the roster. N'ton's there as Weyrleader. And Fandarel snatched Jancis on her way to the kitchens. She's needed to do some drafting but someone's bringing more *klah* and food.' Sebell helped himself to the remaining meatroll. 'This'll make a good conference room.' Then draping one arm around Menolly's shoulders, he steered her out the door.

Lessa shot an intimate look at her own mate and he grinned as he chewed the last of his meatroll and reached for a redfruit.

'Are you already on the list?' Menolly asked Sebell as they made their way down the corridor.

He gave her a mischievous grin, hugging her against his side for she was exactly the size to fit there. They fell easily into step. As he often did, Sebell wondered at his great good fortune to have won Menolly as his mate. He could not mind that part of her heart which was Master Robinton's. Part of his was the Harper's too, and his complete loyalty and respect, but Menolly was the joy of his life.

'How long must we wait?' demanded Oterel, Lord Holder of Boll, scowling deeply as the two harpers passed him where he waited in the hallway.

'The room is small, Lord Oterel, and there is a great deal to be done today,' Sebell said placatingly.

'Small or not, Fandarel and other very minor craftsmen have been in there for hours, and now he has hauled his granddaughter in, too.' Oterel's expression and voice were peevish.

'If you were able to draw clear diagrams as she does, Lord Oterel,' Menolly said for she didn't like the testy old Lord of Tillek Hold, who'd been outspoken against her attaining her Mastery, 'you would doubtless be in there.'

Oterel glared fiercely back at her. Beyond him, Lord Toronas of Benden Hold covered a grin with his hand. 'You're impudent, young woman, far too impudent! You dishonour your Hall.'

Sebell gave him a long quelling look and then pulled Menolly into the small room. It was hot and stuffy, with stools crammed so closely together that she wondered how Jancis, Piemur, Terry and another Smith she didn't recognize could draw at all. Fandarel was hovering over them while N'ton was leaning indolently against the far wall. Then she saw the screen and its display of unfamiliar objects as clearly defined as if the actual item had somehow got inside this Aivas and been magnified.

'Now, once the connections with the F-322RH have been made—' The rich beautifully modulated voice made Menolly gasp in surprise. She glanced around, caught Sebell's grin at her reaction as she tried to locate the source of this voice. '—the circuit will be completed. Add this board to those already installed and come back to me for the next step.'

Obediently the four left, talking to each other in low tones. N'ton came forward then and Fandarel cleared his throat.

'We three, Weyrleader N'ton, I, Craftmaster Fandarel, and Masterharper Sebell, request that you add Master Menolly of the Harper Hall to the roster.'

'Will Master Menolly please speak so that a voice print may be taken?'

'A voice print?' Menolly asked, astonished.

51

'Yes, a human's voice is a more effective means of identification than physical appearance which could be duplicated. Your voice print cannot. Therefore it is necessary for you to speak so that a voice print ID can be registered to the roster file.'

Menolly looked helplessly at Sebell for, uncharacteristically, she was rendered speechless by the unusual request and the glorious voice. Sebell made an encouraging flick of his fingers, grinning cheerfully while N'ton mouthed words at her.

'I'm Menolly, once of Half-Circle Sea Hold, and I'm better at singing than speaking,' she said, stammering slightly in her confusion. Then she fretted that she was letting a stammer be registered.

Master Fandarel made a tumbling gesture with his hands which she took to mean that she should continue talking.

'My rank is Master in the Harper Hall. I compose music and write lyrics. Master Sebell here is my mate and we have two children. Have you heard enough?'

'That is sufficient for a voice which has such a distinctive timbre,' Aivas said. 'Are copies of the music you write available? For the main files?'

'You want my music?' Menolly exclaimed, surprised that Aivas would ask.

'Music was very important to your ancestors.'

'You have some of their music?' She could barely contain her excitement at the prospect.

'There is an extensive file of music, spanning over two thousand years.'

'But you're only one voice?'

There was a significant pause. 'It would be inappropriate to use more than one in conversational mode. This system is, however, adapted to reproduce music in its varied instrumental forms.'

'It is?' Menolly was aware that Sebell chuckled and N'ton was grinning at her reaction.

'We'll get our turn, lovey,' Sebell said softly. 'I promise you that. Master Robinton is as eager as we are but there are more urgent priorities.'

Menolly gulped back disappointment and looked help-lessly at Sebell.

'I must leave now,' Fandarel said. 'We are going to see how to reconstruct that power station, Aivas, and dragonriders have gone to bring my nickel-cadmium batteries, as you call them.'

'Does Master Facenden understand how to connect them to the auxiliary power points shown to him?'

'Yes, I made certain of his comprehension. He will also construct a cage to keep the unwary from touching the fluid or the wires. Come, N'ton, if you'd be good enough to assign us dragonriders to take us up the river to the dam site.'

And Fandarel wheeled about and strode down the cor-ridor, N'ton beside him. Both ignored attempts by those waiting in the hall to stop and quiz them. Sebell gestured for Menolly to take one of the stools before he called Lords Oterel, Sigomal, Toronas and Warbret to enter. Oterel pushed his way in first, wearing a triumphant expression which faded as he looked about him in bewilderment. When all four were in the room, Sebell introduced them to Aivas.

'It is a pleasure to make your acquaintances, my Lords,' Aivas replied courteously. Menolly noticed that his deep voice was subtly deferential. 'Soon this facility will be enlarged so that larger audiences can be accommodated.'

Sebell caught Menolly's eye and winked at her for Aivas's smooth tact.

'You can see us?' Oterel asked, still looking around for something, Menolly wagered, that he could recognize as eyes.

'The visual sensors are registering your individual pres-ences. You will most certainly be recognized again whenever you return.'

Menolly hastily covered her mouth. It wouldn't do for Oterel to see her grinning at his confusion. This Aivas was half-harper. How did it know just how to deal with the old bore? He was one Lord Holder who had outlived his tenure. Had Sebell warned Aivas?

'You don't have any eyes,' Oterel said querulously.

'Optics are the eyes of a machine, Lord Oterel.'

'I understand that you knew our ancestors, Aivas,' Lord Sigomal said while Oterel floundered over the implication that eyes were somehow inferior. 'Can you tell me who mine were?'

'Lord Sigomal,' and Aivas' voice sounded genuinely apologetic, 'no input was received on such details. A list of the names of those settlers who removed to Fort Hold is being prepared and will be available to anyone who requests a copy. Your own Hold Records probably detail who established Bitra. However, you may be pleased to know that your province was named for one of the shuttle pilots, Avril Bitra.'

Menolly wondered at the odd clipped delivery of that information. This Aivas had an incredibly flexible voice, capable of amazing dynamics and nuances. Maybe Master Shonagar, the Hall's eccentric voice teacher, could be pried out of his domain to hear such a wonder.

'Lists of ancestors are the best you can do? That isn't going to be much use to us,' Oterel exclaimed in keen dissatisfaction.

'In your case, Lord Oterel, it is reasonable to assume that Tillek was either established by or named for Captain James Tillek, the captain of the *Bahrain*, a man of considerable acumen and talent as a seaman and explorer.'

Thus propitiated, Oterel began to swell with importance.

'Regretfully, Lords Toronas and Warbret, your Holds were established long after input ceased. Would it be possible to add your Records to the information files of this time period? That would further the understanding of the structure of a Hold. There is so much that must be gathered before what you have created here on Pern can be fully appreciated.'

Master Wansor, mumbling over the page he was reading as he walked in, stumbled into the seated Warbret. Profusely apologizing, he was then confronted by a glaring Oterel and the fact that he had barged in on Lords Holder.

'I've only one small question but it is extremely urgent,'

he said in his gentle contrite voice. He took a breath to deliver the question.

'Master Wansor, you need only place the paper on the plate for it to be read and an answer given,' Aivas reminded him in the most courteous tone.

Menolly raised her eyebrows for few people paid Master Wansor the consideration his true abilities deserved.

'Oh, yes, I keep forgetting,' Master Wansor said, and excusing himself, wove a path past the stools to the control board. He had to bend over, a round little unpretentious elderly man, to see with his weak eyes where to place the paper. The panel glowed more brightly. 'Ah, yes. There!' And he patted the paper into position.

'Lord Toronas, your Hold was obviously named to honour the memory of Admiral Paul Benden,' Aivas said, while several lightning flashes on the panel suggested to Menolly that he was simultaneously attending to Wansor's paper. Then to the amazement of all, a likeness appeared on the main screen, of a fine-looking man, his face full of character. A man to trust, Menolly decided. Then she was stunned by the realization that Aivas had known and talked to that man, so long dead, and so long remembered. 'A fine man, Admiral Benden, holding the settlers together, always encouraging, preserving them through considerable trials to establish a safer haven in the northern continent.'

'And I'm related to the Admiral?' Toronas wanted to know, rather more humble in his request than Oterel. Only Menolly noticed Wansor's discreet departure. 'Our earliest Records are impossible to decipher.'

'It is entirely possible,' Aivas said, 'even likely that you are a direct descendant. Four children were recorded to the marriage of Paul Benden and Ju Adjai. Perhaps if you bring in your Records at some later date, they can be deciphered. A program is available that utilizes a special light which can often restore lost words and phrases.'

Enthralled, Menolly listened as Aivas dealt as cleverly with both Sigomal and Warbret, in as personal a fashion, catering to their self-images.

Then Jancis, Piemur, and Benelek hovered uncertainly in the doorway, each clutching several sheets. Piemur rattled his to get Sebell's attention and the Masterharper deferentially told the Lords Holder that Aivas must be consulted again, and politely gestured for them to leave.

Oterel grumbled but Sigomal rose readily enough and took the old Tillek Lord by the arm. 'It's stifling in here, Oterel. Far too stuffy for comfort. I don't know about you, but I intend to search out those Records and then see what this Aivas thing can tell me. Come along now.'

'He manipulates them like so many string-dolls,' Menolly told her mate in an undertone when he had escorted the Lords into the hallway.

'Master Robinton had advised that tact and flattery might be required,' Aivas replied in as discreet a tone as hers. 'Especially for those who cannot be accommodated with a lengthy interview.'

'How did you hear me?' Menolly asked, dismayed because she'd been careful to whisper.

'Master Menolly, you are sitting beside a receptor. Whispers are clearly audible.'

She caught Sebell's amused glance. He might have warned her about that.

'Don't distract Aivas, Menolly,' Piemur said, arranging his papers on the plate.

'Master Menolly is not a distraction,' Aivas said mildly. 'Next page please, Piemur.'

'Could you really read those old mouldy records?' Menolly asked.

'The attempt should be made. The ink which was used to write the records you were kind enough to bring last night is of an indelible type that will yield to certain techniques available to this facility. Outside manual assistance will be needed, however, to prepare the documents before they can be scanned. That is a project which has been put on hold.'

'On hold?' Menolly was delighted by the unusual but descriptive phrase. 'How explanatory!'

Then she heard the sounds of movement in the hall and saw a file of people, laden with cartons, striding purposefully towards her. She recognized F'lessan and F'nor among them.

'I'd better leave.'

'Hang about,' Sebell told her.

'You seem to be bringing the caves here. Wouldn't it have been easier to move Aivas to the caves?' she asked.

'Negatory,' Aivas said in as sharp a tone as Menolly had yet heard him utter. 'This installation must remain in its present position or it cannot access *Yokohama*.'

'I was being facetious, Aivas,' Menolly said, penitently and rolled her eyes at Sebell for her blunder.

As the dragonriders came in, Menolly moved to N'ton's earlier position against the wall. She didn't want to leave this room and the wonder of Aivas. So she watched as carton after carton was displayed to Aivas, and either dismissed or sent into the rooms where others were attempting to construct the devices which would permit wider access to Aivas's facilities. None of the dragonriders seemed at all surprised to see her there, and F'lessan's grin had lost nothing of its usual impudence in the presence of Aivas. But then the son of F'lar and Lessa took nothing very seriously except his dragon, Golanth. Mirrim followed on T'gellan's heels but then the two from the Eastern Weyr were never far apart since they had declared themselves weyrmates. Mirrim had certainly bloomed and relaxed in the warmth of his preference.

'I didn't see you here earlier,' Mirrim said in an aside to Menolly while waiting for her burden to be assessed by Aivas.

'Oh, I arrived here late last night with the Records of this Pass,' Menolly replied. 'Then Lessa grabbed me for some drudgery.' She extended her strong hands, her callused fingers still showing water-wrinkles.

Mirrim rolled her eyes. 'I'm just as glad we got in on the fetch and carry end of things. Let's compare notes later, huh? I'd better go,' she added with a smug grin, 'T'gellan's waving at me.' She hefted the carton over to Aivas's screen.

When Aivas had delivered a verdict and the riders had left, Sebell then gestured for the Craftmasters to come in and he introduced them. Again they were all courteously, if briefly, addressed, and Aivas again issued the request to see their Craft Records. When they had left, she slipped over to Sebell.

'How on earth will Aivas find time to look at so many Records?' she asked, whispering in his ear.

'He doesn't need sleep, only power,' Sebell replied. 'If we can supply that when the solar panels falter, he'll go on all day and night. You don't sleep, do you, Aivas?'

'This facility operates as long as it has sufficient power to do so. Sleep is a human requirement.'

Sebell winked at Menolly.

'And you have none?' she demanded, jamming her fists into her belt as she faced the screen squarely.

'This facility is programmed to give optimum use at human convenience.'

'Do I hear a tinge of apology in your tone, Aivas?' she asked.

'This facility is programmed not to give offence.'

Menolly had to chuckle. Later she realized that that was when she began to accept Aivas as an individual entity and not as an awesome relic of her ancestors' contrivance.

'Menolly?' called the Masterharper from the top of the corridor which was, for the first time, empty of importunate visitors. 'Is Sebell there with you?' Sebell moved to where he could be seen. 'Take over from him, will you, Menolly? We've got enough here for a conference.'

Sebell put his hand on Menolly's upper arm, giving it a reassuring squeeze. 'You saw how I conducted the encounters,' he said. 'Just introduce them.'

'That didn't work last night when Piemur tried it,' Menolly said.

Sebell grinned, squeezing her arm again. 'Master Robinton and F'lar worked out a necessary alteration in the protocol.'

'Another new word?'

'Aivas for convention or courtesy.' He gave her a quick kiss on the cheek. 'You won't be missing anything in the conference, you know.'

'I do and I'm relieved not to have to sit through another one,' she called after him as he hurried down the hall to Master Robinton. Sebell knew how she hated formal ceremonies. Or would they now be called protocols? She smiled to herself. Then realized that she was alone with Aivas.

'Aivas, would you be able to give me an example of ancestral music?'

'Vocal, instrumental, orchestral . . .'

'Vocal,' Menolly replied without hesitation though she promised she would hear the other categories, too, when there was a chance.

'Classical, ancient or modern, contemporary folk or popular, with or without instrumental accompaniment?'

'Anything while we've got a free moment.'

'Anything is too vague a category. Specify.'

'Vocal, popular, with instruments.'

'This was recorded at the Landing celebration.' And suddenly the room was filled with music. Menolly immediately identified several of the instruments: a gitar, a fiddle and a pipe-like sound, and then voices, untrained but enthusiastic and musical. The melody was hauntingly familiar to her; the words, though clearly sung, were not. The quality of the sound, however, was incredible. These voices and instruments had not been heard for centuries and yet the sounds were as unblurred by time as if the musicians were present. When the song ended, she couldn't speak for the wonder of it.

'Was that not satisfactory, Master Menolly?'

She shook herself. 'It was immensely and incredibly satisfying. I know that tune, too. What did the settlers—' Yes, Lessa was right to call them by that less intimidating noun. '—call it?'

'*Home on the Range*. It is classified as American Western folk music. Several variations were included when the music library was installed in the memory banks.'

She would have asked for more but Piemur came striding into the room, carrying a strange contraption, a thin wide ribbon of coloured strings hanging from one side. The front of it resembled part of the Aivas worktop, a series of depressions in five ordered ranks under a dark sheet of what must be more plastic.

'Kindly hold it over the view panel, Piemur. Level with

your head, please.' There was a long pause for assessment. 'It seems to be correctly assembled. A final check will be its installation and activation but that must wait on a power source and connections to this board. How is Master Terry progressing with the wiring?'

'I don't know. He's in another room. I'll just go and check for you. Here, Menolly, hang on to this. I don't want to risk dropping it,' and, with an encouraging grin, Piemur deposited his load in her arms and half-ran down the corridor.

'Why do you have that?' Jancis asked, arriving with a similar object in her hands.

Menolly told her and watched while Jancis repeated Piemur's antics. Right behind her came Benelek, Lord Groghe's clever son who was now a Smith journeyman. Fandarel had found him so extremely inventive that Menolly was not at all surprised to see him taking an active part here.

When Aivas had approved their efforts, Benelek wanted to know when they could hook up.

'When there is power available. So, Journeyman Benelek, you may as well assemble another keyboard while you're waiting,' Aivas replied. 'Ten are possible with the parts in hand. Two need replacement screens if the Glassmaster will oblige.'

'I really do not understand how you would be able to handle twelve people at once, Aivas.'

'You play more than one instrument, do you not? That is, if this facility has properly understood the training practices of your Hall.'

'I do but not all at once.'

'But there are in this facility many parts, each of which can operate separately and simultaneously.'

Silently Menolly considered that concept and just when it would have seemed rude for her to remain quiet, Master Terry came trotting down the corridor, loops of material strung all over him.

Chapter Three

Down the hall, in the refurbished conference room, seven Lords Holder, eight Craftmasters, eight Weyrleaders and four Weyrwomen were assembled in an extraordinary meeting. Harper Journeyman Tagetarl had been brought in to take full notes of the proceedings.

F'lar stood up to take charge, though everyone could see that Master Robinton would have been happy to officiate. There were those who thought the Harper hadn't looked so animated and vigorous in many a Turn. The rumours of his decline must be vastly exaggerated. Note was also taken that the Weyrleaders looked less haggard, almost cheerful, even optimistic.

'I believe you've all been introduced to Aivas,' F'lar began.

'Introduced? To a talking wall?' Lord Corman of Igen gave a scoffing snort.

'It is much more than a talking wall,' Robinton said tartly, glaring at Corman who rolled his eyes at the Harper's unexpected vehemence and nudged Lord Bargen of High Reaches Hold beside him.

'Considerably more than just a wall,' F'lar said, 'Aivas is an intelligent entity, constructed by our ancestors who first settled this planet. It contains the information which our ancestors needed and used. Valuable knowledge which can teach us how to improve Hold, Hall and Weyr.' He took a deep breath. 'And destroy Thread completely.'

'That I'll believe when I see it,' Corman replied with a disbelieving snort.

'I promised you that, Lord Corman, at the beginning of this Pass and now I can fulfil that promise!'

'With a wall's help?' Corman was now openly derisory.

'Yes, with this wall's help,' Robinton replied, his voice intense with conviction as he glared angrily at the Holder.

'You wouldn't be so sceptical if you'd been here yesterday and heard Aivas!' Larad said, jumping to his feet, his tone trembling with controlled anger, his eyes flashing a challenge at Corman who recoiled at the forceful reaction from the usually imperturbable Holder.

'With all due respect, F'lar, Robinton, Larad,' Warbret said appeasingly, 'we've been called down here so frequently to see useless hulks, empty buildings and caves bulging with shards and artefacts that I personally didn't think that anything could be that urgent this time. I do find it very odd in you, Weyrleader, to be taken in by talking walls spouting archaic legends.'

Robinton rose up out of his seat, bellowing such a protest that Warbret regarded him with amazement. 'Gullible? Warbret, I, Robinton of Cove Hold, may be old but I cannot be considered gullible . . .'

'Nor I,' Fandarel added, also on his feet and looming towards the incredulous Holders. 'This is not a *wall*, Lord Corman,' and the scorn in the usually equable Mastersmith's manner made everyone stare at him. 'This machine, this Aivas, was so efficiently and beautifully crafted by our ancestors that it has survived centuries and still functions. *THAT* is more than the best any present Crafthall can do!' He jerked his big head to emphasize his respect. 'Make no further insult on our intelligence or integrity, Lord Corman. You may not choose to believe in Aivas but most assuredly, I,' and he thumped his chest with his massive thumb, 'Fandarel, Mastercraftsman, do!'

Corman subsided in bewilderment.

'So, why have you called this session then?' Warbret asked.

'So you'd be courteously made aware of the importance of this find as soon as possible,' Lessa said, snapping out the words. 'I'm not letting the Weyrs open to any charge of duplicity or hiding away valuable artefacts.'

'My dear Weyrwoman,' Warbret began placatingly.

'Well, maybe not you, Warbret,' Lord Groghe intervened, 'but I could name some . . .' And he left his words hanging. 'You weren't here, so you didn't listen, as I did, and I'm no more gullible than Robinton, F'lar or Fandarel. But if this Aivas thing really can rid us of Thread, I'm all for giving it every assistance.'

'It says it can do that?' Corman was astounded. 'Then why didn't it do it for our ancestors?'

'Yes, why didn't it?' asked Toronas of Benden.

'Because two erupting volcanoes altered their plans,' F'lar replied with great patience. 'Landing – which is what our ancestors called this place – had to be evacuated. No-one returned from the north to find out what Aivas might have learned.'

'Oh,' and with that Toronas subsided.

'I didn't mean offence, F'lar,' Warbret said reasonably. 'I just think you're all jumping to conclusions on very flimsy evidence that this Aivas apparatus can do the half of what you think it can.'

'Aivas has already proved to me,' Fandarel said, his rumbling voice overpowering others who began explanations, 'that it can restore information that has been lost to my Craft over the last millennium: information that will improve not just my Craft but conditions throughout Pern. You know very well, Lord Warbret, that the depredations of time have rendered many Records illegible. And that many of the conveniences which were our heritage from our ancestors have begun to fail. Further, Aivas has given me plans for a far more efficient power system. One so efficient,' and the Mastersmith pointed a thick forefinger at the Igen Lord Holder, 'that your Hold could be kept cool even at high noon at the height of the summer by the current of your river.'

'Really? I can't say I'd mind that,' Corman admitted but his scepticism remained. 'And just supposing,' Corman added in a sly voice, glancing sideways at F'lar, 'this Aivas does help you get rid of Thread, what will dragonriders do for occupation?'

'We'll worry about that when we have destroyed Thread.'

'So you have some doubts yourself, Weyrleader?' Corman asked quickly.

'I said *when*, Lord Corman,' F'lar said in a grating tone. 'Are you arguing with our eagerness to dispense with accepting your tithes?' F'lar's expression was sardonic.

'No, I mean, we've willingly tithed this Fall . . .' Corman floundered briefly and threw up his hands, recalling the time when he had not willingly supported Benden Weyr.

'And just how will this talking wall of yours destroy Thread, Weyrleader?' demanded the Masterglass-smith Norist, his cheeks red with more than the broken capillaries from facing his hearths. 'By blowing up the Red Star?'

Larad leaned across the table towards Norist, his eyes narrowed in anger. 'Does it matter how it is achieved if it is, Master Norist, so long as there is never another Pass?'

'May I live to see that day,' Corman said in a facetious tone.

'I intend to,' F'lar's voice and expression were steely with determination. 'Now, if we have settled the question as to why at least the dragonriders feel Aivas is important . . .'

'Dragonriders are *not* the only ones, F'lar,' Fandarel said, bringing his heavy fist firmly down on the table, rattling everything on it.

'Nor Mastercraftsmen,' Asgenar added staunchly.

'I, too,' Groghe said when Corman snorted at Jaxom's affirmation. 'Sometimes you can be sharding hard to convince, Corman. You'll change your mind when you've *heard* Aivas. You're not that much of a fool.'

'Enough!' F'lar took charge again. 'The purpose of this meeting is to apprise you of the discovery of Aivas and its inescapable value to Pern as a whole. Which we have done to those of you who bothered to come. Further, I trust you other Weyrleaders,' and F'lar scanned the seven present, 'will join Benden in making full use of the Aivas . . .'

'Now listen here, F'lar, you can't arbitrarily decide something that's going to affect Hold, Hall and Weyr until everyone's had a chance to see for themselves,' Corman began and he glanced at Warbret and Bargen to support him. Larad and Asgenar had made their sympathies obvious.

'I think this ought to be taken up at the Holders' quarterly meeting – which isn't that far off now.'

'Holders may decide for themselves,' F'lar said.

'And Craftmasters,' Norist put in, his expression forbidding. His glare rested longest on Fandarel. 'Our next meeting's not that far off.'

'Decisions on who uses the Aivas ought not to be delayed,' F'lar said.

'C'mon, F'lar,' Groghe said, a gleeful expression on his face, 'you haven't waited on anything. Scrambling about caves in the dark, hauling in apprentices and journeymen from all over the continent to resurrect bits and bobs of strange gear.' He held up a hand when he saw that F'lar regarded him with concern. 'Not that I, personally, don't agree with you, Weyrleader. Deciding anything at the Holders' Quarterlies can try the patience of a dragon. However, I did see and hear Aivas,' and he turned slightly in his seat towards the other Lords Holder. 'The device is amazing and I am convinced of its value!'

'There was a time, Corman,' and F'lar wore the slight smile that reminded the Lord Holder of another occasion when the Benden Weyrleader had faced the massed and armed disapproval of the Lords Holder and bested them, 'when you and all the other Lords Holder urgently required me to put an end to Threadfall. Surely you want me to get on with that task as swiftly as possible?'

'You've done exactly as you ought,' Groghe said, daring Corman to protest.

'Indeed you have, Weyrleader,' Toronas agreed. F'lar found the new Benden Holder a vast improvement on the previous incumbent, Lord Raid.

'However,' F'lar went on, 'it is painfully obvious that we have lost most of the skills our ancestors had. We must relearn them, with Aivas' guidance, so that we can indeed remove forever from this planet the menace of Threadfall.' F'lar looked from Norist to Corman to Warbret and then other Lords Holder who had not taken part in the argument. 'Isn't it sensible to start on the programme as soon as possible? To restore what we have lost?'

'And you expect all of us to take our orders from this

Aivas?' asked Norist, his tone sarcastic. He had been exceedingly reticent when Aivas had queried him about his Craft.

'Master Norist,' Fandarel began in his slow deliberate way, 'if there are opportunities to improve our Craft skills, surely it is incumbent on us to do so?'

'What that Aivas suggested I do in the Craft which I have Mastered, and efficiently, for the past thirty Turns, goes against every established procedure of my Hall!' Norist wasn't going to give an inch.

'Including the now illegible ones in your oldest Records?' Master Robinton asked gently. 'And here is Master Fandarel, fretting to get on with the restoration of an ancestral power station, quite willing to accept new principles from Aivas.'

Something akin to a sneer curled Norist's thick scarred lip. 'We all know that Master Fandarel is endlessly fiddling about with gadgets and gimmicks.'

'Always efficient ones,' Master Fandarel replied, ignoring the disparagement. 'I plainly can see that every craft can benefit from the knowledge stored in Aivas. This morning Bendarek was given invaluable advice on how to improve his paper, Aivas called it, and speed up its production. Very simple but Bendarek immediately saw the possibilities and has gone back to Lemos to develop this much more efficient method. That's why he's not here.'

'You, and Bendarek,' and a flick of Norist's fingers dismissed the newest Mastercraftsman's products, 'may exercise your prerogatives. I prefer to concentrate on maintaining the high standards of my Halls without dissipating effort on frivolous pursuits.'

'You don't, however,' Lord Asgenar said, with a droll grin, 'object to making use of the frivolous pursuits of other Crafthalls. Such as the load of sheets delivered to you last month. Bendarek expects to be able to increase production of paper,' and here Asgenar grinned more broadly, 'so that no one will be kept waiting for supplies.'

'Glass is glass, made of sand, potash and red lead and,' Norist stated stubbornly, 'you can't improve on it.'

'But Aivas suggested ways to do just that,' Master Robinton said at his most reasonable, and persuasive.

'I've wasted enough time here already.' Norist stood up and stalked off down the hall.

'Damned fool,' Asgenar muttered under his breath.

'Back to the important point, F'lar,' Warbret said, leaning forward across the table to the Weyrleader, 'the possibility of eliminating Thread. Just how does this Aivas propose to go about this? F'nor didn't have much luck when he tried.'

F'lar stared at him for a moment, remembering how close F'nor had come to dying in that attempt, collected himself and went on. 'Lord Warbret, until you have first listened to and seen the history Aivas has to tell you, you will not appreciate how much we will have to learn before we can understand his explanations of what we have to do.'

'And Aivas's showing and telling beggars my poor skill,' Robinton said with unusual humility. 'For he was there! He knew our ancestors. He was created on the planet of our forebears! He witnessed and recorded events which have become our myths and legends.' His voice rang with such feeling that there was a moment of respectful silence.

'Yes, you and Lord Corman, you should hear Aivas before you dismiss the gift we have been offered,' Lessa added softly but just as fervently.

'Mind you, I'm not against going along with your course of action,' Warbret said, after a moment, 'if it can help us eradicate Thread. And if you say, Weyrwoman, that we should hold our decision until we've heard this Aivas speak, when will that be possible?'

'Hopefully, later today,' F'lar replied.

'The batteries should be in place now,' Fandarel reminded him, 'but I must go. Aivas is going to need much more power. And I will see that he gets it.' He rose and stood there for a moment, surveying the gathering. 'Some of us will be called upon to change the ways and patterns of a lifetime, which is not an easy thing to do, but the benefits will more than compensate for that effort. We have endured enough of Thread. Now we have the chance to eradicate this menace, and we must grasp it firmly in both hands and succeed! Facenden,' and he turned to his journeyman, 'stay in my stead and report to me later.'

Then he left, his heavy steps audible down the short corridor.

'I think this meeting has gone on long enough, too,' Corman said, rising. 'Do as you wish, Weyrleader. You generally do anyhow,' he said but his comment held no rancour. 'Just see that there is a full report of these activities for the quarterly Convocation.'

He also got to his feet, nudging Bargen to join him. The High Reaches Lord Holder regarded him thoughtfully but did not rise.

'Will you not stay to hear the history, Corman?' Robinton asked.

'In that stuffy little room?' Corman asked indignantly. 'Have my harper learn it and I'll hear it in my own Hold, in comfort and at my own convenience.' And with that he left.

'I will listen,' Bargen said. 'I have come this far. I am by no means at all certain that it is the wisest course to encourage this awesome Aivas thing.'

'At least you will listen,' Robinton said, giving an approving nod. 'Sebell, how many can we comfortably accommodate in that stuffy little room?' He said it blandly enough but several of the Weyrleaders smiled.

'Certainly all here who wish to attend,' Sebell said. 'There are now enough benches and stools and, if a few of us have to stand, I gather no-one minded yesterday. I certainly won't.'

'We don't have to ask this creature's permission?' Bargen asked.

'Aivas is nothing if not accommodating,' Master Robinton said, grinning broadly.

They filed down the hall then, three Lords Holder, the Weyrleaders and Weyrwomen and the Craftmasters. Terry was already there, looking mightily pleased with himself but warding people away from the bundle of cords that wound from Aivas along the left-hand wall and out into the adjacent room. A window had been inserted, high on the right-hand wall so fresh air circulated through the room now. There were benches and sufficient stools to seat everyone, including Lord Groghe who had decided to take a second hearing. Menolly stood beside Sebell. She groped and found his hand when the first vision of Pern in the blackness of space lit the screen.

'Now that's amazing,' Bargen exclaimed but he was the last to speak until Aivas ended his account with the final view of an airsled disappearing through the ash fall to the west. Then, slightly dazed, he muttered. 'Corman's an old fool. Norist, too.'

'Thank you, Aivas,' Groghe of Fort Hold said, rising and shaking out stiffened limbs. 'Of course, I saw it yesterday but it's worth seeing again. And any time I can.' He nodded emphatically at F'lar. 'You know that I'll support you, dragonriders. You will, too, won't you, Warbret, Bargen?' His question was more of a demand and he jutted his chin at his peers, ready to coerce them into agreement.

'I think we must, Warbret,' Bargen said as he rose and turned, courteously inclining his body toward F'lar and then Master Robinton. 'Good day. And good luck.'

The other Lords left with him.

'I don't mean to dash all this optimism,' G'dened of Ista Weyr said, 'but Aivas said nothing to the point of just how we're going to accomplish the elimination of Thread.'

'No, he didn't exactly, did he?' R'mart said, shaking his head as if to clear it. 'The ancestors had a lot more equipment and gadgets and those sleds. If they couldn't get rid of Thread, how shall we?'

'There is a time for all things to be accomplished,' Aivas said. 'As mentioned last night, several conclusions had been made. The most important, for you, is that in four years, ten months and twenty-seven days, it will be possible to jolt the eccentric planet out of its present orbit, permanently.'

The Aivas had the stunned attention of everyone in the room as a diagram of Rukbat's planets blazed on the screen. They moved slowly around their primary and the wanderer crossed at an angle to them.

F'lar gave a weak laugh. 'The dragons of Pern are

strong and willing, but I don't think they could move the Red Star.'

'They will not,' Aivas said, 'for to attempt the feat would be to endanger their lives and their riders. But the dragons are able to perform other, vital tasks that will allow you to alter that planet's course permanently. It will then be close to the orbit of your fifth planet, far from Rukbat though, as you now know, the Thread swarms still follow it past Pern.'

Once again everyone was silent.

'That I might live to see the day,' G'dened murmured fervently. 'I'd go forward another four hundred Turns if we could do that!'

'If that could be done,' R'mart asked, 'why didn't our ancestors do it?'

'The conjunction of the planets was not then auspicious. And,' here the Aivas paused briefly, to add with what Master Robinton heard as irony, 'by the time these calculations had been made, all had gone north and this facility was unable to inform its operators.' Aivas paused again. 'The dragons you have nourished to such size and strength will be critical to the success of the project. If you are willing?'

'If we are willing?' T'gellan and T'bor cried in astonished chorus.

All the dragonriders sprang to their feet, Mirrim hugging T'gellan's arm, her eyes sparkling with determination.

'F'lar's not the only one,' N'ton added, 'whose greatest wish is to exterminate Thread!'

D'ram, the oldest of the riders, had tears streaming down his cheeks. 'We are nothing if not willing, Aivas. Even this old man and his ancient dragon!'

From outside came a chorus of dragons bugling, the rich bass of the bronzes, the thrilling sopranos of the queens and the high piercing tone of Mirrim's green Path.

'It will not be an easy task,' Aivas said, 'and you will have to study assiduously in order to lay the necessary foundations to bring success to that day.'

'Why must it be four years, ten months and whatever days . . .' K'van, the youngest Weyrleader, asked.

'Twenty-seven days,' Aivas corrected him. 'Because that is the precise moment when a window will be open.'

'A window?' Inadvertently K'van looked at the new one in the wall.

'As a rider, you always take your dragon to a precise place when you go *between*, do you not?' K'van was not the only rider to nod agreement. 'It is even more important when one is travelling in space to be precise.'

'We're going to be travelling in space?' F'lar asked, gesturing toward the screen where they had briefly seen what space was like.

'In a manner of speaking,' Aivas said. 'You will come to understand, and correctly interpret, the terms that define the tasks before you. In the lexicon of space travel, a window is the interval which brackets the moment, within which you have flexibility to achieve your objective also travelling in space. If this is to succeed . . .'

'*If?*' R'mart almost yelled. 'But you said it could . . .' And he glared accusingly at F'lar.

'The plan is viable and has every chance of succeeding IF the requisite effort is put into its implementation,' Aivas said firmly. 'But success will depend on the learning of new skills and disciplines. It is obvious that while all dragonriders are dedicated men, you also have little leisure at your command. But the dragons and the riders are requisites to the task, supported by Craftmasters, and those Lords Holder who will lend men and women as support staff. It would be best if everyone on the planet could be involved in the project. As were your ancestors.'

'I still don't see why our ancestors didn't take care of the problem when they had the chance to,' R'mart said.

'Your ancestors did not have dragons the size and intelligence of yours. The species has evolved and exceeded the original genetic specifications. If you will observe,' and two dragons flicked onto Aivas's screen, 'the bronze is Carenath, Sean O'Connell is his rider and the other is Faranth and Sorka Hanrahan. Now,' and two more dragons appeared on screen, three times the size of the first two, 'here are Ramoth and Mnementh. The scale of comparison is accurate.'

'Why, that bronze isn't as big as Ruth,' T'bor said, shooting an apologetic glance at the Benden Weyrleaders.

'No, he doesn't seem to be,' F'lar replied equably. 'You've made the point, Aivas. Now, how do we start this training you speak of?'

'Not today, certainly,' Aivas said. 'The first priority is a proper power source which Master Fandarel has been good enough to undertake in his efficient fashion.' Master Robinton swung a sharp stare at the screen. Or perhaps, he only imagined that Aivas used the adjective in a facetious context. Aivas continued: 'Second, the installation of the additional stations. Third, a supply of paper sufficient for hard copy for instruction and explanation. Fourth . . .'

F'lar waved both hands, grinning. 'Enough, Aivas. When the craftsmen have done your bidding, we'll be ready to take instruction. That I promise you.'

'Good,' and Master Terry rose from his stool, hitching a heavy tool belt to a more comfortable position. 'Are you leaving here now?' he asked amiably. 'Because I've got more connections to make to Aivas and you're in my way.'

'There'll be food and drink in the conference room by now,' Lessa said, encouraging their removal.

Master Robinton waited until all the others were well down the corridor. He glanced at Terry, busy laying out the cables and muttering to himself.

'Aivas?' the Masterharper said in a whisper, 'do you have a sense of humour?'

There was a distinct pause before the reply came. 'Master Robinton, this facility is not programmed for senses. It is programmed to interact with humans.'

'That is not an answer.'

'It is one kind of an explanation.'

With that, Master Robinton had to be content.

The four Eastern Weyr dragonriders glided in a spiral down to the hillside above the dam. All interest in the ancients' settlement had been centred on Landing. No-one had yet had any occasion to wander about the nearby hills looking for evidence of Man's handiwork, so the presence of an obviously man-made lake – for Fandarel had dammed up a few useful streams in his Turns as apprentice and journeyman in the Smithcrafthall and recognized the configuration – was yet another surprise.

The lake stretched back, a glittering long finger, contained between two high ridges, long and narrow. The dam had been built across the neck of the south-east end. Though the structure had been broached and two cascades fell gracefully from the height into the ravine below, it was still the biggest dam Fandarel had ever seen. But then, never since this one had been built, had Mankind needed one on the same scale.

The marvellous thing, Master Fandarel realized, was not that it had been made, but that so much of it had survived for twenty-five centuries. As D'clan's brown Pranith skimmed the top, Fandarel could see that the passage of all that time had taken some toll on the dam. Pieces, like the bites of a creature larger even than a dragon, had gouged grooves on the top through which the falls tumbled. Floods, no doubt, he decided, pushing large boulders or debris relentlessly against it. He pulled on D'clan's sleeve, pointed a thick forefinger vigorously downward. D'clan nodded, grinning, and in the next instant, Pranith tightened his spiral and glided to a neat landing on the left-hand side, the longer intact span.

With a grace and agility most younger and fitter men envied, Fandarel slid from the brown neck and landed lightly on his feet. He was down on his hands and knees, knife blade scraping aside mud and caked dirt to examine the material of the dam. He shook his head.

'Plascrete, Aivas said,' he muttered to himself as the others in his party joined him: Evan, the journeyman who often translated his designs into solid reality, was a self-contained man who hadn't so much as blinked when he took instructions from 'the talking wall'; Belterac, nearly as grizzled as Fandarel was, but wise in his craft and steady in his working habits to offset the apprentice Fosdak who was erratic and troublesome but strong as a draft animal; and Silton, a useful and diligent young man who had shown some of Master Terry's dogged perseverance. 'They built this of plascrete,' he said. 'Stuff that will last for millennia. And it has. By the shell of the first Egg, it has!'

The three dragons were as interested in the dam as the humans, the top more than wide enough for them to walk along, with their wings folded to their backs. Suddenly, V'line laughed and said aloud that his bronze Clarinath asked if there'd be time for a bath here. The water looked so clear and clean.

'Later, please,' Fandarel said, continuing his inspection of the edifice.

'Amazing construction,' Evan murmured, scuffing the surface with his heavy boots on his way to the lake side of the structure. He peered over the edge. 'Water levels are marked, Fandarel. Can't have been high in Turns, though it has been from time to time.'

Then he walked to the ravine side and pointed downwards and to his left. 'There, Master, that's where the ancients had their power station.'

Fandarel squinted, shielding his eyes with one huge hand, and nodded in satisfaction as he saw the remains of the building. Something had smashed into it from a height. Probably the same debris which had breached the dam, crashing down on the place with tremendous force.

'D'clan, if you and Pranith would be good enough to take us down there,' and Fandarel pointed. 'Evan and I will go first to be sure it is safe enough.'

D'clan and Pranith obliged, finding sufficient room to set down by the ruins. What was left were the heavy girders which had supported the roof of the power station, and the inner wall which looked to be cemented to the naked rock. But the floor, despite a thick carpet of pebble encrusted dirt a full knife-blade deep, had remained impervious to the passage of time.

'Those strong young backs can clear this, Evan,' Fandarel said. 'D'clan, can you wave the others down here? Then the dragons may have a swim.'

'They spend more time in the water than in the air,' D'clan replied. 'They're more likely to wash the hide off 'em, if they don't be careful. A hide-damaged dragon's no good *between*.' But his tone was more affectionate than captious.

74

While the others started shovelling away the mud, Fandarel and Evan made careful measurements of the area to be enclosed, and calculated where the new power wheel would be situated. With deft lines, Evan made a preliminary sketch of what the finished installation would look like. Fandarel, watching over his shoulder, nodded approval. Then he looked about him, squinting up at the high smooth face of the dam and the hillsides.

'Now,' Fandarel said satisfied with his analysis of the site's needs, 'we go back to Telgar, to assemble the components.' He grinned at Evan. 'It will be a novel thing, will it not, to work from proper plans.'

Evan merely raised his eyebrows, being long inured to his Master's eccentricities. 'Can't be but more efficient that way.'

'My dear F'lar,' Robinton said reassuringly to the Weyrleader who was patently disappointed at his failure to gain the full backing of the Lords Holder, 'Aivas impressed Larad, Asgenar, Groghe, Toronas, Bargen and Warbret, plus Jaxom. Seven out of sixteen's not bad for a start. Oterel's doddering and Corman always needs time to mull things over. If the various projects for which you will need workers here continue to clear out that beggars' cave of Laudey's, he'll back you.' Then Robinton's expression became understanding and sympathetic. He put one hand on F'lar's shoulder, giving it just a little shake. 'F'lar, you so desperately *want* to eradicate Thread. That's your first responsibility. Managing their Holds is theirs and, sometimes, as we both know, they forget the wider view. Yes, K'van?' The Harper had been aware that the young Southern Weyrleader was hovering in the background. 'Have I been monopolizing F'lar when you need a word with him?'

'If I might intrude,' K'van said tentatively.

'My glass is empty,' and, with a raffish grin, Robinton took himself back to the food-laden table in search of a wineskin.

'Was Lord Toric asked?' K'van said hesitantly.

'Yes, indeed he was, K'van,' and F'lar drew him to one

corner of the room where they were less likely to be drawn into the lively discussions of the other Weyrleaders. 'I charged Breide in particular to let him know.'

K'van managed a fleeting grin for they both knew that Breide's main function at Landing was to report to the Southern Lord Holder everything of interest. Breide's conscientiousness often served up such quantities of trivia that Toric obviously did not read the reports.

'He's trying to get enough men over to the island to shift Denol and his kin. Everyone knows that Toric is furious about the attempt by that band of rebels to take over the island he claims as part of his Hold.'

'I'd've thought he'd accomplished that already,' F'lar said in surprise. 'Toric can be very determined.'

K'van's grin was sour. 'He's also determined to have the Weyr's help.'

F'lar started angrily. 'There's no way he's to have that, K'van!'

'And so I've told him, time and again. The Weyr is not there for his convenience.'

'And?'

'He doesn't take my no as final, F'lar.' K'van faltered and he gave a helpless shrug to his shoulders. 'I know I'm young to be a Weyrleader . . .'

'Your youth is not a relevant factor, K'van. You're a good Weyrleader and I've had that assurance from the older riders in your Weyr!'

K'van was young enough to flush with pleasure to hear that. 'Toric wouldn't agree,' K'van replied, twitching his straight held shoulders.

F'lar could not deny the fact that K'van's slim youthful build would disadvantage him in a confrontation with the tall and powerful Southern Lord Holder. At the time K'van's Heth had flown Adrea's queen, Toric had been enthusiastic about having a Benden-trained Weyrleader. But Toric hadn't had rank rebellion in his Hold at that point.

'At first,' K'van went on, 'he wanted the Weyr to take his soldiers to the island. When I refused, he said that he'd be satisfied that I'd done my duty to the Hold if

I told him where the rebels had made their camp. His argument was that we overfly the island during a Pass so we'd see where they were and that information would assist him in suppressing the rebellion. When I refused, he started to harass some of the older bronze riders, suggesting that I'm too young to know my duty to the Lord Holder.'

'I trust he's had no joy on that score,' F'lar said sharply.

K'van shook his head. 'No, they told him that such action was not a Weyr responsibility. Then . . .' The young Weyrleader hesitated.

'Then?' F'lar prompted grimly.

'He tried to bribe one of my blue riders with the promise of finding him a suitable friend.'

'That is enough!' F'lar's face darkened with his anger and he irritably pushed hair back from his forehead. 'Lessa!' He beckoned her urgently to join them.

When F'lar explained K'van's problem, she was equally incensed.

'You'd think he'd know better by this time not to try to bully dragonriders, of any degree,' she said, her voice crisp with anger. When she saw K'van's apprehensive expression, she gave him a reassuring touch. 'It's scarcely your fault Toric is as greedy as a Bitran.'

'Desperate, more like,' K'van said with the hint of a smile. 'Master Idarolan told me that Toric had offered him a small fortune in gems and a fine harbour if he'd sail a punitive force to the Island. But he wouldn't. And, furthermore, he's told all the other shipmasters that they're not to help Toric in this matter. They won't either.'

'Toric has ships of his own,' Lessa said irritably.

K'van had relaxed enough to grin, a grin that emphasized his youthfulness. 'But none large enough to transport a sufficiently strong force to be effective. His landing parties have been ambushed and either wounded severely enough to make them useless or imprisoned by the rebels.' His grin got broader. 'I've got to hand it to Denol. He's clever. But I wanted to tell you what's been happening before lies or rumours got back to you – or other Lords Holder complained about our attitude.'

'Quite correct, K'van,' F'lar said.

'We'll have to find time to visit Lord Toric,' Lessa said, a steely look in her eyes. Then she smiled, a smile that made K'van relieved that it was not directed against him. 'Lord Toric *needs* a full report on Aivas and what's happening here at Landing. I think we inform him ourselves, F'lar?'

'I'm not sure when,' F'lar said with a sigh. 'But we'll make the time somehow. Just keep your Weyr out of Toric's squabble.'

'I shall!' And there was no doubt in the Benden Weyrleaders' minds that he would. K'van had been a determined and responsible youngster and now, grown to manhood, those traits were refined. He'd stand against Toric simply because Toric didn't think he could.

'Now, place this plug,' Aivas told Piemur, illustrating the appropriate one on the monitor, 'in this female socket.' When Piemur had complied, Aivas went on. 'There should be a green light on the base of the monitor.'

'There isn't,' Piemur said in a voice that was almost a wail. He sighed gustily, hanging on to his patience.

'Then there is a faulty connection. Remove the cover and check the boards, mother, input-output, and memory,' Aivas said. It didn't help Piemur's temper that Aivas seemed totally unruffled by yet another failure. It simply wasn't normal for an entity to be so bloody methodically insensitive. 'Machines must first be properly assembled before they can function as they were designed. That is the first step. Be patient. It is only a matter of discovering which is the faulty connection.'

Piemur found that he was trying to bend the screwdriver in his hand. Which was a childish reaction to frustration. He took a deep breath and, not daring to look to either side of him where Benelek and Jancis were concentrating on assembling their own devices, he removed the cover of his. Once more.

They'd been at this tedious and exacting task ever since Terry had arranged all the wires and connecting cords to Aivas's satisfaction. It soothed Piemur only slightly that Benelek, who had always been mechanically inclined and good with his hands, was not faring any better. Nor was Jancis, though her current ineptitude distressed him for her sake. Piemur's shoulders ached with cramp, his fingers were thick with all the finicky little movements and he was going sour on this whole project. It had seemed such a simple affair. Find the cartons in the caves with the stored units, dust 'em off, start 'em up and that'd be that. But it wasn't. First Aivas had made them learn what each unit was – keyboard, liquid crystal display, computer box, touch keyboard panel, and the codes for the various 'boards' that activated the computer terminal. Fortunately, when it came to soldering broken connections, Jancis and Benelek were adept. Piemur burned his fingers once or twice in practice but he caught on quickly enough. Fingers made dextrous by playing instruments found it easy to adapt to the new task. But the initial enthusiasm which had motivated Piemur since before dawn had long since drained out of him. Only the fact that neither Jancis nor Benelek faltered kept Piemur going.

'Let us begin again,' the inexorable, calm Aivas voice continued, 'by checking each panel to be sure there is no damage or break in the circuits or chips.'

'I've done that twice already,' Piemur said, setting his jaw.

'Then it must be done again. Make use of the magnifying glass. That is why our boards were all made to be visible, serviceable – on Earth it was not possible to check them visually like this. There it was done by facilities in factory outlets. Here we must just proceed patiently.'

Holding his temper firmly in check, Piemur went over the chips, circuit by circuit, scrutinizing the resistors and capacitors. The beads and silvery lines that had once fascinated him had become anathema, called by stupid terms that meant nothing but trouble to him. He devoutly wished he'd never seen the bloody things. Close scrutiny did not disclose any obvious breaks. So, exercising the greatest control on his fingers lest his frustration enter them, he replaced each component as carefully as he could. They all slotted firmly into place.

'Be sure that each card is seated securely in the grooves,' said the ever-calm Aivas.

'I just did, Aivas!' Piemur knew he sounded petulant but, opposed to Aivas's imperturbability, he found it even harder to be objective. Then his captious humour reasserted itself. Machines, he reminded himself facetiously, only do what they are programmed to do. They do not have emotions to interfere with the smooth performance of their duties – once a smooth performance had been attained.

'Before you replace the cover, Piemur, blow gently across the unit to be sure there are no motes of dust clogging the connections.'

Master Esselin had the reconstruction of the Aivas facility in hand but the work roused clouds of dust which sifted into the chamber. The prospect of more room was currently negated by the ensuing mess.

Piemur blew carefully. Replaced the cover. Picked up the plug and inserted it. It took him a full moment to realize that a green light indeed shone on the panel, just where it should and that a letter had appeared on the liquid crystal display. He let out a whoop which startled Jancis and Benelek.

'Don't do that, Piemur,' the young journeyman exclaimed, scowling up at him. 'I nearly soldered the wrong connection.'

'It's really working, Piemur?' Jancis looked up hopefully for she was as frustrated as the two men were. She was very proud of Piemur, who hadn't the training she and Benelek had, for having succeeded.

'Green and go!' Piemur chortled, rubbing his hands together, despite Benelek's sour looks. 'All right, Aivas, now what do I do?'

'Using the letters on the keys in front of you, tap out "readme".'

Hunting out the various letters, Piemur tapped out the phrase. Instantly the screen in front of him blossomed with words, numbers and letters.

'Hey, look, you two. Words! My own screen full of words!'

Benelek spared only an irritated glance but Jancis rose to

stand behind him and admire the result. She gave him an approving pat and then returned to her task.

'Read carefully and absorb the information on the screen,' Aivas said, 'and you will learn how to access the programs you need to reach the information you desire. First you must become familiar with the terms. Being comfortable with these terms increases your efficiency as an operator.'

By the time Piemur had read through the instructions several times, he wasn't much wiser for it appeared to him that familiar words no longer meant what they should. He sighed and started at the beginning of the page again. Words were a harper's profession and he would learn these new interpretations if it took him the full Turn.

'I've got it, too,' Jancis cried elatedly. 'I've got a green light, too!'

'That makes three of us then,' Benelek said in a smug tone. 'And I tap out "readme", Aivas?'

'The initial lesson is the same for all, Benelek. You are to be congratulated! Have more students been enlisted in this project? There is much to be done!'

'Patience, Aivas,' Piemur said, imitating Aivas's tone and grinning at Jancis for his impudence, 'they'll come in their fairs once word has got round.'

'The rider of the white dragon, Lord Jaxom? Will he be one?'

'Jaxom?' Piemur asked, mildly surprised. 'I wonder where he got to.'

Chapter Four

For most of that day, Jaxom had been as thoroughly thwarted as Piemur could have wished. He and Ruth had transported five net loads of cartons from the caves to the Aivas building and just when the last had been off-loaded, Master Fandarel had urgently requested Jaxom and the obliging Ruth to convey Bendarek back to Lemos and his Crafthall. The Woodsmith couldn't wait to initiate Aivas's plans to redesign his paper-making machinery and to improve the quality of the product by adding a rag content to the wood pulp.

When Jaxom and Ruth got back to Landing, Master Terry had needed help in locating cables and wires which, after much scrambling about, were found in an almost overlooked alcove in the caves. Jaxom and Ruth naturally obliged Master Terry in transporting the coils and himself back to the Aivas building. Jaxom tried not to care, reminding himself that he was assisting the overall effort, except that he had had rather different notions of how he and Ruth would spend the day.

The white dragon had looked forward to basking in the hot southern sun. The Winter in the north had been cold and clammy, with little sunshine. Jaxom had especially wanted to work on Aivas's contraptions with Piemur, Jancis and Bendarek.

But Jaxom had made a habit of being accessible, amiable

and helpful. People found it much easier to ask Jaxom and Ruth to oblige than other dragons and riders. As Ruth never objected, Jaxom felt constrained to assist whenever they could. Sharra thought it was because he was so determined to be the opposite of his despotic sire, Fax. She felt Jaxom carried this second generation atonement too far sometimes and she was quick to interfere if she felt his willingness was being abused. But she was back in Ruatha and this was certainly one of those times when amiability was a bloody nuisance.

By the time Terry had off-loaded his coils of wires, Jaxom became aware of a rumbling in his stomach: not surprising, since he had had nothing but *klah* and a meatroll with Menolly and Sebell in the early morning. Sharra always worried about him remembering to take time to eat and Jaxom tried to remember her injunctions. He did wish that her gravid condition hadn't prevented her from accompanying him here but she couldn't risk going *between* right now. So he walked over to the kitchen building, unaware that F'lar was holding the extraordinary meeting, or he'd have been there to lend his support. Jaxom had to help himself to food because the cook and the drudges were busy dealing with an apprentice who had badly burned his hand on a hot spit. That reminded Jaxom that he had promised to convey Master Oldive to Landing. Maybe when that chore was done, he and Ruth could do as they wished.

When Jaxom and Ruth came out of *between* above the great courtyard of the combined Harper and Healer Halls in Fort Hold, Ruth was suddenly surrounded by a chittering fair of fire-lizards, their demands shrill with warning.

'What's the matter with them, Ruth?' F'lar asked.

Master Oldive doesn't want you to land in the courtyard, Ruth replied. *He says the harpers will latch on to you and he'll never get to Landing*. Ruth sounded puzzled but Jaxom laughed.

'I should've thought of that myself. So what does Master Oldive suggest we do?'

I don't know. They've gone to tell him we're here. Ruth discreetly glided to the far side of the big Harper Hall complex, where they would not be so easily seen from either the Hall or Fort Hold, looming to the right of the Hall.

He comes, Ruth said, just as they were once again surrounded by now happily chirping fairs of fire-lizards, doing one of their intricate aerial displays of delight. *They see us from the Hold*, he added, as another full fair of fire-lizards came zooming in on them, shrieking urgently. *No, we have more important things to do than stop at the Hold right now*, Ruth said and added a warning bugle which sent the newcomers whizzing back, their voices thin with distress at his reprimand.

'Lord Groghe's at Landing,' Jaxom said, trying not to feel guilty about ignoring the request. 'He'll tell them all he wants them to know when he gets back.'

His queen fire-lizard has been in and out of the Hold with messages. They know all they need to know about this Aivas. Ruth rumbled in subtle discontent.

Jaxom slapped the white dragon's neck affectionately. 'You wouldn't fit in the room, dear friend. Piemur said his Farli went to sleep, totally uninterested in Aivas.'

Ruth rumbled again. *Here comes the Masterhealer*, and he veered sharply, descending at such an angle that Jaxom reflexively grabbed the riding straps and arched backwards against the steep dive.

'You could have warned me,' Jaxom remonstrated mildly. Ruth had a habit of sharpening up his reflexes with unexpected manoeuvres. Ruth grunted with satisfaction at the success of his trick as he backwinged to land neatly a length from Master Oldive who shambled up to them at an unexpectedly rapid rate for a man with legs of unequal length and a humped back. He had a large satchel thumping behind his normal shoulder but he waved a greeting, a huge grin on his face.

'Ho, there, Jaxom, I feared that you'd forgotten me in all the furore.' He leaned against Ruth for a moment to recover his breath. 'I'm not as fit as I think I am,' he said. They both heard the shouts and saw folk in harper blue charging out of the courtyard archway. 'Quickly. If they catch you, we'll never leave.'

Ruth crouched down on his forequarters, crooking his left foreleg as a step for the Masterhealer. Jaxom leaned down to grasp Oldive's arm. Winded the man might be but he exerted a powerful pull as he hauled himself on to Ruth's back, settling behind Jaxom.

Immediately Ruth sprang aloft, his white wings taking the first important down stroke and beating upwards so that the disappointed cries were quickly lost.

'When you're ready, Ruth,' Jaxom said, picturing the Aivas building and being very careful to detail the alteration of the mounds in front of it so as not to have Ruth land out of time. Enough space had now been cleared for several dragons to land.

The cold of *between* sucked warmth from their bodies and then they were suddenly in the bright, hot southern afternoon sun. A good-sized fair swirled up to welcome Ruth who was the particular favourite of all fire-lizards. As usual in the south, there were as many wild ones as those whose necks were banded in the colours of the people they were beholden to.

'By the first Egg, I don't recognize the place,' Oldive said in an awed voice as Ruth glided in to land more circumspectly than he had with only Jaxom a-back at the Hall.

'I'm not sure I recognize it either,' Jaxom said, grinning as he turned his head over his shoulder so that his words would reach Oldive. 'Master Esselin has already got one annexe up,' he added, pointing to the swarm of men working furiously to erect walls on the right-hand side of the Aivas.

'Oh, you're using parts of the old buildings,' Oldive exclaimed.

'F'lar suggested it. Makes sense instead of having to haul in building materials when there are all those empty buildings.'

'Oh, true, true.' Oldive's tone did not indicate complete approval.

'And only from the smaller buildings, the family units, Aivas called them. There are several hundred of them,' Jaxom went on reassuringly. During their rummaging in the Catherine Caves, Terry had given Jaxom an account of the morning's session with Aivas and the renovations planned.

'Is every Weyrleader here?' Oldive went on, suddenly aware of the long line of sun-bathing dragons on the ridge above the settlement.

Jaxom laughed. 'Since Aivas promises to help obliterate Thread, they wait on his every word.' He held up a steadying hand as Oldive dismounted from Ruth's back.

'How?' Oldive almost lost his footing in surprise, his large and luminous eyes wide with amazement and incredulity. Jaxom braced him, catching the pack before it could swing around and totally unbalance the Healer.

Jaxom shrugged, experiencing another surge of annoyance at being out of things so far today. 'I don't exactly know. I was hoping to find out more this morning but I've been otherwise occupied.'

Oldive put a sympathetic hand on Jaxom's arm, and his expression was apologetic. 'Conveying the curious to the new wonder?'

'Oh, I don't mind, Oldive,' and then he grinned slyly at the Healer, 'if you will remember to ask Aivas about those two patients Sharra's so worried about.'

'They are first on my list, I assure you, Jaxom. Marvellous woman, Sharra, always giving of her own energies and as selfless as you are yourself!'

Jaxom looked away in embarrassment, made all the more acute because he would have preferred to have spent the morning learning new things from Aivas. But he was here now and he eagerly anticipated Master Oldive's reaction to Aivas.

Esselin's craftsmen were making an appalling amount of noise with their hammering. There was dust everywhere as he and Oldive made their way into the building. Jaxom was amazed at how much had been accomplished inside. Walls had been washed clean and their colours were now bright and cheerful. He wondered how colour had been impregnated into the material for it didn't look like any painted surface he had ever seen. Jaxom could hear lively conversations off to the left, F'lar's voice was recognizable, T'gellan's and R'mart's, slightly contentious. He guided Master Oldive to the right and relived the thrill of yesterday's discovery as they faced the closed door to

Aivas's room. He could barely contain his own excitement at the effect Aivas would surely have on Master Oldive.

He rapped on the door in a courteous warning and then opened it on a scene of great industry which reinforced his niggling resentment. Seated in front of a makeshift table, no more than a board supported by empty cartons at both ends, Piemur, Jancis and Bendarek were crouched over the units which he had helped resurrect from the Catherine Caves. And, insult to his sense of injury, the sharding things were working. His three friends were tapping away industriously at the keyboard units in front of them. He inhaled deeply through his nostrils to disperse his pique: a reaction he found unacceptable behaviour in himself.

'Good day to you, Master Oldive,' Piemur had craned his neck around at their entry. 'Welcome to the hallowed Aivas chamber. Where've you been all day, Jaxom?'

'I see you've made good use of *your* time,' Jaxom replied, trying very hard to neutralize his ill feelings. He caught Oldive's sideways glance and made himself smile. 'But I'm here now and you can teach me what I need to know.'

'No chance of that,' Piemur replied with his usual impudence. 'You have to start from the same point we did. Aivas's orders. Correct, Aivas?'

'I'm quite willing,' Jaxom said, trying to see the writing on Jancis' screen, the closest to him.

She had stopped whatever she had been doing at Jaxom's entrance, smiling at Master Oldive. Now she wrinkled her nose at Piemur. 'You are the limit sometimes. The components are all carefully set out in the next room, Jaxom. I'll help you even if he won't.'

Bendarek didn't look up from his work. 'He's to muddle through all by himself, Jancis, or he doesn't learn.'

She rolled her eyes at Bendarek's uncompromising attitude. 'Oh, he'll have to do it himself, but a wink is as good as a nod at times. Besides, I think we'd all better move into the other room. I can't stand it when Master Oldive goes into gory details. And that's what he's here to do with Aivas.' She winked at the Healer whom she knew well. 'Every Craft has its hazards, I suppose.'

'Oh, yes, we certainly should allow him some privacy,' Piemur said, immediately rising from his stool.

'Interruptions, always interruptions,' Bendarek muttered sourly but he got up, too, and carefully began to start the transfer.

'I heard the Weyrleaders back there,' Jaxom began, wanting to effect the introduction protocol for Aivas, 'should I get one in here?'

'Won't be needed,' Piemur said. 'Special dispensation has already been recorded by Aivas. Just go ahead and introduce Master Oldive.'

Which Jaxom did, exceedingly grateful that he'd have no further delay in catching up with his friends at the devices.

'It is a pleasure to meet a man who is so highly praised by all,' Aivas said.

The rich voice, so humanly inflected, caused Master Oldive to stare about him in considerable consternation.

'Aivas is, so to speak, all around you in this room,' Jaxom said encouragingly when he saw how disconcerted the Healer was. 'He's a bit much to get used to at first, I agree. Scared the lot of us.'

Busy disassembling the makeshift table, Piemur shot Master Oldive an indulgent grin. 'You'll get used to a disembodied voice real quick, the kind of sense Aivas talks.'

'Go teach yourself to be sensible for me, young Piemur,' Aivas said in a jocular tone that startled everyone.

'Yes, sir, good Master Aivas, yes sir,' Piemur quipped, bowing humbly as he backed out of the room, carrying the table board, and nearly knocking himself down when he forgot to lower the board to get it through the door.

Jancis, carefully rearranging the cord into the slot cut in the bottom of the door for just that purpose, pulled the door shut behind her as the last to leave.

'Please make yourself comfortable, Master Oldive,' Aivas suggested. 'Did you by any chance bring recent Records from your Hall? Those from the Harper, the Mastersmith, and the Woodsmith have already been assimilated, but for a proper assessment of your society's achievements, records from every Hall, Hold and Weyr are gratefully accepted.'

During this conversation, Master Oldive had absently seated himself, his satchel, heavy with the notes he had indeed brought with him, beginning to slide from his shoulder. He caught the strap and, with a shake of his head, recalled his wits.

'Lord Groghe said that—' and Master Oldive hesitated briefly, not knowing the appropriate form in which to address the entity, '—*you* know – well, everything.'

'The memory banks of this facility contain the most comprehensive data available at the time the colony ships set out for their destination of the Rukbat system. That includes medical information.'

'May I ask how that information is organized?'

'Basic anatomy, micro-anatomy, physiology, autocrinology, medical biochemistry and many more categories, immunology, neuropathology, which, it is fair to suggest, may no longer be known to you.'

'In that you are correct. For we have lost so much knowledge, so many techniques,' and Oldive had never been more keenly aware of the gaps in his Craft.

'You distress yourself unnecessarily, Master Oldive, for all those whom I have met so far are in excellent health and well above what was considered normal weight and height by the medical standards of your ancestors. There is much to be said for a non-industrialized civilization.'

'Industrialized? That term is unfamiliar to me though I recognize the root word.'

'INDUSTRIALIZE,' Aivas intoned, 'transitive verb: to organize large industries in; as, to industrialize a community; to introduce the economic system of industrialization into; as, to industrialize a new nation. An industrialized society in contrast to an agrarian one like yours has been.'

'Thank you. Why would an industrialized society produce less healthy folk?'

'Pollution of the atmosphere and environment by industrial wastes, noxious fumes, chemical effluents, contamination of field grown edibles, among other evils.'

Master Oldive was made speechless by the explanation.

'Those who settled Pern wished to found an agrarian

society. To that end they were receptive to many anti-industrial cultures, like the ancient gipsies, as well as to retired military types. Their objective has been attained in this, your present,' Aivas said.

'It has?' Master Oldive was surprised that Pern had succeeded in anything other than surviving nine Passes of Threadfall.

'In more ways than you might imagine, Master Oldive, being too close to have an objective view. Apart from the inconvenience of the organism, Thread, you have achieved much.'

'Addressing you, Aivas, I perceive that we have also lost much.'

'Perhaps not as much as you think, Masterhealer.'

'In my Craft, I *know* that we have lost the capacity to alleviate much suffering, prevent the plagues which have all but decimated the population from time to time . . .'

'The strong survived and your population was renewed.'

'But so much knowledge was irretrievably lost, especially in my Craft.'

'Those losses can be remedied.'

Master Oldive was caught up short by what sounded very much like a pun to him. But surely a machine . . . He cleared his throat but it was Aivas who continued speaking.

'Would it ease your mind to know that even the most astute medical practitioners among your ancestors sometimes felt themselves helpless against plague? That they constantly sought new methods of easing pain and correcting afflictions?'

'It should, but it doesn't. But, to urgent matters, if I may, Aivas?'

'Of course, Master Oldive.'

'There are several patients, three suffering severe pain which we are unable to relieve, wasting in both flesh and spirit. If I tell you their symptoms, would that be sufficient for diagnosis?'

'Proceed with the symptoms. If they can be matched with cases on record, a diagnosis is possible. As there are three point two billion documented histories that can be consulted, a similarity may be found that would suggest suitable treatment.'

With fingers made momentarily fumbling by the hope that consumed Master Oldive, he opened his case book to the first of Sharra's two patients. He owed Jaxom that courtesy.

'What're you doing?' Jaxom asked, mystified by the way the others intently regarded their grey screens. Aivas' screen was not at all like these which were, among other noticeable variations, much smaller.

Bendarek gave a snort of impatience and bent further over the board. He pecked about with his index fingers in no pattern which Jaxom could discern.

'We're becoming familiar with the keyboard configuration,' Piemur said, with a malicious grin for Jaxom's ignorance. 'We're learning our way through the commands. Don't let us keep you from contrapting your own. You're a half day behind us already.'

'That's mean, Piemur,' Jancis said and, taking Jaxom by the hand, pulled him over to the boxes and cartons that had only been partially unpacked. 'Take a keyboard, then one of those larger boxes. Put them on the table, and take one of the liquid crystal display screens.'

'The what?'

'One of those,' and she pointed, 'and be careful. Aivas said they're fragile and we only have so many of them. Take off the plastic, and you'll need your knife. That stuff is unbelievably tough. Then,' and she handed him a very small-headed screwdriver and a magnifying glass, 'unscrew the big box. You'll have to check over all the circuits to be sure none of them have come adrift. The glass will help you quickly locate any breaks.'

Bendarek suddenly uttered a resounding oath and banged his fists on the table. 'I've lost it all. Everything!'

Piemur glanced up, his expression surprised for Bendarek was not given to outbursts. 'Well, reboot.'

'But you don't understand,' and Bendarek waved his hands wildly above his head. 'I lost all I had typed. And I had it almost done!'

'Did you save?' Jancis asked sympathetically.

'Yes, I did, up until just the last bits,' Bendarek said, his frustration dissipating. Jaxom watched in fascination as he jabbed at various places on the board in front of him and then ahhed in satisfaction at the result.

'Don't dally now, Jaxom,' Piemur said with a wicked grin, 'you must join our jolly band where one misused key can destroy a whole hour's hard work.'

'Aivas did say we'd have to learn many new skills,' Jancis said at her most reasonable. 'Oh, shards! I've done something wrong now, too.' She peered at the blank screen, then frowned down at the keyboard. 'Now what key did I press that I shouldn't have?'

As he drew his beltknife, Jaxom wondered just why he wanted any part of what was obviously an occupation fraught with frustrations.

The quick tropical evening caught them unawares. Piemur, cursing under his breath at any interruption, darted around the room, opening the glowbaskets. But the light was not shining at the correct angle to light up his screen so, still swearing, he altered his chair. Absently, still tapping away, Bendarek followed his example. Jancis and Jaxom were seated at the right angle for they continued with their lessons.

'Who's in here now?' Lessa's voice said from the hallway and she opened the door. 'So this is where you all got to. Jaxom, Master Oldive needs to be taken to Ruatha Hold and I think it's high time you left here. Your eyes are burnt holes in your head. And the rest of you are no better.'

'This is no time to stop, Weyrwoman,' Bendarek said. He had glanced up only briefly.

'This IS the time to stop, Bendarek,' she replied in an uncontradictable tone.

'But, Weyrwoman, I've got to assimilate all these new terms and be able to . . .'

'Aivas!' Lessa raised her voice as she turned her head to the right, 'can you turn these things off? Your students are too diligent. Not that I don't approve – in theory – but they could all use a good night's rest.'

'I didn't save . . .' Bendarek shouted, spreading his

hands in high indignation and staring in horror down at a suddenly darkened and unresponsive screen.

'Your work has been saved,' Aivas' voice assured him. 'You have toiled without renewing yourself all day long, Journeyman Bendarek. Even machines need maintenance. Your body can be considered a soft machine which also needs frequent sustenance. Refresh yourselves. Return tomorrow with energy and concentration renewed.'

From the expression on Bendarek's face, it looked for a few seconds as if he would rebel. Then he sighed and pushed himself back from the table over which he had been bent for hours. He gave Lessa a sheepish grin.

'I will eat and rest. And begin again tomorrow but there is so much to be learned, so much more than I ever imagined.'

'Indeed there is,' Master Oldive said, emerging from the Aivas room, a thick sheaf of papers clutched in one hand and his satchel in the other. He looked from one to the other in bewilderment. 'So much more than I dreamed.' And then he sighed with great satisfaction, holding up the sheaf. 'But this is a good start. A very good start.'

'You will need some *klah* before Jaxom takes you anywhere, Master Oldive,' Lessa said. She took the Healer firmly by the arm and nodded to Jancis and Jaxom to take his encumbrances from him.

He relinquished the satchel readily enough but he clutched the sheaf to him.

'Let me at least tidy them up, Master Oldive,' Jancis said earnestly. 'I shan't disarrange their order.'

'It wouldn't matter anyway,' Oldive said with a weary flick of his free hand. 'They're numbered and separated into categories.' Jancis still had to gently pry his fingers loose. 'I have learned so much, so much,' he muttered with a bemused smile on his face as Lessa led him down the hall. The others followed, suddenly aware of their own fatigue.

You have been in there for six hours, Jaxom, and you had better eat something or Sharra will blame me, Ruth said. *You're very tired, you know.*

'Oh, I know I am. I know I am.' Jaxom wondered if *klah* would be enough to revive him.

'Is it our turn now?' Terry asked as he and several eager-faced journeymen came around the corner from the entrance hall. When Lessa nodded, he urged his followers down the hall at a jog trot.

Their energy appeared almost obscene to Jaxom. No-one had the right to have that much vitality at the end of a day. As they passed him by, he noted that they wore Tillek shoulder knots. So they were actually early in their day. He sighed.

Lessa installed Master Oldive in a chair at the table and gestured for the drudges to supply everyone with *klah* and plates of roast beast and tubers. Never had such a plain meal smelled so appetizing to Jaxom as right now. He almost gobbled down the food and when he was offered a second helping, he took as much again.

There was more colour in Master Oldive's cheeks as he made inroads on his generous serving. Bendarek ate with singleminded intensity, his eyes focused on some obscure distance and occasionally he nodded his head as if approving his ruminations. Jaxom decided he hadn't the energy for thinking right then. He'd think again tomorrow morning. Sharra would understand. He hoped Brand would, since he'd have to leave his steward to cope with the details of running Ruatha Hold yet again. Brand never seemed to mind. On the other hand, Lytol might, but surely Master Robinton would explain the importance of Aivas to his old guardian.

'I must send a message to that young journeyman of Wansor's,' Oldive told Lessa, his enthusiasm vivid on his long face. 'I must have an apparatus similar to the one that was found in Benden Weyr, Lessa. It will magnify blood and tissue so that we can identify disease and infection.' He reached for the neat pile Jancis had made of his papers and started leafing through them. 'Aivas states that the use of a microscope is essential to improve medical diagnosis and even treatment. He has given me the details of how to run other necessary diagnostic tests.'

'A microscope?' Lessa asked indulgently. She thought highly of the Masterhealer who had recently sent her a woman possessed of a miraculous talent for repairing even the most damaged wings or hideous scores.

'That's the word,' Oldive put a hand to his forehead. 'Aivas crammed so much into my poor head today that I wonder I can remember my name.'

'It's Oldive,' Piemur said with an innocently helpful expression on his face, irrepressible even after the long day's stint. He rolled his eyes at the quelling glance Lessa threw him. Jancis poked him in the ribs and he subsided meekly enough.

When they had finished their meal, Jaxom presented himself ready to convey Master Oldive back to the Harper Hall.

'Ah, now, Jaxom, I have advice for Sharra,' and there was a radiant smile of great satisfaction on the Healer's face.

'Aivas knows a cure?' Jaxom asked.

Master Oldive nodded toward his stack, 'Cure? Perhaps. Certainly several avenues of investigation that may provide relief,' he answered cautiously. Then he sighed. 'There was so very much medical acumen lost over the centuries. He didn't say so, of course, but Aivas was clearly taken aback by our lack of remedial surgery. He was, however, most commendatory about our preventive measures and non-surgical techniques. Ah,' and now Oldive made a weary gesture with one hand, 'I could go on and on.' He smiled with self-deprecation. 'With whom should I arrange additional time with Aivas? There are both masters and journeymen who would benefit immensely by consultations with him.'

Lessa looked to F'lar who had joined them during the meal. He shrugged.

'I hadn't thought about apportioning Aivas's time.'

'As soon as we,' and Piemur included Jancis, Bendarek and Jaxom, 'manage to set up these individual stations, there'll be four more links to Aivas.'

'The Healer Hall should have priority,' Lessa added with a frown, scrubbing at her face in fatigue.

'Those are to be teaching consoles,' Bendarek said, scowling.

'For us, maybe,' Piemur said, 'but if they access Aivas,

then they can be used for other purposes. At least that's what I figure.'

'You're a harper, not a journeyman mechanic.'

'I'm a Smithjourneyman mechanic,' Jancis put in, her tone edged, 'and let me remind you that Piemur got his unit up and running before either of us did.'

'Enough!' Lessa brought her hand down on the table with a slap of authority. 'We're all tired.' She rose abruptly. 'Ramoth!' Outside the golden queen dragon bugled a response. 'You're all to leave this building *now*!' She levelled a stern look first at Bendarek and then the others. 'Including us,' and her gaze settled on F'lar who grinned and held up both hands in a fending gesture. 'The two buildings to the left of this one have been set up as dormitories. Go!' and she shooed them with her hands. Then she glared at them until they started to move.

Master Oldive chuckled softly as he and Jaxom made their way out of the building.

'Not that I think I will sleep tonight at all with so much to absorb and review. Why, Jaxom, even what I learned today is only the veriest crumb of the medical knowledge which Aivas had stored. He clarified my understanding of several perplexing conditions. I must have Master Ampris our herbalist bring him our pharmacopoeia.' A weary smile lit Master Oldive's face. 'He said we have made very good use of indigenous plants and he recognized many as those brought by our ancestors from Earth. Earth!' And Oldive looked up at the star-spangled sky. His glance questing, he had to turn his twisted body to scan the dark heavens above them. 'Do we know where Earth is in relation to Pern?'

'I don't think so,' Jaxom replied in mild surprise. 'I don't remember that Aivas gave the direction. Maybe he didn't want to. Our ancestors came here to escape a war, a conflict of such scope and dimensions, waged against an evil far more destructive than Thread, that they wanted to forget Earth.'

'Really? Could anything be more destructive than Thread?' The Healer was both astonished and appalled.

'I find it hard to believe, too,' Jaxom said in an ironic tone.

Ruth glided in from his sunning spot to the cleared area in front of the Aivas building. He ducked his head to receive Jaxom's affectionate slap.

'You must have baked yourself,' he said, shaking his hand as if to cool it.

Yes. It was good. Ramoth and Mnementh are waiting for us to leave this space, Ruth said. *There's really enough room but you know Ramoth. She likes to boss me.*

Jaxom chuckled as he mounted, aware fatigue was making him clumsy in an exercise that was so familiar to him. With no prompting needed, the white dragon crouched down to accommodate Master Oldive. Hauling the Healer up only emphasized Jaxom's weariness. But they'd be home soon. Inwardly he groaned: they'd have to make yet another run to take Oldive back to his Hall.

Sharra will make him stay the night. He'll want to talk so she won't let him go, Ruth said. And Jaxom's thoughts were grateful for that was exactly what was likely to occur.

As Ruth rose from the ground, Jaxom and Oldive were able to appreciate just how busy Landing had become. Glowbaskets lit paths, like the spokes of a wheel radiating out from the Aivas building. Carpenters and joiners were working by glowlight to finish roofing the substantial annexe, doubling the size of the original structure. All of the housing immediately adjacent was lit and the warm evening air was redolent with the aromas of roasting meats. On the mounds beyond, dragon eyes punctuated the darkness with their large vivid blue faceted eyes, like immense jewels on a deep blue background. Two rose and glided beneath Ruth as he continued to rise.

'All right, Ruth, let's go home to Ruatha,' Jaxom said, gratefully focusing his thoughts on the Hold, the big courtyard in front of the wide steps, the smaller court which had been their quarters during their youth. The cold of *between* held a wicked bite on tired minds and bodies. It didn't help to emerge into the weak afternoon sunlight and the chill of Winter. Jaxom could feel Oldive shivering behind him. But Ruth had emerged only a few wing strokes above the Hold and glided effortlessly into the main courtyard, the Hold's fair of fire-lizards in raptures at his return.

Sharra, a thick furry cloak thrown over her shoulders, came running down the steps to them, effusive in her welcome, helping Master Oldive dismount, securing his satchel as it swung off his shoulder, smiling her delight up at Jaxom and with her free hand giving Ruth an affectionate slap. Though she asked nothing, Jaxom knew his wife well enough to know she was bursting with questions. He threw one arm across her shoulders, kissing her cheek, her skin smooth and the scent of her reviving to him, as he guided Oldive up the steps and into the warmth of the Hold.

I'm going inside immediately, Ruth told his rider, *or I'll lose all the benefit of my sunning.* And he took himself off to his quarters in the old kitchen. Jaxom knew there'd be a fire on the hearth to comfort his friend.

Sharra ordered food and drink as she pushed the two men towards the small office where they would have some privacy for eager people came rushing into the hall, hoping to be informed by Jaxom of the ongoing events at Landing.

'Later, later,' Sharra said firmly and closed the door behind her.

Before Oldive joined Jaxom at the fire, he carefully laid his satchel on the wide desk where Jaxom generally managed the details of his Hold. A pile of messages and Records lay waiting for his attention. There was a scratch at the door and the steward himself had brought a laden tray.

'Oh, that's kind of you, Brand,' Jaxom said. 'Lessa made us eat before she'd let us leave, Sharra, but *klah* will go down well. With a lashing of that fortified wine I see you brought along.' Jaxom grinned at the stocky man who had been his friend since his childhood and was now his most valuable assistant. 'No, stay, Brand. You've the right to hear what keeps me from my proper tasks.'

Brand waved his hand in a disclaimer as he helped Sharra pass the hot drinks, the pungent wine masking *klah*'s fragrance. Jaxom took a judicious sip and felt the liquid rushing to restore warmth. Master Oldive, too, seemed to revive somewhat and sank into the chair which Brand placed close to the fire for him.

'My dear, your female patient is suffering a gall bladder

malfunction. Unfortunately, the man appears to have a cancerous growth, as we suspected. We can cure the one for I have been given a specific medication for dissolving the gravel within the organ, but we can only ease the other from life.' Master Oldive paused, his eyes wide and bright with inner excitement. 'Aivas has the most extraordinary fund of medical information which he is quite willing to impart to us. He can even help us revive corrective surgical procedures, which you know I have yearned to do. Our Craft may have been limited to repair surgeries for lack of proper training but he can help us recover much of that lost skill.'

'That would be wonderful, Master, but would we be able to overcome the prejudice in the Hall about intrusive measures?' Sharra exclaimed but her face mirrored her hope.

'Now that we have a mentor of unquestionable probity, I think that once we have proved the benefits to patients who will not mend without drastic measures, we can overcome those scruples.' He drained his cup and resolutely rose to his feet. 'A few moments in your infirmary, my dear Sharra, and we shall have the medication for your gall bladder sufferer. The other poor wight . . .' Oldive shrugged, his expression deeply compassionate.

'Come then and you can tell me all the medical details that would bore Jaxom and Brand to tears,' Sharra said, grinning fondly at her mate.

'You *never*,' and Jaxom paused to give that adverb full emphasis, 'bore me, Sharra.' The loving look that she gave him warmed as the *klah* had not.

'You look tired, Jaxom,' Brand said when the door had closed.

'I am, Brand, and my head aches with what I've seen and heard in the last two days but I feel, I feel,' and Jaxom stopped, clenching one fist, 'that this is *the* most momentous thing that has happened to Pern since,' and he laughed, 'our ancestors landed here.' His second laugh was not as easy. 'Not that everyone will see it that way, I'm sure.'

'There are always those who oppose change,' Brand said

with a resigned shrug. 'Has the Aivas told you exactly how it proposes to eliminate Thread?'

'We are mere babes, Brand, and must put in much hard work and learn many new things before Aivas will give us any details. But you should have seen Fandarel,' and Jaxom's laugh was uninhibited, 'and Bendarek. They were spinning like tops to do everything at once. When Ruth and I got off transport duty, I was allowed to put together one of Aivas's gadgets.' He examined the fingers of his right hand, the solder burn and the nicks where the screwdriver had slipped. 'I'm learning to access knowledge. Tomorrow I may even get to read some of Aivas's stored wisdom. I tell you, Brand, the next few weeks are going to be fascinating.'

'Another way of telling me you'll be frequently away from the Hold?' asked Brand, grinning.

'Well, apart from overseeing Falls, there's not much to do right now in the depths of Winter, is there?' Jaxom said, slightly defensive.

Brand laughed and, with the familiarity of their long and close relationship, he clapped Jaxom on the shoulder. 'That there isn't, lad. I'd be happy to learn if Aivas knew any way of heating stone-cold Holds.'

'I'll ask him!' Jaxom promised earnestly. 'I'll ask him,' and he leaned forward to warm his hands again.

Chapter Five

Against his entreaties, F'lar took Master Robinton back to Cove Hold.

'You need the rest and the quiet, Robinton,' F'lar told the Harper sternly. 'You won't get that if you're allowed to stay at Landing again tonight. You're exhausted.'

'But what a wonderful way to get tired, F'lar. And every time I turn around, I think of something else I must ask Aivas. It's rather like . . .' and Robinton chuckled, 'knowing you have the most fabulous vintage in your glass and being torn between drinking and admiring.'

F'lar shot him an amused look. 'That's apt enough, considering the source.'

'I try! But surely you appreciate why I'm loath to leave?' And the Harper's expression was entreating.

'Oh, I do, Robinton,' and F'lar grinned as he handed the man down from Mnementh's great shoulder. 'But it'd be worth my peace with Lessa if we let you overstretch yourself.'

'But this is giving me new life, F'lar. A new hope that I never imagined to receive.'

'Nor I,' F'lar replied fervently. 'Which is why we must take care of you all the more – to interpret for us.'

'Interpret? He speaks in plain and simple terms.'

'Not what Aivas says, Robinton, but how our people will see what he offers. For me, and all dragonriders, despite the future effects on Weyrs and dragonkind, I cannot but accept Aivas's offer to rid us of Thread. But already there are those who are either frightened or feel threatened by what Aivas can tell us, or give us.'

'Yes, similar thoughts had crossed my mind,' Robinton said solemnly but then flashed F'lar a roguish grin. 'But I also cross them out. The good done us will far outweigh the bad.'

'Get a good night's rest, Robinton. Benden flies Thread tomorrow but D'ram will oblige, I'm sure, to get you back to Landing.'

'Him!' And Robinton was suddenly petulant. 'He's worse than a milk mother as it is.' And Robinton settled easily into D'ram's voice. '"I wouldn't, if I were you, Robinton! Have you eaten enough, Robinton? Now would be a good time to rest in the sun." Tsck! He fusses me!'

'Not tomorrow. D'ram's as eager to see, and hear, more of Aivas as you are, you know,' was F'lar's parting comment just before Mnementh launched himself upwards.

I've told Tiroth to take you tomorrow only if you're well rested, the dragon said. Zair, his bronze tail wrapped about the Harper's neck, his talons lightly clasping his right ear, chirruped agreement.

'Oh, you!' Robinton was torn between irritation at their over-protectiveness and pleasure that Mnementh had a word for him. He could never forget how much he personally owed the dragons who had kept him alive when his laboured heart had faltered that terrible day at Ista Weyr two Turns ago.

He was tired, Robinton was forced to admit to himself. Just walking the short distance to the steps of his lovely residence at Cove Hold winded him. There were lights on in the main hall: D'ram and doubtless Lytol waiting up for him.

Zair chirped again, confirming his guess. Well, they would not tax him and certainly they both deserved a brief report of the day's activities. Only how to be brief? With all that had occurred since he had awakened early this morning. Only *this* morning? It was Turns away in knowledge and understanding.

But when he walked into the pleasant room, well lit with glowbaskets, D'ram, the venerable retired Weyrleader, and Lytol, Jaxom's mentor and a former dragonrider, would listen to no explanations but ushered him to his room with instructions that he was to rest first.

'Whatever momentous events occurred after I left can wait until the morning,' D'ram said.

'Drink your wine,' Lytol added, holding out the Harper's beautiful blue glass goblet, 'and yes, I've added something to make you sleep tonight because just one look at your face tells me you need rest above all else.'

Robinton closed his hand about the goblet. Norist might be a close-minded Craftmaster but he blew elegant glass when he'd a mind to, *and* in the exact shade of harper blue. 'But I've so much to tell you,' Robinton objected, after a sip of the wine.

'All the better told when you've had a good night's sleep,' Lytol said. When he would have bent to undo Robinton's boots, the Harper became indignant and pushed him away.

'I'm not quite that tired, thank you, Lytol,' he said with great dignity.

Laughing, the two left. Robinton took another sip of the wine before unloosening the fastenings of his boots. A third before he hauled his tunic over his head. And another as he loosened his belt with his free hand. *That's enough* he told himself and, draining the cup, lay back. He had only sufficient energy to pull the light blanket over him against the possible chill of a morning sea breeze. He felt Zair nestle down on the next pillow and that was all.

The next morning he awoke slowly, aware that the dream he had had during the night had been both satisfying and confusing but its ephemeral details eluded a conscious effort at recall. He lay for a moment, orienting himself. Sometimes, of a morning, he had difficulty remembering what day it was, or the tasks he had mentally assigned himself to accomplish.

Today he experienced no such disorientation. He remembered everything that had happened the day before with amazing clarity. Ah, that was good. A challenge to stimulate his flagging faculties. Corman and his accusation of gullibility! Indeed! Zair rumbled reassuringly on his pillow and stroked his head against Robinton's cheek.

'Will you pass the word along that I'm now completely refreshed?' he asked the bronze fire-lizard. Zair regarded him, tilting his head sideways, his eyes whirling ever so slightly with the green of contentment. And gave a chirp. Then he rose and stretched, his transparent wings arching over his head before he shook and folded them tightly along his spine.

'So, are Tiroth and D'ram awake to take me?'

Zair ignored him and began to groom his left hind claws.

'I gather that means I must bathe and eat first?' As he rose, Robinton realized that he had slept in his trousers . . . for the second night in a row. He shucked them off, snagged a large towel and, opening the door from his corner room to the wide porch that sheltered Cove Hold from the intense sunlight, strode out. Down the flight of steps with more vigour than he had climbed them the previous night, he jogged down the sandy track to the sea. Zair swirled overhead, crooning his approval as he dropped the towel on the white sand of the cove, and continued on into the pleasant waters. With Zair plunging into the next wave right beside him, Robinton emerged, propelling himself forward with a strong over-arm stroke. A group of wild fire-lizards joined him and Zair in their water-sporting, zipping just above the water alongside him or plunging in just in front of his face, missing body contact by inches. As often as they had seen humans bathing in the sea, they were still fascinated by swimmers.

The exercise was a fine toner, Robinton realized as he turned to retrace his path, allowing the waves to carry his body forward. The sea was gentle this morning. Sometimes he could be turned end over end by the surf but that could also be invigorating.

Drying himself off, Robinton knotted the towel about his waist and strode off toward the house. 'Tell them, Zair, that I'm completely refreshed and in vigorous health.'

'You're awake, are you?' D'ram called from the porch. 'About time. It's well past noon.'

'Noon?' Robinton stopped in his tracks, appalled at having wasted so much time in sleeping. Who knew what he had missed of Aivas's disclosures this morning? 'You should have wakened me!' He did not attempt to keep the irritation out of his voice. He need not worry about offending either D'ram or Lytol with his occasional crotchets: he could enjoy the luxury of ill-temper now and then with these good companions.

'Your body has more sense than you do,' added Lytol, rising from the hammock on the corner of the porch which caught any breeze. 'You got only the sleep you needed, Robinton. Pour him some *klah*, D'ram, while I finish his breakfast – our lunch.'

D'ram poured a cup as Robinton came up the steps and the aroma was enough to remind him that hunger was a need, too. Then he settled himself and, during the substantial breakfast which Lytol served him, he brought them up to date.

'And so, the miracle begins,' he said, finishing his account.

'You've no doubt in your mind, Robinton,' Lytol asked, his sad and graven face reflecting his usual scepticism, 'that this Aivas can effect the annihilation of Thread?'

'By the first Egg, Lytol, one cannot doubt it. The marvels we saw, the very fact that our ancestors made that incredible flight from the planet of our origin, lend credibility to his promise. We have only to relearn the skills we lost and we can triumph over this ancient menace.'

'Aye, but why didn't the ancients rid us of Thread with all their incredible crafts and their full knowledge of the technology lost to us?' Lytol wanted to know.

'You're not the only one to query that, Lytol,' Robinton said, 'but Aivas explained that the volcanic eruptions came at a crucial time and the settlers went north to establish a safe base. So their plans to defeat Thread were interrupted.'

'Why didn't they come back when Threadfall ceased?'

'That Aivas didn't know.' Robinton had to recognize that

105

there were gaps in Aivas' account. And yet . . . a musical instrument can only do what it is constructed to do. Or one of Fandarel's machines. Therefore, a machine, even as sophisticated as AIVAS could only do what it/he was designed to do. 'It/he—' I must really make up my mind how I consider the thing, Robinton thought '– is unlikely to tell lies. Though I suspect *he*,' Robinton made up his mind, 'does not reveal the whole truth. We've had enough trouble absorbing and understanding what he's already told us.'

Lytol gave a snort, a cynical expression on his face which, Robinton was relieved to notice, was not mirrored by D'ram.

'I would like to believe that we can!' Robinton added.

'Who wouldn't?' Lytol said, relenting slightly.

'I believe Aivas,' D'ram said. 'He speaks with such authority. He explained that the time will be right in four years – that is, Turns – ten months and twenty-seven days. Twenty-six today. The time factor has to be correct to succeed.'

'Succeed in what?' Lytol persisted.

'THAT is something we must also learn,' and here Robinton laughed in self-disparagement. 'Not to put too fine a point on it, Lytol, but we're plainly too ignorant to understand his explanation. He did try, something about windows, and leaving Pern at just the precise moment to intercept the Red Star, or rather the planet which appears red to us for so much of its orbit in our skies. He showed us the diagram,' Robinton added, noting the defensive tone he used. He shook himself. 'If you wish to query him, Lytol, I'm sure that you can.'

Lytol cast Robinton a sardonic look. 'There are others with greater reason to consult Aivas.'

'But you *must* hear our history from Aivas, Lytol,' D'ram said, leaning forward across the table. 'You'll appreciate then why we can so unreservedly believe in Aivas and in his promise.'

'He really has got to you, hasn't he?' Lytol shook his head at their credulousness.

'If you listen to what he says, you'll believe,' Robinton said, rising. He had to clutch at the towel to keep it from slipping, which reduced the dignity of his pronouncement. 'I'm dressing to return to Landing. D'ram, will you and Tiroth oblige me?'

'Since you are rested,' and D'ram gave his housemate a long and searching look, 'we will, of course, oblige. Lytol, will you not join us?'

'Not today.'

'Are you afraid of being won over despite your reservations?' asked Robinson.

Lytol shook his head slowly. 'That's not likely. But go. Enjoy your dream of Threadfree skies.'

'The last of the true sceptics,' Robinson muttered under his breath, somewhat disturbed that Lytol would not enter as wholeheartedly as every other reasonable man and woman on Pern in this release from Thread. Did Lytol think old age had dulled Robinson's wits or discriminatory faculties? Or did he believe, like Corman, that the Harper could be taken in by a plausible story?

'No,' D'ram assured him when he voiced the question to the old Weyrleader as they walked toward bronze Tiroth, waiting for them on the strand. 'He's too pragmatic. He told me yesterday that we were far too excited to think logically about the repercussions Aivas will have on our lives. Altering the basic structure of our society and its values and all that twaddle.' D'ram's snort indicated he did not agree. 'He's been through several upheavals himself. He's unlikely to welcome another.'

'But you do?'

D'ram smiled over his shoulder at the Harper as he settled himself between Tiroth's neck ridges. 'I'm a dragonrider, Harper, and dedicated to the eradication of Thread. If there is even the slightest hope . . .' And he shrugged as he broke off. 'Tiroth, take us to Landing!'

'Watch out, D'ram,' the Harper cautioned. 'It's undergone considerable alterations even since yesterday noontime when you left it.'

So Monarth warns me, and although the Harper knew that Tiroth was speaking directly to D'ram, his chest swelled with the privilege of hearing. *I have the altered scene from him. It has changed.*

Was there a note of discontent in Tiroth's tone?

However, Tiroth took them *between* and re-entered on the hill west of the Aivas building, hovering in the air above the line of dragons sunning themselves on the promontory. Robinton looked up at the dragons on the hill, to see if he recognized any of the bronzes or the queens. Then he remembered that Benden Weyr would be involved in Threadfall today.

Gliding down toward the building, the alterations were not visible until the bronze veered to his right and backwinged to land on the wide yard.

'I'd no idea!' gasped D'ram and turned to stare at the Harper who was no less surprised than he.

Robinton hid his own reaction behind a quick smile of reassurance. Obviously, Lytol was in the minority to judge by the changes here: all designed to facilitate access to Aivas. The original wing had been tripled in size, with odd lean-to sheds, like skirts, along all three sides. As Robinton dismounted, he recognized more of Fandarel's batteries housed under the sheds; sufficient power to sustain the entity all the hours of the day and night until the new and more powerful water-turbines were finished.

In the broad new courtyard, several knots of folk were arguing vociferously with each other while, above their heads, fire-lizards made raucous sounds of agitation. Most of the humans wore the shoulder knots of masters and journeymen from various Crafts, while their tunic devices told Robinton that they came from different Holds as well.

'Free for all?' D'ram asked, dropping to the ground beside Robinton.

'That's what it certainly sounds like.' Nor could Robinton see anyone well-known to him among the dissenters. However, at the door of the building, he saw four of Master Esselin's biggest workmen. Furthermore, they were standing in front of closed doors. He wondered if the furtive face he saw peering out was Esselin's or Breide's.

He took a deep breath and strode forward, for all were too busy with their altercations to notice the latest arrivals.

'Now, just what seems to be the trouble here?' he asked in a carrying voice which penetrated the racket. It took only a moment for all the disputants to recognize him before he was encircled with each plaintiff demanding his attention. 'NOW WAIT JUST A MOMENT!' he bellowed. Behind him on the hill, bronze and gold dragons added their authoritative bugle and silence fell. Then he pointed at one man wearing a Masterminer's knot and Crom's device.

'Master Esselin will not let us in,' he said belligerently.

'And my Lord Holder,' said another wearing the head steward knots of Boll and pushing forward from the group, 'insists that we be given the facts about this mysterious being.'

'Deckter charged me to do the same,' said a steward from Nabol in the most aggrieved tone of the three. 'We demand to know the truth about this Aivas. And I'm to see this marvel before I return to Nabol.'

'Yes, you all have been unconscionably slighted,' Robinton said soothingly. 'And those of us who have been fortunate to hear Aivas *know* that seeing Aivas is the first step in believing what he can do for us all, Hold, Hall and Weyr. Why I've only just been allowed to return.' He feigned indignation at such an omission. That the much respected Harper of Pern should be denied access, too, seemed to appease them. 'Now, you must realize that the room where Aivas is installed is quite small . . . though I notice there have been attempts to enlarge the space.' He craned his neck as if trying to see just how much larger it was. 'Hmmm. Yes, working day and night from the look of it. Most commendable really. Now, if you'll just bide here, I'll see what can be done about your quite legitimate requests to see Aivas.'

'I don't want to just *see* it,' the miner complained. 'I want it to tell me how to get back to the main lode of a very rich vein of ore. The ancients located all the ores on Pern. I want it to tell me where to dig since it knows everything about Pern.'

'Not everything, my dear fellow,' Robinton said, less than surprised that Aivas was now considered an omniscient being. Should he emphasize that Aivas was only (only?) a machine, a device which had served their ancestors as the receptacle of information? No, their understanding of machinery, craftsmen though many of them were, was too rudimentary. They would not grasp the concept of so complex a mechanical apparatus: let alone the concept of an *artificial* intelligence. He didn't understand *that* all too well himself. He sighed with resignation. 'And very little about Pern as it is today, though a great deal about Pern as it was twenty-five hundred Turns ago. I suppose none of you heard that you were supposed to bring Hall Records with you? Aivas particularly wants to bring himself up to current times with every Hall, Hold and Weyr.'

'No one said anything about Records,' said the miner, taken aback. 'We heard it knew everything.'

'Aivas will be the first to inform you that while his knowledge extends to many subjects and skills, he is *not*, happily, all-knowing. He is . . . a talking Record, and far more accurate than ours which tunnel snakes, time and other perils have rendered illegible.'

'We was told he knew everything!' the miner insisted stubbornly.

'Not even I know everything,' Robinton responded gently. 'Nor has Aivas even once suggested that he does. He knows a great deal more, however, than we do. And we shall all learn from him. Now, let me speak to Master Esselin on your behalf. There are, let's see, how many of you?' And he did a quick head count. 'Thirty-four. Well, that's too many for one go. D'ram, choose by lots. You all know D'ram here as a fair man. You'll all have a turn – brief it may be, but Aivas you shall see.'

Master Esselin was at first delighted to see the Harper but appalled at Robinton's solution to the matter of the plaintiffs.

'We can't send them away unhappy, Esselin. They have every bit as much of a right to see Aivas as a Lord Holder. More even, because they'll be the *doing* of Aivas's grand plans over the next few years. Who's in there now?'

'Master Terry with masters and journeymen from every Smithcrafthall in the world.' Then his eyes went round with anxiety. 'And Master Hamian from Southern Hold and two of his apprentices.'

'Ah, Toric's finally sent an emissary?' Robinton wasn't

sure if the news pleased or worried him. He had rather hoped not to have to contend with Toric's avarice yet.

'I don't think he comes on Lord Toric's behalf,' and Esselin shook his head, his eyes still wide with apprehension. 'Master Hamian did say to Master Terry that his sister, the Lady Sharra of Ruatha, suggested that he drop everything and come here immediately.'

'And so he should. So he should,' Robinton agreed affably. Hamian would be an excellent man to have involved here. A clever innovator who had already put back to use what the ancients had left behind in a southern mine. 'I'll just see when it's convenient to interrupt them for a few moments. Believe me, Esselin, it's the better part of discretion to give those fellows out there the chance to see Aivas for themselves.'

'But they're only stewards and small miners . . .'

'There are more of those than of Lords and Crafthallmasters and Weyrleaders, Esselin, and every single one of them has the right to approach Aivas.'

'That wasn't what I was told,' and now Master Esselin resorted to his usual obstructive attitude, thrusting his heavy chin belligerently forward.

Robinton eyed him pityingly for such a long moment that even the thick-skinned Esselin could not fail to notice that his attitude was unacceptable to the Harper.

'I think you will find before the day is out that you will be told differently, Master Esselin. Now, if you will excuse me . . .' And with that Robinton strode down the hall to the Aivas chamber.

As he approached, he could hear Aivas's sonorous voice using the sort of penetrating tone that suggested he was addressing a large group. When Robinton quietly opened the door, he was first amazed at how many people now stood in the room, and then that even more occupied the new wings on either side of Aivas' facility. Two doors had been opened into the large annexes on either side. Aivas's two walls were intact, of course, but there was much more space now for larger audiences. This afternoon this was composed of Smiths who were, in general, possessed of large or powerful bodies from working in

111

their Craft. Master Nicat, the Masterminer, was seated at the front on the same bench as Terry and two of his best masters who were all busily copying the diagrams on the main Aivas screen. Jancis was also there, in a corner, bent over a drawing board on her lap. Others in the room were doing their best to draw, too, some using another's back to steady their pads. Robinton could make no sense of the complicated design but it was obvious from the rapt attention it was being given that it was of great importance to the Smithcrafters. Aivas was explaining, adding numbered specifications which also meant nothing to the Harper. The measured voice enjoined its listeners to ask questions on any point that was not clear.

'You have explained in such detail,' Master Nicat said, his swarthy face wearing a most respectful expression, 'that even the most simple-minded apprentice would understand.'

'Ah, if you don't mind, Aivas,' and a Masterminer whom Robinton knew to be the master of the works at one of the larger Telgar iron foundries raised his hand. 'If faulty melts can be remedied up to standard, then can we repair the damage to ones long since discarded?'

'That is correct. The process can be applied to used metals. In fact, quite often the use of old metal improves the final product.'

'Even metals made by the ancients?' Master Hamian asked. 'We have found some in what I understand were the original workings at Andiyar's Stake in Dorado.'

'Once in the crucible, the melt burns off impurities of all kinds.' Then to Robinton's astonishment, Aivas added, 'Good afternoon, Master Robinton. What assistance do you need today?'

Robinton found himself embarrassed by being identified so cordially. 'I do not intend to interrupt . . .'

'You aren't,' Terry replied, rising and stretching. 'Right, Nicat?' he added to the Masterminer who looked like a man hoping that he had understood his orders.

As if released from their thrall, the other craftsmen began low conversations with neighbours and those nearest the door began to file out, carefully folding the drawings and notes they'd been taking.

As Robinton moved further into the room, he caught the pungency of sweating bodies, laced with the taint of metal's acidity and the odd dank smell of deep mine shafts. As the room emptied, he could appreciate what a large room had been achieved overnight.

'Well, well!' he murmured, noticing windows on either ends, opened to a breeze which now circulated freely as the last of the craftsmen left. Jancis alone remained in her corner, furiously scribbling.

She looked up and smiled at the Harper. 'We've accomplished so much today, Master Robinton.'

'And did you get any sleep last night, young woman?'

Her cheeks dimpled in a mischievous smile. 'Indeed we did,' and then she coloured. 'I mean, we both slept. I mean, Piemur fell asleep first . . . Oh, blast!'

Robinton laughed heartily. 'I won't misconstrue, Jancis, even if it mattered. You're not going to let all this fuss and fascination delay your formal announcement, are you?'

'No,' she said most firmly. 'I want to bring the date forward.' She blushed prettily but kept the eye contact. 'It would make things easier.' She gathered up her things. 'The others are all in the computer room. You might want to take a crack at it, too.'

'Me?' The Harper was dumbfounded. 'That's for young resilient minds like yours and Piemur's and Jaxom's.'

'Learning is not limited to the young, Master Robinton,' said Aivas.

'Well, we'll see,' the Harper replied, hedging and running his fingers nervously over his face. He was acutely conscious that he could no longer retain the words and notes of new music and had few doubts that this would extend to other areas. He didn't think himself a vain man, or excessively proud, but he did not wish to show to disadvantage. 'We'll see. Meantime, we have a minor problem . . .'

'With that lot out there, determined against all Master Esselin's prejudice on seeing Aivas?' Jancis asked.

'Hmm, a minor miner problem,' Robinton heard himself saying and groaned.

113

'It is apt,' Jancis said, pleasing him by chuckling. 'They *need* to see Aivas so that they can tell their Lords and Masters that they have?'

'That's about the size of it. Aivas, if you would agree, I shall waft them in and out, with just time enough to say that they've been here.'

'Is that your true wish in this instance?'

Robinton cleared his throat. 'I could wish that as many men and women as possible on this planet could be exposed to your fund of knowledge but even with these enlarged accommodations, that is neither possible nor wise. The parochially minded tend to flog petty issues to a nubbin. The worried assume their problems are uniquely threatening or that you are omniscient enough to solve any problem put to you.'

'It has always been so, Master Robinton,' Aivas said as accepting as ever. 'Mankind has always put great faith in oracles.'

'Oracles?' The word was unfamiliar to the Harper.

'A full explanation of the phenomenon should be kept until you have forty-four hours free, for the file on religion is lengthy. At this moment in time, how do you propose to satisfy the petitioners outside?'

'By sending in small groups to see and question you, however briefly.'

'Then permit them all to enter. The outside sensors indicate the exact numbers which this room is now large enough to accommodate.'

While Master Esselin looked on in dismay and disapproval, the entire gaggle hurried down the corridor.

'Good afternoon, gentlemen,' Aivas said, his mellifluous voice startling them into awed silence. 'Within the walls you are currently facing, there is an Artificial Intelligence Voice Activated System which stores information for retrieval. Or AIVAS, to use the appropriate acronym. It is seen that there are among you those of the Miner Craft. No doubt you noticed that Masterminers attended the previous lecture. It would be of considerable value to you to consult with these men on the new methods of smelting ores. It is hoped that you two stewards from

114

Crom and Nabol have brought with you the Records of your Holds. These will be vital in assessing the present, and future, productivity of the properties you so ably manage for your Lords. You Glass-smiths and journeymen from the Halls at Igen and Ista have, in the sandpits and leadmines of your respective holds, some of the best silicates on this world which account for the fact that you produce the finest, most durable glass on the planet. If this facility may be of service in any way to your Craft-halls, please ask Master Robinton to appoint a time for a longer discussion.'

Most of the attendees simply gawked about them, trying to find the source of the disembodied voice. The Ista Glass-smith took a hesitant step forward, swallowed hard and spoke.

'Master Aivas, Master Oldive asked me to construct the lens of a microscope for him,' the words came out in a rush.

'Yes, such an instrument is of vital importance to the Healer's Hall.'

'I looked up our Records, Master Aivas,' and he pulled from his tunic some mouldering sheets, stained, spotted and more holey than entire. 'But, as you see . . .' He held them out towards the screen.

'Place them over the lit panel on the worktop, Master-glass-smith.'

Looking about him for reassurance, the Istan hesitated until the Harper shooed him forward with a gesture of his hands. The others stared at him for his audacity. Part of one page crumbled off even as the Glass-smith placed it hesitantly over the lighted panel. His journeyman rushed forward and, with the air of a man greatly daring, shoved it into the broken corner.

Instantly the screen lit up with the much damaged drawing. Magically an unseen point connected up the missing lines and, while the watchers gasped in wonder, the instrument became entire on the screen. From the printer slot, a sheet emerged which the dazzled journeyman took at Aivas' suggestion.

'Look! Look! Finer than the best draughtsman we have could render it!'

'Next page, please,' Aivas said and the Glass-smith, with some fumbling, managed to comply.

Very shortly the missing notes and explanations had been restored and everyone in the room had had a chance to see the reconstructed sheets.

'Have you any queries regarding the manufacture of barrel, focusing devices, or lenses?' Aivas asked politely.

There were one or two from the journeyman: his Master was too dazed to be coherent.

'If some should arise during manufacture . . .'

'During what?' the journeyman was startled into asking by the unfamiliar word.

'During the making, either send your question to Master Robinton or return for additional explanation or further demonstration.'

It was easy then for Robinton to deftly lead the group out of the room and speed them on their way down the hall.

'That took ten minutes,' Aivas said in a low tone. 'A useful disposition of time.'

'Have you been advised to appoint me your aide?' Robinton asked in an amused tone.

'Your impartiality is legend, Master Robinton, and your scrupulous sense of fair play has just been demonstrated. Master Esselin's definition of priority is noticeably skewed towards rank. The Glass-smith's need of stored information was indeed a priority which ought to have been immediately scheduled when he arrived early this morning. Master Esselin ignored my wishes.'

'He did?' Robinton was annoyed.

'If you will see to it that he does not exceed his very limited authority, considerable future ill-feeling will be avoided.'

'I will see to that immediately, Aivas,' and Robinton found his irritation enlarging at this further example of Esselin's officiousness.

'If you should be unwilling to act in this capacity, perhaps D'ram, the bronze dragonrider, would assist. He also is held in the highest regard by peer group, Hall and Hold. Is it true that he came forward in time four hundred Turns to fight Thread? That he has already spent a good portion of his life in that onerous task?'

'That is correct, Aivas.'

'This generation, and his, are amazing, Master Robinton.' Though the words were levelly spoken, the tone of admiration was unmistakable and Robinton squared his shoulders proudly.

'We are of one mind in that.' Then brusquely, Robinton added, 'As your aide, Master Aivas, I'll just set Master Esselin straight on the matter of assigning priorities without consultation. You may be sure he will cbey you as promptly as he does myself or the Weyrleaders.'

Back in the hall, Robinton cut short all of Master Esselin's tedious explanations and apologies. D'ram was visible in the room where Piemur, Jancis and Benelek were clattering away at their lessons on the small screens. They were each doing different lessons, although he recognized that Jancis was somehow replicating the diagrams that Aivas had shown the miners.

'Come on, Master Robinton,' Piemur said, looking up from his screen, 'I fixed a station for you to experiment with.'

Robinton held up his hands and backed away. 'No, no, I've appointed myself aide to Master Aivas for the afternoon. You cannot believe how stupid Esselin is.'

'Ha! Yes, I can!' Piemur said emphatically.

'He's as thick as two short planks,' Benelek grumbled. 'And he doesn't like any of us coming and going as we need to.'

'I don't have any trouble,' Jancis said, but her eyes danced with mischief. 'All I have to do is give him a cup of *klah* or something to eat from the tray when I bring it in.'

'And that's another score I'm going to settle with ol' Master fuddy-duddy Esselin,' Piemur said with considerable heat. 'You are NOT a kitchen drudge. He knows you walked the tables to your Mastery! Doesn't he know you're Fandarel's granddaughter and top of your own Craft?'

'Oh, I think he will,' Jaxom remarked without looking up from his board, his fingers flying across it. 'I caught his paternal act this morning and I reminded him that the

117

proper form of address for Jancis now is Smithmaster. You know, I don't think he had noticed the collar tabs.'

'That's no excuse,' Piemur retorted, likely to fume until he himself had settled the score with the old man.

'Perhaps Master Esselin should go back to his archives,' D'ram said. 'That's what he's supposed to be doing.'

'And about all he's good for,' Piemur muttered.

'However, since someone must take over his current responsibility, I think I shall appoint myself in his place.'

'A marvellous notion, D'ram,' Robinton said while the others let out a cheer. 'Actually, Aivas had already recommended you in that capacity. He's heard that you are a well-respected and scrupulously honest character. He doesn't know you as well as I do, of course.' When D'ram glanced apprehensively at him, Robinton broke into a teasing grin. 'In fact, I think we should inveigle Lytol up here, too. Or would three honest men be too much for the job?'

'There can never be enough honest men,' Jaxom said, firmly, this time looking up from the fascination of the screen. 'I think the challenge would be good for Lytol.' His expression reflected a deep concern for his ageing guardian. 'The pair of you already look the better for some proper use of your long experience. And there *ought* to be someone in charge who's got the sense he was born with.'

'I second that,' a voice said from the doorway and in walked Smithcraftmaster Hamian. 'I had to elbow the old fool aside to get back in here. I see what Sharra meant when she said you were all wrapped up in this, Jaxom,' he added, tolerantly grinning at his sister's mate before he nodded courteously to the others in the room. 'I didn't want to cause undue consternation among my peers earlier, Master Robinton, but would Master Aivas be able to tell any of us – me, because I'm dead keen to know – how the ancestors made their durable plastics?'

'Hurrah!' Piemur and Jancis cheered together. And Piemur jumped from his stool and thumped Hamian's back.

The big Smith from Southern Hold was not as tall or quite as massive as Master Fandarel but he was solid enough to absorb Piemur's hearty pounding without giving an inch. He grinned at his friend, his large and even teeth white in his tanned face. 'Glad someone approves. Do you?' And he looked directly at the Harper.

Robinton looked inquiringly at D'ram. 'And thus we make the first test of our authority?'

'I'd say Hamian is exactly the right man to try something so new – new to us at least,' D'ram said, nodding an endorsement.

'So it's now up to him who knows,' Robinton said, and jerked his head towards Aivas's room. 'Let's ask.'

All but Benelek traipsed along to hear what Aivas would say. Robinton beckoned for Hamian to stand squarely in front of the screen. Then prodded him when the big Smith suddenly found it difficult to frame the question.

'Ask him. He hasn't bitten anyone,' Robinton said.

'Yet,' added Piemur, pretending to be worried.

'Ahem, Master Aivas . . .' Hamian began and then faltered again.

'You are volunteering to learn how to make silicate-based plastics such as your ancestors used in building materials, Master Hamian?'

Hamian just nodded, his eyebrows raised in comical surprise. 'How'd he know that?' he said in a low aside to the Harper.

'He's got long ears,' Robinton replied, amused.

'Incorrect, Master Robinton,' Aivas said. 'This facility has far more sensitive receptors than ears, Master Hamian, and since the door to the adjacent room was open, the conversation was audible. To reiterate, you wish, Master Hamian, to learn how to produce the plastics your ancestors used.'

Hamian squared himself in front of the screen, throwing his head up. 'Yes, Master Aivas, that is my wish. There are sufficient of my peers eager to improve the quality of iron, steel, brass and copper, but, having seen the durability of the ancients' plastic materials, I would like to specialize in them. It is my belief that this could be as important a material to us as it was to our ancestors.'

'The manufacture of plastics was a highly refined skill in your ancestors' time. Different polymers produced different end products which could be pliable, semi-malleable or rigid, depending on the chemical formulae. As surface petroleum was discovered near Drake's Lake, there is no reason you cannot revive organic plastic manufacture. However, you will have to understand considerably more chemistry than is currently part of your Mastery training. The manufacture itself can be defined as a continuous mass-solution process. Two units were left in the Catherine Caves by Joel Lilienkamp.'

'Lilienkamp?' Piemur cried, pivoting to point both forefingers at Jancis who also reacted, crying 'Lilcamp?'

'*Who* was Joel Lilienkamp?' Piemur asked Aivas.

'The Expedition's Supply Officer: the person who preserved so many artefacts in the Catherine Caves.'

'Jayge just *has* to be a descendant,' Piemur crowed and then abruptly apologized for his interruption.

'The two large polymerizing units are not marked as having been protectively packaged. Therefore they will have suffered decay and are unlikely to be operative. But they can be used as templates. You will learn much in the reconstruction, Master Hamian, and have more to learn in the chemistry and physics experiments that you will be set.'

Hamian's grin stretched from ear to ear. 'My pleasure, Master Aivas, my pleasure.' He rubbed his big callused hands together, expressing his eagerness to start. 'When do I start?'

'First, you must find the prototype models in the cave,' and Aivas's screen lit up with the pictures of two thick cubes with a variety of curious extrusions. 'These are what you must find. They will be heavy and cumbersome to move.'

'I've moved odder and heavier objects, Master Aivas.'

A paper extruded from the slot which Piemur handed the Southern Smith: the objects were pictured on it.

'You will require a workshop in which to disassemble them and decide what materials you have readily available with which to assemble a modern model. It is advisable that you are not the only one to study these basic sciences: the manufacture of suitable polymers will require a considerable team of workers trained in chemistry and physics.'

Hamian smiled ruefully. 'Study will obviously be necessary, just to understand the unfamiliar words you're using.'

'I think it's safe to say,' Master Robinton put in, glancing pointedly at Piemur and Jancis, 'that you will have at least three or four more students in your class, Aivas. I'm sure, Hamian, that you will want some members of your own Hall trained as well.'

'I've one or two likely fellows in mind, that's certain,' Hamian replied. He drew in a deep breath and exhaled. 'My thanks, Master Aivas.'

'Acknowledged, Master Hamian.'

'How'd you escape your brother Toric?' Piemur asked softly, masking his words behind one hand.

'Escape doesn't enter into this, Piemur,' and again Hamian said with a droll grimace, 'I'm my own Master. I've organized Southern's mines to produce with or without me leaning on anyone. Now I shall broaden my own horizons, as Toric did his. My thanks, Master Robinton, D'ram. I know where the caves are. I'll start right away.'

And he strode purposefully out of the room and down the hall. As soon as he had turned the corner, Master Esselin ducked out of one of the sleeping rooms on the corridor, his expression aggrieved.

'Master Robinton, I told that Smith he wasn't to . . .'

'Master Esselin,' Robinton said, adopting his most charming manner as he put an arm around the man's fleshy shoulders and turned him around. D'ram closed in on the other side so that he was inexorably led toward the entrance hall. 'I do believe that you have been most shamefully treated lately.'

'I?' Esselin's fretful look turned to surprise as he laid one plump hand on his chest. 'Yes, Master Robinton, when bullies like that Southern Smith pay absolutely no attention to my orders . . .'

'You're quite right, Master Esselin. Most shameful and I think your good nature in suspending your invaluable archival contributions to this site has been woefully abused. Therefore, it has been decided that Weyrleader D'ram, Lord Warder Lytol and myself should relieve you of this onerous duty and let you get back to your own responsibilities.'

'Oh, but, Master Robinton,' and Esselin would have slowed his pace if the other two had let him. 'I didn't mean to imply that I was *unwilling* . . .'

'You have been willingness itself,' D'ram said, shaking his head, 'and all to your credit, Master Esselin, but fair's fair and you've been more than kind to officiate. We will now take over from you.'

Master Esselin continued his protests all the way out the door and down the walk to the path which led to the Archive complex. Gently but firmly Weyrleader and Harper gave him a final push, smiling and nodding and totally ignoring his repeated demurrals.

'There!' D'ram said once they were back in the building and he brushed his hands together in satisfaction at easing Esselin out. 'I'll take the first watch, Robinton.' He turned to one of the guards. 'I'm in charge now. What's your name?'

'Gayton, sir.'

'I'd take it kindly, Gayton, if you'd fetch something cool to drink from the kitchens. Bring enough for all of us here. And no, Robinton, he is not going to bring you any wine quite yet. You'll have to have a cool head when you stand your watch, you know.'

'Why, you old coot!' Robinton exclaimed. 'My head remains cool no matter how much wine I take. The very notion.'

'Take yourself off, Robinton.' And, grinning, D'ram shooed him away. 'Get into mischief somewhere else.'

'Mischief?' The Harper grumbled with mock indignation but just then, they both heard a triumphant shout from Piemur so he hurried along to see what had occurred.

'I did it! I did it!' Piemur was still carrying on when the Harper arrived. Jancis and Jaxom both looked slightly envious while Benelek adopted a distant attitude.

'Did what?'

'Made a program all by myself.'

The Harper peered at the enigmatic words and letters on the screen and then at his journeyman. 'That . . . is a program?'

'Sure is. Dead easy once you get the hang of it!' Piemur's elation was infectious.

'Piemur,' the Harper found himself saying, 'I have a few hours to spare right now while D'ram's on duty. Did you or did you not mention that there was a spare one of these contraptions?'

'Indeed there is, Master.' With considerable satisfaction on his face and not a trace of his usual impudence, Piemur spun out of his seat and went over to the shelf where the components were neatly stacked.

'I think I may regret this,' the Harper said to himself.

'It is to be hoped that you will not, Master Robinton,' was Aivas's low reassurance.

Zair nipping his ear roused Robinton from a doze. He came fully awake, at first because of his unfamiliar surroundings and the uncomfortable position he was in. He had been leaning back in the chair, head resting on the support, legs propped up on the desk. He had a crick in his neck and his knees wouldn't at first bend as he lowered them. When he groaned, Zair nipped him again, eyes flaming red-orange.

Instantly the Masterharper became alert. Down the hall, he could hear Aivas' voice explaining something and the lighter voice of one of the students querying. That was as it should be. He looked up at Zair who was staring out of the door into the night. It was then he caught the faint noise, of something cracking and the even fainter splashing of liquid.

He rose, silently swearing at the recalcitrance of ageing joints that no longer functioned smoothly. As stealthily as he could, he moved across the entrance hall and out into the night. It was near dawn: the insect sounds that had lulled him to sleep on his post had ceased and daytime noises had not yet begun. He crept forward, hearing that soft cracking noise again. To his left, where the banks of Fandarel's batteries had been installed against the wall, he saw darker shadows. Two men. Two men busily smashing the glass tanks that held the battery fluid.

'Now, just what do you think you're doing?' he demanded, outraged at such vandalism. 'Zair! Grab them! PIE . . . MUR! JANCIS! SOMEONE!' He ran forward, determined to prevent any further damage to Aivas' power supply.

Later, he wondered what he thought he'd been doing, an unarmed elderly man attacking vandals. Even as the pair came at him with upraised clubs or iron bars or whatever they'd been using to smash the battery tanks, he wasn't afraid: just purely and simply furious.

Fortunately Zair had weapons, twenty sharp talons, and as the little bronze swooped to tear at the eyes of the first man, Farli, Jancis' Trig and half a dozen other fire-lizards joined the battle. Robinton caught a handful of tunic, tried to drag the man to the ground but, with a savage jerk, accompanied by an anguished squeal as fire-lizard claws raked his face, the man broke free and took to his heels. His companion swatted viciously at the aerial attackers and then ran off as well. The fire-lizards followed, dividing into two groups to follow the separating fugitives.

By the time human assistance arrived, even the sounds of the vandals' retreat was lost to listening ears.

'Don't worry, Robinton,' Piemur said. 'We've only to check who got clawed. We'll find them! Are you all right, Master?'

Robinton was clutching at his chest, panting from his exertions and, although he gestured fiercely for Piemur and the others to follow the fugitives, he became their first concern.

'I'm all right, I'm all right,' he cried, trying to avoid their solicitude. 'Go after them,' and he fell into a fit of coughing, caused more by frustration than exercise.

By the time he had convinced them of his well-being, the fire-lizards had returned, looking exceedingly pleased with themselves for having chased the intruders. Disgusted at the vandals' escape, Robinton grabbed up a glowbasket and led the way to the point of attack.

'Five smashed, and if you hadn't heard . . .' Piemur began.

124

'I didn't hear. Zair did.' Robinton was furious with himself for having dosed off.

'Same thing,' Piemur replied with an impish grin. 'And they didn't break enough tanks to jeopardize the power supply. Don't fret now, Master. There're spares in Stores.'

'I'm fretting because it happened at all!' Robinton heard his voice rise in angry stress.

'We'll find the vandals,' Piemur assured his Master and, guiding him back to his chair, poured him a cup of wine.

'We'd better,' Robinton said in a savage mood. He knew there was growing antagonism to Aivas but he hadn't really considered for even a moment that someone would make an attack on the facility.

But who? he wondered, sipping at the wine and feeling its usual efficacious soothing. Esselin? He doubted the fat old fool would dare, no matter how upset he might have been over losing his sinecure. Had any of Norist's Glassmen been at Landing that day?

'Don't fret yourself,' Piemur repeated, regarding his Master with continued anxiety. 'See? Zair's blooded one of them. We'll find them, never fear.'

The men were not found the next morning although Piemur organized a discreet search of the entire complement at Landing. He even went so far as to rouse Esselin well before the indolent man was apt to be awake and his round fat face was blemish-free.

'They must have just kept running,' he had to report to a worried Harper who was overseeing the replacement of battery tanks.

'We must build a barrier across these,' Robinton said. 'We must mount a watch at all times. Aivas cannot be jeopardized.'

'Have you decided who's the most likely suspect?' Piemur asked, watching his Master's tired face.

'Suspect? I've a variety of choices. Proof, no!'

Piemur shrugged. 'Then we watch harder.' Then as an afterthought, he asked, 'Why didn't Aivas sound an alarm? He usually sees what's going on, night or day.'

When queried on that point, Aivas replied that the vandals had been operating under the level of exterior

125

visuals and the sound sensors had picked up anomalous noises, somewhat consistent with usual nocturnal activity.

'What about in here?' Robinton asked.

'This facility is safe. Do not fear vandalism in here.'

Robinton was not all that reassured but could not argue the point as the first of the new day's students were arriving.

'We'll keep this to ourselves for the time being, Piemur,' Robinton said in a tone that brooked no argument.

'What about a message to all harpers to watch out for claw-marked faces?'

Robinton lifted his shoulders briefly. 'I doubt they'll appear in public until they're healed, but send the message.'

Chapter Six

As events over the next few weeks proved, the self-appointment of the Harper, the old Weyrleader and the retired Lord Warder as Aivas' custodians was providential. The management by three men who already enjoyed reputations for probity and impartiality went unchallenged. Certainly the accumulated knowledge of Harper, Weyrleader and Lord Warder was utilized to its fullest in the rebirth and administration of Landing.

Some visitors – the merely curious – became disenchanted when they discovered that Aivas ignored foolish or egocentric questions. Those willing to be enlightened and work hard to acquire the new disciplines stayed on and profited.

Until ten secondary stations were up and running, the three Custodians arranged appointments for Aivas, deftly slotting in emergency consultations without offending anyone. And, because Aivas needed no rest, concentrated lessons, such as those for Master Oldive and other Healers, were scheduled for the early hours of Landing's day.

The major Crafthalls were not the only ones to send representatives; it became prestigious for the Lords Holder to send promising sons and daughters as well as likely candidates from minor Holds. There were so many at first – some so obviously ill-equipped to deal with radical new concepts – that it was kinder and less bothersome to set each applicant a basic test: an aptitude test was what Aivas called it. It certainly weeded out the idlers and those without true scholarship.

Lessa and F'lar never became proficient in their use of a console, because, in the Harper's estimation, they had little time to spend learning the essentials. But they did grasp the fundamentals of accessing information. F'nor didn't try but Brekke joined the Masterhealer's dedicated group in their striving to regain the lost medical techniques. Mirrim, determined to keep up with her mate, T'gellan, had a most distressing start, but struggled on and succeeded. K'van became as adept as Jaxom and Piemur.

To the surprise and delight of his close associates, the taciturn Lytol became an avid user, accessing files from the widest range of topics. He insisted on taking the late shift as he didn't require more than four hours of sleep anyway.

'Lytol's always been a deep person, with unexpected reserves. Or he wouldn't have survived as long as he has,' Jaxom replied to those who commented on Lytol's new obsession. 'Though I don't understand his fascination with all that dry historical stuff when there's so much more that we can apply to *living* and working here and now.'

'On the contrary, Jaxom,' the Harper replied, 'Lytol's investigations may be the most significant of all.'

'Even more significant than Fandarel's new water turbine power stations?'

The Mastersmith had taken great satisfaction in showing off how a model of the proposed generator worked as his foundry laboured all the hours in a day to complete the components of the full-scale machinery.

'That is certainly significant now,' and the Harper chose his reply carefully, 'but there's the problem of general acceptance.'

There had been sufficient time now – and supplies of the special wiring from the Catherine Caves – to make study rooms for different subjects. Two of the larger rooms became laboratories to teach the basic sciences Aivas felt were required as foundation courses, as he termed them: chemistry, physics and biology. There was one room set aside for short consultations, another for general teaching:

a largish one for Healers, the walls of which were covered with various diagrams 'of the most gruesome sort', in Jancis' estimation. Aivas also requested one reserved for special students: those who had concentrated courses in a variety of subjects. Jaxom, Piemur, Jancis, K'van, T'gellan, N'ton, Mirrim, Hamian, three journeymen, an apprentice of Hamian's, four other young bronze riders, two brown, four blue and three green riders were in this group. Other riders would follow when there was space in the classes since, of Hall, Hold and Weyr, the Weyrs were the most eager to take advantage of Aivas.

Occasionally Robinton liked to walk down the hall and listen in on the instructions. One day when he peered in on a lesson including Jaxom, Piemur, Sharra, who was now safely in mid-pregnancy and able to go between, Jancis, and two Smithcraft journeymen, he saw an astonishing sight.

On the high worktop in front of them a ring of dull metal hovered about two inches above it. As they reached forward to touch it with their fingers, it slipped along the bench as if it was on invisible rollers. Aivas's voice continued his explanation.

'The magnetic lines of force in the ring are induced in such a way that they exactly oppose the electro-magnets which are generating the induction field.'

Robinton made himself small against the door jamb so as not to disturb the fascinated students.

'This is far more dramatic at very low temperatures where there is none of the warmth that Jancis felt. At very low temperatures, there is no electrical resistance, the rings are superconducting, and the current passes without any loss. There are not the facilities here to show you this but you will be ready for the superconductivity lesson in three or four weeks. Jaxom will be ready for it sooner, and Piemur might just come up to standard but he must do more on winding electro-magnets with proper toroidal windings. Journeyman Manotti, your metal formers were not up to the standard required but you have a week in which to improve.'

On that note of criticism, Robinton tiptoed quietly away, not wishing to embarrass the students. But he smiled as he sauntered back to the entrance hall: a good teacher should give praise, encouragement and admonition as required.

There were auxiliary workshops for Smith, Glass and Wood Crafts in the larger of the excavated structures at Landing, staffed with Masters, journeymen and apprentices.

One morning, Lytol and Robinton were startled to hear a loud explosion and rushed to the source of the sound which emanated from Master Morilton's glass forge. There, they found Master Morilton helping Jancis to blot the blood from a mosaic of cuts on the face of one of Morilton's apprentices. There were tiny bits of mirrored glass everywhere which accounted for Caselon's injuries. Sharra, her goggles pushed up on her head, was helping another lad remove fragments from Caselon's protective leather apron. Its oil-hardened surface had saved him from more serious lacerations.

'Now,' Master Morilton was saying calmly, addressing his remarks to the others in the forge, 'you appreciate why protective goggles are so important. Caselon could well have lost his eyesight when that thermos glass exploded. As it is . . .' Morilton paused to glance inquiringly at Jancis.

'As it is,' she said, with a wry grin, 'Caselon's going to have the most interesting pattern of scars. Oh, don't worry,' she added as the youth cringed, 'they'll heal to nothing. Don't grimace. You'll only bleed until I've got you properly annointed with numbweed.'

As Lytol turned to deal with the press of the curious who had rushed over, Robinton looked about the place. Master Morilton had certainly set up quite a Hall here. A pump was going tapockety-tapockety in the corner. A tube reaching up to the apparatus had a leather collar at the top, on which were the remains of a mirrored bottle-neck. The rest of the glass was everywhere in the room, a myriad of tiny glinting pieces.

'Shards,' Caselon muttered, trying not to flinch from Jancis' ministrations, 'that was my twentieth!'

Robinton then noticed that nineteen vacuum flasks were neatly racked on Caselon's half of the worktable, only twelve on Vandentine's side. How they had escaped the flying glass splinters, he didn't know.

'We are not in competition mode here, Caselon,' Master Morilton said, wagging a stern finger at the boy. 'What exactly happened? I was concentrating on Bengel's wand work.'

'I dunno,' Caselon said, shrugging one shoulder.

'Aivas?' Master Morilton asked, since there was a direct connection between this workshop and the facility.

'When he moulded the glass, he didn't ultrasonicate it or even tap it as you have taught him, to get the bubbles out of the mix. He was too busy trying to outproduce his partner. There were bubbles in the glass so that under vacuum it imploded. But you may now use two of his vessels to demonstrate the properties of liquefied gases.'

As the numbweed had stemmed the bloodflow on Caselon's face, Master Morilton gestured for him and Vandentine to follow him to another room in the glass forge. Robinton trailed behind. In this room, there was a different kind of pump and, from a nozzle which was absolutely covered in frost, Robinton could see drops of a faintly blue liquid, about three falling into a thick mirrored catch-pot every second.

Aivas continued: 'The blue liquid is the air itself, the air in this room which we are compressing and then rapidly expanding so that it cools again and again, further and further until a tiny fraction of it liquefies.'

Master Morilton said, 'Don't touch the radiator vanes, they'll blister your fingers. This, Master Robinton,' he added, smiling at their guest, 'is a multi-stage refrigerator, quite different from the one you've been using in Cove Hold to chill fruit juice and foodstuffs.'

Robinton nodded wisely.

'This last stage is the most difficult,' Aivas said as Master Morilton gestured for Caselon to fill his flask. The room was filled with mist as the liquid air seethed until it had cooled Caselon's flask. Robinton moved his feet away as some of the pearly drops ran across the floor towards him. 'Now, Caselon, return to your work space and observe the antics of liquid air.'

131

Caselon was already doing so as he left the room.

'Play with air?' Robinton asked, perplexed, and he noticed Master Morilton's knowing smile.

'This liquid helium,' Aivas continued to instruct those in the liquid gas room, 'or rather, these liquids, can flow in opposite directions at the same time, will creep out of the top of a tall vessel and leave none in the bottom, and will even creep faster, much faster through tiny holes than through large ones. You may fill this flask with liquid air yourself, Master Robinton, and experiment on your own, very very carefully observing the properties of liquid gas. This is one of the most dangerous, and therefore educational, exercises for the students to do. Jancis, Sharra, there are flasks for you, too, and this experiment is an important one for both of you.' The way the two girls smirked at each other suggested to Robinton that they didn't know why it would be. 'When you have become familiar with liquid air, we can begin to learn about the special properties of liquid hydrogen, and especially of liquid helium.'

'If it's dangerous, should we be doing it?' Robinton asked, surprised at such a contradictory notion.

'Danger is often more educational for the student,' Aivas replied. 'It is unlikely, for instance, that Caselon will forget to tap his mix no matter how many glass inserts he blows from now on.'

It was an hour before Robinton and Lytol, whom the Masterharper had interested in the liquid-gas experiments, returned to their usual duties.

More and more of the dwellings at Landing became occupied. Many of the artefacts so long stored in the Catherine Caves had been put to use though the Custodians had decreed that samples of each were retained to exhibit in Master Esselin's Archive building for the curious.

Abandoned Landing once again became a bustling community. Where the walks and small yards had been cleared, there were even signs of renewed grasses and weeds.

'Are we a bit mad to re-establish this settlement?' Lessa asked one evening when she and F'lar had taken an evening meal in the Aivas building with Jaxom, Robinton, D'ram,

Lytol, Piemur and Jancis. 'Those volcanoes could erupt again.'

'I did mention that to Aivas,' Lytol said, 'and he replied that he was naturally monitoring seismic activity. He will warn us in plenty of time if there should be a build-up of magma in the volcanic chain. Some of the instruments which the settlers' vulcanist installed are still functioning. He also assured me that there is little activity in the chain.'

'And that is a positive thing?' Lessa asked, still sceptical.

'So Aivas assured me,' Lytol replied.

'I'd hate to lose all we've rebuilt here,' F'lar said, sharing his mate's apprehension.

'Unfortunately,' and Lytol's half-smile was ironic, 'Aivas can't be moved.'

'Then let's not worry about something that may not develop into a problem,' Robinton said firmly. 'We have sufficient immediate ones. Such as how we're going to handle Master Norist. As you know, he has threatened to disavow Morilton's Mastery and to disown all journeymen and apprentices who have produced glass according to the . . . ahem . . . spurious methods and techniques of Aivas.'

'He calls Aivas the Abomination!' Piemur said with a malicious chuckle. 'Aivas said . . .'

'You didn't *tell* Aivas that?' Jancis was aghast at Piemur's tactlessness.

'He didn't mind. I got the feeling it amused him.'

Master Robinton gave Piemur a long look. 'Do you – any of you – ever get the feeling that Aivas is amused by us?'

'Sure,' Piemur replied blithely. 'He may be a machine and all that, and while I know a great deal more about machinery than I used to, certainly, he's a Master machine that interacts with humans so he must have criteria by which he recognizes levity. He may not guffaw as some do at my jokes and anecdotes, but he certainly enjoys listening to them.'

'Hmmm,' was the Harper's non-committal response. 'About Norist . . . As the duly elected Mastercraftsman, guiding his Halls, he can only be replaced at a convocation of all Masters. Unfortunately, the Glass-smithcraft is not a large one and most of the Hallmasters are as dogmatic as Norist. On the other hand, I won't sit by and see Master Morilton disavowed or harassed or humiliated because he has learned something Norist didn't teach him. He's certainly proved adept at the new skills.'

'Norist has also been leaning heavily on poor old Wansor,' Lytol said. 'Fortunately, Wansor appears oblivious both to the criticism and the fact that he might suffer the same discipline as Morilton. In spite of Norist's declaration, Morilton has managed to recruit quite a few journeymen and apprentices who have felt restricted by Norist's rigid adherence to Recorded techniques.'

'If Norist is leaning on Wansor, why don't we lean on him?' Jaxom asked.

'I will,' Lytol replied with a ghost of a smile, 'and I would be happy to. A man who will not see beyond his nose has no right to be Craftmaster!' His smile was replaced by censure.

'Hear! Hear!' came from the Harper.

'I also heard that Norist is denying Morilton the use of the best sandpits,' Lytol went on, frowning.

'That's no problem at all. We've sand aplenty on this coast line,' Piemur responded.

'Dimwit. Beach sand isn't what's used for glass,' Jaxom said with some disdain. 'It's the pits at Igen and Ista that have fine stuff.'

'But those are the ones that Norist has denied Morilton,' Lytol replied.

'He hasn't denied Lord Jaxom of Ruatha Hold!'

'Nor D'ram,' said the aged bronze rider as firmly as the young Lord.

Even Lytol grinned at that solution to Norist's intransigence. 'Microscopes require a very high quality glass, you know, to take the best of grinding and polishing.'

'In any case, I don't see that as a major difficulty,' D'ram said, glancing over to Jaxom. 'Ruth and Tiroth won't mind a little excursion, I'm sure.' Jaxom nodded obligingly. 'You take Ista and I'll get some from Igen.'

'There's nothing on the settlers' map to indicate closer deposits, to reduce transportation time?' asked F'lar.

Robinton held up one finger. 'We'll ask,' and he pecked out the query with considerable speed on the keyboard of the unit in the room.

Immediately a list of locations scrolled out, with the type of sand to be found at each. Those sands which had been used for medical glass were starred, but Aivas recommended the sands found at Paradise River and in an inland sandpit near the site of old Cardiff.

D'ram said he'd go to the Cardiff site as he knew that Jaxom would prefer a chance to see Jayge and Aramina who were holding at Paradise River.

'Hmmm,' the Harper said. 'Aivas reminds me that he wants more green and bronze riders for training.'

'Would he take a big brown or two?' asked F'lar. 'I've several riders who've offered. Seems like Aivas is biased against the medium sizes.'

'I asked him about that,' D'ram said, 'for I thought it odd that he'd want only the largest and the smallest. He says the operation requires them but he won't elaborate beyond stating that he must have enough candidates to allow him to pick the most likely to succeed in the venture and to have sufficient trained back-up personnel.' D'ram shrugged at his inability to explain further.

'I *wish*,' Lessa said, 'that occasionally he would be specific. Then we would have something to tell those we must disappoint. I don't want any resentful dragonriders. Though, in general, I'd say that morale has improved in all the Weyrs. And,' she made a face, 'all the Weyrs want to participate.'

'Aivas did remark that it was easier to teach the younger dragonriders,' D'ram went on, 'since there were fewer set mental patterns. Of course, there are naturally some few exceptions,' he added, rather pleased that he was one of them.

'Is that all right now?' Jaxom asked. 'I'd better get back to Ruatha,' and his grin was abashed. 'I'll bring in Paradise River sands tomorrow but I'd better spend some time in Ruatha.'

'In danger of being disowned?' Piemur asked, with an impudent grin.

Jaxom disdained to reply while Jancis elbowed the young journeyman in the ribs.

'Go on, then,' F'lar said, with a bland sideways glance at his own mate.

'I'll just ask Aivas to print out the location of the sandpit,' D'ram said, rising to leave with the young Lord Holder.

There was a slight frown on Lytol's face as the two left.

'Don't fret, Lytol,' Lessa said reassuringly. 'Sharra's got every right to be annoyed at the amount of time Jaxom's spending here.'

'Especially when I'm sure she's dying to take the Healer lessons,' Jancis said, 'but, Piemur, have you noticed it, too? That whenever Jaxom misses a day, Aivas particularly asks why?'

'Hmm, yes, I had at that,' Piemur replied, momentarily thoughtful and then assumed a careless pose, 'but Aivas sure works Jaxom harder than any of the rest of us, bar Mirrim and S'len.'

'S'len?' asked F'lar, 'isn't he that young green rider from Fort?'

'That's the one. And Aivas insisted on drilling Mirrim to bring her up to a level with the rest of us,' Piemur added.

'Why would the green dragons be so important to Aivas?' Lessa asked.

'They're small, that's why,' Piemur said.

'Small?'

'Well, that's my hunch, and Ruth's the smallest of them all,' Piemur went on. 'There's no doubt in my mind that those two will play a special part in Aivas' Great Scheme.'

Lessa and Lytol both looked concerned.

'Oh, don't worry about Jaxom,' Piemur said airily. 'He's the best of us all. Has a real grasp of all that navigational mathematics Aivas throws at us, and the spatial relationships.'

'Has he suggested *anything* yet?' Lessa asked Robinton and Lytol who shook their heads.

Then Robinton grinned. 'I get literary quotations, such as: "There's a time for some things, and a time for all things: a time for great things, and a time for small things." I am forced to assume that this is the time for small things, like assimilating all those foundation courses from Aivas, while the time for great things is still four Turns, seven months and howevermany days away from us.'

'Literary quotations?' F'lar asked, surprised. His lessons with Avias tended to the practical: tactics, mathematical projections of Threadfall, and draconic healing – though he practised none of the latter, he kept himself informed of Avias' innovations.

'Oh, yes. And Aivas admits he is choosing what he thinks might appeal to my tastes. Our ancestors had fascinating and complex literatures from ever so many cultures that put ours to shame. Some of our epic sagas he has identified as paraphrases of Terran originals. Fascinating.'

'Indeed, my studies have been equally absorbing,' Lytol said, leaning forward on the table, his face lightened with his own enthusiasm. 'I don't think any of us realized that our present political structure was handed down from the very Charter our ancestors brought with them? That is historically very unusual, Aivas told me.'

'Why should it be?' F'lar asked, mildly surprised. 'It allows Weyr, Hold and Hall to function without interference.'

'Ah, but interference was a major factor in Terran politics,' Lytol replied. 'Spurred by territorial imperatives and, all too often, sheer greed.'

Adroitly interrupting another of Lytol's historical perorations, Lessa rose, nodding to Robinton and the two young journeymen. 'We must get back to the Weyr now. Aivas gave me another healing compound for Lisath's wing. It simply isn't mending as it should.'

I told Aramina that we're coming, Ruth said as Jaxom mounted him. *She likes to know, you know*, he added in a confidential tone.

Jaxom rather wished that Ruth hadn't committed them to paying a call on Aramina and Jayge. He really ought to get back to Ruatha *now*.

'Well, we won't stay long, mind.' And Jaxom gave Ruth an indulgent slap.

The white dragon was very fond of the young woman

who, as a girl, had heard dragons on such an incessant level that she had inveigled Jayge of the Lilcamp Traders to take her far away from any dragons to preserve her sanity. Shipwrecked in their effort to reach the southern continent, they had been rescued by shipfish and set ashore. There they had discovered and restored ancient buildings, not realizing the significance of their find. Located by Piemur on his coastline survey, they had been officially named as Holders of Paradise River, and had increased their numbers to a sizeable Hold, including a Fisher Hall. The former trader had been immensely surprised when Piemur and Jancis told him that a paternal ancestor named Lilienkamp had been instrumental in saving so much useful material in the Catherine Caves.

When Piemur and Jancis exchanged formal vows, they had spent a few days up the Paradise River by themselves. Even then, Piemur had been urging Jayge to join the special classes at Landing but so far Jayge had not been sufficiently moved by his blandishments.

As Jaxom had given Ruth the precise coordinates for the ancient sandpit, they emerged over rather anonymous grassland. It wasn't until Ruth had overflown the alleged site several times that Jaxom noticed the declivity well overgrown with grass and shrubs, with the suspicion of white glinting through the vegetation. So they landed and, by kicking and gouging, Jaxom peeled back the obscuring greenery and lifted a handful of sand so fine it was nearly powder. He filled the large sacks he'd brought with him, working up quite a sweat. Then he remounted his dragon.

He had cooled off as Ruth glided to a gentle, faultless halt in front of the gracious ancient residence of the Paradise River Hold.

'And a good day to you, Lord Jaxom and Ruth!' Jayge said, stepping off the wide porch to meet Jaxom. ''Ara started squeezing fresh juice the moment Ruth told her you were coming. And I'm glad you did, because something's come up!'

I'm going swimming. The fire-lizards said they'll scrub my back, Ruth told Jaxom, his eyes whirling with green delight.

That was the real reason Ruth loved to come to Paradise River: he had plenty of bathing assistants. So he hop-glided right into the river, several full fairs of fire-lizards, wild and banded, circling ecstatically above him.

'Off for a scrub, is he?' Jayge asked. He was of medium height, his bare chest burned a fine deep brown, his legs not quite as dark. His oddly flecked green eyes stood out in his tanned face, reflecting a hint of a strong personality and a basic tranquillity, even though a slight frown crossed his face as he gestured for Jaxom to accompany him to the coolness of the porch. 'I'm glad you stopped by, Jaxom. How did you work up such a sweat in *between*?'

'Stealing sand.'

'Indeed?' Jayge regarded him thoughtfully. 'Now what would you need Paradise River sand for? As I'm sure you're going to tell me away.' He gestured for Jaxom to take the hammock while he leaned against the porch banister, arms folded across his chest.

'The settlers had a sandpit back in that scrub land of yours. They thought highly of Paradise River sands – for glass-making.'

'There's enough certainly. Did Piemur and Jancis find those whatchamacallums . . .'

'Chips?' Jaxom supplied the proper term with a grin.

'Chips, then, useful after all?'

'Well, we managed to salvage the usable transistors and capacitors but they haven't actually been installed yet.'

Jayge gave him a long hard suspicious look before grinning. 'As you say!'

Just then young Readis, clad only in a clout, came out on to the porch, rubbing sleep out of his eyes. He eyed Jaxom steadily. 'Ruth?'

Jaxom pointed to where the white dragon, surrounded by industrious fire-lizards, wallowed in the shallow water.

'He's enough of a guardian, isn't he?' Readis asked his father, tilting his head back in a stance that mirrored one of his father's attitudes.

'Ruth's bathing right now and, besides, I'd like you to tell Jaxom what happened to you and Alemi the other day.'

'Did you come just to hear?' There was a certain element

139

of vanity in young Readis' grin. Jaxom was suddenly aware of how much he missed his own son, Jarrol, an engaging three Turns old.

'Well, that was one reason,' Jaxom replied mendaciously. 'So what did happen to you and Alemi the other day?'

Aramina emerged from the house, carrying her squirming daughter under one arm and a tray in her free hand. Jayge sprang quickly to relieve her of the tray, but she gave him two-Turn-old Aranya instead, and served Jaxom a tall cool drink and some freshly baked sweet biscuits. It took a few more minutes until Readis had been sat in a chair, his small glass and two biscuits to hand. As Aramina settled herself, Readis looked to his father for his cue to begin.

'Uncle Alemi took me fishing three days ago in the skiff. The big reds were schooling out there,' and Readis' brown arm indicated a general northerly direction. 'We was to have a beach meal 'cos it was Swacky's nameday and we needed big 'uns to grill. There was only little squids on the edges of the school. Then, all o' sudden, a big one got Uncle's hook and it dragged us, boat and all,' Readis' eyes were shining with remembered excitement, 'right into the current. But Uncle Alemi, he wrestled it aboard and it was this,' he held his arms as wide as they could go, 'big. No funning!' He glared briefly at his father who was hiding his laughter in his hand. 'It was big! You ask Alemi! But he hung on and I helped him gaff it aboard. Then my reel started spinning and Uncle Alemi and I had to put our backs into landing that one. That's why we didn't notice the squall coming up.'

Jaxom glanced anxiously at Jayge and Aramina. Alemi would not endanger anyone and he knew his Craft.

'It was some squall, I can tell you,' Readis said, jerking his chin in the manner of any good story teller emphasizing details. 'We got tossed and spun about 'cos there was no way the sail would have lasted in a blow like that. And then a big wave overturned the skiff and I came up coughing and sputtering, Uncle Alemi hanging on to my arm fit to break it.' The little brown and serious face regarded Jaxom. 'I'm not afraid to admit I was some scared. The sky around us was black and the rain coming down so heavy we couldn't see the shore. But I'm a good swimmer and I can see now why Uncle Alemi always makes me wear my deep water vest even if it is hot most times and rubs my back. See?' And he swivelled his torso, raising one arm over his head, to show Jaxom where the underarm skin had been abraded. 'Then it happened!'

'What happened?' Jaxom asked on cue.

'I had my arms out, trying to keep my head up, when suddenly something came smack-dab into my right hand. AND started pulling me. Uncle Alemi yelled at me that it was all right. We were safe; I was to hang on tight, just as he was doing.'

'Shipfish?' Jaxom asked with an incredulous glance at Readis' parents. He knew that Jayge and Aramina owed their lives to shipfish, and even Master Idarolan swore that the sleek big sea creatures would rescue humans in stormy seas.

'A whole pod of 'em,' Readis said proudly. 'And every time my hand slipped off, there was another one right behind to hang on to. Uncle Alemi says there must have been twenty or thirty. They pulled us far enough in for us to see the beach and reach safety on our own. AND,' he added, pausing to give emphasis to his final words, 'the next morning the skiff was found beached up by the Fishhold, like they knew exactly where it belonged.'

'That is some tale, young Readis. You're a harper born. An amazing rescue. Truly amazing,' Jaxom said with genuine feeling. He glanced at Jayge who nodded supportively. 'The redfish weren't by any chance returned with the skiff?' he asked.

'Nah,' and Readis dismissed that with a flick of his wrist. 'They drowned. So we had to eat ol' stringy wherry 'stead of good juicy redfish steaks. And you know something else?'

'No, what?' Jaxom asked with polite interest.

'The shipfish kept talking to us all the time they was saving us. Uncle Alemi heard them, too.'

'What did they say?'

Now Readis frowned deeply in concentration. 'I don't 'xactly remember the words. The wind was shrieking but I know they were shouting at us. Encouraging us like.'

Until Jaxom caught Jayge's eye, he thought it was a youthful embellishment for a hectic rescue but Jayge nodded a confirmation.

'Readis, why don't you run down and see if the fire-lizards are giving Ruth a proper scrubbing?' Jayge suggested.

The sturdy little boy jumped to his feet. 'Can I? Really?' He flashed a radiant grin at Jaxom.

'Really, you can,' Jaxom assured him, wondering if Jarrol would be as enchanting as Readis when he was five.

'Yahoo,' cried Readis, tearing off down the shore where Ruth was afloat.

'That's exactly what happened to him and Alemi?' Jaxom asked.

'With no embellishments,' Aramina said, obviously proud of her son. 'Alemi said that he didn't panic and obeyed him instantly. Otherwise . . .' And she broke off, her face paling under her warm tan.

Jayge leaned towards Jaxom. 'I wondered if you'd mind asking this Aivas thing of yours what he knows about the shipfish. Alemi also swears that they were speaking words. Over the wind and sea noises, he couldn't distinguish exactly what they were saying, but they used words. He thinks they were giving them directions or reassurances. Piemur gave us a passing mention of the big fish – doll-fins – which Aivas said were brought here from Terra. I asked him to inquire but I guess it slipped his mind.'

These days Jaxom always carried a small pad and pencil in his belt pouch. So he made a notation. 'I won't forget,' he assured them, patting his pouch when he had replaced pad and pencil.

As soon as Ruth had had time to dry off in the sun, Jaxom called him up from the beach. Readis was squealing with rapture for Ruth allowed the lad to climb up on his back for the short walk back. Aramina gave Jaxom a full net of fresh fruit to take to Sharra and Jarrol for which he thanked them profusely.

As Ruth ascended to a safe height, Jaxom came to a conclusion, based on the guilt he experienced in being so long away from Ruatha – yet again!

'Ruth, let's shave three hours off our return. That's safe enough, and we'll be back in Ruatha just as everyone's getting up.'

You know Lessa doesn't like us timing it.

'We haven't in Turns, Ruth.'

Sharra will know.

'I'm hoping she'll be so glad to see me she won't mind – this once.' Jaxom stroked Ruth's neck urgently. 'Let me handle my mate.' Ruth didn't like to deceive either Sharra or Lessa. 'It's not deceiving Sharra. It's getting home early for a change. Not a big thing to ask.'

Oh, I suppose it won't matter this once. I always know when we are.

However, as soon as they came out of *between* above Ruatha Hold, Jaxom had cause to regret coming home at all. A wild blizzard blowing down from the mountains all but obscured the Hold.

A good thing I always know where I am, too, Ruth remarked, craning his neck and blinking wind-blown particles out of his faceted eyes.

'Can you see to land, Ruth? I never thought to check on the weather conditions.' Jaxom covered his cheeks with his gloved hands, feeling the chill entering his bones despite the heavy riding jacket. His legs, clad in trousers appropriate to Southern's Summer, felt like lengths of ice.

I didn't either, Ruth replied forgivingly. *Only a moment or two longer. I'm right above the courtyard.*

Suddenly he backwinged and Jaxom felt the jar as the white dragon landed with an uncharacteristic thud.

Sorry. Snowdrift.

Jaxom wasted no time sliding off his dragon, but his path to the big doors that opened into Ruth's weyr at Ruatha Hold was impeded by the heavy drifts. He had to scoop away the worst of them. Finally, he got one leaf of the door open enough so that Ruth could find purchase for his forepaws. Then dragon strength hauled the stout metal door back through the drifts.

Get inside. Go on, Ruth ordered his rider and Jaxom was all too willing to obey.

Once inside the weyr, which was only warmer by virtue

of being out of the chill and gusting wind, both dragon and rider struggled to pull the door shut. At that, considerable snow got inside.

Rubbing his legs fiercely to restore feeling, Jaxom half-ran across the stone floor of the chamber to the capacious hearth where a fresh fire had been laid. His fingers fumbled with the firemaker before he got it lit. The flames ate hungrily at the dry wood and Jaxom was shortly able to warm himself.

'I don't usually *mind* the cold,' Jaxom said, removing his jacket and shaking off the snow that had caked there even in his brief time in the blizzard. 'It's just coming from all that lovely weather . . .'

Meer says that Jarrol has a bad cold and Sharra's not feeling good with being up all night, Ruth told Jaxom, his eyes tinged with the yellow of worry.

'Young children often have colds this time of year,' he replied, though he knew that Jarrol had had far too many sniffles this winter. Sharra was pulled down nursing him for she refused to allow anyone else to tend their first-born. 'Sometimes, Ruth, I'm very stupid,' Jaxom exclaimed abruptly. 'There's no reason in the world Sharra can't come south, enjoy decent weather, and study with Aivas!'

How? She's uncomfortable astride these days!

'She can come by ship. We'll just find out from Master Idarolan when he can accommodate her on a trip south. They make the journey often enough. Yes, that's what we'll do. We'll all go south. There's nothing here at this season that Brand can't manage without me.'

Suddenly Jaxom felt a great deal better about this solution to his lengthy absences from his family. Surely Sharra would approve.

When he found her rocking their cold-fussy son in the warmth of their apartment, her instant enthusiasm for the removal was as keen as his. The subject of his unusual arrival did not come up at all. As soon as Jarrol was lulled back to sleep and laid down in his cot, Sharra proved to Jaxom's delight just how glad she was to have him home and in bed.

*

144

His face screwed in an anxious grimace, Harper Journeyman Tagetarl came striding out of the Aivas complex to Robinton's desk in the foyer of the building.

'Aivas would like to speak to you and Sebell when it's convenient.'

'Oh? What's he stewing up now?' the Harper asked for the journeyman appeared so uncharacteristically perturbed.

'He wants the Harper Hall to build a printing press.' Tagetarl agitatedly ran his hair back from his face with both hands and heaved an exasperated groan.

'A printing press,' and Robinton gave a gusty sigh. He reached up to nudge his bronze fire-lizard awake. 'Zair, please find Sebell and ask him to join us?'

Zair chirruped sleepily but obediently unwound his tail from the Harper's neck. He walked down Robinton's arm and on to the table, stretching himself as he did so and then leaped away and out the open door.

'Sebell can't be far if Zair's not bothering to go *between*,' Robinton remarked. 'Have some *klah* while we wait. You look as if you need some. Why did Aivas suddenly decide the Harper Hall needs a printing press?'

Tagetarl gratefully poured himself a cup, hooking a chair to Robinton's desk and, once again, smoothing back his long black hair, less urgently this time.

'I asked could we please have copies of the string instrument quartets he played the other evening. Domick particularly wanted to have a transcript. He said he's tired of hearing us rave about ancestral music. Domick added,' and Tagetarl smiled ruefully, 'that, with so many Masters and journeymen working here, he's not able to come and hear for himself.'

Robinton grinned, knowing that Tagetarl had probably edited the Composition Master's acerbic comments.

'Aivas said that he's got to conserve the paper he has left and he has to consider music to be a non-essential in view of the demands on his resources. He's down to the last two rolls. He feels we ought to have our own replication machines.' Tagetarl grinned expectantly.

'Hmmm. That's certainly reasonable.' Robinton tried to

145

sound enthusiastic since Tagetarl was evidently much taken by the idea. But, inwardly, he had considerable concern over just how much more could be added to the 'essential' mechanizations already being undertaken. There were so many people from so many Halls already working full tilt on half a dozen critical projects. 'Undeniably a great deal of information ought to be circulated. Especially for distant Halls and Holds which cannot send representatives here.'

Zair reappeared, chirping in the tone that said his errand had been successful. He had only just settled himself again across Robinton's shoulders when Sebell came running. He had obviously dressed in a hurry and his hair was still wet.

'Easy, Sebell. There's no urgency,' Robinton said, raising a hand to slow Sebell down. 'I hope Zair didn't misinform you.'

Catching his breath, Sebell gave his mentor a salute and a wry grin. 'Obedience to any summons from you, Master, is too deeply engrained to change now.'

'Even when you're Masterharper of Pern?' And Robinton's grin was sly. 'Especially now that you are Masterharper of Pern, you should be allowed to finish your morning ablutions.'

'*Klah*?' Tagetarl suggested, and when Sebell nodded appreciatively, he poured him a cup.

'I'd just finished showering,' Sebell replied, accepting the *klah*. 'So now that I'm here, how can I assist you?'

Robinton gestured to Tagetarl.

'It's really Aivas who wants to talk to you, and Master Robinton. He needs a printing press and he says that, according to his understanding of our present structure, that should be the responsibility of the Harper Hall.'

Sebell nodded his head up and down, accepting the information. Robinton recognized it as a habit of his own which Sebell had adopted when he, too, was absorbing unexpected requests.

'Any form of communication is indeed a Harper Hall function. What exactly is a printing press?' Sebell asked after taking several thoughtful sips of his *klah*.

'An improvement on Master Arnor's crabbed script, I

146

devoutly hope,' Robinton remarked in a bland tone. The other two harpers rolled their eyes. 'Something approximating the readable print which Aivas produces would be an enormous help.'

'Aivas is apparently the only one in the world who easily reads Arnor's script. What's the problem?' Sebell asked Tagetarl.

'Domick's been after me to get copies of some of the splendid music Aivas has been playing for us.'

Sebell nodded understandingly. 'That was inevitable. And certainly the request is only fair when he's had to take over so much Hall management to keep us here.'

'Don't let Domick pressure you with insidious suggestions,' Robinton said, wagging a finger at his colleagues. 'Though he will certainly find the string music utterly fascinating.'

'We all do,' Sebell said as he rose. 'Let's see exactly what this printing press project entails. We are certainly not a mechanically inclined Hall, even if we produce our instruments.' And all three harpers went to consult with Aivas.

'But not without skill or intelligence, Master Sebell,' Aivas replied deferentially. 'Replicating or duplicating written material can be achieved by a variety of methods, of which the current laborious hand copying is the most prone to error. Having scanned the relics of machinery and parts still available in the Catherine Caves, it is possible to assemble a more efficient method of reproducing multiple copies of essential information, and the musical scores requested by your colleague in the Hall.'

Sheets spewed from the print slot which Tagetarl agilely caught.

'The drawings itemize the parts you should be able to find in the caves, and the few that Master Fandarel will need to fabricate for you. It will be in his interests, also, to cooperate.' There followed one of those pauses which Robinton liked to interpret as indicative of the various humours of Aivas. This one, he was sure, was a pointed reminder of how much the Smithcrafthall had already benefited by Aivas's assistance. 'With the intelligence which appears to mark even apprentices in your Hall, you should be able to assemble the apparatus by the time Master Fandarel has finished installing the water turbine station. There will then be sufficient power to run the printing press as well. Master Benelek has admirably succeeded in producing continuous rolls of paper which are also essential to the process.

'The manufacture of the individual letters and numbers to comprise a legible type font, and the musical and scientific signs, should be relatively simple for those with good manual dexterity.' Another page came out, illustrating a highly readable type font. 'Journeyman Tagetarl is a dexterous carver.' His remark astonished Tagetarl for he couldn't think how Aivas had learned about his handiwork. 'There may be others with similar artistic talent who might assist.'

'There isn't a printing press in the Catherine Caves?' Sebell asked, his tone slightly wistful.

'Unfortunately, no. Replication and data storage had developed well past such cumbersome processes. This method will however be sufficient for your needs for some time to come.'

Sebell had taken the type font sheet from Tagetarl. 'It'll be nice not to have to squint or use a magnifying glass to read.' He gave his head a shake. 'Master Arnor won't like it.'

Robinton grimaced and then sighed with regret. 'Perhaps it is time. He's almost blind right now, you know. And those wretched apprentices take terrible advantage of him. Menolly was telling me about a very impertinent incident only last week. One youngster handed in a scurrilous verse in place of the ballad he had been assigned. And poor Master Arnor approved it.'

Tagetarl masked a grin. 'That's not the first time Master Arnor's had that trick played on him.'

'This printing press would help conserve your supplies, Aivas?'

'It will but that was not the basic reason to suggest that you extend your activities to include such a fundamental improvement in data handling. You will find that eventually you will need more than one press so it is prudent to learn the principle and improve on it in your own time.'

'I think,' and Robinton paused, glancing at Sebell since he was encroaching on the new Masterharper's authority with the suggestion, 'that this printing press should first be constructed here in Landing.'

Sebell nodded, intuitively guessing the real reason for his mentor's suggestion. 'That would certainly be less of an affront to Master Arnor.'

Aivas added nothing to that remark: another sort of pause Robinton chose to interpret as 'if you can't say something positive, say nothing'.

Sebell was examining the sheets with Tagetarl. 'Dulkan's already here and he's done some fine brass work for harp plates. There're four more of the older apprentices, waiting for their hour on the General Science Course. We could use them until their appointment.'

Robinton beamed at the two men, already moving forward on the project. He liked that in them. Good men, both of them.

'Terry's down at the Catherine Caves right now, in fact. If we hurry, we can get advice from him, too.' Tagetarl said eagerly.

With the briefest, but still most courteous, of farewells to Robinton, the two young men strode out of the room and down the hall, exchanging ideas on how to proceed.

Sometimes, Robinton thought, as he slowly eased himself down into the nearest chair, such energy exhausted rather than revived him. Not that he wouldn't be delighted with this printing press. Able to run off as many copies as needed? What a concept!

It truly amazed him that there were now so many devices that had never before been required. The effects on Hall, Hold and Weyr, only beginning to filter through, would be profound. Lytol, having delved into the history and politics of their ancestors, had already worried about what he called the erosion of values and the subversion of tradition by new demands. The promise of the eradication of Thread – the possibility, Robinton sternly corrected himself – motivated all but a few dissenters. Even the most conservative of the Oldtimers still alive had swung round to support the Benden Weyrleaders.

And how *were* dragons and their riders to occupy themselves when Thread was no longer the rationale for the Weyrs? Robinton knew, though the notion was not widely discussed, that F'lar and Lessa wanted to lay claim to considerable lands here in the southern continent. But would the Lords Holder – who looked greedily towards the open space of the vast southern continent – be complacent about such claims? Toric's realization that he had settled for such a small portion of the southern lands still rankled in that ambitious man's mind. However, in Robinton's estimation, the Weyrs deserved whatever they requested after centuries of service but would the Lords Holder, and the Halls, agree? That concerned him the most. Yet it seemed to worry the Weyrleaders least. And what if, in the four years, ten months and three days specified by Aivas, the attempt should fail? What then?

Perhaps, and he brightened suddenly, all this new technology would absorb both Hold and Hall, to the exclusion of the Weyrs. Hold and Hall had always managed quite nicely to ignore the Weyrs between Passes. Perhaps, things like power stations and printing presses were indeed valuable but for more abstruse reasons as well as the obvious ones.

'Aivas,' Robinton said in greeting, carefully closing the door behind him. 'A word with you.' Robinton cleared his throat, wondering why Aivas could sometimes reduce him to apprentice nerves. 'About this printing press . . .'

'You do not concur with the necessity of such a machine?'

'On the contrary, I most certainly do.'

'Then what troubles you? For your voice betrays a note of uncertainty.'

'Aivas, when we first realized what you represented, in terms of knowledge, we had little idea of the scope of all that had been lost over the centuries. Yet now, rarely does a day go by but some new device is suddenly on the essential list. Our skilled craftsmen have enough lined up to do for the entire Pass. Tell me, truly, *are* all these machines and devices really necessary?'

'Not to the way of life you had, Master Robinton. But to accomplish what is apparently the desire of the majority of Pern, the destruction of Thread, improvements are essential. Your ancestors did not employ the highest technology available to them: they preferred to use the lowest level necessary to perform the function. That is the level which is presently being reestablished. As you yourself requested in the initial interview.'

Robinton wondered if he just thought he heard a mild reproof.

'Water driven power . . .'

'Which you already had available to you . . .'

'Printing presses . . .'

'The Records were printed but in a laborious and time-consuming fashion that, unfortunately, permitted errors to be made, and perpetuated . . .'

'The teaching consoles . . .'

'You have harpers who instruct by set lessons. You had even managed to rediscover paper-making before accessing this facility. Most paper-making techniques, Masterharper, are refinements of techniques you already employ, now made easier by some basic machinery, and of no higher level than your ancestors brought with them. It is little more than correcting long-standing errors and misconceptions. The spirit of the original colonists is still intact. Even the technology that must be utilized to thwart the return of the wanderer planet will be of the same level as your ancestors. There may be other scientifically advanced methods now available to Earth scientists that could be utilized if there was still communication between this planet and Earth. Great strides in cosmology were being announced at the time the colony ships left Earth's system. These were not, however, incorporated in the memory banks of this facility. Once you have regained the appropriate level of understanding, you may progress, or not, as you choose.'

Robinton pensively rubbed his chin. He could scarcely fault Aivas for doing what had been specifically requested, to bring present-day Pern back to the level of knowledge it had lost. It was also obvious that Aivas obeyed the initial request that only what was really needed be revived. It was just stunning to realize how much *had* been lost.

'This world has survived, Master Robinton, with more dignity and honour than you would imagine. As Lord Warder Lytol is discovering in his exploration of history.'

'Perhaps I have not paid as much attention to his studies as I ought.'

'That statement is a private analysis of achievement, Master Robinton. It is for Lord Warder Lytol to arrive at his own conclusion based on his studies.'

'I wonder if his conclusion will parallel your impartial one.'

'You should delve into history and arrive at your own, Master Robinton.' There was one of the interesting pauses that Aivas affected. 'Printed books would make that much easier for you.'

Robinton glared at the green Active light on the face of the Aivas facility and wondered, once again, what constituted 'artificial intelligence'. On the several times he had asked that direct question, his reply had been a repetition of a translation of the acronym. Robinton now understood that there were explanations which Aivas either could not, or was programmed not to, make.

'Yes, printed books would be much easier. But the settlers had other devices, much more compact.'

'That technology is too advanced to be considered at the present time and would involve processes which are presently beyond your abilities and are an unnecessary refinement.'

'Well, then, I'll settle for books.'

'That would be prudent of you.'

'And you will remain prudent in what you ask us to recreate?'

'That is a corollary to the prime goal of this facility.'

Robinton was content with that answer. But just as he had his hand on the door pull, he turned. 'Would this printing press be able to print musical scores as well?'

'Yes.'

'That would be much, much easier for the entire Hall,' he said, feeling so buoyant as he retraced his steps down the hall, that he began to whistle.

Chapter Seven
Two Turns Later

Lessa roused abruptly, opening her eyes to a darkness in the weyr that suggested daylight was still hours away. F'lar lay sprawled beside her, his forehead touching her shoulder, one arm thrown across her, one leg pinning hers down. Their bed was oversized but he invariably managed to occupy more of it than she did. In fact, there were only finger lengths between her and the edge. She must have told herself to wake up at this barbarous hour: she'd always had that ability. But why? Her mind was too sleep-fogged to provide an immediate answer.

Ramoth was sound asleep, too. And Mnementh! The whole Weyr was asleep, including, she discovered with irritation, the dragon and rider supposedly on watch on the Rim of Benden Weyr. She'd blast him as soon as she figured out why she was awake at this appallingly early hour.

Then she saw the lighted clock-face on the bedside locker. Three bloody of the clock! Progress was a two-edged dagger. Having a reliable time piece that was visible in the dark only made the dark and this early rising harder to endure. But seeing the clock reminded her why she must rise early this morning. She pushed at F'lar who was never easy to wake up unless Mnementh called him.

'F'lar, wake up! We've got to get up. *Ramoth, dear, wake up! We've to be at Landing. Aivas particularly wants us there.*'

She prodded F'lar's shoulder more urgently and, struggling to pull her legs out from under his, reluctantly rose from the comfortable warm bed. 'We've got to get down to Landing early this morning. Early *their* morning.'

There were moments, and this was one of them, when Lessa's enthusiasm for the Project faltered. If, however, this was the morning when Aivas would set in train the results of two Turns of hard studying and work, the early rising would be a minor sacrifice.

In the bigger chamber of the queen's weyr, she could now hear Ramoth mumbling and grunting, denying the summons just as F'lar was doing.

'Well, if I have to get up, you will, too,' she said and callously hauled the sleeping fur off her weyrmate.

'What the . . .' F'lar tried to grab the uncovering fur which Lessa, with a chuckle, snatched from his hand.

'You've got to get up.'

'It's the middle of the bloody night, Lessa,' he complained. 'We don't have Fall for another day and a half.'

'Aivas wants us there at five of the clock Landing time.'

'Aivas!' He sat bolt upright, wide-eyed, pushing his tumbled hair back from his face.

Lessa snorted at F'lar's response to that name.

'My shirt . . .' he cried, shivering convulsively in the pre-dawn cold. 'Heartless woman!'

She snatched shirt and pants up from the chair and tossed them to him. 'I am not at all heartless.'

Then she opened a glowbasket to find fresh clothes for herself. F'lar made a quick stop in the bathing room while she poured *klah* for them both. With her cup in her hand, she passed F'lar on her way in where she washed quickly and replaited the ends of her braids.

'Watch rider's asleep,' she told him when she got back into the weyr where he was stamping into his boots and shrugging on his riding jacket.

'I know. I've sent Mnementh to scare the living lights out of both of them.' He cocked his head then as they both heard a reverberating roar and a startled squeal. 'That'll teach them.'

'One day Mnementh's going to startle one or both of a watchpair off the Rim!' she replied.

He grinned at her. 'Haven't yet! Here!' And he held out her flying jacket and cap. As she stuck her arms in the sleeves, he bent and kissed the back of her neck. F'lar was often amorous when he first woke.

'That makes me shiver!' But she didn't pull away so he kissed her again and hugged her affectionately. Leaving one arm across her shoulders, he guided her out to Ramoth's weyr.

Ramoth's tail was still in the weyr, the rest of her was on the ledge. And, as F'lar and Lessa joined her there, Mnementh lowered his head from the level above the queen's weyr, his eyes gleaming brilliant blue-green in the darkness.

Who did you scare awake on watch up there, Mnementh? Lessa asked.

B'fol and green Gereth. They won't sleep on watch again. The bronze dragon's tone was particularly severe, an attitude with which Lessa had no quarrel for both B'fol and Gereth were well enough on in Turns not to be delinquent.

'Next Fall, B'fol and Gereth will handle firestone sacks,' F'lar remarked, having followed the exchange. This was no time for Benden Weyr to get slipshod. 'Have we time for porridge?' he asked hopefully.

Considering that days at Landing were apt to be spent in non-stop work, Lessa thought a good breakfast was only prudent, even if they were already behind the appointed hour. 'We'll make time.'

He heard the ripple of mischief in her voice for, outside on the ledge, there were only the dragons' eyes for illumination and he couldn't see her face.

'Now, now, Lessa,' he began in a tone of mock reproof, 'if we don't let anyone else time it . . .'

'Rank has some privileges and I'll think the better for a decent breakfast in my guts,' she said. 'So we'll make a little time. Especially since you're so hard to wake up.' She laughed softly when he sputtered a protest. 'If you please, Ramoth!' And the queen crouched to allow her rider to mount. 'You won't mind giving F'lar a lift, will you, dearest? I don't want him falling off that upper ledge, trying to mount Mnementh in the dark.'

Ramoth turned her head towards F'lar and blinked. *Of course.*

Mnementh waited until both riders were settled on the queen's neck before pushing off from the upper ledge and gliding down beside them to the floor of the Bowl. As soon as they had landed, the night lights in the Lower Caverns were visible as well as the banked fire on the small hearth where a big kettle of porridge was simmering. The huge *klah* pot was pulled slightly to one side so that the contents would not become too strong to be palatable. Weyrfolk were particular about the quality of that beverage.

As Lessa filled two bowls with the steaming cereal, she was glad that they had the place to themselves. The bakers must just have left, for the big table near the main hearth was full of cloth-covered breadpans. F'lar brought over two cups of *klah*, spooning an almost indecent amount of sweetener into his, and then sprinkling as much again over the porridge Lessa set in front of him.

'It's a miracle you don't gain weight with all that sweetener,' she began.

'Or lose my teeth,' he said, adding the second half of that long standing complaint. He gave her his widest grin and tapped his teeth with his spoon. 'But I don't and I haven't.' He dug into his breakfast.

Lessa sipped at her *klah* first, wanting to clear the last sleep from her wits.

'Do you suppose that Aivas is going to start the project this morning?'

F'lar shrugged as the question caught him with a hot mouthful. 'I can't think why else he called a meeting of such a group at such an hour. According to the original schedule he gave us, we should be ready to start. Despite what some critics infer,' and F'lar made a grimace which had nothing to do with the piping hot porridge on his spoon, 'he keeps his promises.'

'So far,' Lessa said in a dour tone.

'Well, he has!' Then F'lar looked at his weyrmate. 'You

don't really believe he can keep his promise about Thread, do you?'

'I just can't figure out how he can contrive to have us do what the settlers couldn't!' She glared at him, both relieved and sorry that she had come out with the doubt that had increasingly bothered her.

F'lar covered her hand with his. 'He's done everything he's promised to do. And I believe him, not just because I, as a dragonrider, want to, but because he sounds so very sure.'

'But, F'lar, every time he's been asked, he hasn't *promised* that we will be able to destroy Thread. He's said it is *possible*. That's not quite the same thing.'

'Let's just see what today brings, huh, love?'

F'lar gave her that knowing look of his which sometimes she wanted to scratch off his face. She took a deep breath and held back a scathing retort. Today could prove much, and deeply as she wanted it to prove that F'lar was right to place so much confidence in Aivas, she had to prepare him for possible disappointment.

'But if today is a disaster, that's going to reduce our effectiveness at the Conference at Tillek Hold next week to choose Oterel's successor.'

F'lar frowned. 'I recognize that danger. I'm reasonably sure that Aivas also does. I'd say that's why he scheduled this meeting. His timing so far has been nothing short of phenomenal.'

'He and Lytol are really into the political aspects, aren't they? I could almost wish that Lytol was still Ruathan Lord Warder. That'd give Groghe the support he needs. Even I have heard the grumbling about Ruatha's Lord Holder spending so much time down here instead of in his Hold.'

'Ranrel couldn't be considered too young to be a Lord Holder, Lessa,' F'lar reminded her. 'He's in his mid thirties, with five children. And he's certainly the only one of Oterel's sons who's shown any initiative at all. That port renewal project of his was inspired.' F'lar chuckled. 'Even if he did add insult to injury by insisting on using Hamian's stuff to build the new wharfs and reinforce the piers.'

Lessa had to grin, remembering the fuss Ranrel's innovative engineering had caused among those who derided or downright denied any useful products of the Abomination. F'lar scratched sleepily at his scalp and yawned.

'And when the other brothers tried to belittle Ranrel's project, along comes Master Idarolan, raving about the facilities,' she said.

'That's not going to hurt when the Lords Holder convene. His mate's a Masterweaver. *She*'s interested in having a power loom. I don't know where she found out that such things were possible.'

Lessa threw up her hands. '*Everyone's* gone "power" mad.'

'It sure reduces sheer drudgery.'

'Hmm. Yes. Well, eat up. We'll be late.'

F'lar grinned before he upended his *klah* mug. 'We already are, you know. It's as well you're permitting us to time it.' He laughed at the wicked glare she gave him.

They gathered up their crockery and put it to soak in the main sink. Then, fastening jackets and caps as they left the Cavern, they mounted their dragons.

'We were supposed to be there half an hour ago, Ramoth,' Lessa told her queen, keeping any hint of apology out of her voice. 'We need to be there on time.'

If you insist, Ramoth replied in a disapproving tone.

The others were already assembled in the main hall when the Benden Weyrleaders arrived. Robinton looked sleepy but Jaxom, Mirrim, Piemur, with his queen Farli curled about his shoulders, and the three male green riders all appeared very wide-awake indeed.

Jaxom straightened his shoulders and pulled at the lightweight sleeveless tunic he wore, to free it from his sweaty back. Irrepressibly, Piemur grinned at this evidence of his friend's nervousness, his grin including an equally nervous Mirrim. The other three green riders, L'zal, G'rannat, and S'len, were shifting from one foot to another.

'All present and accounted for, so let's see what Aivas wants with such an ill-assorted crew,' F'lar said, nodding at Lessa to lead the way. As he strode forward, he tossed a reassuring grin over his shoulder at Jaxom and the others.

When Aivas had asked for this pre-dawn meeting two days ago, his special students had been excited by the prospect that he intended to launch THE plan. They had been careful to contain that excitement to prevent even more rumour circulating. Not even Piemur had been brash enough to ask why. Aivas was scrupulous in keeping his own counsel.

Certainly all these young folk had studied diligently over the past two Turns, even if their lessons and drills seemed to be irrelevant or endlessly repetitious until, as Jaxom remarked to Piemur, he could do them in his sleep.

'That may be what Aivas wants,' Piemur had said with a shrug. 'They make about as much sense as the drills he gives me for Farli.'

Jaxom saw him stroking Farli's back as they marched down the hall and into Aivas' room. The lights brightened and Piemur grinned to himself: Master Morilton's 'light bulbs' worked just as the original ones had. Yet another minor triumph for the Masterglass-smith, working from plans of the 'Abomination'. That epithet caused Jaxom to frown for Master Norist was not the only one now to refer to Aivas in that manner. Of course, if today *was* truly the beginning of the assault on Thread, that tune could easily change before there was more cause to worry about the growing number of dissidents.

'Good morning,' Aivas said at his most polite and non-committal. 'If you will seat yourselves, I shall explain today's project.' He waited until they had taken their places and their excited murmurs had dwindled into respectful silence.

Then the screen displayed a clear picture of the view with which they were all familiar now – the bridge of the *Yokohama*. Only this time there was an addition: a spacesuited figure slumped over one of the control panels – similar to the one on which Jaxom had been drilled for the past three months. There was an almost simultaneous intake of breath for all knew now that the body was that of Sallah Telgar who had died so valiantly. This then was the actual bridge of the *Yokohama* – not the view which Aivas had supplied during their training. Then the focus of the picture slid across the consoles beyond the figure to rest on the board marked 'Life Support System'.

Jaxom saw Piemur reach up to stroke Farli whose gaze was fixed on the screen. She gave a little chirp for she, too, recognized the board. She'd been working for a month on a mock-up, pushing at two toggles and depressing three keys in a certain sequence. She could now perform those movements in less than thirty seconds.

Over the past two years, Aivas had subtly collected many facts about both fire-lizards and dragons. The most relevant fact was that both creatures were able to maintain the oxygen levels in their systems for almost ten minutes without suffering undue discomfort or harm. That time could be pushed to fifteen minutes but, in that event, both fire-lizards and dragons would need several hours to recover from the effects of oxygen deprivation. They were certainly able to deal with an oxygen debt as efficiently as humans, if not better. Their human partners would have to direct them in any unusual manoeuvre so both would be involved in this exploit.

One of the exercises with fire-lizards and dragons in which there had been *no* success had been getting them to take an object from one place and bring it to another. 'Telekinesis', Aivas had called it but the concept – patiently explained – confused the dragons as thoroughly as it did the fire-lizards. They would go *between* to get the required object, but they could not bring it without physically collecting it. Aivas had explained that, if the dragons and fire-lizards could transport themselves telekinetically, it logically followed that they ought to be able to use their abilities to *lift* distant items to them.

'Today, Piemur, you are asked to send Farli to the *Yokohama* to manipulate the switches as she has been taught to do. There is no oxygen at present on the bridge and it is essential that the life support system be activated before we can take the next step. Another of the toggles will transmit a report on the general condition of the *Yokohama*.'

'Oh!' Piemur murmured very softly and sighed gustily, stroking Farli who chirped again, her unblinking eyes on the screen. 'Somehow I thought that's what you'd say.'

'She has been an excellent pupil, Piemur. There should be no problem as she is well accustomed to obeying you.'

Piemur took a deep breath. 'All right, Farli,' and he unwrapped her tail from his neck and held up his arm in the position that indicated she was to take a message.

Carefully walking along his bare muscled arm with her talons sheathed, Farli reached his forearm and turned about to face him, her eyes whirling alertly.

'Now,' and Piemur held up his right hand, 'this is going to be slightly different, Farli. I want you to go up in the sky, to the place you see in my mind.' He closed his eyes, focused his thoughts tightly on the scene of the bridge and the particular consoles she was to activate.

Farli chirruped queryingly, looked over her shoulder at the picture on the screen, and burbled once, reclosing her wings on her back.

'No, Farli, not into the screen. Get the "where" from my mind.' He closed his eyes again, concentrating on the exact place he wanted her to go, emphasizing the life support console, next to the slumped corpse. When she chirruped again, this time almost impatiently, he sighed as he turned in defeat to the others.

'She just doesn't understand,' Piemur said, trying not to let his disappointment colour his voice. Not that he blamed *her*. She'd *been* to most of the places he sent her. How could he get across the difference between travelling around the planet and going into space above it. Especially as he couldn't quite grasp the concept himself.

Farli emphasized this by flitting from his arm to the room in which she had been trained, moments later coming back and trying to fly into the picture on the screen.

Piemur's grin was weak. 'What do you bet she's gone and done her exercises again. That much she understands!'

Disappointment was palpable in the room. Piemur kept his eyes straight ahead, on the tantalizingly unreachable view on the screen.

'So?' F'lar asked. 'What do we do now, Aivas?'

There was a long pause before Aivas spoke. 'The mind

of the fire-lizard does not function in recorded animal behavioural patterns.'

'That's not surprising. Your records only cover Terran types,' Piemur remarked, trying not to feel so depressed about his little queen's failure. She was the best of the whole fair; better even than Menolly's Beauty who was certainly very well trained. But he had hoped that she'd be able to make this strange variation of flight. 'It's also a long way to ask her to go when no-one's been there before.'

Another silence hung on the room.

'There's only one dragon in fact,' F'lar said slowly and thoughtfully, breaking the pause, 'who's ever been off the planet.'

'Canth!' Lessa exclaimed.

'F'nor's brown Canth is too large,' Aivas said.

'It wasn't his size I was thinking of,' Lessa replied. 'It's his experience in going above this planet. He's done it so perhaps he can explain to Farli so that she'll understand what's wanted of her.' Her eyes lost their focus as she sought for Canth.

Yes, we can come immediately, Canth replied to Lessa's request.

There was a stir of anticipation among those waiting in Aivas's room. Piemur kept on stroking Farli who had returned to her position on his arm. He murmured softly that she was a marvellous fire-lizard, the best in the world but the toggles she was to pull and the buttons she was to press were really not the ones in the next room but up on the *Yokohama*, far above their heads in the dark sky. She kept cocking her head this way and that, her throat pulsing as she tried her very best to understand what was wanted of her.

'Ah, they're here,' Lessa said. 'F'nor's on his way in.'

Looking as if he had dressed himself in a hurry, F'nor came running into the room. 'Canth said it was important,' he said and, after a puzzled glance around the room, regarded Lessa expectantly.

'Aivas needs Farli to get to the bridge on the *Yokohama*,' she explained. 'Farli doesn't understand her directions. You and Canth are the only two on Pern who have left the planet.

We thought Canth might be able to clarify the instructions so Farli will know what she is expected to do.'

As she spoke, F'nor pulled off his flight cap and shucked out of his heavy riding gear. When she had finished, his expression turned humorously quizzical.

'Well, now, Lessa, that's a problem. I've never been exactly sure how Canth and I managed that abortive flight in the first place.'

'Do you remember what you were thinking?' F'lar asked.

F'nor chuckled. 'I was thinking I had to do something to keep you from trying to get to the Red Star.' Then he frowned. 'Come to think of it, Meron was there, and he tried to make his fire-lizard go. She disappeared in a flash and I don't know if she ever returned to him.'

'Farli's not afraid,' Piemur said staunchly. 'She just doesn't understand where she's supposed to perform what she's been trained to do.'

F'nor spread his hands in a gesture of appeal. 'If Farli can't get the hang of it, I don't think any of them could.'

'But could Canth explain to her that he went off the planet? Into space?' Lessa asked.

'*Could you, Canth?*' F'nor asked the brown dragon. Canth was in the process of draping himself on the ridge above Landing where the rising sun would warm him.

You showed me where you wanted me to go. I went.

F'nor repeated Canth's answer. 'A planet is a bigger target than a space ship we can't see.'

Farli does not understand, Canth added. *She has done the things she was asked to do in the place where she has always done them.*

'*Canth,*' and Lessa asked the dragon directly, '*do you understand what we're asking Farli to do?*'

Yes, you want her to go up to the ship and do the things she has been trained to do there! She doesn't understand where she is to go. She's never been there.

Jaxom squirmed a little on the chair. Considering how hard Piemur had worked with Farli, it was a crying shame that the little creature couldn't grasp the essential point.

'*Ruth, do you understand?*' Sometimes fire-lizards listened to Ruth when they ignored everyone else.

164

Yes, but it is a cold long way for a fire-lizard to go if she hasn't been there before. She's trying very hard to understand.

A lot of thoughts crowded Jaxom's mind just then. But the main one was that Ruth was *not* too big to fit on the bridge: that is, if his wings were folded back and he landed precisely on the floor just in front of the lift door. He'd also have to remain very still for Aivas had said there was no gravity on the bridge. Ruth would be in free fall. Aivas didn't see this as a problem for a dragon, or a fire-lizard, accustomed to being airborne. Jaxom had known that that was one reason Aivas had grilled him so long and hard on the lay-out of the bridge and lectured him on null gravity conditions. But, until Farli had done her exercise on board the *Yokohama*, turning on the bridge's life support system, Ruth and Jaxom could not go.

Aivas had had crews searching the Catherine Caves assiduously for 'spacesuits'. Two had been found or, rather, the perished scraps of fabric and the bright plastic shapes that had once serviced it. Oxygen cylinders had been manufactured, being not dissimilar to agenothree tanks. HNO_3, Jaxom reminded himself now that he knew the precise chemical constituents of the flame-producing mixture. But there was no protection for a frail human body in the absolute cold and airless vacuum of the *Yokohama*'s bridge in its present state.

Jaxom thought that manufacturing proper equipment would prove to be Aivas' alternative. He'd already had several long discussions with Masterweaver Zurg. But alternatives would take time, and more experimentation on the part of both Zurg and Hamian's innovative crew. More time in which the disenchanted Lords Holder could steadily withdraw their support from Landing.

If only Farli could understand, Jaxom thought, searching his own mind for any clues that he, or Ruth, might be able to give her. Ruth had perceived the difference, but he was much smarter than Farli. He understood so much – as much as I do, Jaxom thought with great pride in his beloved friend.

As you understand, so do I, and Ruth's tone was almost accusatory. *It is not really a very long way* between *but it is up far*.

Although Jaxom leaped to his feet, shouting 'No, Ruth, no!' he was too late. For Ruth had already gone *between*.

'Jaxom!' exclaimed Lessa, her face white. 'You didn't send him?'

'I most certainly did not. He just went.' Jaxom was aghast and Farli began shrieking protests, her wings extended, her eyes whirling the startled angry red.

Outside Ramoth and Mnementh bugled their own warnings.

'*Don't, Ramoth! Mnementh!*' Lessa cried. 'We'll rouse everyone in Landing and they'll know something's gone wrong.' Then she turned to F'lar, clutching at him in her fear for Ruth. And for Jaxom.

'JAXOM?' F'lar bellowed, for Jaxom's face mirrored his shock. Mirrim, her tanned face bleached white, had leaped to Jaxom's side as had the other green riders, ready to support him, their faces anxious. Robinton and F'nor were too stunned to react so there was only Jancis to watch the screen and count.

'He's all right,' Jaxom managed to say though his mouth had gone terribly dry. The strong link with Ruth had attenuated to just a faint touch. 'He's still with me.'

'Did you tell him to go?' F'lar demanded, his expression so fierce that even Lessa recoiled.

Jaxom gave the Benden Weyrleader an inscrutable glare. 'He bloody just went and did it! Ruth's got a mind of his own!'

Then Jancis leapt to her feet, gesticulating at the screen. 'There! There! He's there! On the count of ten.'

There, undeniably on the bridge, wings tucked tight, his whole body flattened, was Ruth. Perceptibly he began to drift upward until his head touched the ceiling, peering about him with an expression of astonishment.

'Ah! Well done, Ruth! Jaxom!' Aivas' bellow of triumph cut across the racket of astonishment and surprise that reverberated around the room. 'Jaxom, tell Ruth not to be surprised to float. He is in free fall, with no gravity for up and down. Warn him not to make any energetic movements. Does he understand, Jaxom?'

'I am, I did. He understands,' Jaxom said, staring in fascination at the scene.

'See, Farli!' Piemur pointed excitedly. 'Ruth's led the way for you.' But Farli was so confused by the sudden cheering and shouting in the room that Piemur had to grab her by the cheeks and turn her head toward the screen, and Ruth! 'Go to Ruth!' The little queen gave a squawk and, launching herself from Piemur's arm, disappeared.

'Jaxom, you tell Ruth to get back here right now!' Lessa shouted, recovering from her shock. 'Mind of his own indeed? I'll give him a mind to obey!'

'Restore yourselves to calm observation!' Aivas' voice once again cut through the furore. 'Ruth is unharmed. And . . . Farli has found her way.'

Piemur let out a yipe of surprise, plainly audible in a room suddenly gone very quiet. For Farli had indeed found her way to the bridge of *Yokohama* and, with one talon firmly hooked on the edge of the console, was diligently pulling toggles and pressing on buttons. Lights appeared on the board.

'Mission accomplished,' said Aivas. 'They may return.'

Farli came and has done her job, Ruth said, not realizing that Jaxom could see him. *I'm floating. Let go, Farli. It's not at all like being* between. *A most unusual sensation. Not like swimming either.*

It was also a most unusual sight for those observing Ruth gently drifting across the bridge, a handspan above the arc of consoles, ducking his head to keep from scraping the ceiling.

As Farli released her grip, she, too, began to float. Startled, she extended her wings and gently revolved end over end, colliding with Ruth. He reached out to steady her and both were propelled further away from their original locations, towards the great plasglas window on the bow of the bridge complex. Suddenly Jancis began to giggle, overcome by the humour in what they were seeing, and the tension in the room evaporated.

'I think that's quite enough clowning about now, Ruth,'

Jaxom said, trying to sound stern but he couldn't help grinning along with everyone else over the antics of the two creatures. *'You scared the life out of me! Now get back down here.'*

I knew exactly where to go. I showed Farli. I had no problem at all doing it and this is fun. With a negligent shove of one wing, Ruth executed a complete turn in the air and began floating back toward the lift. *Will we get to come back again?*

'ONLY if you and Farli get your bodies back on Pern this instant!'

Oh, all right. If you say so.

Laughing in a tone that was a mixture of laughter, sheer relief, and fury, Jaxom dashed down the corridor and outside. The others were close on his heels, full of triumph and the laughter of relief for the morning's success. Lessa, however, was raging at the risk Ruth had taken, even to ensure the first step in Aivas' Plan. And she knew from the set expression on F'lar's face that he was of similar mind.

Half down the corridor, F'lar caught Lessa by the arm. 'You may be furious, Lessa, but we can't intervene in this. And I probably lost as many seconds of my life as you did over Ruth's leap.'

'Ruth cannot be allowed to be so irresponsible,' she said, fuming. 'Jaxom isn't. I don't understand how Ruth gets away with such disobedience. Ramoth wouldn't.'

'Ruth and Jaxom were not Weyr-trained. But don't think Ruth's going to get off easily for this escapade.' He managed a droll grin. 'Judging by the look on Jaxom's face, he's had a fright he won't forget. That will inhibit Ruth far more surely than threats from you and me.' He gave her one of his little shakes. 'More important, the less furore there is right now, the fewer rumours will abound.'

Lessa let out a heavy sigh, glared at him, and then gave herself a shake, releasing herself from his grasp.

'Yes, we don't want this bruited about – at least, not quite yet. But, I tell you, and I'll tell Jaxom, too, I don't want to live through another few seconds like that again. All I could think about was how under the heavens would we explain to Lytol.'

F'lar grinned wryly. 'As it's turned out, Lytol can print this up as a turning point in the modern history of Pern.'

'And just won't he!'

Discretion muted the congratulations for the brave venturers but everyone patted Ruth and scrubbed at his eyeridges until they were whirling with delight. When Farli finally settled again on Piemur's shoulder, she also received extravagant caresses. False dawn was just lightening the eastern horizon so there was a good chance that few were awake to wonder at the fuss being made of Ruth.

'I think,' Robinton began when the elation abated, 'that we'd better return to Aivas. I, for one, would like to know what's next.'

'Well, that depends on what Aivas learns from the instrumentation that Farli just turned on,' Jaxom replied. 'If the bridge is intact, warms up and there's enough oxygen left in the tanks that supply that area, Ruth and I go up – together.' Jaxom grinned. 'That's when we initiate the telescopic sequences that will reaffirm the position of the system's planets – most particularly, our old enemy, the Red Star.'

That was, however, not quite all that Aivas had in mind when, late the next day, the bridge levels were satisfactory.

'Piemur, I would like you to accompany Jaxom,' Aivas said when the group reassembled.

'I'm not supposed to go with him this trip,' Piemur exclaimed.

'Originally, no. But, to demonstrate proper respect to Sallah Telgar, it is fitting that her mortal remains be brought back to Pern and properly interred. No doubt, Lord Larad would like to attend to whatever burial rituals are currently practised.'

A profound silence prevailed until Robinton cleared his throat.

'Yes, that would be not only respectful and appropriate, but a long overdue honour for such a valiant lady. I'll inform Lord Larad immediately.'

'Would her spacesuit be usable after all this time?' Piemur asked, curious. When he saw the shocked expression on Jancis' face, he belatedly realized how callous that sounded

169

and, groaning, hid his face against his arm. Farli curled her tail consolingly around his throat.

'With some minor repairs, it is to be hoped that the spacesuit is usable,' Aivas replied into the pause so calmly that Robinton was certain that recovery of both body and suit had been part of this initial stage. 'You are both to dress as warmly as possible as the bridge temperature currently reads ten degrees below zero.'

Jaxom was unmoved by that information since he was used to the absolute cold of *between* but Piemur gave a dramatic shudder and hunched his shoulders as if already warding off the chill.

'Can Farli come, too?' he asked.

'That would be advisable,' Aivas said. 'If Jancis' Trig will accompany Farli, there would then be two fire-lizards who understand this sort of *between* transfer.'

Despite an obvious reluctance, Jancis instructed her young bronze Trig to settle himself on Piemur's right shoulder. Jaxom and Piemur left the building by themselves so as not to suggest this journey was anything unusual. The bulky tanks of oxygen for emergency air supply had already been secured to Ruth's back but Jaxom checked the ropes before he mounted. Ruth had assured him that the weight was not more than he was able for. The two young men mounted Ruth whose eyes were a trifle reddish with anticipation.

'Ready, Piemur?' Jaxom asked over his shoulder.

'As ready as I'll ever be,' Piemur replied, resetting his grip on Jaxom's wide rider's belt. 'But I'm awfully glad Ruth's already been there.'

Tell Piemur not to worry. It's fun to float! Ruth remarked as he launched himself.

As Jaxom passed on that encouraging message, he felt Piemur's spasmodic tug on his belt and knew that the harper was also nervous. Not that he didn't trust Ruth to get them there. It was just such a long way!

Between never seemed so cold nor the transfer so long yet Jaxom, counting mentally, reached ten seconds just as they emerged on to the bridge deck of the *Yokohama*. Jancis' count had been correct.

'Are we there yet?' Piemur asked. His hands were rigid on Jaxom's belt. As Jaxom looked over his shoulder to reassure the harper, he realized that Piemur had his eyes squeezed shut.

He cleared his throat rather than laugh at his friend and turned his head forward. And began to slide sideways off Ruth's neck.

'Shards! What's happening?' Piemur opened his eyes as they both continued to slide to their right until they came up against the cold wall.

Don't make sudden moves, Ruth warned them.

'I heard you, I heard you,' Piemur replied, though the wall seemed to burn through the leathers on his helmet and his shoulder to freeze him.

'I'm going to pull us back up on Ruth, Piemur,' Jaxom said and, carefully grabbing a neck ridge, slowly righted them. Farli unwrapped her tail and peered up at Jaxom, chirping encouragingly.

'That's all I need,' Piemur said wryly, 'is my fire-lizard telling me how to handle free fall!' Farli released all contact with Piemur, pushed off from his shoulder and floated up. Trig squeaked and Farli answered him in an encouraging tone. Trig let go of his perch and, following her example, also drifted away. The two came to rest on the ceiling, chittering animatedly.

'That's enough, the pair of you,' Piemur said, disgusted.

'They're not coming to any harm,' Jaxom said, 'and Ruth says if we move slowly enough, we'll be all right. We've got a lot to do. Look, Piemur, I'll dismount – carefully – and then you can untie the oxygen tanks. Ruth says the tanks are bulky and he doesn't dare move until we've untied them. *He* wants to look out the window.'

'*He* would!'

Jaxom heard the note of self-disgust in Piemur's voice and grinned. 'They did have some practice, you know.'

'Hmmmm! The air here smells peculiar, sort of dead.'

'It'll probably improve with the fresh tanks,' Piemur said cheerfully.

Cautiously Jaxom dismounted on the right-hand side of the white dragon. Keeping between Ruth and the wall might prevent him floating about. There was just room enough.

'*Your placement is perfect, Ruth*,' he told his weyrmate approvingly, hanging on to a neck ridge as he judiciously lowered himself.

It's the only place I'd fit, Ruth remarked, slowly turning his head to his right to observe the margin. *I'll hook my tail so I won't drift when you unload me.*

'*Now I know why dragons have tails!*' Jaxom replied, giving a nervous chuckle.

'Don't laugh,' Piemur said for he had just swung his leg over and had to clutch at Ruth's wing joint to keep from floating up.

'I wasn't laughing at you, Piemur. Ruth's just found out how to anchor himself. Watch his tail. And dismount to the right, not the left. Don't grab that wing joint so hard. Wings are fragile.'

'I know, I know. Sorry, Ruth,' but as Jaxom watched anxiously, he could see Piemur had to make a considerable effort to relax his grip. 'I've done some crazy things in my life, stealing fire-lizard eggs, crawling into carry-sacks, scrambling along shorelines but this is undoubtedly the craziest,' Piemur muttered to himself as he eased off Ruth's back, following Jaxom's example. 'Made it!' he said as his feet touched the deck.

Wedged between the wall and his dragon, Jaxom began to untie the ropes which secured the oxygen tanks to Ruth's back.

'Huh!' Jaxom exclaimed in surprise as the tank drifted to the deck. 'Well, easier off than on! As Aivas said.' He grinned at the young harper who was gaping in surprise. 'No weight at all.' With one finger, he pushed the second tank to the deck.

'Hey, I could get to like a place where work is play,' Piemur said with a grin as he began to relax.

'Here! Let's stack them against the wall. By the first Egg!' Jaxom inadvertently used more force than necessary to lift the tank and nearly launched it over Ruth.

'Wow!' Piemur stretched out to restrain the tank and found himself rising. But he was quick enough to grab

Ruth's wing and corrected the reaction. 'Yeah, this free-fall stuff has distinct advantages! I'll tend to the others.'

While Jaxom watched in surprise, Piemur took a firm hold of Ruth's shoulder neck ridge and executed an effortless flip over the white dragon's back.

'Whee!' The exclamation was part laugh, part surprise as his unorthodox manoeuvre succeeded and he landed neatly in the narrow space between the white dragon and the railing around the upper level of the bridge. 'This is fun!'

'Watch it, Piemur. We don't want those tanks crashing into anything.'

'I'll just tie these down.'

'It is safest to secure any loose object on board a space-going vessel,' answered the voice of Aivas, as calm as ever. 'You are doing well. Bridge temperature is still rising and all proximity alarms are quiescent.'

'Proximity alarms?' Piemur asked, his voice rising in surprise.

'Yes, this facility is now receiving function reports and damage analysis,' Aivas went on. 'Considering its length of time in space, the fabric of the *Yokohama* has not had a significant breach. The solar-powered deflector shields display no operational damage. As you will remember from your studies, these panels provide power to the small thrusters which keep the ship in its geosynchronous orbit. There has been minor penetration of some of the outermost sectors of the main sphere but these were automatically sealed off. None of those sections are now required. The doors on the cargo bay are still open and a malfunction light is on. However, your assigned tasks take precedence. Please proceed. Oxygen remains at a normal level but you will shortly feel the effects of the low temperature, decreasing manual dexterity.

'Gymnastic displays should be curtailed.'

Jaxom smothered a laugh at that reprimand but perhaps only he heard Piemur's insolent mutter about all work and no play.

Moving carefully, Jaxom ducked under Ruth's neck and took a firm hold on the railing. To his surprise, Piemur stood motionless on the wide steps down to the command level of the bridge. Looking up from his circumspect movements, Jaxom, too, was transfixed by what had stunned the harper – Pern lay below them, its blue seas glistening to the port while to starboard was visible the coastline and vivid greens, browns and beiges of the southern continent. Visible, that is, around the minor obstructions of two fascinated fire-lizards who were craning their necks to starboard.

'By the Egg, it's just like the pictures Aivas showed us,' Piemur murmured reverently. 'Magnificent!'

With unexpected tears pricking his eyes, Jaxom swallowed hard, as he viewed his world as his ancestors had once seen it at journey's end! That must have been a triumphant moment, he thought!

'It's big!' Piemur added, daunted by the prospect.

'It *is* a whole world,' Jaxom replied softly, trying to reorient himself to the incredible size of it.

With great majesty, the scene was imperceptibly altering as the planet swung towards the dusk line.

'Jaxom? Piemur?' Aivas' voice recalled them to their duties.

'Just admiring the view from the bridge,' Piemur said briskly. 'Seeing's believing.' Without taking his eyes off the wide window, he floated towards the flight of stairs and grabbed the handrail, to pull himself hand over hand down to the flight deck. Using any available handhold he made his way to the console he was scheduled to program.

'I got more red lights than I like,' he told Aivas.

Even as Jaxom made his way around the upper level to the science positions, he could see the red lights on those boards.

'I've got them, too!' he said, 'but not on the telescope settings.'

'Jaxom, Piemur, key in the override commands and then go to manual.'

Jaxom's board was immediately cleared of over half the red dysfunction lights. Three remained and there were two orange. But nothing to interfere with the program he was to initiate.

He set to work, stopping now and then to flex his

174

fingers and gaze wonderingly at the fantastic view of Pern. Nothing could detract from that spectacle, not even the comical antics of two fire-lizards cavorting in the weightlessness. Oddly enough, their sportiveness, their excited squeakings and chitterings as Farli dared Trig to more and more outrageous manoeuvres helped dispel the unreality of this bizarre environment.

Once Jaxom began to concentrate on setting the program for the telescopes, Ruth released his tail anchor and drifted with great dignity towards the wide bridge windows where he could indulge his fascination in Pern and the star-lit blackness. The fire-lizards continued their chittering conversation.

I don't know what they are, either, Ruth said. *But they're pretty*.

'What's pretty?' Jaxom asked, looking up because the comment was unlikely. '*Can you see the other two ships?*'

No. There are things flowing past us.

'*Things?*' Jaxom asked, craning across his console to see what Ruth was seeing. However, dragon and fire-lizards had their faces pressed against the far right of the bridge viewport.

Suddenly all three creatures flung themselves back, away from the window, floating at some speed towards Piemur and Jaxom.

'Hey, watch out!' Jaxom ducked as Ruth zoomed over-head. At the same moment, there was a distinct pinging rattle.

'Something's hitting us!' Piemur cried and pushed him-self off to the viewscreen.

'What is hitting you?' demanded Aivas.

Piemur bumped against the viewscreen, looking right and left. 'Jaxom, ask Ruth what he saw. I can't see anything.' Pressing his left cheek to the plasglas he tried to see beyond the thick curve of the window.

Things – like fire-lizard eggs, coming straight at us, was Ruth's reply.

'Well, there's nothing out there now,' Piemur replied, disgusted that he had missed the display.

'Aivas?' Jaxom asked.

'The pinging indicated the screens deflecting a small shower of objects,' Aivas replied calmly. 'No damage is reported. As you will have learned from your studies, space is not a barren void. Minute particles are in constant motion through space. Doubtless a shower of some sort startled Ruth and the fire-lizards. You would be wiser to continue your tasks before you become incapacitated by the severe temperatures.'

Jaxom noticed that Piemur, too, was not completely reassured by that explanation. But it was true that the cold was penetrating their layers of clothing.

Both Ruth and the fire-lizards cautiously, and with much conversation, returned to their positions at the window.

Despite the speed with which he worked, Jaxom could feel the cold seeping through down-lined gloves which had always kept him warm through hours of Threadfall. Maybe space *was* colder than *between*.

'Aivas, didn't you say there'd be heat on the bridge? My hands are getting numb with cold.'

'Readings indicate that the bridge heating is not working as efficiently as possible. It is probable that the resistive ceramic of the units has crystalized. This can be repaired later.'

'Mine's done,' Jaxom said when he had double checked the entries. 'Program ready.'

'Activate,' was the order from Aivas.

Jaxom punched that key with considerable satisfaction. Though the Egg knew how he could have got it wrong with the endless drills Aivas had put him through in learning the sequences of attitude, exposure, and sectors. He watched the fast forward scroll of the display as it confirmed his plotting.

'This board's much faster than the ones we use,' he remarked, more to Piemur than to Aivas.

'The equipment on the *Yokohama* was state of the art when the ship was commissioned by the Pern Charter Group,' Aivas said, 'and high speed computations would have been essential in astronavigation.'

'I told you we were using baby stuff,' Piemur murmured.

176

'Before the infant walks, it must learn to crawl,' Aivas said.

'Is everyone hearing all this?' Piemur demanded with some indignation.

'No.'

'I thank your mercy for that! And my program's up and running, too, by the way.'

'Then you must now begin phase two of the schedule. You will find the auxiliary oxygen storage behind Bulwark B-8802-A, B and C,' Aivas reminded them.

Piemur was shaking the fingers of his gloved hands. 'My fingers have never been this cold! I'll give you Bitran odds this bridge is colder than *between*.'

'In point of fact,' Aivas remarked, 'it is not. But you have been in very cold temperatures far longer than you have ever remained *between*.'

'A point,' Jaxom reminded Piemur as they went hand over hand on the stair rail to keep from floating off in the wrong direction. 'Remarkable feeling, this weightlessness,' he said with a comradely grin at the harper.

Piemur gave him a happy grimace of agreement. Just then Farli and Trig came tumbling end over end above their heads, making them duck: a movement which sent them sprawling on to the steps lengthwise, then rising perpendicular to the deck.

'Careful!' Jaxom cried, willing himself not to make a sudden grab for the railing.

'Ohohohohoh!' Piemur continued to float on up to the ceiling.

By the time Jaxom, securely holding on to the rail with one hand, had got the floating Piemur by the ankle and hauled him down, they weren't sure whether to laugh or swear at their clumsiness.

However, the slight mishap made them all the more circumspect with any motions. They located, opened and examined the auxiliary oxygen compartment: carefully removed the one empty tank, manoeuvred the four they had brought with them into the space available, and made the necessary connections to bring the replacements into the system.

Aivas then required Jaxom to test the oxygen supply on the Life Support System console and announced that the new tanks were on line when required.

'Phase three may now be initiated,' Aivas told them.

Jaxom caught Piemur's eyes and the young harper gave him a wry grin, shrugged and turned back to the space-suited figure they had both been avoiding.

'*Ruth, we need you back on the landing, please,*' Jaxom said as he and Piemur solemnly converged on Sallah's body.

Jaxom swallowed against his repugnance for phase three. He could not look at Piemur who was also evading eye contact. As they lifted it from the chair it had occupied for twenty-five hundred Turns, the rigid spacesuited body retained the position in which it had collapsed across the console.

Jaxom tried to feel reverence for the personality that had once inhabited the frozen shell they were handling. Sallah Telgar had given her life to prevent the defector, Avril Bitra, from draining the *Yokohama*'s fuel tanks in her bid to escape the Rukbat system. Sallah had even managed to repair the console Bitra had wrecked in her thwarted fury. Odd that a Hold had been named after such a woman but then, Bitrans had always been an odd lot. Jaxom chided himself for such thoughts. There were some very honest, worthy Bitrans who were not given to gambling and other forms of gaming which fascinated many of that Hold. Lord Sigomal kept to himself but that was preferable to the late Lord Sifer's well-known unsavoury appetites.

With the ropes which had held the tanks in place, Jaxom and Piemur strapped the bent body between Ruth's wings. Sensing their mood alteration, Farli and Trig had ceased their falling about and, when Piemur again mounted the white dragon, they quietly settled on to his shoulders.

When Jaxom slid astride Ruth, he could no longer control his jaw and his teeth chattered. Had Sallah felt the creeping cold as she died? Was that what had killed her, abandoned so far above the planet? He could barely feel Ruth's neck ridge with chilled fingers.

'*Let's get back to Landing before we freeze solid, too, Ruth,*' he said.

'Can we go before we freeze solid?' Piemur asked wistfully, unable to hear Jaxom's request of Ruth.

'NOW!' And Jaxom longingly projected a vivid scene of warm, balmy Landing to his dragon.

As they entered the chill blackness of *between*, Jaxom was still not sure which was colder!

Much later in the evening of that momentous day, when Lessa had a chance to sit down and think about it all, she wondered just how Aivas – quite likely with Lytol's connivance – had contrived such an extraordinary and timely event as Sallah's return. This would have considerable impact on the entire population, both north and south, on the doubters and the believers. Sallah Telgar's heroism and self-sacrifice had become a favourite harper ballad, repeatedly requested at all Gathers and evening entertainments of any consequence. To be able to bring her back from her lonely crypt should be considered a significant vindication of the Landing effort. It might even win the support of some doubters.

Lord Larad was absolutely dumbfounded when Robinton, conveyed by Mnementh and F'lar to Telgar Hold, apprised him of the retrieval of his ancestress' remains.

'Yes, yes, indeed, Sallah must be honoured. There must, of course, be some ceremony fitting such an occasion.' Larad looked helplessly at Robinton.

Burial services were usually brief, even for the most honoured being. The deeds and goodness of unusual persons were perpetuated in song and harper tales, which were considered the most fitting of memorials.

'A performance of "The Ballad of Sallah Telgar" would certainly be appropriate,' Robinton said. 'Full instrumental accompaniment to chorus and solo voices. I'll speak to Sebell.'

'I never thought to have the chance to honour our brave ancestress,' Larad said and floundered once again.

Fortunately Lady Jissamy, Larad's astute and capable wife, stepped to his side. 'There is that small cave, just to the north of the main court, the one which that recent rock slide revealed. It is just large enough . . .' She faltered and then recovered, 'and certainly accessible, easy to reseal.'

Larad patted her hand gratefully. 'Yes, the very place. Ah . . . when?' he added tentatively.

'The day after tomorrow?' Robinton suggested, resisting an urge to grin in triumph for that would be just the day before the Lords Holder convened about the matter of Oterel's successor.

Larad shot him a quick glance. 'You couldn't possibly have planned it this way, could you, Masterharper?'

'Me?' Years of practice made it possible for Robinton to affect genuine surprise. He waggled his hand in denial.

F'lar came to his assistance with a disgusted snort. 'Hardly, Larad. We knew she was there. So did you. Aivas included her sacrifice in his historical narrative. Yesterday Piemur got his queen fire-lizard up to the *Yokohama*. She's been training for the last few months and Aivas felt that she was ready to make the attempt. We had to wait until there was sufficient oxygen to initiate some necessary procedures but today Jaxom and Piemur went up. It just didn't seem proper to . . . well, just leave her remains there.'

'To give her rest after all that long time in cold space,' Jissamy said with a delicate shudder. 'It's time and past it. Should we make it an open ceremony?'

'I think that only proper. Telgar, of course, should have the honour but many will wish to be respectful,' Robinton said with a properly grave mien, hoping that the occasion would spark considerable interest through Hold and Hall. Those who weren't merely curious would have to come to see who else attended.

When Jaxom, Piemur and Ruth arrived back at Landing, they had gratefully turned their burden over to Master Oldive and two of his Masters. They had handled matters then and now the mortal remains of Sallah Telgar rested in a finely joined coffin of Master Bendarek's best wooden panels.

Shown the cleansed spacesuit, Aivas assured all that the heel of the spacesuit and the other small tears could be mended. Aivas remarked to Lytol that it was fortunate indeed that superstition was not a facet of Pernese culture. Lytol disagreed. He and Aivas immediately became involved in a discussion of primitive religions and arcane beliefs so that Robinton was just as glad that he could leave for Telgar Weyr with F'lar. Robinton wondered if he'd have done better to have stayed to listen to what was certain to be a fascinating debate. But he was deriving considerable satisfaction in being the bearer of such remarkable tidings.

One of the older Telgar sons brought in a tray with wine glasses and a fine crystal decanter which Robinton decided must be one of the new designs Master Morilton produced. The next son arrived with a tray of piping hot little pasties and some of the good Telgar mountain cheeses. With a glass of white Benden in his hand, Robinton was rather pleased, after all, that he had come.

'You said, did you not,' Larad began, 'that someone had actually been on the old ship? Was that judicious?'

'Necessary,' F'lar said. 'No danger involved. Piemur's little fire-lizard did exactly as Aivas taught her. So there's air on the bridge, and it's warmed up. Ruth will take Jaxom back again tomorrow to find out why the cargo bay doors have remained open. Probably a trivial malfunction according to Aivas. All in all,' and F'lar paused to sip his wine, 'a most auspicious beginning. Most auspicious.'

'I'm glad to hear that, F'lar,' Larad said, nodding his head, his expression solemn, 'I'm very glad to hear that.'

'Not half as glad as I am to be able to report it,' replied the Benden Weyrleader.

Chapter Eight

'*K*eep a grip on me, will you, Ruth?' Jaxom said as he carefully swung his right leg over Ruth's neck ridge. Manoeuvring in free fall had been easier yesterday when he and Piemur had each other to hold on to. He'd got the hang of it then, of the slow controlled movements. Today the clumsy suit impeded him and he felt ungainly. His feet in the heavy magnetic soled boots were especially unwieldy. He clutched at Ruth's neck suddenly as he felt his body moving in a direction other than *down*. Ruth caught him by the ankle and suddenly he was down, the boots anchoring him safely to the deck.

Knowing that his fellow students were observing him made him hope devoutly that he didn't look as ridiculous as he felt. Sharra had repeatedly told him that yesterday he hadn't looked at all foolish coping with weightlessness. He should relax in satisfaction that both he and Piemur had handled themselves most creditably, though she wished they could somehow have seen the view of Pern which had so transfixed them.

'I've never seen that particular look on Piemur's face before. Jancis was impressed.'

'So how did I look?'

'Dumbstruck, just like Piemur,' she replied, giving him a mischievous grin. 'About the same way you looked at Jarrol the first time.'

At least today, Jaxom knew he had some control over his movements. As long as he could keep his feet on the deck. He took the first step forward, wrenching the heavy boot's grip off the floor and stamping it down in front of him. Ruth had landed in the same spot as yesterday, right by the lift door. Jaxom had only to duck under Ruth's neck to reach the control panel. Aivas had assured him that it was in working order.

I'll move out of your way, Ruth said obligingly and, picking up his hind legs, flipped over and over backwards, coasting towards the window. *It's better than the view from the Star Stones on Benden or the fire-heights at Ruatha.*

Ruth was completely undaunted by a vista which awed both Jaxom and Piemur. By the time Jaxom had pressed one thick-gloved finger on the pressure panel, Ruth had his nose on the thick plasglas, staring out into space.

Jaxom still could not dispel the sense of intrusion which he had felt keenly the day before; walking where his ancestors had, manipulating switches, toggles and keyboards just as they had once done. He'd told himself that that was partly because of the gruesome errand he and Piemur had been on, retrieving Sallah Telgar. He had hoped the feeling would have altered now that he was here on another errand.

Though they had, miraculously, been able to log into their respective consoles and complete their tasks, Aivas had not been able to discover why the cargo bay doors remained open.

Today, having had a brisk tutorial session from Aivas, Jaxom's assignment was to descend to the cargo level and attempt to use the control console there. Or the manual override.

'It is to be hoped that one of those two systems is operational,' Aivas said.

'Why?'

'You would have to venture outside the ship to discover what was keeping the doors from closing.'

'Oh!' Jaxom had seen enough footage of Aivas' training tapes to wonder if he would have the nerve to space-walk.

The lift opened and he stepped in. The door shut. Once

again consulting the diagram in his hand – though he had memorized it – he punched the button marked CB for cargo bay before he noticed how many levels the lift served. Although Aivas had assured him that the solar panels of the *Yokohama* contained sufficient power to operate the bridge lift, he had a nervous moment before the long-unused mechanism rumbled into action.

'The lift is operational,' Jaxom told Aivas in what he hoped was a casual tone. 'I'm descending.' He had also been instructed to keep up a running commentary. Jaxom was not by nature garrulous: it seemed inane to keep reporting simple actions, even if they did not take place under normal conditions. Aivas had merely repeated that this was a normal operating procedure for a single operative in what was a hostile environment.

'Proceed,' Aivas said, his tone approving.

The lift descent seemed to take both a long time and no time at all. A warning note sounded and a red sign, 'Danger/Vacuum!' appeared on the door of the lift.

'What do I do now, Aivas?'

'Press the "Pump-down" button on the right of the sign, and wait for the danger lights to go out.'

He did this. He noticed that his suit puffed out and seemed slightly less wieldy. As he was getting accustomed to this alteration, there was a melodious 'ding' and the door slid silently aside. And Jaxom looked out at a vast blackness that framed an even blacker area which was punctuated by star lights. There was no reassuring sight of sunlit Pern below him. He didn't move a muscle.

Don't be nervous. I'd come after you if you fell out, Ruth said encouragingly.

'I've reached the cargo bay,' Jaxom said, belatedly remembering Aivas's instruction. 'There's insufficient light.' And that, Jaxom said to himself, must be the single most stupid understatement he'd ever made!

'Feel to the left of the door. There will be a panel,' Aivas's steadying voice said in Jaxom's ear and he let out his breath, only just realizing that he had been holding it in. 'Wave your hand across the panel and emergency lights will come on.'

We hope, Jaxom said to himself. Moving with extreme care, Jaxom obeyed and was unutterably relieved to see a line of lights come up all around the immense cargo bay. The effect did heighten the blackness of space but he felt better with the partial illumination. 'Yes, I now have light. *It's bigger even than Fort's Hatching Ground,'* Jaxom told Ruth, looking about him and awed by the dimensions.

'There is a handrail all around the inside wall of the cargo bay,' Aivas went on conversationally. 'To your left you will see a bank of lights and the console should be visible under them.'

'It is.'

'It will be faster to go hand over hand, Jaxom,' Aivas went on, 'and quite safe. Otherwise you would exhaust yourself needlessly.'

Jaxom wondered if Aivas knew just how scared he was. But how could he? So, Jaxom took a deep breath and lifting his left foot, reached out and caught hold of the handrail. It was round and firm in his grip and amazingly reassuring for a mere thin rail of metal. 'I've got the rail. I'm proceeding as directed.'

Holding very tightly with both hands, he kicked off his right foot, balanced the reaction against the solid rail, and began to move hand over hand, hauling his weightless body after him.

'How did my ancestors manage to load ships working like this?' he asked, unable to think of anything else today.

'Your ancestors worked in half gravity in this area during loading but the rest of the ship was on normal gravity.'

'They could do that? Amazing,' Jaxom replied dutifully. He was nearly halfway to the console. The curve of the bay now hid the unnerving sight of star-studded space. He wanted to increase his pace but sternly held himself to the rhythm that did not cause untoward body reactions. He could feel the sweat on his forehead and then the little suction fan in his helmet turned on and the moisture was evacuated. That phenomenon occupied his mind until he was actually at the lighted console.

He activated it and a range of red and orange lights

flickered into being. Jaxom experienced a slight shock and then began reading the dials. Well, some of the red lights were perfectly in order since they indicated that the cargo bay doors were open. He sighed in relief and applied his lessons to deciphering the rest. When he was sure of what sequence to use, he entered the appropriate code. The orange light began flickering. The legend above it said 'RTC'. He reported this to Aivas.

'That explains why the cargo bay doors remained open. They were on a remote time control and ought to have shut. That is not a serious malfunction. But the simplest method now is to use the manual release, Jaxom,' Aivas told him. 'It is found under the terminal. Open the glass lid and pull.'

Grabbing the handle of the manual release, Jaxom gave a yank. When nothing happened, he gave a second more forceful yank. Fortunately he was still holding on to the handle for he experienced the reaction of the force of the yank. At arm's stretch, he dangled above the deck. A strange gargling noise echoed in his ears.

'What has happened, Jaxom?' Aivas asked, his voice as calm as ever and Jaxom's momentary panic subsided.

In chagrin, he explained and Aivas replied helpfully, 'Pull yourself towards the deck by exerting a downward pressure on the handle, and very slowly tuck your feet forward.'

Jaxom did so and was relieved to feel his soles restored to a firm contact with the deck. Engrossed in recovering from his hasty action, Jaxom did not at first notice the alteration in the light on the deck. Motion caught his peripheral vision to the right and, remembering to turn his head slowly, he saw the great cargo bay doors folding slowly inward, wrapping him in more complete safety.

The door lights on the panel turned from red to green. And suddenly the aggravating orange light winked out.

'Operation completed,' Jaxom said, wanting to shout in relief.

'That is enough for today. Retrace your steps and return to base.'

*

Later that afternoon, when Robinton, Lytol and D'ram arrived for a private meeting, Aivas had further interesting disclosures to make.

'Your wandering planet is flagrantly erratic,' he told them. 'There has been time to study most of the Records presented to this facility. Even the most illegible ones have been deciphered, using available restoration techniques. The Red Star, as it is inaccurately called, has an aberrant course and does *not* cross Pern's path every 250 years. The orbit varies by almost ten years in four Passes, three were 258 and one was 240. Thread Passes alter from forty-six years in the Second Pass to fifty-two in the Fifth and forty-eight in the Seventh. The two intervals of 400 years each appear to suggest that the planet did not in fact orbit as far as the Oort Cloud. Or was, in some inexplicable fashion, diverted from its usual orbit. The former theory is more acceptable than the latter. Another possibility,' and the resonant voice indicated this was most unlikely, 'is that it passed through attenuated portions of this cometary reservoir. Of more importance and based on calculations from the *Yokohama*'s bridge, this Pass will be short by three years.'

'Now *that* is very good news indeed,' D'ram said. 'But, I don't understand how such inaccuracies could have slipped into the Records.'

'That is not at issue,' Aivas replied. 'Though the method of dating on this planet promotes error.'

'Then that would account for the need to position the Eye Rocks, wouldn't it?' Lytol asked. 'Because no matter if dating was faulty, the Weyrs would always know exactly when a Pass was imminent.'

'An ingenious method of ascertaining the correct position of a planet, though by no means original,' Aivas replied.

'Yes, yes,' Lytol said hastily, 'you told me about Stonehenge and the Triangles of Eridani. Do the inaccuracies have any other importance?'

'That information is still being correlated and updated. Optimistically, it augurs well for the success of the plan.'

'And we can reassure Holds and Halls on that account?' asked Robinton, his voice buoyant with hope.

'You can indeed.'

'This briefing is, then, to decide on what information can be made public.'

'Yes.'

'What else can we tell them?'

'As much as you know.'

Robinton chuckled. 'Which is very little.'

'But significant,' replied Aivas. 'The two expeditions to the *Yokohama* have been extremely successful. You may also report that the next exercise will extend to the four green riders. It is vital for them to make bridge transfers and continue the research which Jaxom and Piemur initiated. Each will have an objective during his time on board.'

'*Why* did Jaxom have to close the cargo bay doors today? Especially when you said that that area will not be used for some time,' D'ram asked, curious.

'It is necessary for someone to get practice in working in free fall and to become accustomed to using the spacesuit. Jaxom is the most adept computer operator and Ruth is the most courageous of the dragons.'

Robinton noticed that Lytol perceptibly preened himself on hearing such praise of his ward.

'Does the fact that he is also a Lord Holder and can report on his expedition come into your consideration in his choice?' Robinton asked, amused.

'That did figure in the choice, but competence, and being a dragonrider, were more important.'

Robinton chuckled. 'So who goes next?'

'Now that Ruth has led the way, the green dragons will feel compelled to follow where the littlest one of them has gone before. They will be sent in pairs: Mirrim and Path, G'rannat and Sulath. They have complementary temperaments and skills.'

Robinton chuckled. 'You are indeed well versed in manipulating people.'

'It is not manipulation, Master Robinton. It is understanding the basic personalities of those who are being trained.'

'The cargo area is large enough for bronze dragons to transfer,' D'ram suggested.

'Not until there is also sufficient air for them to breathe.

They will play a major role in future steps, D'ram,' Aivas said. 'But the next step will be to reestablish oxygen producing algae in the hydroponics area to purify the air of the few usable areas on the *Yokohama*. The telescope will have to be adjusted periodically. There is one probe left which may or may not be operational. It could be useful. Failing that, it would be helpful if perhaps a bronze dragon and his rider could venture to obtain samples from the Oort debris.'

'WHAT?' The exclamation came in a chorus from all three startled men.

'A sample of pre-fall Thread was never obtained by the colonists though several attempts were made. An analysis,' and Aivas raised its voice over renewed protests from the three Custodians, 'would be carried out in the one remaining operational laboratory on the *Yokohama* in the cold sleep facility. The rewards of a proper scientific analysis of the Thread material far outweighs any risk. From what I have seen of the abilities and intelligence of the bronze dragons and their riders, the risk would be minimal. Once, of course, they have the exact directions for such a flight. And when protective gear is available for the rider.'

The three regarded the screen with varying degrees of stunned amazement.

'Thread in its nodular form is not dangerous,' Aivas continued as if oblivious to the effect of this statement on the Custodians. 'It is only when it finds a hospitable environment that it alters. For the purpose of analysis, it can be kept safely contained in one of the sleep capsules. Seven of the most promising biology students are already sufficiently trained to handle such investigations, Lady Sharra being the best of them. Much equipment for the investigation of frozen human and animal tissues is still up there. Even an electron-microscope is in place in the cryogenic laboratory – making it the ideal site for our purpose.'

Aivas always sounded so perfectly reasonable, the suggestions always logical and forthright, but Robinton instinctively baulked at the mere notion of such an undertaking. He didn't dare glance at D'ram, or Lytol.

'To destroy a menace, one must perceive it as a whole and in its separate manifestations,' Aivas continued in its most persuasive voice.

'How can we possibly destroy Thread, if what you have told us about this Oort Cloud that surrounds our system is true?'

'What you have been told is fact.'

'Fact is not the only truth,' Lytol reminded them all.

'Now, let's not deviate from the subject at hand,' Robinton said, eyeing Lytol sternly. He and Aivas could indulge in semantics and philosophy in their own time.

'One alters the facts,' Aivas went on as if Lytol had not interrupted. 'That is the plan.'

'I wish,' and Robinton leaned forward in his earnest petition, 'that you would tell us the whole of this plan of yours.'

'Master Robinton, to use an analogy, you would not expect a new student to read a score of music perfectly, would you?' When Robinton agreed, Aivas continued, 'Nor would you expect that same student, no matter how talented, to be able to perform to a high level of competence, playing intricate passages on an unfamiliar instrument, would you?'

'I take the analogy,' Robinton said, raising both hands in surrender.

'Then be reassured by the successes already achieved: the lessons learned and understood. Progress towards the high level which must be achieved is being made but it would be harmful to overwhelm your valiant people before they are properly prepared by education and experience.'

'You are right, completely right, Aivas,' Robinton said and continued to shake his head at the folly of his impetuous demand.

'How critical to Pern, and to this project, is this Lords Convocation, Master Robinton?' Aivas asked.

Robinton gave a wry smile. 'That's the debatable point. But when all the Lords Holder assemble, minor irritations have a habit of flaring up into roaring debates. We – Sebell, Lytol, D'ram and I – have good reason to believe that Landing, and this project, may be called to question by some of the dissatisfied and conservative elements. We'll be better able to gauge reactions after Sallah Telgar's interment tomorrow.'

'Will many attend that ceremony?'

Robinton's grin turned broad and slightly malicious. 'Anybody who is anybody on Pern will be there! Master Shonagar has been relentlessly rehearsing apprentices and journeymen: Domick has been killing himself to produce suitable music, including a splendid fanfare of trumpets. Dragons will fill the sky to do her honour.' Robinton felt an unexpected closure of his throat at the thought of the tributes arranged for this fabled ancestress. 'Perschar, among others, will be on hand to illustrate.'

'Such scenes would be an unusual addition to the archives of present day Pern,' remarked Aivas.

'You shall have them, of course,' Robinton promised earnestly.

'As well as your individual verbal accounts of the proceedings.'

'All of us?' D'ram asked surprised.

'Different perspectives often supply the full dimensions of an event.'

By the next evening, Robinton wasn't certain if the *full* dimensions of Sallah Telgar's interment would ever be properly recorded. It had been quite a day and, for once, he admitted that he was very very tired.

Larad and his lady had organized a splendid occasion, with master instrumentalists under the direction of Domick himself and singers from all over the continent to sing 'The Ballad of Sallah Telgar'. The large Telgar Gather pits had been utilized to feed those who began arriving the day before. Most had thoughtfully brought their own rations but Telgar stinted no-one and anyone of consequence was accommodated in the portions of the great Hold that had not been tenanted since the last plague. Robinton rather thought that every holder in Telgar had been drafted in to clean though Lady Jissamy was by no means lax in her duties and even the furthest corner of her domain endured inspection once a Turn.

191

The interment had been set for mid-afternoon to allow time for those who wished to attend to arrive. Every dragon came laden with as many passengers as it was safe for them to convey. Toric himself arrived on K'van's Heth, and his seldom seen wife, Ramala, accompanied him. He immediately began to solicit the other Lords Holder for guards to help him with his rebels. From the expression on the big southerner's face, Robinton surmised that he met with little success. When the Harper had a chance to compare notes with Sebell, it appeared that the Lords Holder, without exception, felt that this was an inappropriate time to recruit a punitive force. That meant that Toric would air that problem at the conference. That was another debate sure to be heated. Robinton was of two minds about attending: he was no longer obliged to but the invitation had been made to him, and he was far too curious to stay away. He trusted Sebell to report accurately but he preferred to make his own observations whenever possible.

However, all minor rifts and major controversies faded into insignificance as the interment ceremonies commenced. The Ballad, well known, was magnificently performed for those who gathered on the site. Then, cued by Ruth and Jaxom, the massed Weyrs appeared in the skies above Telgar. Robinton felt tears well up in his eyes, as much in remembrance for the previous occasion nearly twenty Turns ago when the five Lost Weyrs had reappeared in Telgar skies to meet Threadfall with Benden's valiant wings as for the honour the massed Weyrs did Sallah Telgar. Today, Lessa on Ramoth and Telgar's senior queen dragon, Bedella's Solth, carried between them the hammock containing Sallah's coffin. The sun glinted off the gold plate, trim and handles, causing the throng to gasp as it seemed Rukbat itself was honouring the gallant woman. Ranged above the two queens the Weyrs formed seven sections in a close formation that was a feat of wingmanship in itself. The dragons must be touching wingtips.

The entire mass followed the two queens down, hovering above as Ramoth and Solth delicately placed their burden on the bier, the hammock falling gracefully to either side.

An honour escort of Holders stepped forward to bear the coffin the last few lengths to its final resting place.

The massed dragonriders swirled, each keeping its Weyr formation, and came to rest either on Telgar's fire heights or as a border to the assembled. Then Larad stepped forward, his sons behind him, for Aivas had affirmed that they were, indeed, the direct descendants of Sallah Telgar and Tarvi Andiyar.

'Let this be a day of rejoicing that this valiant Lady has returned to the world she gave her life to protect. Let her rest now with others of the Blood in the Hold that bears her name and honours her above all its ancestors.'

With those simple words, Larad stepped aside, and the coffin was lifted to the shoulders of the escort and carried in measured steps towards the tomb. As the coffin was placed inside, the dragons, one and all, lifted their heads to keen. A heart-tearing sound on any occasion but to Robinton, with tears streaming down his face, the notes had an oddly triumphant ring. As if in response to that, an immense flurry of wings and what must be every fire-lizard in the north and south, wild and tame, swooped down in a deep wide aerial veil, just above the heads of the escort, across the still open tomb, adding their high voices as counterpoint to the dragons' deeper tones. They swept up and at the top of Telgar's precipice abruptly disappeared.

Robinton had wondered where Zair had gone to, and only now realized that those around him who were usually adorned by a fire-lizard had had empty shoulders from the moment the massed dragon wings appeared in the sky.

The escort, somewhat stunned by that final flourish to the solemn event, stepped back and the Telgar masons, their Gather-best clothes protected by new aprons, moved forward to seal the opening.

In respectful silence – for even the youngest had been awed by dragon and fire-lizard displays – the assembled waited until the tomb was completely closed and the masons stood aside. Larad and Lady Jissamy both moved to face the tomb and bowed deeply, as did the escort. The obeisance was repeated by every one present.

Then Larad, his Lady, and the escort stepped back and

processed towards the broad court of Telgar Hold. Domick's musicians began to play a solemn and majestic piece to signal the end of the ceremonies. They followed behind the last of the crowd dispersing to enjoy the hospitality of Telgar Hold.

Robinton was looking forward with great anticipation to tasting one of the roast beasts turning on the great spits and a fine vintage of Benden wine which he was certain Larad would provide when he felt a touch on his elbow.

'Robinton!' Jaxom said in a low voice, his eyes sparking with fury. 'They tried to attack Aivas. Come!'

'Tried?' Robinton was shocked and confused. The Harper found it very hard to take in what Jaxom had just said.

'Tried!' Jaxom repeated grimly, guiding Robinton by the elbow towards the edge of those sauntering along towards the court. 'Farli brought just a scribble so I know no more than that but I for one can't stand about *here*.'

'Nor I!' Nothing would settle Robinton's pounding heart until he saw with his own eyes that Aivas had suffered no damage. The very thought of being deprived of the knowledge they were daily gaining from the facility was enough to give him another heart attack. He also decided not to spread this information until he had reassured himself. Shards! He was getting old. Why hadn't he realized that today would be the perfect time to make a direct attack – when Landing was nearly deserted. Everyone who could come was up here in Telgar.

'Edge over further, Master Robinton. We're almost to Ruth now. We'll just get to Landing and see for ourselves. I don't think anyone should ruin this,' Jaxom said, gesturing to mean the Telgarian reverence for Sallah.

'Properly said, Lord Holder.' Robinton moved with more alacrity to where Ruth had been edging towards them as inconspicuously as possible. No-one would think it odd that the white dragon would save Robinton the walk back to Telgar Hold court. So they mounted and Ruth, swinging upward and over Telgar cliff, abruptly went *between*.

The white dragon came out right above the clearing in front of the Aivas building. Those crowding the entrance made room for his passengers. While Robinton took note of their expressions, he was puzzled for their anger was understandable but their amusement was not.

Lytol had chosen to take the duty that day to see that the students appeared for their scheduled courses, permitting D'ram and Robinton to attend the Telgar ceremony. He was sitting in his customary seat, but he wore a bandage on his head, and his clothing was torn. Jancis and the Landing Healer were in attendance, but she grinned reassuringly at the new arrivals.

'Don't worry! His skull's too hard to crack,' she said gaily, and with an expansive wave, directed their attention down the corridor to Aivas, 'and *he's* got a few tricks he never bothered to mention.'

'Go look,' Lytol said with a most uncharacteristic grin of pleased malice.

Robinton was first down the corridor but he stepped two strides in and stopped so that Jaxom bumped into him. Standing guard were Piemur and six of the sturdiest students, hefty clubs held ready for any excuse to use. Two of them also wore head bandages. On the floor were the unconscious bodies of the attackers, the heavy axes or metal bars with which they had intended to wreak havoc on Aivas piled beyond reach.

'Aivas protects himself,' said Piemur, grinning, swinging his club in a circle on its thong.

'What happened?' Robinton demanded.

'We were taking a meal break,' Piemur said as Jancis joined him, 'when we heard the most awful noise. We rushed back and found Lytol, Ker and Miskin knocked down and then this lot acting as if their brains were on fire. Which, from the residual sound *we* heard, is a fair description.'

'But what . . .'

'This facility was provided with resources to prevent tampering,' said Aivas, its voice reaching down the corridor. As matter of fact as the tone was, Robinton also 'heard' a faint note of satisfaction, certainly permissible. 'There are sounds which emitted at volume can render humans unconscious. When the intruders attacked Lytol,

195

Ker and Miskin, it seemed advisable to initiate this defensive measure. Regrettably, some permanent aural damage may result but most should regain consciousness within a few hours. They took more sonics than is, was, normally required in dissuasion.'

'I . . . we . . . had no idea you had *defences*,' Robinton said, struggling with both relief and surprise.

'A built-in feature of any Aivas, Master Robinton, though seldom required. These units are programmed with industrially and politically valuable information which dissidents would find useful: unauthorized access and/or destructive actions must, therefore, be actively discouraged and this has always been a minor function of an Aivas facility.'

'Well, I must say, I do feel better knowing that but why didn't you tell us?'

'The question didn't arise.'

'But you knew there'd been that attempt to ruin your battery power,' Jaxom began.

'The facility was not in any danger from such crude vandalism. You were quick to provide effective measures against a repeat of such sabotage.'

'But why didn't you . . . do whatever you did today then?' Jaxom wanted to know.

'Such measures are best invoked during a direct assault when they are most effective.'

'What exactly did you do?' Jaxom asked, gesturing to the limp bodies.

'Sonic barrage,' Piemur said, grinning. 'Pure and penetrating sound. Must have hurt,' and he gestured to one man who lay face up, his contorted expression suggesting the pain he had endured before unconsciousness relieved it. Piemur gave the body a contemptuous push with his toe. 'I don't know where Norist got them . . .'

'Norist?' Robinton exclaimed.

Piemur shrugged. 'Has to be Norist. He's the one who's most vocal about destroying the Abomination. And look . . .' He bent then and lifted a limp hand for them to examine. 'Those look like glass pipe calluses and he's certainly got old burn scars on his arms. He's the only one who has them. But once they wake up, we can ask a few questions. And get answers!' Piemur's voice took on a harsh edge.

'Who knows about this?'

'Everyone presently in Landing,' Piemur said with a shrug and then grinned impishly, 'which isn't many since everyone who could grabbed a dragonride to Telgar. How'd that go?'

'Impressively,' Robinton said, almost absently as he moved to check the other would-be vandals. 'The dragons AND the fire-lizards accorded her their own tribute.'

'Ruth didn't even warn me,' Jaxom added with a wry grin.

It was fitting. The dragons were in agreement. The fire-lizards imitated them, but that was fitting, too, Ruth told Jaxom who told the others what he had said.

Completing his examination of the unconscious men, Robinton didn't recognize a single face among this rough lot who had obviously been chosen for bulk. Gloomily he wondered if Norist indeed had planned and organized the assault.

'Lytol's truly all right?' Robinton asked in a lowered voice, glancing back at the front entrance.

'He's got a terrible bump,' Jancis said, 'and the Healer says he cracked a rib, falling on the edge of the desk but his pride's more injured than his skull. You should have heard him complaining that Ker and Miskin were too slow on their feet to be of any assistance.'

'Against eight men armed with axes and bars?' Robinton said, appalled at the possible harm such implements could have done to his friend, much less to Aivas. He found himself swaying a bit on his feet.

Immediately Piemur grabbed him, roaring at Jaxom to take the other side, at Jancis to get the Healer and some wine, and they supported him into the nearest room and into a chair.

Protestingly, he flailed at their hands, but even to his own ears his voice had a quaver of weakness which he was appalled to hear. He didn't like to admit that the day was supplying too many shocks.

'It's time to bespeak Lessa and F'lar,' Jaxom said, 'and I don't bloody care what excuse they give Larad. Ruth!'

Even as Robinton lifted a hand to object, Jaxom's expression told him that he had given Ruth the message to forward. Jancis arrived with a huge mug of wine which Robinton sipped at gratefully while the healer fussed at him.

'The Masterharper has taken no harm, for his vital signs are restored to acceptable levels,' Aivas said, his voice pitched to penetrate to the room but his tone was kindly reassuring. 'Do not distress yourself, Master Robinton, for there has been no lasting harm done to humans and none to this facility.'

'That is not the point, Aivas,' Jaxom said, whirling towards the entity. 'No harm should have been considered, much less attempted.'

'The winds of change create a climate of resistance. That is to be expected.'

'By you?' Jaxom asked, irritated by Aivas' imperturbability. Why hadn't they realized how ideal this day was to dissidents like Norist who would have known that Robinton and D'ram would attend the honours done Sallah Telgar: that anyone who could grab a ride a-dragonback would be gone from Landing?

'And me. Ease up, lad,' Lytol said, entering the room just then. 'I figured an attempt might be made. That's why I made Ker and Miskin stay back. I didn't think there'd be so many of 'em. Rushed us and we'd no chance.' He looked keenly at Robinton. 'Humpf. You look much the way I feel, Robinton,' he added as he lowered himself carefully into the nearest chair. 'Master Esselin was with me at the time but he fainted when that gang barged in. I hadn't thought to arm the students. They were near by and fifteen of 'em should have been sufficient deterrent.'

Just then two of Esselin's young apprentice archivists came running down the corridor, shouting for Piemur.

'Quietly!' Piemur let out the single bellow, grimacing in apology for the noise he had himself made.

'Harper, we found their runners, tied up in a copse just off the old sea road,' the older lad reported. 'Silfar and I rode a pair back after we'd moved 'em from where they was in case someone escaped. Trestan and Rona stayed 'cos Rona has a fire-lizard.' His eyes were big in his flushed young face and he was panting with excitement as well as exertion and the eyes of the bronze fire-lizard clinging to his shoulder were whirling in violent patterns of red and orange.

'Well done, Deegan,' Piemur said. 'Have you winded your runners?'

'No, sir, harper.' Deegan's expression became indignant at the thought of injuring a valuable beast. 'They're sweet movers. Cost a pouch or two for that sort of runner, sir.'

'Send your bronze to reassure Rona and go back and bring in the others. We might find something interesting in their gear.'

'All they had in their saddle packs was food, sir,' Deegan added apologetically. 'I looked 'cause I thought there might be some clues.'

Again Piemur nodded approval of his initiative. 'Off you go then.'

Then he turned grimly to the others. 'There're more in on this than Norist and his cranks. How'd expensive runners get south? Who put up the marks to buy eight and send 'em here?'

'Meaning a dissident Fishermaster is also involved?' Jaxom asked.

'That's the one Craft that has not benefited very much from Aivas' stored information,' Piemur said, frowning.

Robinton shook his head but it was Lytol who spoke. 'Not at all, Piemur. Master Idarolan was exceedingly grateful to Aivas for the detailed charts of depths and current which Captain Tillek compiled. The overviews from space are truly astounding.' Lytol paused in respectful awe. Then gave a shrug. 'Of course, there have been alterations in coastlines since then but the accuracy of the charts makes it all that much easier to update them. Every Master has been given copies and specific area charts are being supplied to every fisherman. What Master Idarolan approves is accepted by every Master of his Craft.'

'True enough,' Piemur replied but added in a sardonic

tone, 'though I can think of one or two extremely conservative and hidebound Fishmasters without naming any names who might sympathize with Norist's discontent. Look at how many people made it to Southern who weren't supposed to.'

'A full purse can close many a mouth,' Lytol added cynically.

'Let us not make rash assumptions,' Robinton said.

'Lessa says it's impossible for either herself or F'lar to come,' Jaxom said at that point, 'but F'nor can. The Weyrleaders're both livid and want to know why such an attack could occur.'

One of the assault group stirred, moaning.

'We'll find out!' Jaxom and Piemur said simultaneously and exchanged grimly determined glances.

'Might I suggest we tie these fellows up before they regain their wits?' asked Robinton, eyeing the sizes and comparing them to the slighter frames of the student guards.

'Yes,' Piemur said, 'and we've just the thing to hand.' He reached for a coil of thick flex, a savage grin on his face. 'C'mon, you lot,' and he turned to the students, 'let's truss these sharding dimwits up properly.'

Once restraints were in place, each man's clothing was searched but that proved fruitless. Old scars, thick ears and broken noses suggested that five of the eight had fought often. Only the one bore marks of the Glass-smith Craft but the remaining two were equally rough livers.

'Swacky might know some of 'em,' Piemur suggested. 'He's been sergeant at arms in enough holds over the Turns to know many regulars.'

'They'd hardly pick men we'd recognize, now would they?' Robinton said, 'but if Swacky could identify any one of them, that might give us a direction for inquiry. How long will they remain unconscious?'

He addressed that to Aivas who said that the period was variable. 'The duller the subject the more sonic barrage is required. As you see, they survived to the very threshold.'

'I don't like that at all,' Robinton said explosively.

'However, they would not have passed the threshold,'

Aivas remarked in a fashion that left no doubt in anyone's mind of the truth of the statement.

Robinton shuddered and drank down the rest of his wine, feeling an urgent need for more of such consolation. 'Let's get them out of the hall. Surely we have some secure building to hold them in. It's almost . . . almost obscene leaving them sprawled in the hallway like this.'

'Assistance just arrived,' Jaxom said and they all heard the bugling challenge of many dragons.

So F'nor, T'gellan, Mirrim and nearly a full wing of Eastern Weyr riders appeared in a timely fashion.

'From now on there is full dragon surveillance for Aivas,' F'nor said when he had listened to Lytol's concise report.

'Eastern insists on the honour,' T'gellan said.

'I just wish it hadn't come to this,' Robinton said, shaking his head, weary in body and heart.

'My dear friend,' Lytol said, placing a consoling hand on the Harper's shoulder, 'it was bound to happen. You should have taken time to read the histories as I did. You would then have been better prepared for the cultural upheaval which is occurring in every Hold, Hall and Weyr.'

'I had hoped that Aivas would ensure a bright future for us all . . .' Robinton began, raising his arms in an expansive gesture before letting them fall limply to his knees.

'That's because you're the eternal optimist,' Lytol said with a sad smile.

'That's no bad way to be,' Piemur said firmly, shooting Lytol a quelling glare. It pained the young journeyman to see his Master so depressed and listless. The Warder shrugged and turned away to hide his cynicism.

T'gellan dispatched a rider to bring Swacky from Paradise River Hold in the hopes that he might recognize one of the intruders. Jayge, reckoning that he might be of some help since he had seen so much of the Eastern Holds and Halls during his trading days, arrived with Swacky.

'Yeah, I recognize this pair,' Swacky said, turning one lolling head from side to side. 'Bitrans, if I remember rightly. Bitrans'll do anything if you give 'em enough marks.'

'Any name come to mind, Swacky?' F'nor asked, frowning.

Swacky gave a shrug of his thick shoulders. 'No. Bitrans aren't friendly and I don't think you're going to get much out of this lot. They're too stubborn to give in and too stupid to give up. They do stay bought,' he added with grudging respect.

Jayge, kneeling by another man, shook his head. 'I know him. I don't know where but I know him. I'll tell you one thing, though, he's worked fishnets. Look at these three-corner tears on his fingers and palms. That's net damage.'

Robinton heaved a long sigh and Lytol looked grimmer than ever.

When the first of them finally regained consciousness late that evening, he stared around with such bleak panic in his face that it soon became obvious he had lost his hearing. To written questions he shook his head and seemed far too depressed over his deafness to wish to better his situation by contributing any information. Consultations between Aivas and the Healer about a return of hearing produced no helpful results.

'To prevent their entry, it was necessary to raise volume and intensity beyond the normally preventative decibel rate,' Aivas said. 'As a consequence of the extreme deterrent required, regrettably permanent damage may have been inflicted.'

When their animals arrived, none of the gear indicated its source. The saddles were new but bore no leatherman's stamp nor were the runners ear-notched or branded for identification, and they handled with the nervousness of very green animals.

'Probably stolen from Keroon or Telgar herds before Spring culls,' was the opinion of Masterherder Briaret who came the next day to assist in the inquiry. 'Whoever chose them knew his runners and further picked those that don't show any particular characteristics from sire or dam. They was rough broke,' he added, looking into the mouth of one, and pointing out biting scars, 'never been shod and came by sea,' and he pointed to marks on hips, rumps and shoulders from being rubbed about in the narrow stalls used to transport animals by ship. 'Don't think we'll find out where they was stolen from, but I'll put the word out to my halls.'

The tack he said was all apprentice-made, pointing out the flaws which would have made them unsaleable from any reputable Tanner Hall.

'These could have been picked up from various Halls over the course of a Turn or two from 'prentices needing Gather marks. I'd say that whoever planned this has planned long and well,' was Briaret's opinion.

The sturdy but worn clothing was of a style and fabric available all across the continent and the camping equipment had seen considerable use.

'Could've staked out here for a spell, just waiting for a good opportunity. Like the ceremony at Telgar.'

In one saddle bag the searchers found a small collapsible telescope, of the sort used by fishermen but it had no other mark than the usual Telgar Smith one on the metal rim of the eyepiece.

When Master Idarolan was asked his opinion, he was outraged that any of his Craft could have been involved though it was obvious one had to have been part of the plot. He promised to investigate, admitting that there were some who were unfortunately no credit to their calling and were not above making a clandestine voyage for a full purse of marks after a bad season. He'd name no-one now but he knew who to watch, so he did.

Swacky volunteered to stay at Landing as warder of the invaders. His notion was that, recognizing him as another guard, he might yet get one of them to confide in him. They might be deaf but six of them still had wit and tongue.

Jayge lingered, too, finally admitting to Piemur and Jancis that he would very much like an interview with Aivas if that was at all possible.

'No problem, Jayge,' Piemur reassured him and grinned broadly. 'Beginning to think all this new technology has some use?'

Jayge gave a wry chuckle. 'I need to know if Readis and Alemi are both losing their wits. They swear they've had more conversations with shipfish, with the dolphins. The dolphins say they came with the original settlers.' Jayge set his jaw as if waiting for derision.

'Dolphins did come with the settlers, Jayge,' Piemur reassured him, Jancis nodding as well. Then the young Harper's expression turned rueful. 'We've been so busy with space we really still haven't caught up on other important details. C'mon. Everyone else's busy with the intruders right now so Aivas is free.'

'The dolphins are indeed capable of communicating with humans,' Aivas told Jayge. 'Mentasynth enhancement is genetically transmitted so that the ability would have survived through any number of generations. They were the most successful of the mentasynth experiments. It is good to know that the species has survived. Are they numerous? It would appear from the question, Holder Jayge, that contact has not been maintained. Is that so?'

'No,' Jayge admitted apologetically, 'though my wife and myself as well as my son and Masterfisherman Alemi owe our lives to them.'

'The species has always been considerate of human-kind.'

'And they do speak a language we humans could learn?'

'Since humans taught them the language, yes. But it would be the language of your ancestors, not that which is in current usage. This facility was able to make linguistic adjustments which would not be available to the dolphins, despite their great intelligence.'

'The shipfish have great intelligence?' Piemur asked in surprise.

'They possess an intelligence measurably equal to, if not surpassing, most human intellects.'

'I find that hard to believe,' Piemur muttered.

'Believe it,' replied Aivas in the sort of definite way that all its students had learned meant its opinion was incontestable. 'Holder Jayge, if you are interested in reviving the communications link with dolphins, this facility would be glad to assist you.'

Jayge grimaced. 'It's not me, Aivas. I was just here and wanted to know. It's my son, Readis, and our Masterfisherman Alemi, who thought the dolphins were speaking.'

'The resumption of that link could be of great value to fishermen and all who use the seaways. Time can be allotted to that study.'

'I'll tell Alemi. He'll be delighted to hear it.'

'Your son?'

'Oh, Readis is a child . . .'

'A child has fewer inhibitions in learning new languages, Holder Jayge.'

Jayge's eyes bulged in surprise. 'But he's seven!'

'A most receptive age. This facility would take great pleasure in instructing young Readis. Piemur, see that time is allocated. Contact should be resumed between the dolphins and humans as soon as possible.'

'I'd really thought you all were embellishing your accounts of that Aivas of yours,' Jayge said in a low voice to the grinning pair who escorted him out of the room, 'but you were harper-true this time.'

'Aivas doesn't need embellishments,' Piemur assured him smugly.

'You will bring Readis, won't you?' Jancis asked. 'Tell Ara that I'd take very good care of him while he's here.' She giggled. 'I think it's the best thing I've heard yet. Shipfish are smarter than us humans!'

'I think we better keep quiet on that score,' Piemur said, his expression solemn. 'We've got enough trouble as it is. That opinion'd really start a snake hunt. Even with folks who've got a lot of common sense.'

'I think it's marvellous,' Jancis repeated, grinning in broad malice. 'It's perfect. Alemi'll be over the moons.'

Jayge looked chagrined. 'Ara'll beat him there. She swore blind the dolphins talked to her when they saved us from drowning.'

'Then bring Ara, too,' Piemur suggested. 'There ought to be more than just two to learn dolphin talk. Say, you know it might be smart to teach more kids than just Readis . . . not meaning to detract from him, Jayge, but, if say, we put it about that Aivas was teaching mainly *kids*, no adults would get suspicious. Because I'm serious, people. I don't think we ought to spread this intelligence thing about.'

'I agree,' Jancis said.

Jayge shrugged. 'I'll accept that judgment. And I'll bring Readis, Alemi and whoever else he thinks we should include. Talking to shipfish! Wow! That's a real stunner.' And he shook his head slowly, in time with his step as his friends escorted him back to where V'line and bronze Clarinath waited to convey him back to Paradise River Hold.

The day before the Lords Holder Conference, the Benden Weyrleaders held a short meeting at Cove Hold to decide whether or not to bring up the matter of the attempt to disable Aivas.

By then all eight men had recovered from the sonic coma: two would never be of use to anyone, none had recovered their hearing. Three wrote messages asking for relief from unbearable headpains which finally abated after considerable dosing of fellis juice. Since none of them were willing to divulge any information about those who had hired them to attack the Aivas, his guardians had no recourse but to have them all transported to the mines of Crom to work underground with other incorrigibles.

'Why do we have to bring the subject up at all? Let's just let rumour work for us,' Master Robinton suggested with a devious smile. 'Let them ask us for explanations. That is, if any are required.'

'Seeing it my way for a change?' asked Lytol with a sardonic smile.

'The rumours are alive and exploding with inventiveness,' Jaxom said with a grin at Piemur.

'I'm not sure that's altogether the wisest course,' Lessa said, scowling.

'Who has ever controlled rumour?' Robinton demanded.

'You!' Lessa retorted promptly, her scowl disappearing into a wide grin at the person who had so often deliberately spread rumours.

'Not really,' Robinton replied with a smug smile, 'not after I sent off the original version.'

'Well, then, what's being bruited about right now?' F'lar asked.

'That Aivas perceives the motives of anyone approaching

206

him and has withered the unworthy,' Piemur answered eagerly, ticking off the variations on his fingers, 'that he had horribly maimed some innocent petitioners who had the audacity to approach him one early morning because they overheard him plotting with Lord Jaxom . . .' Jaxom had apparently heard that variation and only snorted. 'That we had installed a squadron of Gather champions to defend the place and they'd beat up anyone they didn't like the look of, that there is a full wing of dragons constantly on guard and that they are somehow under Aivas's complete control, that fire-lizards are afraid of their lives to come near Landing any more, that the Aivas had deadly and powerful weapons that could paralyse anyone not totally committed to his intentions for Pern's future. That Aivas has control of all Weyrleaders and Lords Holder . . .' Piemur had to wait until the indignation of the attending Weyrleaders subsided, 'And was going to take over the running of the planet, and that all too soon the three Dawn Sisters were going to come crashing down on Pern, causing irreparable damage to any Hold or Hall that won't support Aivas. And if the Dawn Sisters lose their position in the sky, all the other stars will go out of control so that's how Aivas will prevent any further Threadfall because Pern will be totally destroyed and not even Thread will find it hospitable.' Piemur took a deep breath and, his eyes glinting with amusement, asked, 'Heard enough?'

'All I care to, certainly,' Lessa said with considerable asperity. 'Absolute twaddle!'

'Is anyone taking any of it seriously?' F'lar asked, leaning forward.

Lytol sucked in his breath. 'Some of that foolishness would account for the extreme tenseness of that delegation from Nerat, that group who applied for advice on how to counteract a blight. Masterfarmer Losacot had to chivvy them to enter the room. I mentioned the fact in my day report.'

'Did Aivas notice their reluctance?' asked Lessa.

'I certainly wouldn't ask Aivas a question like that. Totally irrelevant,' Lytol said, somewhat surprised and indignant and he gave Lessa a sharp look. 'The important aspect was that they apparently received a positive answer for they were discussing the ways to implement his advice when they left. Master Losacot stopped to thank me for slotting them in so promptly. I thought the matter quite urgent.'

'I still maintain that the more people who encounter Aivas,' Robinton said, 'the more support any plan of his will receive.'

'Not always,' Lytol said in a low-voiced contradiction. Then he smiled at the Harper. 'But you and I have agreed to differ on that score, haven't we?'

'We have,' the Harper replied affably but there was a sad shadow in his eyes as he gazed on the old Warder.

'So, what attitude do we take at the conference tomorrow?' Lessa demanded, 'presuming of course the Weyrleaders will be allowed into the meeting.'

'Oh, you will be,' Jaxom said. 'Larad, Groghe, Asgenar, Toronas and Deckter wouldn't permit exclusion of Benden and High Reaches Weyrleaders!' And he grinned. 'I think we ought to wait until *they* bring up the subject.'

'Tomorrow's a solemn occasion, Jaxom,' Lytol said, favouring his former charge with a stern look.

'Not all of it and I really can keep countenance when I need to, old friend.' Jaxom grinned engagingly at Lytol. He ignored Piemur's snort. 'Since so many of us should be in attendance, T'gellan and K'van have doubled the dragon guard here.'

'D'ram's in charge,' Robinton added. 'Insisted since both Lytol and myself ought to attend the conference.'

'As if you'd miss it,' Lessa replied, her eyebrows raised.

'This one least of all,' Robinton remarked affably.

Chapter Nine

I n the Spring of the year, Tillek Hold was at its most
attractive, for the vivid blue skies seemed to brighten
the Hold's granite cliffs and the sun often glinted
off surfaces that were momentarily silver-gilt. From its
position on the heights, the uppermost level of the Hold
provided north and south views: on clear days, as today,
one could see across the promontory to the southern
coastline where the terrain fell away from the Hold height.
Today banners flew from every window, brilliant panels in
audacious colours against the grey stone.

Below the Hold, the natural deep harbour and the smaller
holds and cots on the terraces that made up the large Tillek
settlement were also decorated with banners, streamers
and even garlands of the various yellow blooms of Spring.
Ranrel's recent labours to improve docking facilities were
being put to the test. Many people had elected to sail up
the western coast to attend the conference and the festivities
following the confirmation of a new Lord Holder. But so
spacious was the anchorage that not even the mass of craft,
small and large, strained its capacity.

To Jaxom's surprise, Ruth came out of *between* over the
harbour waters, giving himself and Sharra an excellent view
of the activity below them. It would appear that every small
craft that could be paddled or rowed had been drafted to do
lighter duty between the visitors' ships and the new wharf.

There was even a line of craft bobbing at each landing stair waiting to discharge passengers, gay in their festal attire.

Then Jaxom appreciated why Ruth had elected to bring them out over the water, for the congestion of dragons above the Hold itself would have taxed even the white dragon's vaunted ability to avoid collision.

'We really should have brought Jarrol to this, Jax,' Sharra yelled in his ear. 'He would have adored all the colour and excitement.'

Jaxom shrugged for he was as glad Sharra had been dissuaded from that notion. Today was going to be full enough without having to worry about the antics of an active and inventive four-Turn-old child. And he wanted Sharra at his side without an encumbrance.

'There'll be other investitures, love, when he's old enough to appreciate it more,' he said, shouting over his shoulder at her.

Ruth descended, moving with more decorum than usual, to prevent Sharra's heavy formal skirts from billowing out. The riding straps which the couple used when they rode tandem on Ruth helped contain the folds but they still flapped vigorously in the wind.

'The unexpected perils of dragonriding,' Sharra muttered as Ruth circled slowly to find a place in the crowded forecourt. Then, continuing the conversation that they had broken off to go *between*, she added, 'And I really am to go up to the *Yokohama* with you the day after tomorrow?'

'Yes, indeed,' and Jaxom was pleased by the excitement in her voice. 'Aivas says we've got to have the oxygen recycling to spend our time aboard efficiently. Even in the few areas we'll be using. Putting breathable atmosphere in the cargo bay and the engine room is going to take a lot of oxygen and we can't keep lugging tanks up and down. You and Mirrim will do just fine setting it up. You know the programs and the instructions for starting the algae by heart. I heard you muttering the steps in your sleep.' He grinned back at her because he wanted very much for her to share the incredible experience of viewing Pern from space and to have a part in the project that absorbed him: almost, he admitted with private candour, to the exclusion of everything else. 'Besides, Aivas says the whole program is foolproof but we need the computer controlled porous-technology CO_2/O_2 to supply sufficient oxygen for our needs. The system just wants starting and then regular checks. Once you and Mirrim understand the system, you'll teach other green riders. And with Path and Mirrim, you and Ruth, there'll be proper control on the system. Meanwhile the greens'll be hauling oxygen in tanks to tide us over until the system's fully operational again.'

'Ruth would take anyone you asked him to,' she reminded him because, while she wanted more than anything to do the ultimate exploration, the *Yokohama* itself in space, she was also very much aware that the mission could be dangerous. She had two children to think of now, not just herself, and it was a question in her mind of the priorities of her responsibilities: to Jaxom as his mate, to her sons as their mother.

But I like taking you better, Sharra, Ruth said ending that argument. *Maynooth says it's my turn in the forecourt but you're to dismount as quickly as you can,* he added. *Maynooth's rider is terrified of having a collision while he's on duty.* Ruth added a contemptuous snort for that possibility.

Jaxom helped Sharra unclip the riding straps and dismount, careful that the full skirts of this brand new gown did not become entangled in the harness, or excessively rumpled in the process. The colour was an amazing, vibrant blend of green and blue that complemented Sharra's colouring and the fabric was cut to a pattern found by Master Zurg when he had an opportunity to access Aivas' files on matters pertaining to his Craft. On first seeing his wife dressed in her splendour, Jaxom had been once again slightly stunned by her subtle beauty and was torn between pride in his beloved and anxiety that others might monopolize her when the dancing began.

Her descent accomplished with no hazard to her attire, Jaxom helped her remove the equally fetching jacket, its leather dyed a slightly darker shade than her dress, its fur lining too warm to wear now in Tillek's sun. Then he offered his Lady his arm and Ruth was free to find himself a spot on the sun-warmed heights. As the tall, handsome couple made their way across the forecourt to the Hold entrance, they acknowledged the greetings of the many people they knew.

They caught glimpses of Oterel's two older sons, and exchanged courteous nods, but both Blesserel and Terentel knew Jaxom as a lost cause in the Holder voting for he had made perfectly plain his preference for Ranrel.

Sharra chuckled softly. 'I see that everyone who could afford it has been spilling marks into the Weavercraft coffers.'

'I thought Master Zurg looked excessively smug when we passed him.'

'He should be. Everyone, including that wretched dandy Blesserel, is wearing new clothes: either tailored by or made from fabrics bought from good Master Zurg. Except you.' Sharra said that with a sniff of disapproval. 'It wouldn't have taken much time to have a new outfit for today.'

'Why? I'm not exactly threadbare or colourless,' Jaxom replied, for he was fond of the deep brown and russet he wore – which colours he thought went well with Sharra's azure. 'And these clothes aren't all that old. They were new for our last Gather day.'

Sharra sniffed again. 'Half a Turn ago. You don't care what you wear so long as it's comfortable. Just look at the variety of style and hue others are wearing.'

Jaxom closed his right hand over hers on his arm and gave it a squeeze. 'You look grand enough for both of us.'

Sharra gave him a droll sideways glance. 'If you'd ever taken the time to be fitted for what I wanted you to wear, we'd outshine everyone else, love.' She gave a resigned sigh. 'As it is, it's just too bad the Craftmasters can't vote on the succession.'

'They should, you know,' Jaxom replied. 'They're as vital to the smooth management of Pern as any Lord Holder.'

'Sssh,' Sharra said, though her eyes twinkled at his heresy, 'you upset sufficient Lords Holder without suggesting *that* innovation.'

'It'll come! It'll come,' Jaxom said, 'once the conservative element among the Holders are replaced.'

'What if Ranrel doesn't make it? Brand did say that there would be protest over his use of the Abomination's materials.'

Jaxom snorted. 'With bloody near everyone else wearing them? Besides, Ranrel's the only one of Oterel's issue who's ever worked. And he's improved the Hold's facilities. That has to count heavily in his favour.'

'Yes, but he's also a journeyman which men like Nessel and Corman take as an admission that he himself knows he's not Holder material.'

'And Blesserel and Terentel with their soft hands and steep debts are? A journeyman's knot in the Fisherman's Craft at least says a man has skill, strength and endurance. And he's had more of managing *men*,' Jaxom stressed the gender, 'than either of that useless pair.'

'Brand mentioned that Blesserel's been actively striving to get support from Corman of Keroon, Sangel, Begamon, and even went to see Toric.'

'Well, if he's promised to help Toric with Denol's island rebels, he'll be working against himself,' Jaxom said scornfully.

'I don't know about that, Jax, I really don't,' Sharra said, frowning slightly. 'My brother's devious as well as plain contrary at times.' Then abruptly she smiled as she saw Toronas and his wife heading in their direction.

'Four votes wouldn't be enough anyway,' Jaxom murmured with a reassurance he didn't really share before the young Benden Holders joined them.

Robinton had wanted to arrive early at Tillek, to have a stroll round and get the feel of the assemblage. Somehow or other, Lytol had managed to delay their departure so that T'gellan deposited them only just before the actual conference was due to start. Lytol secured him an oversized goblet of Benden white and insisted that he be seated on one of the few wall benches on the forecourt, 'for an overall view'. Granted he had that, but he would have preferred to mingle with the crowd and sense the general mood.

'You're fussing over me, Lytol!' Robinton said, his voice querulous.

'You'll have enough excitement . . .'

'There are people I wish to speak with down there . . .'

'You can't alter the outcome of today's proceedings a half hour before they start, Robinton,' Lytol replied.

'But you can!' Robinton knew himself to be testy with his old friend, and jealous.

'I will do as common sense dictates, Harper, and when that will be most effective.' Briefly he caught sight of Blesserel, Oterel's first born son, today clad in sober dark colours in a conservatively cut outfit. 'As if that garb is going to counteract his years as a gaudy guy!' Lytol muttered contemptuously.

'I don't see Ranrel,' Robinton complained.

'To your left, on the third riser, speaking to Sigomal,' Lytol said, indicating the direction.

'Well, good for him. He's not afraid to parade his accomplishments,' Robinton said after a moment's regard, for the youngest of Oterel's eligible sons had dressed in Fishcraft colours and wore his journeyman's knot fastened to his Tillek rank cord. 'Ista and High Reaches will appreciate the compliment. And Master Idarolan.'

'For all the good it does.'

'Now, if only Craftmasters were allowed in on the voting . . .' Robinton said that half to tease Lytol and half in wishful thinking. Lytol merely grunted at this reference where, in previous times, he had been deadset against such an innovation. Was Jaxom having some effect on his former guardian after all?

'Idarolan's a sound man and manages to keep most of a very wayward lot in line – most of the time. But inlanders would not be swayed by his opinions . . .'

'Sangel of Boll is scarcely an inlander,' Robinton protested.

'That doesn't mean he thinks with his wits,' Lytol replied. 'And it's the undecided Holders that must be swayed one way or another: Sigomal, Nessel and Deckter.'

'Deckter will appreciate Ranrel's harbour reconstruction. He's got a merchant's mind on such matters, and Terentel has done nothing to improve Tillek Hold.'

'Sigomal will side with Blesserel, if only to recoup the

boy's gambling losses. You know the way Bitra always turns: markward.'

The Hold bugler appeared at the massive entrance and blew the ten minute warning. The babble of the crowd briefly abated and then increased with excitement as the fifteen Lords Holder began to make their way towards the steps. Lytol watched for Jaxom, Sharra still on his arm, to emerge from the throng and unobtrusively beckoned him over. Jaxom's face lit with a big smile as he saw the Harper beside his former Warder.

'My dear Lady Holder, you outshine the day,' said Robinton, rising to take Sharra's hand warmly in his. She laughed at his outrageous compliment. Though she was a tall girl, she had to stand on tiptoe to plant a kiss on his cheek.

'Has everyone made Zurg markedly richer to-day?' he added, admiring her new dress. 'Even Master Norist,' she whispered in his ear, giggling as she indicated with a nod of her head where the Masterglass-smith could be seen in the crowd, resplendent in red and yellow. 'Did anyone have the nerve to tell him how much Zurg's craft has been enhanced by the Abomination's data?' Robinton let out a bellow of laughter, beginning to feel happier in spite of Lytol's machinations. Then she took an admiring pinch of his gracefully belled deep-blue sleeve. 'I see you endured the fittings and pinnings, too.'

'I was excused them,' Robinton said loftily. 'Master Zurg has had my measurements all these years and presented me these gladrags as a token of his Hall's appreciation for time well spent with Aivas.'

Sharra affected a shocked expression. 'And here I thought you were Pern's most honest man.'

'Not even Lytol is,' and Robinton gestured to the former Ruathan Warder's back, for Lytol was just entering Tillek's Great Hall with Jaxom. 'But then Lytol, as a former weaver, has always been particular in matters of dress.'

'I wish he'd managed to install that particularity in Jaxom,' and Sharra sniffed. 'I'd chosen such a beautiful fabric, one of the new brocades in marvellous dark blue-green and he never managed a single fitting.'

'I fear he fit in other things,' Robinton replied, unable to forego the wordplay.

'Oh, you!' And Sharra rolled her eyes dramatically, laughing at his whimsy.

A singularly lovely ripple of laughter, Robinton thought, grinning back at her. Zair, watching everything from the Harper's shoulder, chirped agreement.

Just then the Tillek steward pulled shut the great Hold doors with a finality that echoed across the forecourt. The Harper and Sharra were close enough to hear the clang as the lock was spun shut. Conversation was momentarily stilled but the distinctive noise was also the signal for the kitchen doors to open. Drudges streamed out, carrying trays of *klah*, chilled fruit juices and finger foods to ease the tedium of awaiting the decision.

The clang signalled the Lords Holder within the Great Hall to take their places at the round table. Before them were fine glasswares and small pitchers of *klah*, wine beakers and bowls of succulent fruits.

The night before Jaxom had been the object of a special meeting which included the Benden Weyrleaders, Lytol, Master Robinton, D'ram, and Sebell. He was the youngest Lord Holder and while he was as capable as any of the much older men, perhaps more so than some, to manage a Hold efficiently, he was not yet forgiven his age.

'Especially,' Sebell continued, holding Jaxom's eyes with an apologetic glance, 'as you're working so closely with Aivas.'

'That figures,' Jaxom said with deep contempt. 'And just how many of the oldsters refer to Aivas as the Abomination?'

Grinning at the epithet, Sebell winked at Jaxom. 'The ones you'd expect: Corman, Sangel, Nessel, Sigomal, Begamon.'

'Five, huh?' Jaxom replied. 'That means no clear mandate for Ranrel and I'll be stuck all day in Council.'

'With little to say,' Lytol added grimly.

Jaxom threw up his hands and, jumping from his chair, began to pace the room. 'And how much longer do I have to play the idiot before my opinions,' and he jabbed a thumb into his chest, 'bear any weight?'

'It's what you don't say that will bear weight on this occasion,' Lytol replied crisply.

'Lytol!' Robinton said warningly, raising an eyebrow at the old Warder. 'His actions speak louder than words . . .'

'Even if they do get me deeper into trouble with those hidebound relics,' Jaxom said bitterly. 'All right, all right,' he added, spreading his hands to pacify the others before he received another lecture. 'I *appreciate* the circumstances. I'll content myself with voting as I see fit. I'll be polite when they cast aspersions on Aivas and all we're doing but, by the first Egg, I know more about Hold precedents and procedures than they've forgotten.'

Although he had not mentioned that meeting to Sharra, it still rankled: rankled more because the climate against Aivas, and himself, was so changeable.

With a suitably dignified reserve, Jaxom seated himself between Lord Groghe of Fort and Asgenar of Lemos. He was not of a temperament to hold a grudge or keep a sulk, so he was amused that the known pro-Ranrel group had ranged themselves together in one quadrant of the table. Predictably, the supporters of Blesserel and Terentel had also seated themselves in blocks, though he wasn't sure how many supported which older son.

He nodded pleasantly to those opposite him – Sangel of Boll, Nessel of Crom, Laudey of Igen, Sigomal of Bitra, and Warbret of Ista: the ones reputed to favour Blesserel, the eldest son of Oterel. Begamon of Nerat, Corman of Keroon and, surprisingly, Toric of Southern were said to prefer Terentel. Toric was probably being perverse since he didn't know any of Oterel's sons well enough to have made a value judgement. Enough for Toric that his sister's husband was for Ranrel along with Benden, Nerat, Telgar and Lemos.

Jaxom took a deep breath, determined to be on his best behaviour no matter how sorely he was tempted to *explain* to some of the old idiots. He picked up the *klah* pitcher, glancing courteously at Groghe with an offer to pour which Groghe declined with a nod of his head. The portly Lord

217

Holder was pulling at his pursed lips as he looked about the table, though his glance, Jaxom noticed, seemed to veer back to Toric.

Bronzed, with hair bleached almost blond by the southern suns, Toric was quite a contrast to the older Lords on either side of him. By comparison, Sangel looked more wizened than ever and Nessel desiccated. On Nessel's other side, Laudey of Igen, his face as tanned as Toric's, looked the healthiest of the group.

'D'you think Toric'll support Ranrel?' Groghe asked, shielding his mouth as he bent toward Jaxom.

Jaxom gave a slight shake of his head and replied with equal discretion. 'Toric's been in a perverse state of mind ever since Denol went to the Big Island two Turns back. Then, too, Ranrel used Hamian's material and Toric's annoyed with his brother, furious with the dragonriders for not assisting him in ousting Denol from the Big Island. So, since I've made no bones about preferring Ranrel and I'm a dragonrider, Toric is making his protest public.'

Groghe gave a snort. 'He's making too much of this Denol affair.'

'You tell him then, Lord Groghe. As I understand the tradition of Holding, he doesn't lose the island no matter who's improving it – it remains incontrovertibly his as part of his Hold grant. No-one can usurp his title to it. Especially not someone like Denol.'

Groghe swivelled round in his chair to gaze with some astonishment at Jaxom. 'Are you sure of that? I mean, about the Holding? That no-one can supersede his claim?'

'Of course I am,' and Jaxom grinned slyly, 'that sort of irrevocable grant is mentioned in the settlers' Charter. And, remarkably enough, Pern still operates, and enforces, the rules and restrictions of that Charter, even if half the world doesn't know it. So, once given, a grant can't be rescinded. It can't even be ceded out of the Bloodline of the original grantee. When the last of the Bloodline dies, challenge decides the new Holder.' Jaxom noticed how grimly Groghe smiled at that reminder of how F'lar and Fax had duelled to make Jaxom the heir to Ruatha Hold. 'Toric was awarded those specific southern lands in compensation for Holding during the Oldtimers' incumbency of Southern Weyr. If you'll remember, the Big Island is within the borders of that Grant. No act of Denol's can alter Toric's title to the Island.'

'Even if Toric's not put his own holders there?'

Jaxom grinned. 'When Denol first came south, he agreed to hold for Toric. He can't disavow that. I'm sure he thought that because others have been granted, mind you, granted the right to hold in their own names, he could simply cross the water and claim the Big Island. It doesn't work that way.' Jaxom was rather pleased to note the respect in Groghe's eyes as he explained the ramifications. He'd always been lucky to have the Fort Holder's good opinion but he felt that he had reinforced that today. He'd rather have Groghe's approval than any of the other's so this little conversation was doing much to restore his pride. 'Meantime, Denol's been improving the place with every cot and shed he's built, every crop he's planted. In fact,' and Jaxom's grin was slightly wicked, 'if Toric gave Idarolan the word, Denol's marketable goods could be collected and sold north but the profit would be credited to Toric!'

'Well, that would solve that problem, surely.'

'Yes, but Toric's not listening, and certainly not reading any messages from Landing,' Jaxom said ruefully.

'Hmmm, yes,' and Groghe pensively fingered his full lower lip. 'Well, he'll listen to me, by the first Egg! Best thing about getting old is that you've got the authority to make people listen to you.' Groghe nodded his head sharply, emphasizing his remark.

Jaxom did not grin nor did he add that getting older did not always give a person something worth listening to. But Groghe was more open minded than some of his contemporaries, for which Jaxom often gave thanks.

'Heard you went upstairs again yesterday?' Groghe added. 'What'd you do this time?'

'Closed some doors,' Jaxom said with a diffident shrug. He'd also spent a long time, Ruth beside him, looking down at the splendour of Pern as seen from space. Not even Piemur, harper-trained as he was, had been able to adequately describe the scene: certainly not how deeply it affected him. Nor had Jaxom, though he'd managed to tell Sharra something of the grandeur he'd seen and the awe he'd felt. He kept the vision solidly in one bedazzled corner of his mind. If only more of these Lords Holder would see, they'd stop their petty bickerings.

'Closed doors? Was that all?' Groghe asked in surprise.

'There's a lot to be done to set the *Yokohama* to rights. It's dangerous up there,' Jaxom replied. That was a slight exaggeration but Aivas had steadily repeated the fact that space was a hostile environment and humans must learn the necessary cautions to prevent accidents. 'When the safety measures do check out, it would be our pleasure, Ruth's and mine, to take you up there.'

Groghe was clearly astonished and hemmed and hawed nervously. 'We'll see, lad, we'll see,' he finally said.

So Jaxom nodded and asked amiably, 'Do you think this will take all morning?'

'Likely to.' On this safer topic, Groghe gave a snort and then covered his mouth so that only Jaxom would hear his next comment. 'Sigomal needs Blesserel to be confirmed or he'll never get his money. That young fellow was gambling on succeeding and having the Hold's mark-coffers at his disposal.'

Jaxom had already suspected that Oterel's oldest son was heavily in debt to the Bitran Holder.

'Does Terentel have any support?' Jaxom found it hard to imagine who. Some people are losers: Terentel was one.

'Actually,' and Groghe's eyebrows went up in surprise, 'I believe Begamon will support him. Corman, too, but probably only because he dislikes Blesserel and is feeling testy about the amount of interest in the Landing projects. He's still not convinced.'

'No one from Keroon Hold itself is involved but enough from the minor holds so that no-one at Landing's worried overmuch about his opposition,' Jaxom replied. 'Keroon's more agriculturally oriented anyway.'

'And Corman's a stubborn old fool,' Groghe added, eyeing Jaxom critically.

Jaxom contented himself to a grin. Then Asgenar touched his arm and he turned to his right.

'Larad says that we have Deckter of Nabol who, of us all, appreciates Ranrel's harbour repairs, ourselves, you and Toronas. Which way will Lytol go?'

Jaxom gave a shrug. 'Where his conscience leads him.'

'Then he'll be for Ranrel,' Asgenar said smoothly. 'We think Bargen of High Reaches is with us, too.'

'Really? I'd've thought he'd go with the other . . . ah . . . older Lords.'

'He was impressed with Aivas, remember. He's got an odd twist of mind and wouldn't hold with Blesserel's profligacy or Terentel's apathy.'

'That gives Ranrel eight votes on the first ballot. Not bad. Maybe it won't take too long after all.'

'How did yesterday go for you?'

'Easy enough,' Jaxom replied diffidently, 'just had to close the cargo bay doors.'

'Doors, huh?' Then Asgenar leaned closer. 'What was it like, Jaxom, bringing Sallah Telgar back?'

Asgenar's soft words reached only his ears but he felt himself go rigid in surprise. He hadn't thought Asgenar had a penchant for the macabre.

'I've been sent on some odd errands now and then, Asgenar,' he replied, 'but that was the most unusual.'

'Aivas said she'd've been frozen as she died. Could you see her face? What did she look like?'

'We could see nothing,' Jaxom lied. Even from Larad, Sallah's descendant, such morbid curiosity would have been unacceptable. 'The face plate of the helmet was clouded.'

Asgenar seemed disappointed. 'I just wondered if she looked anything like we do.'

Jaxom gave a snort. 'Of course she did. All the settlers were humans, just like us. What were you expecting her to be?'

'I don't know but I . . .' Asgenar faltered.

Jaxom was exceedingly glad that Lytol took that moment to call the meeting to order. In his position as the retired Lord Holder of Ruatha, Lytol had been chosen as the meeting's arbiter. He was also still entitled to vote, as a mark of respect for his probity and integrity in raising Ruatha's heir to his majority.

'We know why we're here and that the accession to this Hold has been challenged by the legitimate sons of the late Oterel. Proposing themselves, as is their right, are Blesserel, Terentel and Ranrel.'

'Get on with it, Lytol,' Groghe said, testily flapping his fingers at the man. 'Put it to a vote and let's see where we stand.'

Lytol regarded Groghe a moment. 'There are procedures and we will adhere to them.'

'Thought you'd plunged headlong into all the new ways,' Sangel said sarcastically.

Lytol regarded the Boll Holder with narrowed eyes and expressionless face until Sangel stirred restlessly and glanced at Nessel for support. With a slight smile, Nessel turned to his right-hand neighbour, Laudey, and murmured something.

Imperturbably, Lytol continued: 'You might be interested to note that the manner in which this Council conducts the business at hand has not changed since it was first instituted twenty-five hundred Turns ago. The Charter was carefully promulgated and every contingency addressed. We will go on as usual.'

Warbret of Ista looked surprised and, covering his lower face, leaned to Laudey to make a comment. Laudey's disapproving expression did not alter.

'If there are no further comments,' Lytol said, having scanned the faces around the table, 'let us cast the first vote. I do not need to remind anyone at this table that twelve votes are required to confirm a candidate. Signify your choice by number: one for Blesserel, two for Terentel and three for Ranrel.'

When he resumed his seat, he picked up the ink pen and, shielding the pad with one hand, made a brief inscription. Folding the sheet, he tore it from its glued backing.

Jaxom noted that everyone at the table was similarly employed and wondered if any of them realized that they were using 'new' products to exercise their traditional franchise.

The votes were passed around to Lytol who mixed them up even as he received them so the order in which he then opened them would not indicate the origin. He sorted them in three neat piles, one much thicker than the others. Meticulously he counted each pile before announcing the result.

'For Blesserel, five votes, for Terentel, three, for Ranrel, seven. No clear majority.'

Jaxom inhaled a long breath. As he expected, but seven on the first ballot was a minor triumph for Ranrel. Lytol made a wad of the voting papers and put them in the brazier, watching them burn before he again rose to his feet.

'Who will speak for Blesserel, the eldest?' Lytol asked as required.

Jaxom slumped down into the heavy chair, glad of the cushions that gave him a small measure of comfort. He hated this tedious part of the proceedings: his stomach had a tendency to roil through speechifyings. The older Lords would go on and on, given an opportunity. Then he remembered his covert role.

'Ruth, please tell Master Robinton that the vote went seven to Ranrel, five to Blesserel and three to Terentel, and I'm reasonably sure Toric voted for Terentel. He can't be serious but he can be a nuisance,' Jaxom told his weyrmate.

I told the Harper. He expected this outcome.

'We both did but it's going to be a long day. Are you comfortable in the sun?'

I am! It is a fine day.

'For you!'

There will be time for feasting and dancing later. Now you must be Lord Holder.

Hastily Jaxom turned his inadvertent chuckle into a cough and reached for his cup, displaying an innocent expression when frowns were directed at him. He nodded apologetically at Sangel for interrupting his measured remarks supporting Blesserel's claim. Then Begamon rose and, in rather disjointed comments, tried to sway votes in favour of Terentel. Privately Jaxom thought anyone else

223

would have done better for Terentel than the Neratian Holder.

The second vote proved that, indeed, Terentel lost two supporters, who had both gone over to Blesserel. The eldest son polled seven votes while Ranrel received eight. As before, Lytol burned the papers. Too close, and Jaxom tried to stop his leg from jiggling for that habit was a sure sign to anyone of his inner tension.

Groghe signalled that he wished to speak and Lytol consented.

'I'm not the oldest of you but I have held Fort for longer than any of you others, bar Sangel,' and Groghe accorded the Boll Holder a bow and a smile. 'Tillek was the third Hold to be established . . .'

'Word of the Abomination?' Sangel asked slyly.

'Aivas has now seen, and restored, the records of every Hold which can scarcely be called an abominable duty – boring, probably, if your ancestors enscribed as much trivia as mine did . . .'

'What's your point, Groghe?' Laudey asked in a testy voice.

'My point is that James Tillek who founded this Hold was a forward-looking man who charted the coastline and started the first Fish Hall. Tillek has always been the safest harbour on the western coast, with the biggest fleet and more Masters sailing: its Lords Holder have always encouraged and assisted our fishermen. Ranrel thought enough of his heritage to take a journeyman's knot from the Fisherman's Hall . . .'

'He did that because Oterel threw him out of Hold,' Sangel retaliated.

'Order!' Lytol's voice boomed out with unaccustomed force and Sangel subsided.

'Be that as it may, he's certainly the only one of Oterel's sons who's ever done a day's hard work. I think he deserves to Hold now. Fort'll support him as Tillek's Holder in every way it can, so we will!'

Murmurs of 'well-said' caused Groghe to flush with pleasure as he seated himself.

Larad then asked to speak and did so concisely, adding

that in his last months Oterel had been too ill to attend
to many matters but the only one of his sons to take
an interest in Hold management had been Ranrel. If
Blesserel however, or Terentel, had done anything to take
Hold in their father's name, he would like to hear of
it.

'Clever point,' Jaxom murmured to Asgenar beside him.

Sigomal asked to be recognized.

'Blesserel had the onerous task of caring for his ailing
father, scrupulous in all duties to ease Oterel in his last
illness. He is a man of integrity . . .'

'He pays his gambling debts,' Asgenar whispered to
Jaxom, 'when he could squeeze the marks out of Oterel's
purse.'

'. . . with four fine strong sons and a fine woman to be
his Lady Holder . . .'

'Ranrel's wife is not only a Masterweaver but considerably easier to get on with than Lady Esrella . . .' Asgenar
added quietly.

'Put in your mark's worth, Asgenar,' Jaxom said.
'Why don't you speak?'

'And ruin Ranrel's chances altogether?' Jaxom tried to
sound as if he didn't mind.

Asgenar inclined his head, accepting what Jaxom implied:
that he was the youngest of the Lords Holder and his
opinion not much sought by the oldest of the Lords.

Meanwhile Sigomal wound up his peroration and sat
down, glaring at Jaxom who turned his head to regard
Asgenar as he stood to speak for Ranrel.

'When a man does not wait for honours to be given him
but works with his hands and achieves a mastery in a Hall,
he has learned many of the skills needed to make a prudent
and resourceful Holder under whose guidance Tillek will
prosper. We can ask for no better qualified a man than
Ranrel. On all counts.'

'I'd heard,' Toric began, standing without benefit of
Lytol's permission, 'that Ranrel had quarrelled with Oterel
and was told never to show himself in Tillek Hold again.
Can a father's express wishes be so totally disregarded by
this Council?'

Bargen jumped to his feet, glancing belatedly at Lytol for permission.

'In my presence, Oterel retracted that statement two sevendays before he expired. Ranrel is the only one of the legitimate male heirs who has achieved merit on his own cognizance. At the last, Oterel was proud of the boy which is why Ranrel has my complete support.'

'But he did not name him successor?' Toric continued, an enigmatic half-smile on his face. 'And he had disavowed the third son.'

'Do you doubt *my* word?' Bargen demanded, scowling at the Southern Holder whose slightly condescending manner was almost an affront.

'Doubt doesn't enter into it, Bargen. The incident is recorded fact.'

'Which is why the succession has been challenged,' Lytol said, 'and the right of any male descendant to challenge the succession, no matter what bad feeling existed between father and son, has been upheld on numerous occasions.'

Groghe leaned across the table toward Toric and spoke in the blandest possible tone: 'I'm sure Lord Toric appreciates that fathers and sons may agree to disagree.'

Toric stared at the Fort Holder hard enough, Jaxom thought, for his gaze to have burned holes through the man. Groghe affected a shrug. Now, how had Groghe known that Toric had stormed out of his family's fishhold in Ista? That wasn't generally known nor would Sharra have been so disloyal to her brother as to mention it.

'But it is as Lord Toric has said,' Sigomal was saying, rubbing his hands together nervously, his expression one of specious regret. 'Oterel disavowed Ranrel and that should be noted. His challenge should be nullified.'

'Blesserel must owe Sigomal a great deal,' murmured Asgenar to Jaxom, his expression bland.

'Does anyone support Terentel's claim?' Lytol asked into the pause. When Begamon did not respond, he added, 'Then let us vote between the two remaining candidates: Blesserel and Ranrel.'

This ballot raised Ranrel's support to ten but, with

Blesserel still polling five, the requisite number had not been attained.

'I am calling a brief adjournment, my Lords Holder, for private discussions,' Lytol said and, rising, moved away from the table.

The others followed his example.

'We need two more votes,' Groghe murmured to Jaxom, Asgenar and Larad as they made their way to the tables where food was available.

'Toric has to have been the third vote for Terentel. I know Corman and Begamon espouse him,' Larad said. 'Is Toric hoping that loon Terentel will give him guards for that armed assault he wants to make on the Big Island?'

'Something like that but I've a word for his ear alone,' Groghe said, winking at Jaxom and grinning broadly.

'C'mon, Asgenar,' and Larad hauled the Lemosan Holder after him. 'We'll bear you out, Groghe.'

Jaxom took a plateful of the spice cakes he knew Lytol liked and served his old guardian, all the while surreptitiously watching the three in close conversation with Toric. He looked quickly away when Toric suddenly swivelled in his direction, an indecipherable stare on his broad tanned face. Jaxom wondered if Groghe had identified the source of his information. Toric then asked Larad a sharp question. Groghe responded, Larad added a few words while Asgenar nodded his head, a slight smile at one corner of his mouth.

'I think we just obtained one more vote for Ranrel,' Jaxom murmured to Lytol, being careful to keep his expression bland.

Larad and Asgenar stayed talking to Toric while Groghe made his way back to the Ruathans.

'That seemed to go down with no trouble, Jaxom. Clever of you. Though I don't think Denol should attempt to have a meeting with Toric when he finds out he can't make any profit for himself. Who else can we approach?'

'I'm not approaching anyone. Remember? I'm deeply involved with the Abomination,' Jaxom said with a disgusted snort. 'I'm not about to ruin Ranrel's chances by speaking up'

'You do yourself a disservice, lad,' Groghe said kindly.

'I'd rather not do Ranrel one, Lord Groghe.'

As Groghe turned away, Jaxom took the opportunity to inform Ruth what was happening, asking him to tell Sharra.

Master Robinton thought it would go that way, Ruth replied. *He asked have you told Toric? He didn't say what.*

'Groghe did, with Larad and Asgenar backing him up,' Jaxom replied. 'Certainly it's giving Toric something to think about. More'n I could get him to do. There's a recess on right now. The west coast contingent needs more* klah *to wake up enough to listen. I'll keep you all informed.'

Shortly thereafter, Lytol called the Lords to order again and asked if anyone wished to add or supply new information to the Council.

'Another vote, Lytol,' Deckter said, 'there is other business to be discussed.

Jaxom had noticed Deckter in deep discussion with Warbret and hoped for success in that area. Two votes were all that was needed – unless Toric decided to be more difficult than usual.

This time everyone appeared to be counting as Lytol sorted so all knew before his formal announcement that Ranrel had won the honours. Sigomal looked ready to spit nails, glowering at Toric and Warbret who had abandoned his cause.

'Ranrel has polled the requisite number of twelve votes and is duly elected to succeed to his father's honour as Lord Holder of Tillek.' Lytol gave Jaxom a warning sideways glance which the young Ruathan had no trouble understanding: he was not to make any premature announcement through Ruth.

'There are two other important reports to discuss in this Council. I now call upon Lord Jaxom of Ruatha Hold to inform us of any progress made toward the end of destroying Thread.' Lytol inclined his head courteously to his former ward and sat down.

Jaxom stood abruptly, catching the attention of the entire table. The phrases he had rehearsed so often piled out of his mouth and continued even when he heard someone mumbling imprecations about the 'Abomination's corruptions'.

'Having received extensive training from the Aivas, Journeyman Harper Piemur and myself rode Ruth safely *between* and landed on the bridge of the *Yokohama*. We completed the programming of the telescope for use by Aivas from the Landing facility and initiated a damage report on the space vessel. We retrieved the remains of Sallah Telgar which have since been suitably interred at Telgar Hold,' and he bowed deeply to Larad. 'The next day Ruth transported me back to the bridge. I then proceeded to the cargo bay area to close the outer doors which had not shut due to a malfunction in the remote closure program. Once the doors closed, I returned to the bridge and from there to Landing. Additional journeys to the *Yokohama* will be necessitated to improve the basic life support systems, namely, replant the algae tanks. Additional personnel must become acclimated to free-fall conditions and there will be several missions composed of different teams, using green dragons, in order to alter the telescope to maximize its use.'

'And just what does that all mean when translated into normal speech?' Corman wanted to know.

'That the *Yokohama* can be used as a base from which to attack Thread in space, Lord Corman.'

'So all the dragons are going up to the spaceship to attack Thread at a distance from the planet?' His sarcastic remark must have seemed as silly to himself as it did to the others for he flushed and looked away from Jaxom.

'No, that is not the plan, Lord Corman. The plan is to divert Thread from ever falling to the surface.'

'And how far are you toward that desired end?' Laudey asked, not quite as contemptuous as Sangel had been.

'There are still two Turns, five months and seven days before that end is achieved, Lord Laudey.'

'And I suppose that you're here to ask our permission to draft more journeymen from our Halls, more drudges from our Holds?'

'No, sir, we don't "draft" anyone,' Jaxom replied and couldn't help grinning. The problem was turning unsuitable people away from Landing without giving offence.

'And I suppose you're unhappy that those lower caverns

229

of yours are pretty much empty of beggars and layabouts?'
Groghe asked pointedly.

'And will they all stay usefully employed two Turns,
five months and however many days from now?' Laudey
demanded.

'Do you, or do you not, wish to be rid of Thread, Lord
Laudey? Lord Corman?' Jaxom demanded. 'Admittedly,
in two hundred and fifty Turns, *you* won't have to care
whether or not we succeed. But your descendants will!'

'Are you speaking as a Lord Holder or a dragonrider,
Jaxom?' Nessel asked in a snide tone of voice.

'Both, Lord Nessel!'

'Then we won't need dragonriders any more!' Sigomal
roared. 'What're you dragonriders going to do then?'

Jaxom grinned back. 'I think you will find, Lord Sigomal,
that you will always *want* to have dragonriders on Pern.'

'And how do you arrive at that?' Sigomal demanded.

'They do a lot more for you, and everyone here, than
rid the skies of Thread. Think on it, Lord Sigomal.' Jaxom
smiled enigmatically. Let them cudgel their brains over
that one. 'Lord Toric knows what I mean, I'm sure.'

Startled, Toric swung his piercing gaze to his sister's
husband and began to frown.

'I don't get what you mean, young man,' Sangel said in
some agitation.

'My Lord Sangel, I would have thought that was too
obvious to require explanation. May I continue, Lord
Lytol?' When he had received the nod, Jaxom went on.
'I will also tell you that Harper Piemur and I have seen
this lovely world of ours, turning in space, from day
towards night. It is the most incredible sight!' He knew
his voice trembled slightly but he wasn't ashamed of
the emotion that view had evoked. 'Once we are certain
that the life support systems – oxygen and heat – are
stable, I will take it upon Ruth and myself to bring
any Lord who wishes to the bridge of the *Yokohama* to
see for himself what a splendid world we live on and
how essential it is for us to rid ourselves of Thread
for ever.'

Jaxom looked around, inviting someone to take up his

offer. Daring anyone when his first round of the startled faces produced no other responses than nervous throat clearings and foot shiftings.

'I'd like to go,' Larad said quietly, and Asgenar held up his hand as well.

'And I,' added Lytol.

'One doesn't see too much of the north from the *Yokohama*'s bridge,' Jaxom admitted, 'but Aivas is hoping to repair the damaged portside viewers. That should make some of the east coast visible from space.' He looked pointedly at Toronas who, after visible hesitation, raised his hand.

'How much of the southern continent is visible?' Toric asked in a hoarse bark.

'More if we can repair the stern viewers,' Jaxom replied, delighted that Toric had responded.

'I don't see what good'll come from all this,' Begamon began querulously. 'Risking lives on foolish sundreams of destroying Thread. It's been with us for hundreds of Turns. And I say again, if the ancients knew so much why didn't they get rid of the stuff in their time? Huh? Why didn't they?'

'Aivas has answered that to my satisfaction,' Lytol said firmly, 'and every task we have undertaken since his discovery has benefited everyone on this planet.'

'How? Tell me, how?' Begamon demanded.

Lytol held up the pad, the ink pen, a sheet of the weather reports which Aivas had been producing for the past two Turns to the delight and relief of Holders, major and minor. Then he pointed to the ornate clock on the wall, ticking away the minutes of the meeting, and to the new clothing in which Begamon was dressed, made from one of Zurg's latest fine fabrics.

'I also heard that you've new power to irrigate your fields and portable stoves to heat your orchards during frosts,' Lytol replied. 'Not to mention the fact that your youngest granddaughter owes her life to Master Oldive's new surgical techniques.'

'They're things we can use, see, touch, Lytol,' and then

231

Begamon waved his hand over his head, 'not something beyond our reach and our ken.'

'Then let the things you can use, see and touch reassure you that there is more to be learned, more to be explored, more to be understood to improve our lives, to ensure our lives,' Jaxom said, speaking so earnestly that even the oldest, most hide-bound Holders listened with something akin to respect for his sudden authority.

'Thank you for your report, Lord Jaxom,' Lytol said smoothly breaking the long pause. 'Let us now address the subject . . .' When there was a murmur of disagreement over his method, he held up his hand, 'You will all have plenty of time to speak to Lord Jaxom after the business of this Council is over. The second matter to be brought to your attentions is a notification from the Mastercraftsmen of Pern . . .'

'Not *all* the Mastercraftsmen,' Corman said, jutting his chin out belligerently.

Lytol neither glared nor stared but he made Corman feel abashed at having interrupted so rudely. 'The Mastercraftsmen of Pern, with one exception, that of Master Norist of the Glass-smithcraft, notify this Council of their intention to form two new halls: Printer Hall, to be loosely allied with the Harper Hall but independent and autonomous, with three main Crafthalls: the main Hall to be at Landing, with additional installations at Ruatha which harbours no Crafthall, and at Lemos in conjunction with the paper industry of Masterwoodscraftsman Bendarek. The second new hall is to be the Technician Hall, loosely allied with the Smithcraft Hall, to deal with problems arising from the new equipment . . .'

'I'll say no to that one immediately,' Sigomal said, jumping to his feet. 'That's catering to the Abomination and . . .'

'There will be no vulgar epithets at this table, Lord Sigomal,' Lytol said at his most censorious. 'Nor should I have to repeat that the Mastercraftsmen have no need of your permission. You have only to abstain from the purchase of any materials produced by a Crafthall which distresses you. Since it comes to my notice that certain projects of yours have benefited from new gadgetry of which only Aivas could be the source, you would be wiser to refrain from uttering such arrant hypocrisies in the Council.'

Gawping, Sigomal sank back.

Jaxom managed not to smile at the Bitran Lord's discomfiture. One of the men who had tried to attack Aivas had been a Bitran but that was scarcely proof the Lord Holder had been connected with that attack. Bitrans hired out to anyone who would pay them enough to make the job worth their while. Still, this was the first time Sigomal had publicly labelled Aivas an Abomination.

'We will be duly informed when the new Mastercraftsmen are chosen and the parameters of their professional spheres set. Let me further remind the Lords Holder that such additions to the Crafthalls require no ratification by this Council since the Halls have, by long custom, been autonomous. This is a formal notification of intent.'

'Is that in the original Charter, too, Lytol?' Sangel asked nastily.

'No,' Lytol replied, not the least bit perturbed, 'the Crafthall scheme was originated shortly before the end of the First Pass by Fort, Ruatha and Benden Holds to preserve skills and educate young men and women in the various urgently needed crafts. Originally,' and Lytol affected a slight smile, as he glanced toward Corman, 'Ruatha Hold played host to the Masterbeastman and Masterfarmer until the wide plains of Keroon were explored and found more suitable to animal husbandry.'

Larad rose to address the Council. 'It is also worth noting that both Mastersmith Fandarel and Masterharper Sebell are completely within their rights to propose additional, separate Halls without even consulting other Mastercraftsmen. But they have done so and received full support . . .'

'It isn't full if one Mastercraftsman abstains . . .' Nessel took up the complaint in his peevish whine of a voice.

'Master Norist did not attend the meeting though he was duly notified,' Larad said. 'Both the Printer and Technician Halls will supply the special training now required and unavailable elsewhere. We have all benefited by the new machineries, especially clearly printed instruction books and records. For more people to enjoy these benefits, additional Craftsmen must be trained up in the skills.'

'Why can't the printers work under Master Sebell and the repairers under Master Fandarel,' Corman demanded. 'Why all this fuss to create new Crafthalls?'

'Master Fandarel is working all the hours of the day already, filling orders for new equipment,' Larad said. 'He does not have the time, or the personnel, to oversee a new Craft.'

'Well, this printing could be handled by your Master-woodsmith, Asgenar,' Corman replied. 'He's not over-worked.'

Asgenar laughed. 'He is, I am, and we still can't keep up with the demand from every single Hall and Hold for paper in the sizes, qualities and styles you all seem to feel you must have.' He shook his head. 'Master Bendarek has a Hall full of apprentices, only two journeymen, and no other Master yet. He needs every pair of hands he can employ but he can't oversee the printing as well. Paper-making takes all his time and energy.'

'Master Fandarel wished me to explain that specialist technicians will be required to keep all the new machinery operating at peak efficiency,' Larad continued. 'Right now we have machinery only a few people can understand or repair while others are able to operate, but not repair, them. Eventually, we'll have men and women who can do both but not right now.'

'Then why don't you walk before you start running?' Corman demanded with a snort. 'In my experience you can't race a yearling runner nor force an immature herd beast to breed or lactate.'

Jaxom started to rise but felt Groghe lay a warning hand on his arm. It took a great deal of self-control for Jaxom to obey that tacit command. He fervently wished that he could speak for himself but grimly recognized that the older Lords were not going to accept him as a peer. When he really had helped destroy Thread, would they consider him an equal then? Or would he still be classed as Holder by default?

'Machines *are* slightly different, Corman,' Groghe replied, grinning patronizingly at the Keroon Lord. 'Once a machine is built, it does what it was designed to do. When it breaks down, you replace the worn part. You can't do that with livestock.'

'No, damaged livestock can be slaughtered and eaten. Whaddya do with worn-out machinery? First thing you know we'll have piles of rusting scrap in every Hold and Hall. And probably the Weyrs too since this is all their fault.'

'Lord Corman!' Trembling with outrage, Jaxom wrenched his arm from Groghe's grip and sprang to his feet, his fists clenched. 'You may not disparage the Weyrs in my presence . . .'

He was only barely aware that Lord Groghe had risen beside him and clamped both hands on his left arm while Asgenar was on his feet, restraining him on the other side. Larad was loud in protest and so were Toronas, Deckter, Warbret, Bargen and, to Jaxom's immense surprise, Toric.

'Lord Corman, you will immediately apologize to this Council for that remark!' Lytol roared.

With ten Lords on their feet in protest to his aspersion, Corman had no option but to apologize. When he mumbled a phrase, Lytol icily demanded that he speak loud enough to be heard. Then Lytol stared at each of the standing Lords until they sank back into their chairs.

'If we are to eliminate the menace of Thread, it will be necessary to have the equipment, manufactured by our own hands which we can make, operate and service, with which to achieve that elimination. That has already been the ambition of every Weyr since Fort was first established. It is the end to which every Hold and Hall have all worked. If to destroy Thread completely causes some re-evaluation of ways and means, a displacement of useless or archaic traditions, the price is not too high for the reward of Thread-free skies.' Lytol paused a moment, as if surprised by the vehemence of his own rhetoric. 'There will be no mention of this incident when the Council is adjourned.

'Now,' and he continued briskly, 'let us show some unanimity of purpose and encourage the two new Halls. How say you, Lords? Write "yea" or "nay".'

Corman sat hunched in on himself, glowering, and his was probably the one blank sheet turned in to Lytol. There were two boldly printed 'nays' but the 'yeas' signified the approval which would be passed on to the two Mastercraftsmen involved.

'Who decides who's to be Craftmasters and pay for the establishment of these Halls?' Nessel wanted to know.

'Craftsmasters have not yet been chosen but there are suitable candidates. Empty buildings at Landing have already been altered for both new Crafts,' Lytol said, consulting his notes, 'and the additional Halls will be built by those seeking to apprentice themselves to the new Crafts. Anyone wishing to transfer to either the Printer Hall or the Technician Hall will need the permission of their Mastercraftsman and the Master of their present Hall.'

'What about those working without their Mastercraftsman's permission?' Sangel asked in his disparaging way and everyone knew he meant Morilton.

'That is an internal Craft matter,' Lytol said, 'and will be resolved by the parties involved, not this Council.'

'But what if we can't get glass . . .'

'There's no shortage of glass,' Groghe said, curtly. 'We buy what we chose from whom we chose. Simple as that! And there's many of us who patronize one Hall in preference to another. Always have, always will. It's only sensible, human nature being what it is.'

Master Robinton wants to know what's delaying the announcement, Ruth said to Jaxom.

'*Talk. The choice has been made but Lytol'll peel me if I usurp his prerogative.*' Just hearing Ruth's voice helped to calm Jaxom who was seething at the subtle, and not so subtle, currents. At least he now knew which Lords to watch: Corman, Nessel, Sangel, and Begamon. Corman was blunt enough to speak his mind but the others had been nursing their resentment and grievances and that wasn't healthy. Did it stem more from fear of Aivas or a stubborn intractable resistance to change?

'Is there any other business before the Council?' Lytol asked as procedure dictated.

'I have a question,' Toric said, rising to his feet.

236

'Yes, Lord Toric?'

'Who is to be Lord Holder of Landing?'

For once even Lytol lost his composure and gawked at the Southern Lord Holder who gave a faint smile of satisfaction.

'Certainly a place which seems as important as Landing cannot be left without proper supervision.' Toric sounded eminently reasonable but Jaxom almost guffawed at the shock registered on lordly faces. The expressions were even more indicative of which Lords felt Landing was important: Jaxom noted those who did not, confirming his guesses; Sangel, Nessel, Sigomal, Corman, Begamon and Laudey, though the Igen Holder seemed more diffident than antagonistic.

'You've not been keeping up with such minor details in the east,' Jaxom heard himself saying in an amused drawl. 'Lord Warder Lytol, Masterharper Robinton and D'ram, Tiroth's rider, jointly administer Landing and equably represent the interests of Hold, Hall and Weyr. The shared authority works well. You have always been welcome at Landing, Lord Toric.'

'Immediately the discovery of the Aivas was made,' Lytol said, firmly taking charge of this awkward query, 'a meeting was called on the site. The eight Lords Holder, eight Craftmasters and seven Weyrleaders unanimously decided that, in view of its historical significance and its current educational status, Landing would remain an uncontested area.'

Corman growled irritably to Nessel but when Lytol gestured for him to speak up, he morosely subsided.

'How much of an area?' Toric all but pounced on Lytol with the question.

Lytol regarded him in subtle rebuke before answering. 'The same area that was encompassed by the Landing site on the settlers' maps, of course.'

Toric flicked a grimace at Lytol and sat down, his enigmatic stare checking the expressions of those at the round table. Jaxom, scrutinizing him under cover of a hand on his brow, could not guess what thoughts might be going through Toric's covetous mind. Surely the man knew that further territorial acquisitions would be met with resistance from Hall, Hold and Weyr: especially the Weyrs. Jaxom began to regret that he had given Toric a solution to the problem of the Big Island: *that* had kept the man from looking eastward for over two full Turns. Jaxom sighed. Sometimes you solved a problem to create a half dozen more.

He was considerably relieved when, with no more ado, Lytol called the Council meeting adjourned. There were protests and reproaches from certain quarters but Lytol chose to ignore them, as was his right. However much Jaxom would have liked to storm out of the Great Hall, there was one more ceremony to be performed before he could.

'*We're adjourned,*' he told Ruth.

Lytol led the procession, Jaxom deftly inserting himself between Larad and Asgenar, grinning an apology at Groghe when he sort of insinuated his body ahead of the Fort Holder. Lytol gave the traditional three pounds of his fist on the door and it was immediately opened by the Tillek Hold head steward. Privately Jaxom decided that stewards must have some arcane instinct for the ending of meetings. Lytol nodded and the men at either side of the great doors wrestled to turn the metal lock wheel and hauled the halves apart. The bright sunlight was almost as dazzling as the finery on people crowding the steps. Foremost of these were the three contenders: Blesserel commanding a position in the exact centre, looking far too smug; a length to his left was Terentel wearing an almost imbecilic expression, while Ranrel just stood quietly, at the far right of the broad apron. Just behind him stood Master Robinton, Sharra, Sebell, Menolly and the Benden Weyrleaders.

Jaxom lifted his lips in the merest of smiles and saw the relief on their faces even as Lytol began his formal announcement.

'On the third vote, the requisite twelve votes was achieved,' Lytol said when the crowd's babble had died sufficiently for his voice to be audible. 'The Council has elected a new Lord Holder. Lord Ranrel, may I be the first to offer my congratulations on your succession to the honour.'

While jubilant cheers echoed off Tillek's granite walls, Ranrel looked genuinely stunned and none too sure he believed what he heard. Blesserel looked murderous and Terentel merely shrugged and, turning on his heel, pushed his way through the crowd to the nearest wine keg. From the fire-heights, the dragons bugled their congratulations and the air overhead was made hazardous by fire-lizards, zipping and darting, singing their high descants to dragon sound.

Lord Ranrel was immediately surrounded by good wishers, thumping his back, pumping his arms, shouting congratulations. Blesserel was surrounded, too, by Sigomal, Sangel, Nessel and Begamon. Jaxom didn't bother to see if Blesserel was apologizing or demanding explanations. Sigomal's face was frozen with displeasure and a cunning that boded no good for anyone crossing him today.

'Was it very bad?' Sharra asked in his ear as she embraced him. 'Ruth said you were angry and upset but he didn't know why.'

'I was and I am. Give me your cup,' he said, needing a steadying draught. 'Let's get to Sebell and Master Robinton. There're things they should hear as well. Your brother wanted to know who'd be made Lord Holder of Landing.'

Sharra rolled her eyes in dismay. 'He'll never learn, will he? So, what was he told?'

'The truth,' Jaxom replied. 'You'll remember we asked Breide to be sure Toric knew Aivas was an important discovery.'

Sharra wrinkled her nose, a mannerism Jaxom still found engaging. 'He was so livid over Denol occupying his island that he could think of nothing else.' Then she cast a sharp look at her husband. 'You told him about the irrevocable grant?'

'I didn't. Groghe did. We needed his vote cast for Ranrel.'

'He wasn't voting for Blesserel, was he?' Sharra was aghast.

Jaxom gave her a flash of a grin. 'What happens in Council is not to become public knowledge!'

'Since when is your wife public!'

They made their way out of the crowd who were waiting to congratulate the new Lord Holder and to the quiet corner where Robinton and the others waited for him to summarize the proceedings.

'My harpers, too, report resentment from those Holders, Jaxom,' Sebell said. 'I told Master Robinton and Lytol as much earlier today. And I've every apprentice with any wit whatever keeping his or her ears open here today.'

'It's almost a relief to have the dissenters identified,' Master Robinton said.

'Is it?' Jaxom asked sceptically for the retelling had depressed him. They had so much to hope for in the future – if they could only get over the pitfalls and trivial machinations in the present.

Sensing his mood, Sharra leaned against her tall husband and he allowed himself to be comforted. After all, they had voted Ranrel in despite the opposition. The dissenters were few in number, and all of them old.

Chapter Ten

Master Idarolan got legless before anyone else on Lord Ranrel's celebratory day. He rarely imbibed but, having the most to lose if Ranrel was not elected, had been under great stress. He had evidently started drinking at his Hall over the breakfast meal and continued all through the long morning until the result of the convocation was announced. Since the Masterfisherman was also extremely popular, his uncharacteristic inebriety was kindly ignored. When he lurched over to the courtyard corner where Jaxom, Sharra, Robinton, Sebell, Menolly and Tagetarl were seated, his gaiety was a welcome change from their gloomy conversation.

'There was no way,' Idarolan announced in drunken joviality, 'that we fisherfolk would have been happy to keep our Hall here with Blesserel Holding. He'd mortgage us, mast, spar, hull and anchor when we wasn't looking!' His exuberance was so infectious that Jaxom was not the only one to grin at his antics. 'I'd've moved me, Hall, Master, journeyman and apprentice down to that fine harbour the old maps call Monaco. Yessur, that's what I'd've done had anyone but Ranrel become Lord.'

'But Ranrel is Lord so you don't need to worry now,' Robinton assured the Masterfisherman. The Harper gestured for Sebell and Jaxom to find the man a stool before his legs buckled. Menolly and Sharra offered

241

him choice portions to eat in the hope of counteracting the wine.

'I won't waste time eating what'll doubtless return on me all too soon,' Idarolan said, waving aside their plates. Then he belched and apologized. 'Don't mind me, ladies. I'm a relieved man and I think that's what I'd better do, if you'll pardon the expression. Lord Jaxom,' and he leaned at a dangerous angle towards the young Holder, his eyes unfocused, 'before I continue my drinking, would you be good enough to indicate the proper direction?'

Jaxom signalled to Sebell to help and, with both lending Idarolan support, they steered him towards the nearest heads, just past the busy kitchens.

'I was fearful worried, I was, my ol' friends, that that Blesserel would take the honours. We'd be done for then, we would, we decent hardworking fisherfolk,' Idarolan rambled on. 'I couldn't've borne the waiting sober, could I? So I'd had to take a heartener, or three or four,' he added, grinning with a fine appreciation of his present state, 'but you know me, lads, I never drink on board. Never. Nor do any of my Masters . . . them as are on the Crafthall rolls, that is.'

Jaxom got him into a stall, Sebell deftly adjusting his clothing. Then they both politely looked away. Idarolan began to sing some sort of a sea song but, although his speech was clear for a man well gone in wine, he couldn't do more than mouth the lyrics in a hoarse bass voice. He took his relief for such a long time that, despite themselves, the two old friends locked eyes in amazement at his bladder's capacity. Jaxom's grin became a chuckle and then Sebell started to laugh. The pair of them were overtaken by mirth while, oblivious to them, Idarolan continued his wild garble as counterpoint.

Abruptly, Idarolan completed his business and sagged between them.

'Oops! Hang on to him,' Jaxom said urgently, just managing to throw Idarolan's limp arm across his shoulders as the man started to slide to the paving between them.

'He is gone, Jaxom, gone,' Sebell said, grinning broadly and shaking his head. 'It might be kinder to just leave him here to sleep it off.'

'Master Robinton would never forgive us. Slip into the kitchen, Sebell, and grab a pot of *klah*. We'll sober him up. Why should he celebrate only half a day? The best part's still to come.' Closing the lid, he eased Idarolan on to the stool, one hand on the Fishermaster's chest to keep the flaccid body from falling.

'Be right back.' Sebell slipped out of the stall, carefully closing the door behind him. Jaxom heard his boots scraping on the stone floor and then the outer door opened and closed.

Jaxom rearranged Idarolan into what he felt would be a more comfortable, or at least manageable, posture but the man was as slippery as a fish on a deck.

Jaxom adjusted boneless arms and hands on the man's lap, all the while holding his torso upright on the stool. The knees were together and the toes pointing in. Even in the soft court leather boots, Idarolan had big feet, Jaxom noticed for the first time.

Just then the outside door slammed inward, the brush of footsteps on the flagging indicated the arrival of several men; men shod in leather shoes, not workboots, Jaxom decided, pleased with his power of observation. Wishing to spare Idarolan embarrassment, Jaxom quickly leaned forward to slip the bolt of the stall door shut.

'Well, he's not the only heir. He's not even the direct heir,' one man was saying.

'We know that,' a second man said in a gravelly voice. 'His dam was only a third cousin, once removed, of the Blood. But the second cousin's alive, known to be of the Blood and it's her son we'd support in his place. The lad'd be dead easy to manipulate. Fancies himself as a true Blood.'

'Which he is,' said a lighter voice.

'Don't forget her son has sons who're in the direct line even if his mother disqualified him to the succession,' said gravel voice.

Jaxom couldn't figure out who they meant for there had been no question of Ranrel's lineage. He had his father's light eyes and the rugged features of his maternal grandfather. But the tone of their discussion about this

243

facile rearrangement of sons and true Bloods was distinctly unsettling.

'That doesn't disqualify him,' the first man said in disgust.

'He's weyrbred, not Holdbred, and a dragonrider so he can't hold.'

'His sons are too young to be considered, even with a warder. No, this local lad will suit the purpose. He only needs encouragement.'

'So all we have to do is arrange a convenient accident to bring the Hold in contention again?'

'That's all,' said gravel voice.

'Yes, but how?' asked the light voice.

'He flies Thread, doesn't he? And he goes up to the Dawn Sisters, doesn't he? That's dangerous. We just wait for the right moment and . . .' He had no need to finish his grisly sentence.

Incredulous, Jaxom shook his head, not wanting to believe this conversation. He was also aware of a paralytic chill oozing from his guts to his gorge as he realized that these men had to be referring to himself, Lessa and F'lessan. The 'local lad' could only be Pell, for his mother, Barla, was of the direct Ruathan Bloodline.

'I'm not going off good solid earth, I'm not,' the second man exclaimed. They were moving away now, their business completed.

'You won't have to,' the first man said with an icy chuckle. 'We've . . .' and the closing of the door cut off the rest of his sentence.

Jaxom realized he'd been holding his breath and expelled it. He was shaking. Lack of oxygen, he told himself, drawing in deep breaths. Idarolan groaned and began to slide out of a grip Jaxom had inadvertently relaxed.

'C'mon, Sebell. Hurry up!' If Sebell arrived *now*, he'd see who had just left the heads. A sensible man identifies enemies. '*C'mon*, Sebell!'

I'll tell his fire-lizard, Ruth said suddenly, his tone anxious. *What's worrying you? I can feel it. Is the fisherman ill?*

'No, Ruth, he's only very drunk. Ask Kimi to tell Sebell to get a move on. Though I think it's too late now,' he added glumly.

244

He hadn't recognized any of the voices and they'd not spoken in any particular twang that would suggest which Hold, or Hall, they came from.

He heard the door crash open. 'Jaxom? What's wrong?'

'You didn't happen to see three men leaving here, did you?' Jaxom called anxiously.

'What's wrong? Kimi said it was urgent. Which three men? Everyone and his cousin is packed into the court-yard.'

Sebell fumbled with the stall door until Jaxom threw the latch over. Anxiously Sebell looked down at the comatose Masterfisherman and then in astonishment at Jaxom. He had a pitcher in one hand, a mug tucked under his arm.

'Never mind, too late now,' Jaxom said, feeling defeated by circumstance. He also decided not to worry Sebell with a conversation that might well have been just disgruntled speculation. Talking was harmless, though he couldn't quite convince himself the conversation he'd overheard had been in the least respect *harmless*. He sighed in fateful resignation to that interpretation.

'What happened?'

Sebell's harper instincts were very good, Jaxom thought grimly. But then, the man was trained to observe, to hear the unsaid.

Jaxom managed a detached manner. 'I suppose one has to expect that not everyone is happy about Ranrel's lording.'

Sebell gave him a shrewd look. 'No, but here's one who is. Hold his head up. Maybe the aroma of *klah* will revive him. And we've got reinforcements coming.'

'I don't mind . . .' Jaxom began for he hated people to think him pretentious and unwilling to cope with an inebriated friend.

Sebell grinned as he passed the full cup of *klah* back and forth under Idarolan's nose. The man began to stir. 'Yes, you're good about such things, Jax, but his people are worried about him so let them handle it discreetly.'

Once again the door crashed open and several men entered in haste. 'Master Sebell?'

Sebell swung the stall door open. 'In here!'

The switch-over of attendants was quickly made and just

as Sebell and Jaxom swung out of the place, they heard the unmistakable sounds that Idarolan had foretold and grinned at each other.

'My timing has always been excellent,' Sebell said. 'Even Master Shonagar agreed. Ah, the music has begun.'

In the doorway, Jaxom hesitated, seeing very well why Sebell would not have noticed three men emerging from the heads. In just the short time they had been assisting Idarolan, the courtyard had filled up with celebrants. Indeed they had to squeeze past and around knots of boisterous folk, all merry with wine and stuffing themselves on whatever was on the trays the drudges were serving.

'When are you and Menolly doing a Turn?'

Sebell winked. 'Whenever the good Lord Ranrel asks us to!'

'A new song?'

'What else for a Lording!'

Jaxom took heart from Sebell's merriment. No use borrowing trouble. It had probably been just talk. And he'd just keep his eyes open.

The day wore better the longer it went, Jaxom decided by the time he and Sharra reluctantly retired from the dancing square. Threadfall was scheduled to begin over water but creep forward over the southern border of Ruatha Hold. Jaxom never missed that duty no matter how involved he was with Aivas at Landing. He obligingly joined in with T'gellan's Eastern Weyr when Thread fell there. It wasn't simply a point of honour with Jaxom: both he and Ruth were stimulated by the implicit danger of Fall and revelled in being part of a fighting Weyr: especially Fort. N'ton was an excellent Weyrleader, perhaps a little more flexible in dealing with his wings than F'lar, but equally as scrupulous in fulfilling his traditional duties.

'Look, Jaxom,' Sharra said, as they readied themselves to leave the Hold. She pointed upwards, to the mass of dragon bellies just visible in the glow of the myriad lights that had blossomed at sundown on every wall, hold, cot and ship. 'I'll bet that's all of Fort Weyr going home!'

Jaxom was trying to adjust the riding straps so as not to

damage Sharra's gown and spared only a glance. 'You'd be right about that.'

'Don't worry about my skirts, Jax, not after all the dust they've picked up from the dance square.'

Jaxom humphed and felt Sharra's hand ruffling his hair. Then he grinned for he had worried that she'd worn herself out with the dancing. If she was still so playful, she wasn't too tired. They'd get back to Ruatha in good time. *'Ruth?'*

I'll time it for you for good reason, but that isn't.

'Oh, and isn't it?' Jaxom swung up on the white dragon with a huge grin on his face. Sharra grinned back as she wrapped both arms tightly about him, trying to work her fingers up under his flying jacket to his bare skin.

You've time enough in hand. And Ruth sprang lightly from the ground, his wings making that crucial downward sweep.

'It's so beautiful!' Sharra shouted in his ear to be heard. 'Ask Ruth to hover. We'll never see Tillek look so beautiful again.'

Ruth considerately began to glide in a wide slow circle, head down as he also enjoyed the sight. Jaxom could see that the white dragon's eyes were sparklingly blue and each of the many facets of his multiple eye were tiny points of the bright lights of Tillek. The Hold, all the cots, and every ship in the harbour were outlined in radiance. There couldn't be a glowbasket left indoors.

Jaxom felt Ruth's sigh through his buttocks and, replacing this dazzling sight with a vision of Ruatha's unadorned heights, told Ruth to take them there.

It was not easy to climb out of bed the next morning even if Sharra had already left it to comfort young Shawan who had cried fretfully about dawn. The Fall was due in the early afternoon so Jaxom took a few more moments to savour the first morning cup of *klah*. Sharra came in with Shawan, once more a cheerful child. Jarrol appeared immediately he heard his father's voice and bounced across the bed, demanding a tickle, his cheeks still rosy with sleep and his curly hair mashed on one side of his head. The tickle duly administered, Jarrol followed his father as he washed and

247

dressed. By then, breakfast was ready in the main room of their apartment.

Jaxom sent Jarrol to request Brand's company. He could clear up any urgent Hold business that might have come up in the past sevendays of his latest absence from Ruatha. With Sharra and Jarrol accompanying him back to Landing in the next day, there were also details to be arranged for the absence of both Holders.

It was while Sharra took the boys off on her own rounds that Jaxom remembered the strange conversation in the Tillek kitchen heads.

'Tell me, Brand, what's young Pell, Barla and Dowell's son, doing with himself these days?'

'Learning his Craft from his father but he'd rather be in Landing.'

'Like half the northern youngsters,' Jaxom replied, leaning back in the fine wooden chair Dowell had carved for him. Wood was much kinder on the bones than stone. 'Has he any ability as a joiner?'

'He's capable enough when he gets into a task.' Brand shrugged carelessly. 'Why do you ask?'

'In the heads at Tillek, I heard a rather odd conversation. It could be no more than disgruntled supporters spouting disappointment with the decision. Pell would have a good claim to Ruatha, wouldn't he?'

Brand sat up, a look of consternation on his face. 'What are you talking about, Jaxom?' he scolded, much as he had when Jaxom was an erring boy 'There's not a thing wrong with you and you've two fine sons, and probably more to come.' He scowled then. 'What exactly was said? Have you told Lytol?'

'No, and you're not to either. This is between us, Lord to steward as well as friend to friend, Brand. I want that understood?'

'Yes, of course,' Brand hastily assured him, then waggled a finger, 'but only if you tell me what you heard.'

It was a relief to do so for Jaxom trusted Brand completely. He had hoped that, in the telling, the sentences would lose their burden of dread but Brand took the implications quite seriously.

'Could anyone plan an accident for you or Ruth up there?' Brand asked.

Jaxom gave a snort. 'I assure you that from now on, I intend to pick my companions carefully. But I don't think an accident could be easily contrived.'

'The two trips you've already made were not without dangers . . .'

Jaxom shook his head vigorously. 'Not with Ruth so close at hand. Not with Aivas in constant communication with me. Piemur as well as Farli and Trig were with us the first time. Sharra's to go up tomorrow – you knew that? Good. Mirrim and S'len are scheduled for the day after. None of them would conspire against me. Besides which, Ruth wouldn't let anything happen to me.'

You may be very sure of that!

Jaxom grinned and Brand began to relax, allowing himself a slight grin for he knew the signs of a Ruth-Jaxom exchange.

'Clearly they underestimate both you and Ruth and, now that you're forewarned . . .' Brand halted, frowning his eyes into slits. 'I'll have a word or two with young Pell. And young he is, proud of his heritage but not so foolish as to wish to become Lord by way of your demise. Besides you and your sons, there're also those three lads of F'lessan. Their claim to Ruatha is direct through Lessa, even if she did defer to you at your birth. I can't see the older Lords Holder denying their claim because F'lessan's a dragonrider. The Bloodline would be the important aspect so I don't think Pell would have a chance. At least with the present composition of the Council. Not that the circumstance will ever arrive!' Brand's conviction did much to assuage the niggling anxiety in Jaxom's mind. Then Brand squared his shoulders in a characteristic change of topic. 'That was quite an inauguration,' he said for, as chief steward of Ruatha, he had also been invited to Tillek Hold. 'Can't say as how Tillek Hold ever looked as inviting. We'll see some grand changes now Ranrel's Lord. Good for you to have another Holder nearer your age.'

Jaxom grimaced. 'Yes, maybe then I can speak now and again at these councils.'

Brand smiled broadly. 'I heard that Toric finally got your message.'

'Hmm, yes, even if it was Groghe who delivered it. Now, what have you for me? I've Fall after the noonmeal.'

'More or less minor details to be discussed, Lord Jaxom. Let's see,' and Brand lifted the top sheet from the pile he had brought with him.

As Jaxom and Ruth circled down to Fort Weyr, Jaxom once again wondered what had it been like for the first dragonriders who inhabited this old crater? Had they ranged themselves in preparation for their leader's commands as this century's dragons did, along the Rim, from the Star Stones to where Fort Weyr's bowl had crumbled in an ancient landslip? How many dragonriders had there been before they needed to expand into Benden Weyr? Whatever way had been followed, for Jaxom, it was always a breathtaking sight to see the Weyr displayed. And Fort was right now at full strength with this Turn's young riders taking their places through the wings. Green, blue, brown ranked in their wings beyond the bronze wingseconds, every hide glistening with health in the midday sun.

N'ton on bronze Lioth stood statuesquely in front of the Star Stones. Ruth answered Lioth's bugle of welcome and neatly took his customary position to the right of the Fort Weyrleader. N'ton gave him a salute and pointed down to the Bowl where the four queenriders were being accoutred with the flamethrowers.

A blue rider, returning from a preliminary sweep, emerged abruptly into the air, giving the ancient two-armed signal that Thread was imminent. N'ton acknowledged that even as the assembled dragons, almost simultaneously, turned their heads to receive firestone from their riders. The queens bellowed their readiness and one by one lifted from the floor of the Bowl and spiralled up to take their positions to the left of N'ton and Lioth. The big bronze was carefully masticating the first of the many lumps of firestone that he would chew before the end of the Fall. Jaxom offered Ruth his hunk and listened, as ever awed, by the sound of draconic teeth chomping on the phosphine-bearing rock.

Knowing the scientific process by which dragons digested the rock in their second stomach and belched the phosphine gas forth in flame did not in the least destroy his reverence for dragonkind.

Jaxom watched the process carefully for now and then every dragon chewed on his tongue or his cheeks and that would disqualify him from flying that Fall.

When Lioth had finished his chewing, he let out another roar, and N'ton pumped his arm in the age-old motion to take to the skies. With a powerful upward lunge, Lioth left the Rim, Ruth a breath behind him. The queens with effortless grace were airborne the next second. Making height, Lioth veered to the south east, and one by one the wings became airborne, manoeuvring into their fighting positions: three on the level above, three just behind N'ton and Ruth, and the third carefully on a lower level while the queens' wing dropped below them.

All human eyes were trained on N'ton, all dragons listened for Lioth's word. As often as Jaxom had seen the flights of dragons go *between*, as often as he had himself been a part of that transfer, it never ceased to thrill him.

'*Between is colder than space,*' he told Ruth and a breath later they were above Ruatha's southern border, the expanse of the river a silver snake below them. And to the east was the silver rain they had come to destroy.

The wings met Thread, breathing fire on the thick strands, watching them curl and twist in flame and drop harmlessly as ash on the ground far below. The upper wings streaked across the sky above them and far below the queenriders sent flaring gouts of liquid fire after those few Threads that escaped the upper wings.

Once again, Jaxom and Ruth were part of the ancient defence of Pern, falling into its rhythm, escaping its hazards, flicking in and out of *between*, weaving across the breadth of Thread, flaming swathes through the deadly rainfall. For this pair, it had long been a matter of reflexes acting apart from conscious direction of either partner.

They had done at least eight transverses of the Fall, drifting further and further south and east when a blue dragon just ahead of them screamed and ducked *between*.

Jaxom tensed, waited a heartbeat, scanning for the blue's return. He might need assistance. Jaxom had had a glimpse of the left wing entangled in Thread. Hundreds of lengths below his point of exit, the blue re-entered, his left wingsail dotted with Threadchar.

He's badly hit, Ruth told Jaxom as the blue winked out again, returning to the Weyr and to waiting weyrfolk who would drench his injury in numbweed, ending his pain. *One of the new young riders. There's always one who doesn't keep his eyes open.*

Jaxom wasn't sure if Ruth meant the rider or the dragon. Suddenly, Ruth veered, the riding straps cutting into Jaxom's left thigh as the white dragon evaded a thick clump. He did a reverse turn, almost on his tail and flung himself down at the receding cluster, blowing mightily. Righting himself, he turned his head peremptorily to his rider and Jaxom obediently offered more firestone. Chomping as he rose to see where his flame would next be useful, Ruth swerved to his right, once again throwing Jaxom's weight against the riding straps. Abruptly Jaxom felt the front strap stretch, leaving him far too loose in the saddle. Quickly, he grabbed a neckridge with his right hand, clamped his legs tight to the saddle and hung on tight to the left-hand straps.

Ruth reacted on the instant, halting mid-air, allowing Jaxom to regain his balance. A dribble of flame escaped his lips as he turned wondering eyes on his rider.

The strap broke? Ruth's query was laced with astonishment.

Jaxom felt along the length of it with gloved fingers. The worn spot was easy to locate, right below the belt clip, the leather stretched but not parted. It had been a very near thing. A little more pressure and the strap would have snapped, flinging the rider dangerously out of the saddle.

All too clearly now, Jaxom remembered the ominous conversation he'd overheard. Surely they could not have implemented their plan overnight? 'An accident', they'd said. What would be less suspicious than a rider's faulty harness?

A dragonman maintained his own riding straps, renewing

them frequently, testing them every Fall for signs of wear or strain. He cursed himself. He hadn't actually looked at his harness this morning, merely lifted it from its peg in Ruth's weyr, a place open to anyone in Ruatha. And to any casual visitor.

One thing was colder than *between* or space – fear!

'It's not broken, Ruth. But the leather is badly stretched. Let's get back to Fort and I'll cadge a replacement from the Weyrlingmaster. Tell Lioth why we're leaving. We won't be long.'

Jaxom endured a scolding from H'nalt, well deserved as it was, for when they examined the leather strap, it was plainly cold-hardened, brittle enough to stretch and crack. At least, the metal work of the toggles was bright enough to pass old H'nalt's scrutiny. Relieved that in this instance only wear was the problem, Jaxom and Ruth rejoined the Weyr and fought till the end of the Fall.

The first thing Jaxom did when he reached Ruatha was to cut new straps from the thick well-tanned leather made in his own Hold. That evening, with Jarrol's assistance, he oiled and sewed the straps on to the turnbuckles. He said nothing about the close call to Sharra who, fortunately, was accustomed to such an evening's occupation. Jaxom often mended riding straps in the company of his family. That evening, when he saw that Ruth was comfortably bedded down in his weyr, Jaxom put the mended harness on the peg but thereafter he concealed the one he was using as well as the double harness he and Sharra shared. Forewarned is forearmed.

Waking hours before dawn in Ruatha for the trip to Landing, Jaxom helped Sharra wrap a sleeping Jarrol in his warm flying gear. Shawan was far too young to be exposed to the cold of *between* and would be tended by his nurse during his mother's absence. There were enough enticements on this trip to pry Sharra from her maternal duties: she'd see first hand why Jaxom was so preoccupied with this venture; she'd have a chance to practise her profession and she'd be with her dearest friends, for Jancis had agreed to mind Jarrol with her Pierjan while Sharra was on the *Yokohama*.

Her two fire-lizards, bronze Meer and brown Talla, were even more excited than she was and were rebuked for their agitation by Ruth as he launched himself from the dark courtyard at Ruatha.

The weather at Landing was chilly as the southern continent was in its winter season but the land was never as bleakly brown and bare as winters in Ruatha. Not that Sharra didn't love Ruatha for it was Jaxom's home and where her children had been born. And she rather liked the variations of each season.

As soon as they entered the Aivas building, Mirrim pounced from where she had been waiting, chatting to D'ram.

'I'm ready when you are,' she announced to Jaxom and Sharra.

'Easy, girl!' Jaxom laughed. Her association with T'gellan had calmed her considerably but she tended to become zealous in her enthusiasms. Not necessarily a bad trait, just wearing on those also involved in the same project.

'Well, I am ready, with only the two barrels and tanks to be positioned on my green Path. And if we don't know what we're supposed to do,' she shot a glance at Sharra, 'we never will. It's so simple. Open the packets, add water and stir.'

'Not quite,' Sharra said, grinning to take the sting from her qualifier. 'It's the setting of the mirrors that'll take time and their positioning is crucial to the success of the algae propagation.'

'I know, I know,' and Mirrim impatiently dismissed that with a flick of her fingers.

'Is S'len ready, too?' Jaxom asked.

'Him!' And Mirrim gave an amused grunt. 'He's studying the photos of the bridge area in spite of the fact that we're supposed to get our placement directly from Ruth.'

'Who's to carry the water barrels?' Sharra asked and, taking Mirrim by the hand, led her away to check on that detail.

'Heard you told Toric what to do,' D'ram said, and the old Weyrleader's eyes sparkled with mischief.

'No,' Jaxom replied smoothly, 'Lord Groghe told Toric. Anything else I should know about Landing?' he added pointedly.

'Aivas will tell you what you need to know about Landing,' and D'ram shooshed him down the corridor. 'He's expecting you.'

Just as if Jaxom had not been absent for several days, Aivas outlined the schedule.

'There is sufficient oxygen in the environment sector now but the duties are to be carried out as expeditiously as possible. The fire-lizards are to accompany Lady Sharra and Greenrider Mirrim. They would be sensitive to any sudden drop in pressure or in oxygen level. It is also an integral part of these exercises to accustom as many fire-lizards as possible to the act of transferring from the planet to the *Yokohama*.'

'When will you explain *that* particular wrinkle in your master plan?' Jaxom asked as he silently mouthed the expected response.

'In due time. If you knew the answer, why did you ask, Jaxom?'

Jaxom batted both hands at the Aivas. Little escaped the entity in this room – even silent flippancy.

'Just checking,' he replied amiably, 'in case due time had arrived while I was gone.'

'There is a great deal to be prepared before that time is accomplished. Surely you, of all people, who have been on the *Yokohama* should realize that.'

'Two more Turns?'

'Five months and twelve days, with respect to the position of the eccentric planet. Meanwhile the fire-lizards can become messengers even as they are here on the surface: transporting items required on the *Yokohama* which are within the scope of their abilities.'

Jaxom kept his resignation to himself. They had no option but to proceed at the pace Aivas set. But what – eventually – did Aivas intend the fire-lizards to transport? He hadn't given up his efforts to get them to bring items to them, rather than go for. It was a piece with the difficulty of explaining to Farli to go to the bridge of the *Yokohama* to perform her drill on toggle and pressure plate. It had taken a dragon as intelligent as Ruth to appreciate the distinction.

There were willing hands to help them load Ruth, Path and S'len's Bigath with oxygen tanks and water barrels, although Mirrim fussed inordinately about how the tanks were situated on her beloved Path.

'You're wasting time, Mirrim,' Jaxom finally said when she insisted on padding the knots across Path's back. 'The load sits fine and we're not flying straight, you know.' Privately he wondered if Mirrim was covering up a case of nerves. Sharra was composed enough and so was S'len, though his face was flushed with excitement.

'I just don't want them shifting,' Mirrim replied stiffly.

'Shift they will. All the way to the *Yokohama*,' S'len remarked, grinning at her.

'Enough. We go! Now, Ruth!' Jaxom said and felt Sharra's hands work tighter on to his belt. Then he gave Ruth the mental vision of the bridge and heard the white dragon pass the instructions on to Path and Bigath.

If there were many things Jaxom did not understand about Aivas, the artifical intelligence had some problem understanding dragon capabilities. For instance, how much weight could a dragon carry? For which the answer was how much weight the dragon *thought* he could carry. An answer Aivas found specious – certainly not helpful when what was needed was numbers.

And for the question, how do dragons know where to go? 'Their riders tell them' did nothing to explain the process to Aivas. While Aivas did accept teleportation, he could not understand why telekinesis was so impossible a concept to explain to the dragons and fire-lizards. Especially when Ruth had indeed understood what Farli had not: to go to the *Yokohama*.

In checking the details of this joint trip to the space ship, Jaxom had asked Ruth if he could carry two riders as well as two padded barrels, one of pure water and one of carbonated water. Ruth's reply had been affirmative although, as Aivas saw the load, it was more than the dragon's slight frame ought to be able to bear.

'If Ruth thinks he can, he can,' Jaxom could only reply. 'And it's not that far.'

It might be easier, the white dragon remarked to his rider as he did so, *to just go* between *from the ground instead of lifting.*

'Is the load too much for you after all?' Jaxom asked, teasing.

Of course not. Just bulky! Everyone's set. Here we go!

There was a squawk from the five escorting fire-lizards and the next moment the tanks clanked against the bridge walls. Exclamations of surprise from the three newcomers punctuated their arrival. Ranged neatly in front of him, green dragon bodies occupied the remaining space on the broad upper level of the bridge. Jaxom heard Sharra inhale in astonishment. Grinning at her response, he skewed about on Ruth's neck and saw her wide-eyed, an expression of awe on her lovely face as she viewed the incredible vista of Pern spread out beneath them, framed by the vast blackness of space beyond. Meer and Talla, her fire-lizards plus Mirrim's three, Reppa, Lok and Tolly had made the successful transfer and were tumbling about, shrieking with delight at the experience of free fall.

'Oh!' she said, her eyes luminous with the dazzle she beheld, 'now I understand, dear heart, why you're so involved with this! Pern is so beautiful, so serene from up here. If only some of those contentious sour old men could see our world from this vantage point . . . Isn't it incredible, Mirrim? . . . Mirrim?'

Jaxom turned then to the green rider who was staring out the wide window with bulging eyes.

'That's Pern?' Mirrim asked in a cracked voice. 'Down there?' And a limp hand pointed a finger to the deck.

'That's Pern! Isn't the view great?' Jaxom tried to sound reassuring because Mirrim was patently overwhelmed. 'S'len? You all right there?'

'I th . . . think . . . ssso,' the other green rider said with little confidence.

Jaxom grinned back at Sharra.

'It is awesome,' he agreed with the nonchalance of one who has overcome astonishment. 'But stir yourselves.

Remember how Aivas keeps reminding us we can't waste oxygen.'

'Why not?' Mirrim demanded in her assertive way. 'All we have to do is haul more tanks up here.' With crisp motions, she unbuckled her riding straps.

'Careful now, Mirrim. You're in . . . ah . . . oops.' Jaxom broke off for Mirrim had forgotten how she was supposed to move in free fall and was drifting ceilingwards. 'Just hold out one hand, and ve-ry care-ful-ly push away from the roof. That's right.'

Mirrim had been too startled to make any outcry, as well as having no great wish to show to disadvantage. She did as directed and managed a weak grin as she grabbed Path's helpfully extended muzzle. The green was fortunately wedged fairly tightly between guard rail and wall and was not susceptible to the whimsies of free fall.

'Make every motion slow and easy, S'len, when you're dismounting. Hang on to a neck ridge or something,' Jaxom advised, and nodded to Sharra to follow the same advice before he detached his riding straps.

Keeping up a running line of encouragement and advice, he supervised the unloading. S'len crowed in delight when he realized that heavy tanks could now be shifted by the judicious prod of one finger.

'They're still awkward,' Mirrim said, poking one of the tanks towards the storage area. Then she grinned. 'T'gellan should see me now. But I understand why Aivas specified green dragons.'

'For once greens get the best assignments,' S'len added proudly.

'Green dragons are far more versatile than anyone knows,' Mirrim added staunchly. 'Can't say the same for green fire-lizards,' she went on, sourly observing the absurd antics of Reppa and Lok who were tumbling end over end overhead, chittering ecstatically. Meer, Talla and her brown Tolly had abandoned such nonsense and were plastered against the window, their wings limp in their utter fascination with the view. 'When this is done, can we go have a look before we do the algae, Jaxom?'

'We've time for that, I'm sure. I would construe it as part

of your initiation. Besides,' and he grinned broadly at them all, 'it's rather magnificent.'

As soon as the dragons had been unloaded, Ruth encouraged Path and Bigath to join him at the window. While the white dragon floated serenely from the upper level, Path and Bigath had a few problems that were hilarious to the observers.

'They get the hang of it quickly enough,' Jaxom said, watching approvingly. 'After all, they're used to flying.'

Once the oxygen tanks had been secured, the others could view the magnificence of the vast planet beneath them.

'Does the view stay the same?' Mirrim asked. 'I can't see Benden from here.'

'Or Ruatha,' Sharra added.

'I can make out Eastern Weyr,' S'len put in, 'and I thought it was pretty big!'

'That's what a geosynchronous orbit means, my friends, the ship stays in the same position relative to the surface of the planet,' Jaxom said. 'However, if you'll move over to that first position – easy does it,' and he grabbed Mirrim before she could propel herself too forcefully away from the window. 'We can see the coast of Nerat and something of Benden from the rear view screen, but,' he nodded to Sharra, 'Southern Hold's over the horizon.'

'Then don't let Toric up here because all he wants to see is Southern spread out before him,' Sharra said with a wry grin.

They had all managed to transfer without incident to the navigation console on which Jaxom called up the rear screen view.

'That's nothing,' Mirrim said in her usual blunt fashion. 'Too small.'

'Just a minute,' Jaxom replied, holding up one hand, as he mentally rehearsed the procedure for altering the view on the main screen. He tapped it out and was gratified to see the screen alter.

'By the Egg, that's incredible!' sighed S'len, eyes round with amazement. 'How'd you do that, Jaxom?'

Jaxom recited the sequences and S'len nodded his head, repeating them in a mutter.

'Now, I'll help the girls get the barrels to environment. If you'd rather Ruth and I accompanied you to the *Bahrain* . . .'

'No, no, that's hardly necessary,' S'len said, affronted, and started to fasten his jacket.

'The board on the *Bahrain*'s the same,' Jaxom said, 'if you want to see the views from there, though they're not much different from the ones you get here.'

S'len mounted Bigath.

'*Ruth, check their direction, would you?*' Jaxom asked his dragon.

Bigath knows exactly where he's going. Be easy, Ruth replied without turning his head from the window.

When Bigath and S'len had departed, Jaxom clapped his hands briskly.

'All right, girls, let's get these barrels down to environment,' Jaxom said, beckoning to them. 'The section we're using is only one level down. It would keep the bridge supplied in case of emergency.'

They got the barrels into the lift and down to the next level. This section of the level was sealed off by airtight doors so that the lift only accessed the environmental section.

'I thought you said Aivas warmed this place up,' Sharra exclaimed, rubbing her arms vigorously.

Jaxom grinned. 'It's warmer than it was, believe me.'

Mirrim's teeth started to chatter and she rolled her eyes and hurried to palm open the double doors just in front of the lift. 'Wow! This is bigger than I thought it would be,' she said as she entered the white room, glancing at the cabinets that lined one wall and the huge spirals of trays which would slowly revolve on their posts to allow each section the required amount of deflected light to propagate the algae.

'Come back here, Mirrim,' Jaxom said as he gently kicked a barrel out of the lift.

It didn't take the three long to set up the supplies. Jaxom offered to help prepare the trays with the padding that would be wet to moisturize the algal spores but the girls shooed him away. He watched while Sharra and Mirrim found the supplies they needed, the packages of algae and nutrients that must be carefully added to the fluid.

'Where's the con . . .' Sharra began and then spotted the console which had been meticulously covered by whoever had decommissioned this facility. 'All right, dear,' she said, and smiling absently at her bemused husband, flicked her fingers at him to leave, 'we've all we need. You'd best get on with your chores.'

Hunkered down by the shelves, Mirrim glowered when Jaxom made no move to leave. 'Git!'

Back on the bridge, Ruth and the five fire-lizards were still plastered to the window. Jaxom activated the link between the two ships, and located S'len as he was painstakingly soaking the padding in a tray, holding one hand to prevent water flowing from the barrel to float free.

Jaxom then settled himself at the navigation board, activated the telescope and began his day's chore. He opened the channel to Aivas and received the new sequences for the telescope which he was programming to scan the visible stars above Pern. This program would alternate with observations of the retreating Red Star.

By the time he and Aivas had double-checked the installation of the program, Sharra and Mirrim returned to the bridge, moving with considerably more confidence in the weightlessness.

'S'len's working away?' Mirrim asked. 'Time for us to do the *Buenos Aires* then,' she said, buckling up her jacket and nodding at Sharra to do the same. 'Aivas? Farli has turned on the life support systems there, hasn't he?'

'Yes, there is now oxygen in the relevant areas of the *Buenos Aires*.'

Sharra gave Jaxom a look that was tolerant of Mirrim's predilection to take charge of any work she was involved in.

'*Ruth* . . .' Jaxom began for although he did really trust Mirrim and Path, it was Sharra they'd be taking to the *Buenos Aires*.

If Path caught me looking in, Mirrim'd never forgive you, was the white dragon's reply and this time he gave his rider a doleful stare.

'All right, all right. I trust her or I don't. And I do. I'll restrain myself.'

So will I! And the white dragon dropped his jaw in a draconic grin.

When the girls were mounted on Path, Mirrim gave him a salute. 'Don't wait for us. We'll go straight back to Landing.'

Before he could protest, Path disappeared and so did the fire-lizards. Jaxom's fingers flew on the console, calling up the link to the *Buenos Aires*' bridge just as Path, with the girls and the fire-lizards, arrived.

Ruth gave such a scornful snort that he blew himself slightly away from the window.

'All right then, big eyes,' Jaxom said, closing down the console, 'since my work's finished, we can go back to Landing.'

When Sharra and Mirrim returned to Landing, Brekke and Master Oldive were there.

Brekke, the introverted wife of F'nor, had agreed to learn more about the treatment of wounds since she also helped Benden Weyr's Healers.

'Master Morilton delivered the petri dishes today,' she told them. 'Aivas says that if you are not too tired, he can elaborate on his last lecture about bacteria and how to overcome them with what he calls antibiotics.' She pronounced the unfamiliar word syllable by syllable.

Sharra and Mirrim exchanged glances but they were more exhilarated by their morning's work than tired. Sharra had been fascinated with the concept of isolating certain bacteria, and finding ways to combat infection by developing special bacteriophages.

So they filed into the laboratory room, exclaiming with pleasure at the sight of sufficient microscopes, one at each work station. Brekke smiled in her quiet fashion, for that was the day's big surprise.

'We won't have to take turns,' Mirrim cried. 'For my eye only!' And, slipping on to the high stool, peered through the eyepiece. 'Hmmm. If you're looking at nothing, that's what you see.'

'Please take positions at the microscopes,' Aivas told them in a tone that meant they should listen carefully. 'Not only has Master Morilton been able to deliver the petri dishes in which you may culture the bacteria of your choice, and the microscopes so that each of you may progress at your own speed, but Master Fandarel has contrived an ultra-sound device by which we can break the bacteria up so that we may examine their structures chemically. Master Fandarel has put to good use his studies in electro-magnetics. This is only one application but for you a very important one.

'The bacteria collected for today's lesson come from wounds . . .' Mirrim made a grotesque face. 'Wounds which you will have seen in your independent areas. Wounds that become infected. By separating the bacteria, it is possible to discover the parasites – mostly symbionts – which exist in the bacteria. By altering these symbiotic little parasites into pathogenic forms, making them like predators – you do recall the lesson on determining which is a predator and which is a parasite?'

'Yes, indeed, Aivas,' Mirrim said, grinning, 'whether you admire them or they disgust you.'

'You can always be counted on to remember such distinctions, Mirrim. It is to be hoped that such skill will extend into this area of your studies.' Mirrim wrinkled her nose impudently but Aivas continued. 'So, one can disimprove a symbiotic parasite, turning it into a predator, and have a useful organism to destroy that particular bacterium. This is often more useful than using antibiotics as you will see.'

'How many bacteria are there?' Brekke asked.

'More than there are grains of sand on all your beaches.'

'And we have to find every one of them?' Mirrim was not the only one aghast at that prospect.

'You will have ample chance for independent study to do so if you desire. This is, however, one step to take along the road towards the reduction of bacterial infections. Now, you will begin by culturing the effluent from a wound on a blood-containing medium, then isolating one kind of bacterium.'

Chapter Eleven
A Full Turn Later

'I suppose we should be grateful that there are still so many youngsters who'd prefer to be dragonriders in spite of the competition from Landing,' Lessa said wryly as she looked out over the sixty-two candidates standing in the Hatching Ground.

F'lar looked down at his diminutive weyrmate and grinned. '*Anyone* is available for Ramoth's clutches. Groghe was almost dancing when his youngest daughter was chosen on Search.'

'He'll be insufferable if she Impresses the queen,' Lessa said with a chuckle. 'Such a pretty child. Wonder where she got her looks.'

'Lessa!' F'lar said, pretending shock. 'Groghe shouldn't expect a clean sweep of the honours. After all, Benelek was elected first Master of Technician Hall and he's got another son and a daughter doing very well in Aivas' study group.'

'At least Groghe keeps his sense of proportion. Here he comes now,' and Lessa pointed to Lord Groghe who was leading the Fort Hold contingent into the Hatching Grounds. He was almost soberly dressed in comparison to some of the other gaudily dressed folk. Lessa nodded approval. 'And he's sensibly wearing boots,' she went on as she watched the sturdy Lord Holder striding out across the hot sands while others in his party minced, lifting their feet high in an effort to cool their leather soles. 'The Dance of The Hatching Ground Sands,' she added, stifling a laugh at their antics.

'Come, we'd better get to our seats,' F'lar said, extending his arm to her. 'And see if the insoles Master Ligand's so proud of really do insulate the foot against heat as well as the cold of *between*.'

Lessa spared a critically admiring look at her new red boots before she took his arm. 'It's the plant fibre he felts that provides the insulation for either extreme.'

Lessa had a complete new outfit in a deep wine-red for this Hatching – Ramoth's thirty-fifth – especially as this clutch included a queen egg, the first in twelve seasons. Even so, the great queen rarely laid fewer than twenty eggs and this clutch, appropriately, numbered thirty-five.

The eight Weyrleaders had already agreed on the necessity of the foundation of a ninth Weyr. The existing eight were completely full, with some two-year-old dragons still living in the Weyrling cavern for lack of space. While Weyrleaders were proud to be flying at strength, dragon dignity required independent quartering. Not only were there no more suitable sites in the north but so many people were taking up holdings in the vast lands between Southern and Eastern Weyrs that a new one should be located in the vast southern continent: preferably equidistant between K'van's Southern Weyr and T'gellan's Eastern. The grubs might protect the land and vegetation but dragons were needed to repel Thread from human and beast holds. A little reshuffling among the existing Weyrs and there'd be plenty of older dragonriders to balance out the young ones: dragons and riders who'd appreciate quarters in the south where the climate was kind to old bones and stiff injuries.

Lessa experienced a flush of pride for what had been achieved over the past Turns by an ex-drudge from Ruatha Hold and the bronze Benden rider no-one wanted to believe. She glanced up at her mate, noticing that there were even more silver strands amid F'lar's crisp black hair. The sun creases around his eyes had deepened, additional touches of ageing even if he seemed to have lost not a jot of his vitality. Maybe they should resign Benden to the energy of younger riders. With fewer responsibilities, they could devote time to all the splendid projects at Landing. Not that she thought she'd a chance of coaxing F'lar away from Benden until he'd eradicated Thread from the skies for ever.

F'lessan spent some time telling her that, once there was a breathable atmosphere in the cargo bay on the *Yokohama*, even as big a dragon as Ramoth would be able to jump *between* to view Pern from space. Lessa wasn't sure either of them wanted to go that far though she was more than pleased to find her ebullient son becoming a responsible and dedicated part of the Aivas team. She was genuinely fond of the only child she had been able to bear F'lar, but she had no illusions about him.

'Gone *between* in thought, love?' F'lar murmured, leaning down to her, amusement in his amber eyes. 'Groghe's waving at us.'

Spreading her best welcoming smile on her face, Lessa located the Fort Holder and acknowledged his salute. They had reached the tiers, already packed with folk here to see a son or daughter Impress a dragon or merely to attend what was invariably a magnificent occasion.

'Those new insoles work,' F'lar said as he handed her up the stairs.

'Hmmm, don't they!' Then she noticed Larad and Asgenar with their wives and their older children on the second tier and waved cheerfully at them. Master Bendarek was on the same row as they were but he and the recently appointed Masterprinter Tagetarl were deep in a private dialogue.

Lessa surveyed the ranks behind her, looking for Master Robinton and D'ram, a pair who rarely missed an Impression. And difficult to miss for they were resplendent in their Gather finery. Becoming so involved with the Aivas project had given both them, and Lytol, stimulation and new purpose. Why was it that these older men throve on the challenge while others, like Sangel, Norist, Corman, Nessel and Begamon rejected all that the new information provided Pern? No, not new, *retrieved* information. And

266

just at the time of a Pass when everyone needed such an infusion of hope.

Absently she responded to several other salutes before taking her place in the first tier.

It's almost time, Ramoth told her rider, swinging her head possessively over the queen egg.

'Now don't scare the girls, dear.'

Ramoth's eyes glittered in a rainbow gamut as she looked straight at her rider. *If they scare, they're not worthy of my daughter.*

'You liked them well enough yesterday.'

Today it is different.

'Yes,' Lessa agreed affably, versed in her dragon's whimsies, 'today your daughter Impresses.'

The humming had already begun as the massed dragons of Benden chanted their welcome. Feeling the sound along her bones, Lessa turned to smile softly at F'lar who returned it and took her right hand in his. This moving overture had become a special moment for them, an affirmation of their own love and a rededication to their own dragons.

An abrupt hush rippled down the tiers as the audience became aware of the distinctive sounds. Fire-lizards darted in and, though Ramoth followed their progress with her brilliant eyes, she no longer bellowed a warning if the creatures entered the Hatching Ground. They did, however, seek a roost on the very topmost ridges. After Lessa heard Aivas' account of the fire-lizards' reception of their huge cousins at the first Hatching, she had told Ramoth and both had been more charitable.

Some of the eggs in the main group were rocking slightly and the fifty-seven young males closed in about them, hope and eagerness mirrored on their clean shining faces. The five girls moved slowly but resolutely towards Ramoth, an immense form cosseting the mottled queen egg.

'Move back, dear,' Lessa said gently.

Not quite growling, Ramoth took one backward step, flicking her tongue over her egg.

'Ramoth!'

'Up to her usual tricks?' F'lar asked.

'Hmmm. *Two more steps, please, dear and do keep your*

tongue in your head. Such an undignified posture.' Lessa spoke firmly and, though Ramoth swung her head in a last show of reluctance, she did step back, five times, deliberately more than requested before she crouched down, glaring with orangey-red flashes through her faceted eyes.

Then Lessa cast an appraising glance over the five young women confronting the queen egg. Groghe's daughter, barely fifteen Turns old, was the smallest, a daintily made child. She had already Impressed two bronze fire-lizards and Lessa hoped that they'd contain themselves until after Impression was over. Ramoth might tolerate the creatures in the Hatching Ground but not flying about her head. Still, Nataly had been sensibly raised and her two fire-lizards had behaved themselves admirably since arriving at Benden.

Breda, the wraithlike blonde, came from Crom. Odd that Nessel did not object to Search, for all he opposed the Weyr's energetic support of Aivas. She was very quiet, a journeyman weaver and the oldest candidate at twenty-two.

Cona was Neratian and Manora had reported that, in the sevenday that she'd been in the Weyr, she had already been in the weyrs of three bronze riders. That was not a bad trait in a queen's rider: it was certainly preferable to a lack of sensuality.

Why the dragons had chosen Silga was a bit of a puzzle for the girl had been terrified by her first flight *between* and that wasn't a good omen.

The final girl, Tumara, was a cousin of Sharra's and so delighted to leave the isolated fisher's island off the Istan coast that Manora said the girl wore her out, trying to be useful.

Compliancy was a good trait but too much became subservience and that was not one of the more desirable qualities. A Weyrwoman had to be firm, fair and sympathetic with her queen. Not that this pairing was certain to become senior in any Weyr.

Much had to be done, besides finding a suitable place. Then, whichever junior queen in whatever Weyr next rose to mate would be flown by all unattached bronzes. The triumphant pair would only be temporary Weyrleaders until they had proved themselves. As fully three quarters of the other queens on Pern were likely to come into season over the next few months, this was as fair a method as any to determine the leadership.

The humming had increased to a frantic pitch and the first egg – Lessa breathed a sigh of relief that a bronze head and wing emerged – had split cleanly and the hatchling was up and out. A fine strong bronze, unsteady on its feet, of course, but able to extend its wet wings and swivel its head to and fro, trying to focus its bleary eyes on the figures before it.

With a shriek of triumph, it made a tremendous leap and landed in front of a stocky lad; from a Smith Hall in Igen, if she recalled him accurately. Sometimes their eager young faces seemed to blend with the candidates from the many Impressions held in this Hatching Ground over the past twenty-three Turns she had been Weyrwoman. Holding her breath, she watched that magical moment when the boy realized that the dragon had chosen him: ecstacy wreathed his face as he knelt to caress the imperious creature butting at him. Tears of joy streamed down his cheeks as he threw his arms about the damp bronze neck.

'Oh, Braneth, you are the most beautiful bronze in all the world!'

The audience let out a cheer and applauded while the dragons interrupted their hum to bugle a welcome.

After the initial Impression, other eggs cracked or split or crumbled to tip their inhabitants on to the warm sands, to match brown, blue and green dragonets with compatible personalities.

'Good, twelve bronzes,' F'lar said, keeping track of the pairings. 'We could do with more browns, only four, but the distribution of blues and greens is exactly right.'

Lessa hadn't been paying that much attention past the first three, for the queen egg was beginning to rock. Tentatively at first and then with considerable energy. No cracks showed on the shell, a fact which was beginning to worry Lessa. Usually the queens were impetuous in their arrivals. Then the tip of the nose broke through, both wing claws appeared and, as if the little queen had given a tremendous shrug, the shell parted vertically and she stood there, framed by the casing, looking about her with great dignity.

'Oh, she's a darling, that one,' F'lar murmured to Lessa. 'Just look at her, queen of all she surveys.'

With the unusual suppleness of a hatchling, the little queen tilted her head backwards almost to her spine and gave Ramoth one long look before she swung her head forward again. Now she regarded the five girls facing her and, daintily, stepped away from her shell. With a calm arrogance she swept her coruscating glance once more at those awaiting her decision. Lessa wondered if any of the girls was actually breathing at this crucial moment.

'I'll wager you a mark on Cona,' F'lar said.

Lessa shook her head. 'You'll lose. It's Nataly. The two are perfectly matched.'

However, the little queen was quite an individual. Now she stalked to one end of the semi-circle of the girls, giving each a close scrutiny as she passed. She didn't make it to Cona and Nataly for she paused at Breda, extending her neck and pushing her head very gently against the tall girl's body.

'That,' and F'lar snapped his fingers, 'for our choices.'

Lessa chuckled. 'The dragon always knows.' Then she gave a little gasp for Breda's rather plain face had taken on a beatific glow that transformed her into a radiant beauty as she knelt to clasp the little queen's head to her breast.

With luminous eyes, Breda looked up at Lessa. 'She says her name is Amaranth!'

'Well done, Breda. Felicitations,' Lessa called, having to shout above the applause that greeted the queen's Impression. '*Are you satisfied?*' she asked Ramoth who was staring dourly at the pairing.

The girl wouldn't have been Searched if she wasn't suitable. We'll see how she copes with Amaranth. This one is a true daughter to me. From his high perch, Mnementh added a stunning triple-noted bugle. Ramoth craned her head up at him, her eyes dazzling with pulsating colour. *You flew me well.*

F'lar grinned at Lessa for they had both heard the remark. 'We'd better get on with our day's duties, love,' he said, using that excuse to put an arm about Lessa's slender waist and guide her down the stairs and out on to the Hatching Ground sands.

In an unusual display of maternal approval, Ramoth followed Lessa and F'lar as the Weyrleaders helped Breda escort Amaranth out of the immense cavern.

'Never for a moment did I think I'd be chosen, Weyrwoman Lessa,' Breda said. 'I've never been out of Crom, not even to a Gather.'

'Did your family come?'

'No, Weyrwoman Lessa, my parents are dead. The Hall raised me . . .'

In an uncharacteristic gesture, Lessa laid her hand with tacit sympathy on Breda's arm. 'And you are to call me Lessa, my dear. We are both queen riders.'

Breda's eyes widened at the thought of such temerity.

'Who knows, my dear?' F'lar said, half-joking, 'you may be a Weyrwoman, too, one day soon.'

Amaranth pushed at the girl who had stopped in her tracks at such a prospect. The little queen urgently creeled her hunger.

Lessa tightened her hand on Breda's arm and led her briskly to meet the weyrfolk bearing the huge bowls, heaped with herdbeast flesh. 'It is a possibility, you know. But first, we'll show you how to feed Amaranth. Don't let her bleating bother you. They always think they're starving after they've hatched.'

Breda needed little instruction in feeding Amaranth, settling to the task with such ease that Lessa thought the girl had probably had to feed youngsters in the Hall that raised her. Life in the Weyr was going to be quite different. Breda had just acquired a huge family.

Then Lessa turned to discharge the less enjoyable task of an Impression day – comforting the unsuccessful candidates. F'lar had already begun that process among the young men and boys. When Lessa looked about her for Nataly and Lord Groghe, she found them in a family knot at one of the tables. Manora was there before her, serving wine, *klah* and fruit juices. Nataly was struggling to hide her disappointment and managing nobly, Lessa decided. Better than Silga and Tumara who were in tears with their families not really knowing what to say to console them. Cona was nowhere to be seen. Lessa wondered who had spirited her away but decided that her preferred kind of consolation might mend matters more effectively than any other available method.

She paused long enough to speak to Nataly and Lord Groghe and then moved on to help assuage the disappointment of Silga and Tumara.

The harpers had started to play and, although there were some long faces among the visitors, the music would soon brighten them. Weyrfolk were already busy with wine sacks and with serving huge platters of the pit-roasted herdbeasts and wherries. Food was so often a sovereign remedy.

Finally, once the sated hatchlings were asleep on their pallets in the barracks, the Weyrlingmaster permitted the new dragonriders to join their families. With the honoured guests present, the festivities went into full swing.

'A most positive young queen, hmmm?' Robinton said, sliding into an empty space beside Lessa. He raised his cup in a toast to F'lar opposite her. 'Made rather an entrance, didn't she?'

Lessa smiled and offered to fill Robinton's glass from the skin of Benden white that hung on her chair.

'Is Amaranth why F'lessan's been so interested in the vacant Stakeholds in the south?' Robinton delivered his query in the guileless fashion that told Lessa and F'lar that he guessed a new Weyr was required.

F'lar gave a knowing snort. 'He offered.'

'He's more in Landing than he is here,' Lessa added wryly. With three sons by as many weyrgirls, F'lessan had need to be absent from their entreaties. He had provided well for each of his children but he was no more ready to settle to one than any young, handsome, and popular bronze rider. Manora had even suggested that the absence of that young charmer for a while might result in one or more of the girls settling for an older rider in a more stable, lasting attachment.

Robinton cocked an eyebrow which suggested to Lessa that he already knew about the demands on F'lessan. 'He's an excellent choice of explorer. Is a Weyr situation the only thing he's to investigate?'

F'lar picked up on that. 'Why? Is Toric restless again?'

Robinton took a judicious sip from his cup. 'Not really. Now that Denol's tenure of the Big Island has been settled, he's making up for lost time with Aivas.'

'And?' F'lar prompted him when the Harper paused.

'He hid his chagrin rather well when he discovered just how . . . mmm . . . less than vast the southern continent actually is. Fortunately he's decided that Southern must have Halls of both new Crafts. I believe that he and Hamian had rather a vociferous confrontation over the filler plant Hamian's been developing as an insulating material.'

'The fibrous stuff that Bendarek's been on about?' Lessa asked. 'You knew that he's genuinely concerned about the amount of trees that are needed to supply the demand for paper?'

'Indeed,' Robinton said, nodding vigorously. 'I do see his point that a weed that grows rampant in Southern should be utilized instead of chopping down those magnificent forests of his.'

'I thought that Sharra discovered the plant and recognized its usefulness,' Lessa added.

'I believe that's Toric's contention,' Robinton replied, his eyes sparkling with mischief, 'that she found it on his holding while on a sweep for him.'

'Will the man never be satisfied!' Lessa demanded with some heat.

'I doubt it,' Robinton replied equably.

'Will we end up having to fight him for holdings in the South?' Lessa went on, shooting him a fierce glance for his casual manner.

'My dear Lessa, no-one, absolutely no-one, is going to challenge a man, or a woman, mounted a-dragon! And let us devoutly hope that there never is a point at which that is even remotely possible.'

'Southern Weyr?' F'lar reminded the Harper severely.

'Well, yes, now but that was not aggression: it was

abduction.' Robinton had good cause to remember the time Ramoth's egg had disappeared from the Hatching Ground and how very nearly Benden dragons had come to fighting the Oldtimer Southern dragons. Not wishing to remind the Weyrleaders that they had ostracized him at that point in time, Robinton held up his glass, looking plaintively at the wineskin hanging on Lessa's chair. She filled it for him. 'Mind you, I think you're wise to send F'lessan to explore the tantalizing potential of Southern. When is he going?'

Lessa grinned, lifting her eyebrows expressively. 'He should be there even as we speak.'

The great plains rolled on below F'lessan and Golanth as the big bronze glided on a sou'sou'west path, aided by the high thermals. A slight twinge of guilt marred F'lessan's happy contemplation of the scenery. He really should be working up those equations for Aivas who would be under the impression that the young bronze rider's presence was required at the Benden Hatching. As F'lessan had no wish to have to explain to Nera, Faselly and Brinna why he couldn't choose among them, he was glad enough to spend this free day obeying the injunction of F'lar and Lessa.

Golanth was so thoroughly enjoying himself that F'lessan decided it was unsuitable to belabour himself with unnecessary remorse. He had, for him, been unusually diligent in his studies: even enjoyed them. In truth, as F'lessan looked back over the past two Turns, he had devoted more time to Aivas than to the Weyr – save for Threadfall. He often flew as wingsecond with T'gellan and the Eastern Weyr and with K'van in Southern. He liked fighting Thread and he and Golanth were exceedingly deft at escaping injury.

One thing he hadn't dared to ask Lessa and F'lar: if he found a suitable site for another Weyr, was he in line to be Weyrleader? He dismissed that notion almost instantly. F'lessan had few illusions about himself: he was, however, a good wingleader; he understood draconic abilities, he knew which were the best riders in every Weyr and who were the most likely weyrlings in Benden, but he didn't think he was anyone's immediate choice for the next Weyrleader. And he was well aware of how such matters were decided: open mating flight for all unattached bronzes.

I'm big and strong, Golanth informed him with just the hint of boasting in his tone. *I'd've caught Lamanth that time if Litorth had not done that clip-and-run dive manoeuvre. He'd been practising with the greens!* he added in petulant disappointment.

F'lessan soothed his dragon with hand and voice. He'd been a bit provoked about that himself. Mind you, Celina was nearly as old as Lessa but it was becoming a matter of honour for Golanth to fly a queen and Celina was a nice sort. Anyone could get along with her.

A dust cloud caught F'lessan's attention and he asked Golanth to veer toward it.

I'm not hungry just now, Golanth replied as they got near enough to distinguish the rumps of fleeing herdbeasts.

'Get in a little closer, would you, Golanth? I've never seen any like these. Brown and white, and black and white. Big beasts. Nice and juicy.' F'lessan said the last coaxingly.

If they are big now, they will be bigger when I am ready to eat.

F'lessan chuckled. There were times when Golanth couldn't be diverted. He glanced at the dial strapped to his arm, checking the time it registered with his reading of the sun. Accurate enough. Aivas called it a watch – and F'lessan found that he had indeed watched, mesmerized, as the long second hand made its way around the dial. Jancis presented it to him on his birthing day. She had designed and executed the device for him personally. There weren't many of these and F'lessan had felt both honoured and elated to be the proud possessor of a wrist watch. In one of his superior tones, Aivas had remarked that digitals were far more reliable and accurate. F'lessan didn't care. Jancis had only made six: Piemur, of course, wore one, so did Lord Larad and Lady Jissamy; Master Robinton and Master Fandarel were the other lucky recipients.

He and Golanth had been a-wing for the past five hours. If they didn't sight their objective soon, he was going to ask Golanth to land so he could eat his lunch and stretch his legs. A six-hour stint during a Fall was one thing – you were actively involved. Flying straight to a new location was a different matter altogether: always tedious but necessary – unless you had excellent detail about where you were going or could grab the destination from another dragon or rider's mind. This was not the case today. Golanth was making good time, catching the thermals and air currents which increased his speed but it was a weary way to go.

Still and all, F'lessan enjoyed being first at something. He wasn't by nature an envious sort but it did seem that Piemur and Jaxom had the larger portion of luck with their discoveries. He was very pleased that Lessa and F'lar had entrusted this search to him. They could have sent one of the older bronze riders, or F'nor. Nevertheless, it was F'lessan and Golanth who were winging over the great plains, towards the huge inland sea which the settlers had named Caspian, to a Hold called Xanadu.

Suddenly, off to his right, the sun dazzled him, reflecting off – water?

'To our right, Golly,' F'lessan said excitedly.

A very big water, Golanth added, an opinion F'lessan did not dispute since his dragon was farseeing.

As he often had, F'lessan wondered if he would see clearer, better, farther if he had faceted eyes. Dragons had so many useful abilities.

I can see anything you wish for you, Golanth replied meekly.

F'lessan pummelled his neck affectionately. 'I know, big fellow, and I'm always grateful for your help. I was just thinking what it might be like, that's all.'

Golanth began to stroke the air, beating upwards. Thermal, he said cryptically and F'lessan leaned down against the great bronze neck so as not to impede his ascent. The young rider felt the alteration in the wind current and let out a triumphant yodel when Golanth flattened out and set his wings to glide on the hot air.

'And that's something else you can do which I can't. Tell where the air currents are. However do you know where the thermals are?'

276

My eyes see the variation of air, I smell the difference and my hide feels the altered pressure.

'Really?' F'lessan was impressed with the explanation. '*Been listening in on my aero-dynamics' lessons with Aivas?*'

Golanth thought that over. *Yes. You listen to him so I thought I should. Ruth does, and Path certainly. Ramoth and Mnementh don't. They prefer to sleep in the sun while Lessa and F'lar are here. Bigath listens, Sulath and Beerth. Clarinath occasionally but Pranith always and Lioth whenever his rider's down. Sometimes the listening is very interesting. Sometimes it's not.*

Not only was that an unusually long speech for Golanth but it gave F'lessan such food for thought that he was kept occupied with the ramifications until the edge of the vast inland sea became visible.

'*How are the air currents, Golanth? Shall we cross it or fly around?*'

We cross it, was the immediate and confident answer.

'*We need a nor'nor'west heading, Golanth, to reach the point where the ancients settled. Not that I think we'll find much.*'

They passed through several squalls on their way, noting all the little islands and the strange pinnacles of rock upthrusts, like bony fingers or clenched fists. On some, odd-shaped trees had managed to find soil enough in the rock crevices to support their roots. In two instances, naked roots twisted down the spires, seeking additional dirt and sustenance. The trees, with their odd closely packed heads, leaned precariously away from the prevailing winds. Or were those branches which were seeking the summits and sunlight? Sharra would want to know about these. She liked such oddities. F'lessan was genuinely fond of Jaxom's wife.

The western coastline was now visible, a high palisade of cliff. The inland sea must have been formed in a vast subsidence, F'lessan decided, recognizing the geological formation from Aivas's survey lectures. That would also account for the spires and islands, the tops of sunken mountains. Now if those distant cliff faces also held caves, this would be a splendid place for a Weyr. All that water! You'd never have a dry dragon in your Weyr.

He was to be disappointed, however, once they got close enough to see the solid granite composition of the high bluffs.

Dragons don't have cliff weyrs in Southern or Eastern and they don't complain, Golanth said helpfully.

'I know but I was asked to find a useful old crater or two.'

The sun will find me in a clearing and there are some very good smelling trees on this continent.

F'lessan thumped Golanth, grinning at the bronze's effort to console him for the disappointment.

'This isn't the only place I'm supposed to check out. There was a settler's hold, called Honshu, in the foothills of the southern barrier range. However, since we're here, let's look about for this Xanadu Stake Hold.'

Golanth's sharp eyes spotted unnatural outlines on a slight prominence, not far from where a wide river had worn a deep gorge from the outer sea to this inner one. F'lessan wasn't sure about ruins but he had to accept that wide steps had been cut in the palisade face. Someone had wanted an easy access to the lake shore. Golanth landed neatly beside his alleged ruins. At first F'lessan thought the dragon had been mistaken in seeing any shape whatsoever beneath the heavy vegetation.

This is not natural, Golanth insisted, tapping a vertical thicket of twisted vines and moss. Extending his wing, he hooked his wingfinger claw on a twisting branch and pulled away the obscuring greenery. Myriad creatures scuttled away from exposure to the sun. F'lessan could scarcely deny that the tall chimney had been made of worked stone. So the rest of the ruin had to be the remains of the walls of a large dwelling.

F'lessan shook his head for those foolish enough to build with so much vegetation all around them, making them twice as vulnerable to Thread. Taking a meatroll from his pouch, he ate as he walked around the hold walls, using his belt knife to scrape down to long-hidden dressed stone. It would have been a large dwelling. Golanth had shouldered his way into the thick forest and now called his rider to inspect more ruins.

'Sizeable place right enough,' F'lessan said, kicking at

some rubble. 'Xanadu, huh!' He turned back to the main building, snagging a ripe redfruit from a hanging limb as he walked. Chewing the juicy fruit, he contemplated the prospect of sea and distant shore that the long dead inhabitants must surely have enjoyed, too. Magnificent! If there hadn't been Thread to worry about, it would have been an endlessly beautiful vista. 'We've another place to investigate, Golanth,' he said abruptly, throwing off a sense of regret on behalf of those long dead holders.

He asked Golanth to wheel over the site so that he could imprint the details in his mind for future visits. If . . . no, F'lessan corrected himself defiantly, *when* Pernese skies were Threadfree, this would be an admirable situation for an open-air weyr.

Golanth caught an updraft that put them quickly back into the westerly current. They'd a long way still to go. Shielding his eyes, F'lessan glanced at the lowering sun and then, berating his forgetfulness, looked at his wrist watch. Four more hours until the dusk. Not that flying at night bothered Golanth but F'lessan wouldn't see what he had flown all this way to lay his eyes on. Nor would it be the first night F'lessan had curled up in a bed made by his dragon's forepaws.

They flew onwards, Golanth's wings tirelessly carrying them, until the great southern barrier range developed from a pale lavender smudge to vast purplish blue massifs, dominating the horizon.

'Big,' and F'lessan drawled the adjective, '*mountains! Higher than anything we have in the North until you reach the Icy Wastes.*'

The air would be very thin up there. Will we have to cross them?

'I don't think so,' and F'lessan rummaged in his jacket pocket for the map Aivas had printed out for him. It flapped so badly in the wind of their passage that he had trouble reading it. '*No, this Honshu holding is in the foothills below the real range. We're just not close enough to distinguish them.*'

In fact, the last of the brilliant sunset illuminated the general area of their destination. Only because sharp-eyed Golanth saw a line of herdbeasts ambling through a wide doorway in the foot of the cliff did they locate Honshu.

'Are you sure you saw what you said you saw?' F'lessan asked in surprise. 'Surely they would have taken their beasts with them when they left.'

Maybe wild ones found the way into a place of safety, Golanth suggested and, speeding up his wing strokes, reached the foot of the sheer cliff just as the last of the sunset drained from the western skies.

There was no mistaking the wide track worn smooth by usage that led to the cliff face and through a wide entrance angled into the cliff. Peering inside, F'lessan coughed at the stench of the place. High in the walls, window slits did not give him light enough to see much – and the smell was enough to discourage investigation. The herdbeasts bawled in surprise at his entrance and milled anxiously deeper into what must be an immense cavern. Choking and with eyes streaming from the intense ammoniac smell, F'lessan backed out. Leaning against the cliff, he breathed deeply of the fresh evening air.

'Looks like you found me Honshu, Golanth,' he said, running his hand up the beasthold entrance. 'This was cut as neatly as a hot knife in cheese. Just like Fort Hold and the Weyr. When the ancients still had power for their stone cutters. So this has to be Honshu.' His fingers also located a door, neatly retracted into the wall. 'They left the door wide open after all. Well, Golanth, let's find us a place to camp for the night. A fire would be right cheerful on a black night like this. I don't know if those big felines Sharra and Piemur talked about range this far south, but . . .'

No feline would challenge me!

'Not one who wishes to see tomorrow,' F'lessan said with a laugh and peered in the dark for some place to settle down.

Follow me, Golanth said and ambled to the left of the cliff face.

'You're better than a torch,' F'lessan said and followed, making certain he didn't tread on his dragon's tail.

Dead wood was easy enough to find, and rocks to contain a fire, so very shortly, F'lessan was comfortably settled against Golanth's shoulder, munching at his travel rations and sipping some Benden wine he'd talked Manora into putting in his bottle. Then, because there was little else to do in these surroundings, F'lessan unrolled the fur that padded Golanth's neck ridge, nestled himself snugly between Golanth's forelimbs and went to sleep.

He woke up just as the eastern skies were brightening. Enough embers remained from his fire to be coaxed back into sufficient warmth to heat his morning *klah* and he broke his fast with a meatroll. Golanth ambled down to the river and drank deeply.

This will be a good place to swim – once the sun is up, he said with the air of an expert. *And the cliff a good place to warm after a swim. The sun will catch the stone and radiate heat.*

F'lessan grinned as he sipped his hot *klah*. 'You have been learning a thing or two from listening.'

Only the things that make sense to me.

Then F'lessan heard the low bleating and moaning of the animals sheltering in the hold.

'Stay there, Golanth, or the animals won't come out and I want to investigate this place.'

I don't mind if I do, Golanth replied equably, *but they have nothing to fear for I am not hungry yet.*

'Somehow I doubt they'd believe you, dear heart.' F'lessan made a second cup of *klah* and then kicked dirt and gravel over his little fire lest the smell of burning wood alarmed the beasts.

He did not have long to wait. Once the sunlight hit the entrance, the animals began to file out, ready for a day's browsing or grazing. For there was more than one species of herdbeast among those that sheltered in the ancient hold. Most of them had younglings at foot. Not stirring a muscle, F'lessan watched the exodus. When all had made their way down the track, spreading out on their separate ways, the bronze rider approached the opening.

'Faugh!' The reek discouraged F'lessan from entering but he could now see that the dung had accumulated to a considerable depth, up to the level of mid-thigh.

It was a huge stinking cavern of a place to judge by what he could see from the patches of early morning light filtering from the high windows. It was then that he noticed a flight of steps to his right, though the first few were covered in the manure of ages.

'Golanth! I'm going in. There're steps here.' And drawing his collar across his nose and mouth, F'lessan darted towards the steps and ran up to the first landing before he stopped. There was a large door to his right, a door that had once been secured by a lock, now a rusted shell that fell into dust at his touch. He pushed open the door and stood on another landing, with steps leading down to a large high-ceilinged room. From window slits he could make out a bulky object, half a dragon length in size, which appeared to be covered.

'I've found some sort of an ancient artefact!' he told Golanth as he took the steps two at a time in his excitement.

The covering was of ancient manufacture, soapy and slick to the touch once he brushed aside the film of dust that had turned a bright green fabric to grey. Flipping a corner up, F'lessan peered at the unmistakable prow of a vehicle. Struggling to uncover more of the incredible object, F'lessan recognized it from some of the tapes Aivas has shown them as a sled: one of the larger sort.

'Just wait till Master Fandarel and Benelek see this thing, Golanth! They'll go spare!' F'lessan crowed with delight and anticipation at the stir this beauty would cause. He rolled more of the cover back, noticing how carefully the craft had been stored by its owners, wondering why they had left it. 'No more fuel to fly it, probably.'

It's a cumbersome looking thing, Golanth remarked.

'Don't worry, love. I'd never trade you in for one of these. Cranky things from what the records tell us. Always needing to be serviced and have parts replaced. Don't have that worry with a dragon.' F'lessan laughed heartily at how Smithcrafters would swarm over this sled – for all the good it would do them. Still, it was quite a relic to find lovingly stored away. So few of the settlers' everyday implements had been discovered. Then he noticed the racks of dust-shrouded tools on the wall, a pile of empty plastic sacks such as the settlers had used to store all manner of items, and, under their layers of fine dust, plastic containers in the settlers' favourite bright colours.

'Well, when I tell Aivas what we've found, he won't be so upset,' F'lessan added. 'So I'd better survey the whole place for a complete report. Aivas respects complete reports.'

Then he bounded up the steps to the landing and proceeded on upwards. He noticed that there were piles of dung on some of the steps and the muddy hoof marks that, fortunately, ended at another closed door.

This one slid back into the wall – not without some grunting and shoving on F'lessan's part. Having achieved a wide enough gap to squeeze through, he stepped on to yet another landing, with stairs leading down to a huge cavern, a work room, to judge by the variety of tables and cabinets. Slightly amazed, he identified both a forge and a huge kiln as well as the work benches. There he saw his first signs of a hurried departure for some cabinet drawers were half-out of their slides and there were odd cartons, not quite lidded shut on three work surfaces. He didn't go down to investigate further for yet another flight of stairs led up to a higher level of this incredible place.

'I'm moving up in the world, Golanth, with more marvels to report to Aivas. Oooowhee, but this place is a treasure trove. The people may have left but, for once, they didn't take much with them. Robinton and Lytol are going to be fascinated!'

Golanth's response was a deep grunt that echoed in F'lessan's ears but, laughing at his dragon's lack of enthusiasm, the bronze rider galloped eagerly up the steps.

Nor was F'lessan disappointed. The door on this level gave on to what must be the main entry to this hold. Through a graceful archway, he could see into what must have been the central living area. For the first time, F'lessan felt like an intruder as he stepped into the immense room. And stopped. He heard the slither of tunnel snakes, retreating from his presence. He could distinguish little beyond shrouded forms in the darkness but he could see the thin lines of light around window apertures.

Retracing his steps to the hall, he threw open the wide double leaves of the main door, blinking at the brilliance of the early morning sun. The hold faced north east, as a

southern hold should, and an early breeze ruffled the thick
cushion of dust on the floor. With that light to help him,
he found the windows, and also found the long pole that
opened them as they were set above his head. Five of the
ten large windows he had opened before his eyes fell on
the space above them.

'Golanth! You should see this! It's amazing!'

See what? Where are you now? Is there room for me?

'I . . . th . . . think so.' F'lessan heard his own stammer
echo back from the vaulted ceiling: a ceiling which had
been decorated in brilliantly coloured murals which had
lost nothing of their brightness. And he now knew part of
the story they depicted. 'This ought to shut up the doubters
– an independent verification of what Aivas told us!' he
murmured, more to himself than to Golanth, as he gave
the walls a fleeting glance before beginning a more studied
perusal. So involved did he become with the mural scenes
that it took him a moment to realize that the scrabbling
noise was Golanth's claws on stone.

This door is not wide enough for me, and Golanth sounded
distinctly annoyed. F'lessan glanced around and stifled
a guffaw. Golanth had got head and neck through the
opening but not his massive shoulders.

'You're not stuck, are you?' the bronze rider asked
solicitously.

*They could have made the door a little bit higher and wider
since they made it as big as they did.*

'I don't really think they had dragons of your size in
mind when they built, Golanth. But can you see the murals?
There's even a scene about dragons . . . right overhead. Oh,
you can't quite see it but these murals are amazing. There
are panels for every major event,' and F'lessan pointed out
the appropriate panels as he explained, 'the actual landing
in the shuttle craft, the ones in Ship Meadow, and yes, there
are sleds just like the one down below, and the building
of holds, and people working the land, and then Thread.
They did that panel too graphically. Turns my stomach just
to look at it. They've got lots of sleds, and smaller craft, and
flamethrowers and . . . Ah, high up in the ceiling, they've
even got Rukbat and all its planets. If only we'd found this

place a long time ago . . .' F'lessan was silent a long moment, his eyes moving from one beautifully painted panel to the next. 'They'll all want to see this place,' he said at length with infinite satisfaction. 'We did good, Golanth dear heart. And we were first here!'

He looked around one last time, deciding not to investigate further so that others might have the pleasure of seeing the place as it had been left. Then he carefully closed the windows.

Golanth had been trying to see what he could, crammed into the doorway. Now, as F'lessan approached him, he carefully backed out on to the broad shelf that jutted out from this level. F'lessan closed the doors behind him, marvelling at the workmanship that allowed the heavy metal to pivot so easily after so many centuries of disuse. He gazed up at the sweep of the hold: three more levels of windows were visible.

'Neither weyr nor hold but it would serve,' F'lessan said, remembering the point of his search. 'That is, once the artefactors and Craftmasters get their look-in.'

Dragons would find this spot eminently suitable, F'lessan, Golanth assured him. *There is the river which is deep, clear and tasty to drink, and there are many ledges that face the sun all the day long,* and Golanth swung his head to left and right to bring those places to F'lessan's notice. *This would make a very good Weyr indeed.*

'And so we shall report.'

Chapter Twelve

The discovery of Honshu was partially eclipsed when S'len found eighteen usable spacesuits in the *Yokohama* ready room. In Master Robinton's opinion, Aivas had received that news with a great deal more excitement than he had displayed when hearing about Honshu's state of preservation. Aivas said the suits gave his schedule considerably more flexibility and dispensed with some rather awkward and possibly dangerous alternatives. However, some folk in the Smithcraft, and many in the Harper Hall, considered Honshu the more important, and certainly more immediately useful, discovery.

While Aivas was revising his plan, Jancis and Hamian were appointed by Master Fandarel to inventory the tools at Honshu and, if their use was not immediately apparent, to decide what function they had had. Aivas did take time to print out a manual for the sled, out of respect for the keen interest shown, but added the qualifier that any investigations were esoteric since he could give no assistance in powering it. That provoked some resentment in those who felt that aerial transportation should not be restricted to dragonriders and a 'chosen few'.

Aivas' rebuttal to that accusation was to enumerate all the skills and technological improvements (which those same complainants objected to in theory) that would be necessary to produce powered aerial vehicles, including the development of an alternative and reliable power source.

'The settlers used power packs, a technology developed and zealously guarded by one of the Federation's alien members,' Aivas reminded them, for the subject had arisen before. 'These units were rechargeable but no recharging mechanism survived. The preservation of the sled itself is astonishing, due to the care with which it was decommissioned and the dry climate at Honshu's altitude.'

'But can't you tell us how to make the power packs?'

'No, and for this reason! There are two kinds of science. One invents its own rules, like a technology: physics and chemistry are such sciences. They only work within the rules they themselves make, as you have been learning. The physicist works things only within the rules he chooses to use. Any anomalies he disregards or gives to the engineer who might be able to use them somewhere. The fabric of knowledge that is available to this facility, and thence to you must be contained within the framework, like the physics you have learned. It makes its real world, it doesn't discover it; it uses a small sub-set of real-world rules to make its own real world.

'The second kind of science works with the world as it really is – and is much more messy. Which is essentially what you do with dragons. The problem with that kind of science is that the world as it is doesn't only use *your* ideas, it uses *all* the laws: the ninety-nine per cent you, and the alien physicist who gave the idea away to an alien engineer, don't know about.'

'In other words, we're stuck with this world and what's in it?' Jaxom asked.

'Precisely. And it is up to you to work this out for yourself, or to gain help from Lytol rather than from this facility.'

And that was as much time as Aivas would spend on Honshu. With additional spacesuits available, he initiated new projects which, it was made clear, were much closer to the major task in hand, the destruction of Thread.

Now that the life support systems on the *Bahrain* and the *Buenos Aires* were fully operational, Mirrim and S'len on their green dragons could make the necessary links between the bridge consoles on the two smaller ships and the *Yokohama* link with Aivas. The two smaller space vessels had, however, sustained more damage over the centuries than the *Yokohama*, losing antennae, exterior optics, considerable areas of the outside skin from impacts which the shields had been unable to deflect. Damage, Aivas was quick to state, which would not interfere with the plan.

Terry, Wansor, three of the Glass-smith's brightest journeymen and Perschar were ferried up by green dragons for long sessions on the *Yokohama*'s telescope, mapping the Red Star for any distinctive features. The vid-link down to Aivas was still imperfect though Aivas had been unable to discover the problem so that he had to rely on human observations. They soon reported to Aivas that only one side of the planet was turned towards them. Perschar was to do large reproductions of whatever geographic features the surface of the eccentric planet presented. Wansor had to be peeled away from the console, so exhausted by his lengthy efforts that he actually fell asleep *between* on the return trip.

Teams made up of green and bronze riders – with the green dragon of the one transporting both – explored the deserted levels of the *Yokohama* in case anything else had been left behind. But the ancients had stripped an amazing amount of material from the ship. The spacesuits – and the banks of coldsleep capsules – were all that had been deemed useless on the surface.

Then Smithcraftmaster teams were sent to familiarize themselves with the cargo bays and engine rooms of all three ships, starting with the *Yokohama*.

The four Smiths – Fandarel, Belterac, Evan and Jancis – were fascinated by the ship's construction, pausing to examine the way struts had been secured, how walls, ceilings and floors had been fitted into the skeleton of the ship. They were amazed to learn from Aivas that the *Yokohama* had been assembled in space at one of old Earth's gigantic satellite shipyards. It was difficult for them to assimilate the fact that the heaviest portions had been pushed into position by single workers, with computer-controlled machines, taking advantage of the lack of gravity. This relative ease of positioning heavy objects was an experience they were also learning.

Master Fandarel made full use of the *Yokohama* as a schoolroom, getting Aivas to explain the designs and the safety aspects of the compartmentalization. He was truly amazed at the rationale behind the odd design of the space-going ship and had many questions to put to Aivas about the apparent anomalies.

The main section of the *Yokohama* was a huge sphere of many levels, each of which could be closed off as could sections of each level to sustain life, Aivas told them, should the main hull be breached. Thus heat and oxygen could be laid on where necessary, as was being done now, to conserve supplies. The bridge area, the environmental section and the lift accessing it, a small infirmary and Airlock A were the most heavily shielded and could protect occupants against a variety of space hazards. There had been escape pods attached to Airlock A before the *Yokohama* was recommissioned as a colony ship when those pod positions had been altered to access supply drones.

The huge matter/anti-matter engines were housed on a long shaft, attached to the midsection of the main sphere, but separated by the heaviest shielding on the *Yokohama*. Two great wheels on either end of the engine shaft had held the fuel and cargo pods which had been wrapped around the engines. Those had, of course, been emptied during the journey and launched to splash down in the seas off Monaco Bay. Retrieved, the basic metal had been smelted down and reworked. The ceramic fuel tanks had been put to different uses. Very little of the superstructure of the *Yokohama* and the other two colony ships remained. The narrower stern wheel on the end of the engine shaft still held its band of manoeuvring jets which, powered by the solar panels and in conjunction with those around the main sphere, were what kept the *Yokohama's* orbit stable. One of the first checks Aivas had commissioned was how much fuel remained in the *Yokohama's* main tank.

At that remark, Fandarel wondered why the settlers had

dared to leave the colony ships in an orbit that must ultimately decay. Aivas replied, in a curt fashion that bordered anger, that that was not an immediate concern. So far, the orbits had not decayed and the surface of Pern was not at risk – at least from ship debris.

It was while Jancis was busy patching the main engineering board into Aivas and the others were examining the 'readiness' run of the great propulsion units that one of the greens riders activated the red alert from the bridge.

Jancis' bronze fire-lizard, Trig, became so agitated that she had a time calming him down enough to make sense of his response. Nor could Jancis raise either S'len or L'zal on the com, as the red alert signal kept blinking in the engineering facility.

'Thread attacking the *Yokohama*?' Jancis got that much from Trig's chaotic thoughts. 'It can't, Trig. It can't. We're safe here! No, don't you dare breathe fire in here!'

Jancis then bellowed directions through the speaker to the bridge until S'len hit the right sequence of buttons and they had voice contact.

'It's Thread, Jancis, I'm sure of it. Not space debris,' S'len replied. 'There's this flood of egg-like things of varying sizes streaming towards us. Looking just like the stuff Aivas described to us in his lecture. Space debris wouldn't come in a steady flow, would it? This stuff goes back as far as we can see from the window. Only none of it ever hits the window and the pilot's board is all lit up and the engineer's station is beeping at us,' he went on, words tumbling out in his haste to describe the situation. Then his voice became agitated. 'Bigath and Beerth are demanding that we go *outside*. They say it's Thread. I never should have even *thought* what I thought it is!' Then in an explosive aside, 'No, Bigath, we *can't* fly this sort of a Fall. It's not Thread yet, if that's what it is! We haven't any firestone and there's no air out there and you wouldn't fly outside anyway – you'd float, just like in here. Shards! Jancis, I can't make her understand!'

S'len didn't panic easily and Bigath was not as erratic as some greens. In the background, Jancis could also hear Aivas's loud reassurances. If Bigath wasn't obeying her rider, she certainly wouldn't be disciplined by the Aivas. Her bugling challenge at Thread took on a frantic edge.

'Tell them Ruth says they're not to go! They obey him!' she said, latching on to an authority the greens respected. She didn't know a green dragon who wasn't partial to the white dragon.

'When is Ruth coming, Bigath wants to know!' S'len had graduated from dismay to desperation. Aivas's calm voice continued to exhort the green dragons to listen to reason, which the dragons were in no state to hear.

Jancis was scribbling a note to Jaxom to come at once when S'len, with a cry of relief, added, 'Ruth's here and everything's under control!'

Jancis looked at the note and then at her fire-lizard who cocked his head at her quizzically. She considered the matter for a moment longer and then made a decision. There was absolutely no way in which Jaxom and Ruth would have known to come to the bridge. He was at Ruatha today and Aivas was not in communication with him there. She checked the exact time on her watch and wrote it down on the note. Then added a final phrase in big letters: 'TIME IT!' Then she sent Trig off to Ruatha and Jaxom.

'But if Ruth and Jaxom are here, why send the note now?' Fandarel asked.

Jancis smiled at her grandfather. 'Trig needs the practice, Grandda.'

Trig almost met himself going he was back so quickly, looking inordinately pleased with himself.

'He needs more than practice,' Fandarel said, dismayed at the apparent disobedience.

'I don't know about you,' Jancis said as a diversion, striding over to the lift, 'but I want to see this "attack". I've never been allowed out of Hall or Hold during a Fall so now may be my only chance. Aren't any of you interested?'

The reaction to her challenge was immediate and, when Jancis found herself crammed into the lift with three big Smithcraft bodies, she was sorry that she had issued it.

Then the lift door opened to a curious bedlam: two green dragons, wings plastered on the window, were so fiercely hissing and spraying saliva that the view was obscured while Ruth, his wing fingers on those of the two greens, putting him at full stretch, overlapped their bodies. He was loudly emitting some sort of a croon that was only just audible through their angry sputters.

Jancis managed to grab Trig before he took off to join them in their futile posturing. She pinned him firmly under one arm while she hung on to the railing lest his violent attempts to free himself send her into a spin. Ruth turned his redshot eyes in their direction. His peremptory bark made the bronze fire-lizard submit to his restriction.

The view, even partially blocked by green and white dragon bodies, was awesome: the objects blanketed the entire panorama. Jancis had to exert a firm control over an urge to recoil as the shapes, zooming straight at *Yokohama*, were deflected at seemingly the last moment before impact by the ship's shields. But gradually, she and the Smiths became accustomed to the spectacle and could appreciate it with detachment. Not that any of them found it as amusing as Jaxom did. He was clutching the pilot's chair with one hand to keep from floating off but he was nearly doubled up with laughter. S'len and L'zal, moving circumspectly out of reach of furiously swishing dragon tails, looked on in chagrin and embarrassment.

Fandarel, being the tallest man there, had a reasonably unobstructed view over the draconic obstacles. He shook his head sadly. 'An amazing spectacle. Aivas, is this one of those meteor showers you've told us about?'

'What you are seeing is not a meteor shower,' Aivas replied. 'Comparing the present onslaught with the reports made by Pilot Kenjo Fusaiyuki during his reconnaissance flights and pending examination of a sample, it is reasonable to believe that Thread, in its space-travelling form, is flowing past the *Yokohama* on its way to your planet.' Everyone was silent.

'But where will it fall?' Jaxom asked, unable to remember which Weyr was scheduled to fly Fall next.

'On Nerat in precisely forty-six hours,' Avias replied.

Jaxom let out a long whistle.

'This swarm has a long way to go yet to reach the atmospheric envelope of the planet,' Avias continued.

'Hmmm,' Fandarel said, moving closer to peer out the window. 'Fascinating! To be amid Thread and unharmed by it. Truly astounding. It's a great pity we can't do something to stem the tide here, before it reaches the surface.'

S'len groaned. 'Please don't even think that,' he said, flicking his hand at the willing creatures whom Ruth was visibly restraining at the window.

'Thread doesn't look so dangerous right now,' Jancis said thoughtfully as she watched the ovoids sweep in and abruptly disappear.

'In it's frozen state, it is unlikely to be life-threatening,' Avias said.

'But you don't know for sure?'

'Attempts were made by Nabhi Nabol and Bart Lemos to secure specimens but their ship disintegrated before they were able to return with them.'

'We could get some now,' Jaxom suggested. 'There're plenty out there.'

There was a significant pause and Jaxom winked at Jancis. It wasn't often that Aivas was caught speechless.

'You fail to recognize the hazards of such a venture.'

'Why? We could stash the thing in Airlock A, for instance, and it would stay frozen. As you keep telling us, it takes the friction of the atmosphere for Thread to metamorphose into its dangerous state.'

Jancis was mouthing words at Jaxom, shaking her head violently, while, under her arm, Trig struggled to free himself from restraint with renewed vigour.

'The *Yokohama* is moving at approximately 38,765 nautical miles per hour or about 20,000 mph relative to the Thread ovoids are travelling in excess of that speed. To attempt to capture one would be an impossible manoeuvre even for persons trained in extravehicular activities. It would also be essential to have non-heat conducting tongs.'

Trig squawked.

I would capture a Thread egg for you, Ruth said, turning his head at an impossible angle over his shoulder to his rider.

Jaxom looked in alarm at his white dragon and regretted his facetious suggestion. 'Oh, no, you don't.' When Ruth looked crestfallen he added, 'No-one else can keep those greens under control.'

'Did Ruth just offer to go get a Thread?' Jancis asked, holding more tightly to the writhing Trig. 'Let Trig go.'

'You heard what Aivas said about the velocities and non-heat conducting tongs.'

'It doesn't look as if we're travelling anywhere near that speed,' she replied, then sighed, 'even if I know we must be. Fire-lizard talons aren't exactly heat-conductive, are they? Trig seems to think he can.'

'WHAT!' Belterac demanded, his eyes bulging with horror. 'Bring one of those . . . those things in here with us?'

'Not in here,' Jancis replied. 'Into the airlock, where we can examine it closely. In its frozen state, it poses no danger.'

'Do you think Trig would be able to manage?' Fandarel asked, his insatiable curiosity getting the better of an ingrained revulsion to Thread.

'If he thinks he can,' Jancis said. She looked down at the struggling fire-lizard. 'Letting him do something about Thread may calm him down.' She looked out at the barrage.

'It has been noted,' Aivas said slowly, 'that fire-lizards are particularly courageous in the presence of Thread. It has also been noted that, in both fire-lizards and dragons, the *thought* becomes the deed by some method which does not bear investigation. If Trig should *think* he can retrieve a specimen, despite the obvious difficulties, it would greatly facilitate a useful examination of the organism. Placing it in Airlock A would, of course, keep the specimen frozen, dormant AND impotent,' Aivas stressed that conjunction. 'Then it could be examined at leisure: a procedure your ancestors scheduled but did not implement. It would complete their biological investigations of this organism.'

Jaxom looked warily at Jancis. All in all, he wasn't sure they should ask this of Trig. Didn't they know as much as they needed to know about Thread? And yet, to have a Thread impotent, at their disposal, locked in a primal form, would be subtly gratifying.

It wouldn't be at all hard to do, Ruth told Jaxom.

'Ruth!' Jaxom vetoed that with a sharp chop of his hands. 'You stay out of this fire-lizard assignment. Show-off!'

To his surprise, Jancis laughed. 'Does Ruth think he'd fit in Airlock A?' she asked, grinning at Ruth's reproachful expression. 'First, let's see if Trig is certain he can manage. Now, dear,' and she lifted Trig up level with her eyes, took his triangular head and pointed it towards the window, 'we want you to go get one of those big eggs and put it in Airlock A. You remember where that is. It'd be like catching a wherry mid-air.'

I'm telling him too, in case he doesn't understand, and Ruth turned a reproving eye on his rider. *I'd be perfectly safe. I'm much bigger than the Thread eggs. I wouldn't be thrown off-balance as a little fire-lizard would be. And it's no more than a jump between.*

Trig gave a cheep, turning his head towards Ruth and cheeping again, the whirling of his eyes speeding up with anticipation and resolve.

He understands. He says he can easily do that.

'Ruth has now briefed Trig thoroughly,' Jaxom told Jancis.

'You're sure you can do this, Trig? You don't have to, you know,' Jancis said, but Trig's eyes were orange-red with challenge and confidence. With a sigh, she bounced Trig off her arm. He disappeared. A moment later they all saw him through the bridge window, catching an ovoid nearly as large as himself. Briefly the force of the capture sent him spinning backwards but before he had come near the window, he abruptly flipped out of sight again. Three heartbeats later, he reappeared on the bridge, chittering with satisfaction.

'His hide is so cold,' Jancis said as she stroked him. 'He's got stuff on his talons! Freezing! Ugh!' But, for all of that, she didn't dislodge him from her shoulder.

Everyone made much of him, including Ruth, with the notable exception of the two greens who were sullenly rumbling their discontent at being kept inside the *Yokohama*.

'Apparently the extravehicular activity was successful?' Aivas asked.

Jaxom activated the optics in Airlock A and saw the

ovoid floating gently above the lock floor. Eyes widening in surprise, Jancis jiggled her finger at the screen showing the airlock. 'Look!' she exclaimed. It took a moment for the others to realize that the ovoid was gliding across the lock. It hovered briefly by the wall and returned to approximately the same position in the centre of the facility.

'Excellent demonstration of incident of magnetic levitation,' Aivas remarked. 'And congratulations from Master Robinton and D'ram. Warder Lytol is already mobilizing a team to examine the specimen.'

'Is he indeed?' Jaxom asked flippantly, wondering who Lytol would tag with this unenviable task.

'The extent and density of this stream would be useful knowledge,' Aivas went on. 'Jancis, such readings can be taken from the navigator's console by activating the exterior optics, using the EXAM.EXE code.'

'It occurs to me, Aivas,' Jaxom began, winking at Jancis as he spoke, 'that this phenomenon was not on your agenda for today in space?' He was amused to see Fandarel regard him with astonishment for such an impudent question.

There was so profound a silence from Aivas that everyone on the bridge exchanged amused glances. Twice in one day they had confounded Aivas? Fandarel began to chuckle, a deep rolling sound, when an answer finally came.

'Regrettably, this facility did not compute that possibility though calculations now indicate that the *Yokohama* and her sister ships have been in the line of Thread showers every fourth Fall.'

'Well, imagine that!' Jaxom remarked, his eyes glinting with mischief. He hadn't ever thought to catch Aivas unprepared.

With what Jaxom decided was considerable aplomb, Aivas asked, 'Is the shield destroying the ovoids or is it deflecting them?'

'Deflecting,' Jaxom replied and then absorbed the nub of that remark. 'The shield has a destructive mode? We could destroy what's raining down on us? What an ingenious concept! There'd be just that much fewer to fall on Nerat tomorrow. And that might persuade old Begamon that all this,' and he gestured about the bridge, 'is worth the effort.'

'Jaxom, the destruct capability can be activated from either the captain's chair or the pilot's console. Call up the shield function program and alter DEFL to DEST.'

'I hear and obey,' Jaxom said eagerly, finding his breath quickening as he slid into the pilot's seat and activated the console. 'Program altered.' For a moment, he let his finger hover above the enter tab. 'Engaged!'

In the next instant, the pellets streaking towards them dissolved in puffs, clearing a path so that the width and depth of the stream became all too visible.

'If you will activate the rear view screen, Jaxom,' Aivas went on, 'you will see how effective the destruct mode is.'

Plainly a wide swathe of Thread had been eliminated.

'That's beautiful! Just beautiful! Charring Thread in the air is one thing! THIS is much better. Much better!' Jaxom muttered, then he turned the forward view back on and continued to watch the visible destruction of Thread with intense satisfaction. The green dragons had stopped spitting and begun to rumble in delight.

'Is there any way to extend this destruction beyond the *Yokohama*?' Master Fandarel asked.

'No,' Aivas replied. The shield's main function is to deflect ordinary space debris. Considering the width, breadth and depth of the stream, it would be analogous to trying to destroy a snow shower with a candle,' Aivas added.

'Then how, Aivas, do you propose that we shall destroy this menace – as you promised we would?' Jaxom demanded.

'By removing the vector that brings Thread to Pern. That should have been obvious to you all by now,' Aivas chided them. 'The path of the eccentric planet must be altered sufficiently so that it does not come close enough to the inner system to spin Thread into Pern's orbit.'

'And how can we possibly do that?' demanded Master Fandarel.

'That will become apparent as you continue with the plan. Everything you have learned, every seemingly simple exercise either here or on the ground is directed towards preparing you for that end.'

No amount of wheedling or blustering could move Aivas

to elaborate. 'You cannot run before you walk,' he repeated to almost every rephrasing of that question from Fandarel, Jaxom, Jancis and Belterac.

Finally, Jaxom desisted and turned to the immediate situation. 'Don't the *Buenos Aires* and *Bahrain* have similar shields?'

'They do,' Aivas replied.

'Well, then,' and Jaxom rubbed his hands together in anticipation.

'Now wait a moment, Lord Jaxom,' Jancis said. 'You're not going to have all the fun today. I want my turn at destroying Thread.'

'And I,' said her grandfather, a rapturous grin replacing his usual composure.

'It would be a dangerous task for a young woman, a young mother,' Belterac said, moving forward and glancing anxiously at Fandarel to support him.

'I will not be done out of my opportunity on those grounds,' Jancis said, her eyes flashing as she confronted Belterac so belligerently that he nearly recoiled in surprise. 'Besides, I fit into a spacesuit. You're much too big, Belterac.'

'I'm not,' Evan said, speaking up for the first time.

'I thought that life support systems had been reactivated on both the smaller ships,' Fandarel said. 'Am I not correct, Aivas?'

'You are, Master Fandarel.'

'Well, then, spacesuits are not required.'

'A knowledge of the sequence is, Granddad, and you always leave console work to someone else.'

Fandarel drew himself up to his full height, swelling his massive chest importantly. 'It did not seem too difficult. A few pecks and then the enter.' He threw a quizzical glance at Jaxom.

'Cease!' Jaxom said, throwing up his hands and nearly propelling himself out of the pilot's chair by mistake. 'As Lord Holder, I outrank everyone else so I will make the decision. Master Fandarel deserves the chance for many reasons, and Jancis, too. However, Bigath and Beerth brought all you Smithcrafters up here so they can just haul you across to the other ships as well. You,' and he pointed at Belterac, 'can be trusted with switching the screen from deflect to destroy, and you,' he indicated Fandarel, 'can then engage. Jancis, you reprogram the shield and Evan, you can hit the enter key. So you'll all take part.'

'It must be pointed out,' Aivas said, 'that the amount of Thread that would be destroyed, even utilizing the destruct mode of the shields on all three ships, is only 0.09 per cent of an average Fall. Is this trip necessary?'

'That's 0.09 per cent the dragonriders don't have to worry about, Aivas,' Jaxom said jubilantly.

'Then let us make this efficient use of the available technology,' Fandarel said, patently eager to do so.

'It is apparent that such participation would give immense psychological satisfaction, far outweighing either the risk or the actual destruction ratio,' Aivas said.

'Immense satisfaction,' Jaxom agreed.

'Raising morale to a new height,' Jancis put in, 'and to think I can have a part in it!'.

'That is,' and Jaxom turned courteously to the green riders, 'if you and your dragons are amenable . . .'

S'len and L'zal were more than amenable, deciding that any action for their dragons was preferable to their current frustration.

Jaxom drilled everyone on the steps necessary to alter the shield to destruct mode. Aivas did insist that everyone was to take along emergency oxygen equipment. The atmosphere on the two smaller ships was only minimal and oxygen deprivation could not be risked.

When the greens, well laden with riders, departed, Jaxom found the bridge remarkably quiet.

'Jaxom,' Aivas began, 'how much weight can the green dragons carry? Their burdens today weigh more than their body weight.'

'A dragon is capable of carrying as much as he thinks he can,' Jaxom replied, with a shrug, for Aivas experienced difficulty in accepting draconic abilities.

'So, if the dragon thinks he can carry any object, irrespective of its actual weight, he will?'

'I don't think anyone's actually tried to overload a dragon. Didn't you tell me that the earliest ones were used to transport loads out of Landing following the eruption?'

'That is true. But they were never, as you surmised, permitted to carry great weights. In fact Sean O'Connell, the leader of those early riders, resented the fact that the dragons were used in such a capacity.'

'Why?'

'That was never explained.'

Jaxom smiled to himself. 'Dragons can do a lot of inexplicable things.'

'For instance,' and Aivas's voice altered subtly, 'arriving in very timely fashions?'

Jaxom chuckled. 'That's one.'

'How did you contrive such a serendipitous entrance?'

'Jancis was clever enough to put down the time. When I visualized the bridge for Ruth, I also visualized the bridge clock,' and Jaxom pointed to the digital face, 'at a minute before the one she gave. So, of course, we arrived,' he chuckled again, 'in time!'

Tell Aivas that I always know where in time I am, Ruth said and Jaxom duly repeated the message to Aivas.

'A most interesting ability.'

'Mind you, Aivas, that is for your ears only.'

'This facility has no ears, Jaxom.'

Any further discussion concerning unusual draconic abilities was interrupted by the jubilant return of the teams, the green dragons looking as gratified as their passengers.

'When Thread has passed by,' Aivas said, 'someone must return to the ships and reset the shield to deflect. The solar panels do not supply unlimited power and will need to be fully recharged.'

There was a unanimous agreement to that suggestion. By then, Aivas had accessed all the data he required, the Thread flow had diminished to a few stray globules and the green dragons returned the teams to reset the shields.

'Aivas,' Fandarel began when they were once again assembled on the *Yokohama*'s bridge, 'has the matter of our excursions to the other ships been mentioned on the surface?'

'Master Robinton was on duty and approved,' Aivas replied.

Fandarel cleared his throat. 'No students listening to the exchange?'

'Only Master Robinton was in the chamber at that time. Why?'

'We can count on his discretion, then. This interesting facet of the *Yokohama* should be discussed before it is made public,' Fandarel said. 'I found it most exhilarating to initiate the destruction.'

'Wouldn't it serve to convince the doubtful that these projects are useful?' Jancis asked.

'That is the question that must be discussed,' Fandarel said.

So Jaxom and Ruth made their farewells and left the bridge. As Jancis and the other Smiths returned to the engine room and their disrupted tasks, she fleetingly wondered if he timed it back to Ruatha.

Jaxom did not return immediately to Ruatha. He felt obliged to inform the Benden Weyrleaders of the incident. Ruth was thoroughly in favour of a Benden destination as he always enjoyed visiting his native Weyr.

Ramoth and Mnementh are happy to see me, he told his rider as they circled in to land at the queen's weyr. *Lessa and F'lar are within*. Then he turned his head up to Mnementh and the two dragons touched noses. *Mnementh says that F'lar will be very pleased to hear what we did on the* Yokohama. *He and Ramoth are.*

As Jaxom entered the queen's weyr, Ramoth was watching for his appearance and rumbled a greeting.

She greets you as the bearer of very good tidings, Ruth told him.

'How about letting me deliver my own surprise?' Jaxom muttered with mock irritation.

'And what surprise is that?' Lessa asked, looking up from reinforcing a join on a long strap. F'lar had his harness stretched from a peg set high on the wall, rubbing oil into the thick neck strap.

These reminders of his near escape from cold-damaged leather sobered Jaxom. He hadn't seen any further indication that the conspirators at Tillek were carrying out their threat against him. But then, he'd been careful not to provide opportunities.

'Oh,' Jaxom began casually, 'just that the Fall over Nerat won't be as heavy as usual day after tomorrow.'

'How's that?' F'lar swivelled about, giving Jaxom his complete attention. Lessa's stare suggested that Jaxom had better be quick with his explanation.

Grinning because it wasn't often that he could astound this pair, he related what had happened. When he had finished, and the two Weyrleaders had questioned him closely on details, Lessa looked less than pleased.

'I'd say we were very lucky not to have lost two green dragons. And don't tell me you didn't time it, Jaxom.'

'Then I won't,' Jaxom replied. 'Bloody lucky Ruth's so clever at it.'

Lessa opened her mouth to remonstrate with him but F'lar held up a hand.

'And there can be a reduction in the density of Fall, using the destruct mode of the shields?'

'It certainly looked that way to us out the back window . . . as it were.' Then Jaxom halted in dismay. 'You know if I'd had the sense of a fire-lizard, I'd've reprogrammed the telescope and gotten a good look.'

'It takes time to become accustomed to using all this new technology. Anyway we'll confirm it at Nerat,' F'lar said, smiling as he pushed back his errant forelock. 'This'll be heartening news, Jaxom. Fall's right now at its densest and, unless Thread can reform – which I doubt – during its descent through the upper strata, the wings will have a brief breather. And that'll cut down on our casualties.'

'It may increase them,' Lessa said with a scowl. 'If we decide to take advantage of this capability. Riders'll become inattentive, expecting a lull.'

'Oh, come now, love,' and F'lar gave Lessa's long thick plait an affectionate tug, 'you can be downright ungrateful for a favour.'

She paused, reconsidered, then gave a grudging smile. 'Sorry. I do tend to be gloomy just before a Fall.'

'In that case, Lessa, you'd best come up to the *Yokohama* the next time this happens. I found it tremendously satisfying to be able to destroy so much Thread without endangering Ruth or myself!' Jaxom paused and added. 'We also have a specimen of Thread on the floor of Airlock A.'

'WHAT?'

Jaxom grinned at her startled, horrified expression. 'Oh, it's safe enough. Airlock's got no oxygen and it's the same temperature as outside. Aivas assured us that it's impotent in this form, can't alter. At that, we managed what the settlers never could – we captured Thread in its dormant stage.'

Lessa shuddered in revulsion. 'Get rid of it!' she said with a dramatic gesture of her hand. 'Get rid of it!'

'Lytol's already assembling a team to dissect it.'

'Why?' Lessa flinched again.

'Curiosity, I suppose. Though Aivas could merely be responding to another of those earlier imperatives of his he's so determined to implement.'

F'lar gave Jaxom a long hard look. Then he held up the *klah* pitcher, gesturing for Jaxom to join him at the table for refreshment. Jaxom nodded gratefully and took the chair F'lar indicated while the steaming *klah* was poured.

'I don't care what Aivas is implementing,' Lessa was saying, 'I don't like the idea of Thread on the *Yokohama*. Suppose . . .'

'Aivas would not expose us to danger,' F'lar said, giving her a soothing smile. 'I find Jaxom's comments on Aivas's mandates extremely perceptive.' He settled in a chair and, cradling his *klah* cup, leaned across the table. 'I'm curious, Jaxom, and you're more in Aivas's company these days than we are: this dissection business makes me wonder if Aivas's basic imperatives conflict with ours?'

'Not where the annihilation of Thread is concerned. Though sometimes I don't understand at all why he has us doing some of those endless drills and exercises. Especially now that Aivas has been revealed as fallible.'

F'lar grinned. 'Did Aivas ever say he was not?'

'He likes to give the impression that he's never wrong,' Lessa said in a sharp tone, looking alarmed.

Jaxom grinned. 'Good teacher image, and that's necessary when he has to pound all these radical ideas into our parochial heads.'

'Is his fallibility a danger to us?' F'lar asked.

'I don't really think so. I'm just commenting on it since we are private today,' Jaxom went on, 'and because I was so surprised when Aivas did not know that Thread's descent passed so close to the *Yokohama*.'

F'lar blinked, absorbing that information and Lessa's frown deepened. 'Surprised? Or worried?'

'Well, it's not his fault. The ancients didn't know it either,' and their lapse gave Jaxom a certain satisfaction.

F'lar grinned back at him. 'I see what you mean, Jaxom. Makes them more human.'

'And Aivas not so inhumanly perfect.'

'Well, it doesn't please me,' Lessa said, her eyes snapping. 'We've believed everything Aivas has told us . . .'

'Don't fret, Lessa. So far Aivas has not lied to us . . .'

'But if he doesn't know everything, how can we now be sure he's guiding us in the right direction with this great plan of his that's supposed to destroy Thread for ever?' she wanted to know.

'I'm beginning to figure out what that's going to be,' Jaxom said so confidently that Lessa gave him a long look. 'Aivas is obviously teaching us at the rate at which he feels we'll be able to absorb the revolutionary ideas; these exercises are what we have to perfect before we can achieve his goals, which are ours, and were our ancestors.'

'And will you let us in on your conclusions?' Lessa's tone was as caustic as Jaxom had ever heard it.

'It has to do with having a Thread in the airlock and being able to analyse it unemotionally, the way Sharra, Oldive and the others can identify bacteria and develop ways of combating infection. It has to do with becoming accustomed to moving in free fall or in airless space, in using sophisticated equipment as if it were a third arm or an extra set of brains. That's all Aivas is, you know. An extra set of brains with a phenomenal, and infallible, memory.' F'lar regarded Jaxom with growing respect. 'And possessing a knowledge of the advanced technology we have lacked, so we couldn't do more than hold Thread at bay. But it's the dragons, and their riders, that Aivas needs to demolish Thread.'

'That's obvious, considering the questions Aivas keeps asking us,' Lessa put in sharply. 'I'd feel happier if we knew what he wants our dragons to do.' Ramoth gave a crisp bark of agreement. 'I'd also like to know when he'll let the larger dragons up on the *Yokohama*.' Both Ramoth and Mnementh bugled their agreement.

Jaxom grinned at Lessa. 'Now, Lessa, don't be mean. It's not often that the greens get the jump on their bigger clutchmates. Allow them their moment of glory. At any rate, your chance comes soon. Sharra and Mirrim are monitoring the oxygen levels in the cargo bay and, as soon as the atmosphere's at the proper consistency, you'll be very welcome. Of course, you can always ask a green to fly you up there.'

Emitting an angry rumble, Ramoth turned on Jaxom eyes that whirled with occasional flickers of red.

'There! You know what Ramoth thinks of that idea,' Lessa replied but there was a glint of amusement in her eyes. 'As if I'd consider for one moment being conveyed by a green,' she added to soothe her weyrmate.

'A white?' Jaxom offered slyly.

Ramoth rumbled again but not quite so angrily and sneezed, giving a poor opinion of that option.

I'd be exceedingly careful carrying Lessa, Ramoth, Ruth said. *I fit on the bridge which is warmer than the cargo bay and Lessa would see much more on the bridge than in that dark cavern.*

'I heard,' Lessa said when Jaxom opened his mouth to relay the message.

'I know that Aivas wants all the bronze and brown dragons to get used to free-fall conditions. The bay's the only large open area that they'll fit in. The algae farm is developing beautifully so it shouldn't be long now.'

Lessa cocked her head at Jaxom, her expression thoughtful. 'Does Aivas plan for the dragons to move those ships?'

'Move the ships?' Both Jaxom and F'lar were surprised by that question.

'Why? How?' F'lar asked.

'Remember, F'lar, when Aivas insisted that the dragons should be able to move things telekinetically?'

'Dragons can only move themselves, their riders and what they carry,' F'lar said in a categorical manner. 'They cannot move things they're not holding. And what good would come of moving the ships? If his plan is somehow to use the ships to blow up the Red Star, I don't see what good that would accomplish. Not as I understand his lessons in spatial mechanics.'

'No more do I.' Jaxom took the last gulp of his *klah* and rose. 'Well, I've delivered my report of today's surprise.'

'For which you have our gratitude,' F'lar said.

'If that kind of pre-destruction turns out to be beneficial, we can set up a regular schedule to switch the shields,' Jaxom said. 'You can even have a chance at programming the mode yourselves.'

'I'm sure it will be feasible, Jaxom. Anything that destroys Thread is helpful,' F'lar said, rising to accompany the young Lord to the ledge.

'You won't worry about Aivas' fallibility, will you, F'lar?' Jaxom asked in a lowered voice when they were in the short corridor beyond the weyr.

'Me? No, certainly not,' the Weyrleader assured him. 'We've learned so much already from Aivas that, even if his vaunted plan fails, we'll surely find our own ways of ridding Pern of Thread by the next Pass. But, somehow, Jaxom,' and F'lar gripped his arm hard to show his implacable resolve, 'I know we'll manage do it in this Pass! Make no mistake about that! We'll do it in my lifetime!'

When the Smithcrafters returned to Landing, thoroughly elated by their time aboard the *Yokohama*, there was some contention over who should be allowed the opportunity to initiate the destruct mode. And of a more immediate nature, who would have the opportunity to dissect the Thread specimen.

'You'd have to choose carefully,' Lytol said, 'for too many

folk believe that just being in the presence of Thread is followed by a terrible death. I've sent quite a few messages off to find qualified persons to perform the task and, so far, there's been no response.'

'You might not get one,' Piemur said. He had been waiting for Jancis' return, a sleeping Pierjan limp in the backpack. 'I suppose the knowledge would be useful even if it'll become academic by the end of this Pass.'

Master Robinton held up his hand. 'I'll go if no-one else will.'

He was so besieged with protests that he grinned. 'So long as I can visit the *Yokohama* at some point in the very near future. And DON'T,' he glared about him, 'tell me that my health won't permit it. I found data in the medical files on how heart patients were frequently sent to free-fall wards on satellites to recuperate. A visit to the *Yokohama* would, therefore, be *beneficial* for my health and it could do my heart good to stab a sequence that destroyed Thread! Did one of your messages go to Oldive or Sharra, Lytol? Well, then, they're both busy folk but they'll get back to you in time. And if one of them goes, why I'd have my Healer at hand.'

Considerable consternation was roused when it became more widely known that a Thread ovoid had been procured. Aivas obliged with scenes of it reposing in Airlock A. It remained there unchanging for several days, proving that in its present state it posed no danger to anyone.

More importantly, Lessa and F'lar reported favourably on the reduction of Thread density during the latest Fall over Nerat. There had been three long columns entirely free of the deadly rain. So Lessa and F'lar came to Landing to discuss adding that task to the on-board duties. Aivas had a tape of the incident so the Benden Weyrleaders could view it, and did so several times.

'Incredible to think Thread can be destroyed without dragon assistance,' Lessa murmured in a low voice.

'Too bad there aren't a dozen more colony ships up there,' Piemur said.

'Then dragons wouldn't have been needed, and *that* doesn't bear thinking of,' Lessa snapped back at him.

'I spoke as a harper, Weyrwoman,' Piemur said courteously, 'as I for one am very glad dragons do exist.'

'I think, F'lar, that we should go to the *Yokohama*,' Lessa remarked. 'There's enough oxygen for Ramoth and Mnementh in the cargo bay by now, isn't there, Aivas?'

'There is. It is essential that the larger dragons become accustomed to the conditions that pertain in space,' Aivas replied. Lessa and F'lar exchanged meaningful glances. 'The next stream should intersect with the *Yokohama*'s orbit in three days' time, at precisely 15.22 hours ship time.'

'That's late morning, isn't it, Benden time?' F'lar asked, turning to Lessa. 'We'll go then, direct from Benden.'

'Who's going to take me then?' Robinton asked, sitting straight up in his chair and looking aggrieved.

'I will,' said D'ram. 'Surely there's enough air for three big dragons, isn't there, Aivas?' The old Weyrleader's tone implied that there had better be.

'Certainly,' was Aivas's prompt assurance.

'Well, then,' Robinton said, brushing his hands together in complete satisfaction, 'that takes care of that.'

Chapter Thirteen

Lessa was just a trifle put out when Ruth, with Jaxom, Sharra and Oldive astride, joined the three big dragons the morning of their first ascent to the *Yokohama*.

'Sharra and Oldive volunteered to dissect the Thread egg,' Jaxom said without any apology for what Lessa clearly considered an intrusion, 'and I'm to man the telescope and give Aivas fore and aft views of the Thread stream.'

What Jaxom didn't say was that Ruth might need to give the big dragons a few helpful hints on how to manage themselves in free fall. So far, none of the green dragons had experienced any difficulty with the unusual sensation of weightlessness. The fire-lizards had been totally fearless and almost casual about coming up to see what the dragons, especially Ruth, were doing on the *Yokohama*. Mirrim was scheduled for algae farming on the other two vessels that day so that, with Ruth, that gave the party two dragons suitable for bridge-to-bridge transfer.

Going *between* from the brilliant sunlight and balmy air of Landing to the big dimly lit cargo bay on the *Yokohama* brought exclamations from all the initiates.

'Jaxom, I thought you said there were lights,' Lessa said.

'There are,' Jaxom said, agilely dismounting and expertly pushing himself towards the main switches on the wall by the lift. He was rather pleased that, with such an audience, he arrived effortlessly at the exact spot. Being well aware of the load soon to be taxing the solar panels, he activated only the ring lights, not the overhead globes which ate power.

'Amazing!' Master Robinton exclaimed, staring around the immense and empty facility.

Ramoth made an odd little noise in her throat as she viewed her surroundings, her eyes idly whirling. Mnementh lowered his head, sniffing at the scarred deck plates, peering into the corners, his eyes calm. D'ram's Tiroth stretched his neck until his head reached the ceiling. At that point, his feet lifted slowly from the floor, startling the big bronze into a bellow of protest.

You are in free fall, Tiroth, Ruth said casually, *every action has a reaction. Gently push yourself back to the floor with your snout. See? That was easy.*

Then Ramoth swung her head too rapidly to see what was happening to Tiroth and she started to drift.

Don't fight the motion, Ramoth, Ruth said, *just relax and let yourself go with the movement. Now, easily swing your head back. See, it's not hard at all. Look at me.*

'Ruth!' Jaxom said repressively, 'don't you dare show off.'

I'm not showing off, I'm showing! Ruth executed a slow back flip, being careful that his wings were tight against his spine and wouldn't interfere with his progress. *We weigh no more than a fire-lizard up here!* And then he twirled around on his tail end.

'Ruth!' Jaxom bellowed, his voice echoing back to him from the walls of the bay.

'I think you've made your point, Lord Jaxom,' F'lar said, a ripple of suppressed amusement in his voice. 'Easy does it, right?' Moving carefully, F'lar swung out of his accustomed perch between Mnementh's neck ridges and found that he had propelled himself deckward in a floating motion. 'An incredible feeling! Try it, Lessa. I know you don't weigh much under any circumstances but- I just drifted down! Amazing sensation! No strain for you, Robinton.'

There were a few misjudgements as the passengers experimented. Sharra, discreetly assisting Masterhealer Oldive to the deck, made for the lift to start their day's project – a close examination of the egg in the airlock. For they had felt it their duty to set an example for their faint-hearted colleagues. Aivas had recommended that they take the Thread to the medical station on the top coldsleep deck. Laboratory facilities were still in place, including a microscope more powerful than anything they had yet managed to build. The section had air, and while not yet warm, that would be to their advantage. For an unemotional piece of machinery, Aivas was exhibiting an odd insistence for what Sharra would have thought a relatively unimportant element of the total project.

When everyone had gotten somewhat accustomed to the vagaries of free fall, Jaxom escorted them to the bridge.

Certainly Jaxom was as eager to show Lessa, F'lar, Robinton and D'ram his familiarity with the *Yokohama*'s bridge as Ruth was to discreetly supervise the big dragons. Jaxom's novices did not disappoint him for they were as genuinely awestruck by the view of Pern as he could wish. He let them absorb the wondrous sight of the sunlit continent, the brilliantly blue sea. Then he gently shooed them out so that the lift door could close. They clung for a while to the guard rail, coming to terms with their experience.

Propelling himself smoothly to the captain's chair, Jaxom fed the telescope program, checked the ready room where Sharra was helping Oldive into a spacesuit, and tuned one of the ceiling screens in to the laboratory's occupant. Sharra had adjusted one of the optics so the tank was under observation.

'It's not as big as I thought it'd be,' F'lar said, dragging his gaze away from the riveting view of Pern.

'No, it's not. That's why it'd be interesting to see how a big long Thread fits into such a confined envelope,' Jaxom replied.

Lessa shot one glance at it before turning back to the more compelling panorama. 'Can we go to the window?' she asked.

'Just push yourself off gently . . . don't worry,' he said when she started to float and tried to stop herself. 'Just flow. Don't struggle.' She went by him, rotating, and he reached up and halted the motion. Then, with a gentle shove, aimed her at the window.

Robinton, having observed her mistakes, did not commit them and shortly was beside her at the window, his feet dangling a handspan above the floor. D'ram gave a grunt and went hand-over-hand down to the nearest console, strapping himself into the chair.

'How long before the stream starts to intersect the *Yokohama's* path?' he asked.

That had been configured so Jaxom set D'ram's screen at its highest magnification and called up the appropriate sector. The lessons and drills Aivas had heaped on him were now at his fingertips. He was quite at ease using the *Yokohama's* command console.

As D'ram's screen refocused, the old bronze rider reared back in his chair, his expression blank with shock as the ragged beginnings of the wave appeared so immediately in front of him.

'It's not that close to us yet, D'ram. I just gave you an enhanced image. I'll give you the actual perspective,' and Jaxom altered the magnitude. Now the incoming stream was a sun-lit smudge dropping towards them from the fourth quadrant.

'How near is it?' D'ram asked, his voice dry and cracking.

'Proximity monitor suggests we've a good ten minutes before contact,' Jaxom said.

F'lar cautiously made his way to D'ram, hanging on to the chair back, his legs almost horizontal to the floor. Then he levered himself into the other station, strapping in.

'Are you all right down there?' Jaxom asked Ruth as privately as he could so as not to be overheard by Ramoth.

She's far too busy enjoying free fall, Ruth replied, his tone amused. *She's better at it than Mnementh and Tiroth for all she's bigger. She's not using as much shove. I think they are doing much better without their riders watching. Watch your wings, Ramoth! Not much room in here.*

Jaxom covered his grin with his hand. Then froze as he caught movement in the lab. It was only Sharra and Oldive entering: Sharra moving as gracefully as the magnetic boots allowed, one gloved hand guiding Oldive's jerkier progress.

Their attempts to penetrate the hard shell of Thread almost made Jaxom miss the stream's rapid approach. But D'ram had been watching and Mirrim, on green Path, arrived on the bridge.

'Who'm I taking to the *Bahrain*?' she asked, grinning at the sight of Lessa and Robinton stretched across the window.

'Whoever will go with you,' Jaxom said. 'Lessa? F'lar?'

Lessa made an injudiciously sharp movement of her head and flattened herself against the window. 'I'll go with you, Mirrim. No, Ramoth, it's perfectly all right. I assure you that you would NOT fit on the bridge here, much less on the *Bahrain*'s. You learn to keep your balance down there in the bay where you have some space to manoeuvre.'

Jaxom asked Ruth to oblige F'lar and the white dragon jumped *between* to the bridge, at the opposite end of the level from Path.

'You know the drill?' Jaxom felt he had to ask the Benden Weyrleaders.

Lessa gave him a hard stare as she floated across to Path but F'lar chuckled and replied meekly, 'I assure you, we've been practising hard, Jaxom. My thanks, Ruth,' he added as he glided up to the white dragon's back and settled himself.

'Bit easier to bestride than that great hulk of yours, isn't he?' Jaxom replied, grinning at the mild surprise on the bronze rider's face. 'Have a good destructive time! You've got three minutes before contact.'

'Where do I sit, Jaxom?' Robinton asked eagerly, pushing himself off from the window.

'Where F'lar was.'

Much as Jaxom's fingers itched to insert the command, he found it equally gratifying to watch the expression on the Harper's face as he performed the task. As the Smiths had on the previous occasion, both men recoiled as the ovoids hurtled towards the window. D'ram grunted as the first puffs signalled the destruction. Then sat with arms folded across his chest, eyes narrowed and a look of deep satisfaction on his face.

'You know, D'ram, we really ought to get Lytol to come here one time,' Robinton said. 'It might ease his heart to destroy Thread. He never had the chance as a rider.'

'Might do him some good at that,' D'ram remarked thoughtfully.

'Aivas?' Jaxom opened the channel to Landing, 'are the pictures coming in clearly enough?'

'Yes, Jaxom, and the density is up by 7 per cent or more on the previous Fall.'

'Then this pre-destruction will be welcome.'

Jaxom could then turn his attention to the efforts of Sharra and Oldive in the coldsleep laboratory. Despite the magnetic soles of their boots which kept them firmly attached to the deck, the two Healers were finding it difficult to penetrate the shell of the Thread with the instruments they had brought with them.

'We've pounded, we've chipped, we've scraped,' Sharra told Jaxom, 'and we've not so much as scratched the surface.' She sounded disgusted, waving a chisel in frustration.

'So much for those who fear it would leak out and devour us,' Oldive said. He sounded more amused than frustrated. 'Amazing envelope. Impervious to everything we thought would easily cut through it.'

'Diamond cutters?' Jaxom suggested.

'You know, that might be just the thing,' Oldive said, well pleased with the suggestion. 'Well, I certainly don't mind coming up here again. I've never felt so mobile.' Although Oldive paid no attention to his physical handicaps, his hunched back and crushed pelvis had given him uneven leg lengths and a crabbed gait. In weightlessness these problems were neutralized. No wonder he found free fall attractive.

'This is an instance,' Aivas said at his blandest, 'when the teleportational abilities of the fire-lizards would come in exceedingly useful.'

'Neither Meer nor Talla wouldn't know a diamond cutter if it bit them,' Sharra said ruefully. Then Jaxom heard her ruffled breath of a sigh. 'I doubt if even that sort of an edge will have any effect on this thing. Its casing is impervious.'

'Not to heat,' Jaxom reminded her.

'There is no way, Lord Jaxom of Ruatha,' Sharra said, and in the screen Jaxom saw her settle her hands to her hips in a characteristic posture, 'that you will get us to heat that thing up to simulate the friction of an ovoid's passage through atmospheric levels. Not that one could use a flamethrower in such a confined space as this lab.'

'You do not have the technology necessary to produce a narrow heat beam such as a laser that would be effective on such a casing,' Aivas added. 'Another area in which you will have to make great progress over the next Turn.'

'Oh? Why?' Jaxom asked, noting that both Robinton and D'ram reacted to that announcement as quickly as he did.

'There is no point, at this juncture, to elaborate on device or need,' Aivas replied. 'It is a matter which has been placed in the Mastersmith's hands but does not have priority over other, more essential, projects.'

'Haven't you any helpful suggestions for us?' Sharra asked Aivas in a caustic tone.

'The diamond cutter edge will be effective.'

'Then, why on earth, didn't you suggest that we bring one along on this trip?' Sharra wanted to know.

'The question was not put to this facility.'

'The trouble with you, Aivas,' Sharra continued with some asperity, 'is that you only tell us what you think we should know: not necessarily all we *need* to know or what we *want* to know.'

A long silence ensued, during which she and Oldive left the laboratory, sealing the door behind them.

'Sharra's right, you know,' D'ram remarked, breaking the ensuing silence.

'Indeed,' Robinton said.

'But would we have thought that a diamond cutter would be necessary, considering the selection of edged tools Sharra and Oldive did bring with them?' Jaxom asked, though he agreed completely with his mate. That was a corollary to what he'd said to F'lar and Lessa. In one sense, he was rather proud of her for speaking so bluntly. Aivas hadn't refuted the accusation. That was also significant.

Robinton shrugged in answer to Jaxom's question. D'ram, however, pulled at his lower lip.

'Diamond cutters are used for gemstones and glass etching. Why would we think to use them to cut open a Thread capsule?' the old Weyrleader asked. Then he lifted his hands, expressing inadequacy.

'Master Fandarel would have,' Robinton remarked. Then he sighed. 'We have so much still to understand, to learn, to appreciate. Is there ever an end, Aivas?'

'To what?'

Master Robinton turned a wry smile to Jaxom. 'The question was rhetorical, Aivas.'

From Aivas, there was silence.

Later, when the group returned to Cove Hold, the consensus was that the sojourn on the *Yokohama* had been eminently successful. The dragons had become comfortable in free fall: the humans had had the gratifying experience of cutting ship-shaped tunnels through incoming Thread at no risk to themselves or their dragons. Once their riders had dismounted, the dragons headed for the warm water of the Cove lagoon and the humans were by no means averse to a relaxing swim. Fortunately, Lytol had anticipated this so the meal he had ordered could be delayed until all had been refreshed.

Ramoth had got so accustomed to fire-lizards by now that she did not object when wild ones came to assist the riders in scrubbing their dragons. In fact, Ramoth insisted that because she was the biggest, she needed more to help Lessa scrub her, Lessa not being as big as the other riders. *And Ruth has Jaxom and Sharra to bathe him,* she added imperiously.

When a laughing Lessa repeated Ramoth's remark, Robinton announced that he was more than willing to scrub a queen. Then D'ram said that there were far too many fire-lizards helping Lessa, whereas Robinton had been flown to the *Yokohama* by Tiroth and so the Harper ought, out of courtesy, to wash the bronze. In the end, all the apprentices and journeyfolk working at Cove Hold, save Lytol, waded into the waters and helped bathe the five dragons.

After a very pleasant evening meal spent in most congenial company, Jaxom, Sharra and Oldive reluctantly departed for Ruatha where Oldive would spend the rest of that day in the Ruathan infirmary. Jaxom was as accustomed to these long days as Sharra. Making use of the extra hours allowed him to acquit his Hold responsibilities while indulging himself in the Aivas schedule. While Sharra and Oldive dealt with the sick and infirm of the Hold, he located Brand and oversaw the enlargement of the beasthold at Riverside, and checked over the improvements to two more minor Hold properties.

Having put in a twenty hour day, he was not best pleased then to be awakened in the black of the night by an urgent message from F'lessan, relayed to him by Ruth.

Golanth says that the roof of Honshu caved in and something very curious, and quite possibly very important, has been discovered in a secret room. Ruth said, faithfully repeating what he had been told. *Golanth has informed Lessa, F'lar, K'van and T'gellan. Messages have also been sent to Master Fandarel, and for Master Robinton to relay to Aivas.*

Jaxom did not move for a long moment, though his mind actively considered the information. He resented being roused from much needed rest and yearned to go back to sleep.

Golanth does not ever bother us unnecessarily, Ruth added almost contritely.

'I know that!' Jaxom replied wearily. 'Any indication of Aivas's response to this message?'

If you are not in Aivas's presence, I can't hear what he says. Ruth was silent for a long moment while Jaxom argued with himself about leaving the warm bed and his sleeping wife and making an adequate response to this new summons. *Tiroth is bringing all three from Cove Hold with him. He says that Lytol believes this could be very important. Aivas was insistent that these sacks be investigated as soon as possible. Ramoth and Mnementh will come. Everyone who was asked is coming.*

The unspoken inference was that Jaxom had better be there, too. Stifling a groan, Jaxom eased himself out of the bed, careful not to disturb Sharra. She needed the sleep as much as he did. Maybe this wouldn't take long and he could get back before she discovered him gone again. She and Oldive were keen to return to the *Yokohama* with a diamond cutter. He would hate to disappoint them because he'd been called elsewhere.

He dressed, light clothing under his riding gear, for it would be warmer in Honshu. He was pleased that, sleepy as he was, he could remember such details. He did not, as he frequently did, check the riding harness which he left openly on the peg in Ruth's weyr. With the deftness of long practice, he rigged his covert gear on Ruth and, throwing open the wide doors to Ruth's quarters, followed the white dragon out to the courtyard to mount. The watchdragon, the watchwher and some of the Hold's resident fire-lizards silently observed their departure, their bright eyes gleaming blue or green spheres in the night.

What a time to send for folk, Jaxom thought as Ruth leaped skyward.

What time is it in Honshu? Ruth asked.

'Sun-up, probably!' Jaxom replied testily, envisioning the facade of Honshu Hold that F'lessan had vividly described to him.

Between, Jaxom shivered despite his fur-lined riding jacket. Two breaths later they were hovering above a sea of mist, with dawn just breaking. Around them were other dragons, clinging to pinnacles that rose above the obscuring vapour. Rather than hover, Ruth descended to the nearest vacant spire and nodded greetings to the other dragons.

'And where is Honshu?' Jaxom wanted to know.

Ramoth says it's obscured in the river mist to our right. I knew where I was going. It just isn't visible yet, Ruth replied. *Today begins beautifully, doesn't it?* he added unexpectedly, gazing to his right, eastward where the sky was a lighter blue.

Grudgingly, Jaxom agreed as he contemplated the view. To his left, both moons were visible, half full, hanging in a sky of an unusual clear and cloudless blue as night retreated westward. Where he should still be in his bed. He suppressed the urge to lean forward in his saddle, rest his head on Ruth's neck and go back to sleep until the mist cleared. But the longer he looked on a today so beautifully beginning – he didn't know that Ruth could be so lyrical – he found it increasingly difficult to look away.

More dragons arrived, hovered, surprised to discover their landing site obscured, for the whole valley in front of Honshu was mist-clad, and eventually they settled wherever they could.

Golanth apologizes, Ruth informed Jaxom. *The mist rolled up from the river just as day broke. He says that once the sun is up, this will clear away. He says he will go stand near the place where the roof collapsed.* Ruth turned his head in the appropriate direction and Jaxom, seeing with his dragon's eyes, spotted Golanth's bronze shape, rising out of the mist as the bronze settled on a still invisible surface. *Golanth says that there is hot* klah *and porridge waiting and so few of us have seen Honshu that we have a nice surprise coming. He says there is very good hunting in the valley. When it's visible.*

Ruth's qualifier touched Jaxom's sense of humour and he chuckled himself out of irritability just as the sun rose, shooting bright, hot rays across the mist. Then a breeze picked up energy and very shortly the mist indeed cleared away, and Honshu's cliff face became visible: Golanth perched on the heights.

Golanth says for us to land you on the upper level by the Hold's main door. There should be enough room for all. More of the roof might collapse and, on the lower level, the beasthold hasn't been completely cleaned out yet. F'lessan doesn't want anyone entering that way.

Almost as one, the waiting dragons lofted themselves to comply. Perhaps it was the downdraft of great wings wafting away the last tendrils of mist, but by the time the dragons were ready to land, the vapour had cleared right up to the second tier of window slits.

F'lessan and the other weyrfolk who were making Honshu liveable waited at the wide doorway, cheering the arrivals.

'Thanks for coming so promptly,' F'lessan said, grinning broadly. 'I don't think you'll be disappointed. Sorry to get you out of your bed, Jaxom, because I know you had a long day, but you'd hate me to leave you out of this.' The young bronze rider threw a companionable arm about Jaxom's shoulders, his expression so uncharacteristically anxious, that Jaxom felt obliged to reassure him.

'It's thoughtful of you to have food and *klah* laid on, F'lessan,' Lessa said as she crossed the entrance hall, 'but I'd rather see your discovery first.'

F'lessan pointed to plastic sacks on the long table in the main room. 'You can see the secret room, too, if you don't mind a long climb up winding stairs.'

Everyone but Jaxom hurried to the table. Jaxom, however, stood on the threshold, staring up at the amazing murals, their colours as brilliant as the day they'd been first applied. Vaguely he recalled Lytol and Robinton talking about the decorations at Honshu but he hadn't expected anything as magnificent as this.

'Rather spectacular, isn't it?' F'lessan said, turning back to his old friend. He spent a long moment admiring it, too. 'The place is not really big enough for a Weyr, though Golanth says that there're plenty of good ledges to lie on. And good eating.'

'Southern Weyr had less than this originally,' Jaxom reminded him.

'True. But it's arranged as a Hold. I just don't want anyone lording it in here,' F'lessan said with unexpected fervour. 'People know they can come and go freely in a Weyr. C'mon. You'll want to see the stuff I found. And now that I've got you here at last, you're going to see the whole place. It is remarkably well preserved and full of the most fascinating tools and equipment. All the Smiths are drooling over them.'

'I've had the complete inventory from Jancis,' Jaxom said with a wry grin.

F'lessan's find was most unusual. Liquid carefully stored in plastic bags. Each had been tied shut around the neck by rigid strips which ended in wide tabs. These were inscribed with strokes in odd patterns, the like of which neither Robinton nor Lytol had seen in all of Aivas's records.

'I opened one,' F'lessan said, pointing to the sack sitting in the bowl, its mouth carefully peeled back so that its contents were accessible. 'I thought at first it had to be water but it's not. It's got an odd sheen to it and anyway, water would long since have evaporated, I think. It smells funny. I didn't taste it.'

Lytol and Fandarel nearly bumped heads as both leaned over to sniff the liquid. Fandarel dipped in a finger and smelled it, grimacing.

'Definitely not drinkable.'

'We should take this sack to Aivas for examination,' Lytol said. 'Is this all there were?'

'No,' F'lessan replied blithely. 'Thirty-four more, plus the six here. They don't all contain the same amount of whatever it is. There were a few empty sacks in the attic so some leakage occurred. Or maybe tunnel snakes chewed their way through. They'll eat anything.'

'You said something about a stairway?' Lessa asked.

'Well, the steps weren't completely cut. Just a toe hold up the final curve. We didn't bother to explore that level . . . until Benmeth crashed through.'

'You didn't say whether she hurt herself or not,' Lessa said, almost accusingly.

F'lessan grinned, rarely affected by his mother's moods. 'Scraped her right hind leg but J'lono's slathered numbweed all over her. She's down in the workroom.'

'Show me where the stairs are, F'lessan,' F'lar said, and when the young bronze rider had indicated the doorway, the Benden Weyrleader led the way, followed closely by Fandarel, Lytol, K'van, and T'gellan.

'Oh, no, you don't,' Lessa said, grabbing Robinton by the arm. 'Free fall's all right but stairs are not, Robinton. And you won't have eaten yet if I know you.'

Not fancying a long hike, Jaxom added his persuasions to Lessa's and F'lessan insisted that Robinton would insult the weyrfolk if he didn't sit down right now and enjoy Honshu's hospitality.

'It is fuel,' Aivas said and Robinton had never heard such ringing tones from the facility. 'Fuel!'

'Yes, but is it any good after so many centuries?' Fandarel wanted to know.

Jaxom had a brilliant vision of the three shuttles lifting

off the ship meadow and cancelled it almost immediately as a total impossiblity. Those ships would never fly again. Pern hadn't the technology necessary to repair them properly.

'The fuel does not deteriorate with age, nor does the sample you brought appear to have suffered any contamination. Since this discovery is in Honshu, Kenjo Fusaiyuki's Stake Hold, it is logical to assume that this is part of the fuel he had diverted for his personal use. Mention was made of this cache by Captain Keroon when the *Moth* was readied for its abortive attempt to collect Thread specimens from space and a search for the fuel was conducted at Honshu but was never found.'

'But the sled was so well preserved, couldn't we . . .' Fandarel began excitedly.

'The sled used power packs, not fuel. The forty sacks which have been recovered will be put to excellent use,' Aivas said.

'Where? Why? In what?' Jaxom demanded.

'The shuttles in the field?' Piemur asked, his face flushed with anticipation. And Jaxom realized that he was not the only one who had had dazzling visions.

'Even were you technologically more advanced, they have deteriorated past repair,' Aivas said. 'This unexpected dividend will be put to very good use when the alternatives have been thoroughly reviewed.'

Jaxom and Piemur exchanged expressions of disgust.

'Let me guess, Aivas,' Jaxom said, 'we could put all the fuel in the *Yokohama*'s tanks, or split it up between all three ships. There'd be enough to give us half-grav, some manoeuvrability – that is, if we wanted to go anywhere in those ships . . .' He finished on a querying note.

'There is insufficient fuel to reach the Oort Cloud,' Aivas said. 'Or to follow the direction of the Thread stream and use the destruct capability of the shields to reduce the density of the ovoids.'

Trying not to let his frustration show, Jaxom made himself grin at Piemur, 'Well, he thought of one course that I didn't.'

'Who are we to outguess Aivas?' Piemur asked but Jaxom noted the suppressed anger in the harper's eyes.

'One of these days . . .' Jaxom said just loud enough for Piemur to hear and Piemur nodded.

'But, Aivas, since there is this sample,' Fandarel said urgently, 'can you not analyse its composition so that we can duplicate it. Surely we can make enough fuel to take at least one ship to the Oort Cloud?'

'For what reason?'

'Why, to blow up the Oort Cloud! Destroy the Thread organism that is generated there!'

Another of Aivas' curious silences ensued and then suddenly the Rukbat system came up on the screen, the sun dwarfing its satellites. Abruptly the picture altered and the brilliant sun diminished to a pinpoint of light, the planets reduced out of visibility on the new scale and the swirling nebulosity of the Oort Cloud flowed across the screen, blotting out even the distant Rukbat. As had been demonstrated often before for students to comprehend spatial distances, a red line began to describe the orbit of the Red Star, through the Oort Cloud and back into the system, swinging around the primary, inside Pern's conventional path.

'Aivas certainly knows how to cut us down to size,' Piemur murmured.

'Oh!' Fandarel said, resigned. 'It is indeed difficult to appreciate the massive scale of the Cloud and the insignificance of our tiny world.'

'So how DO we destroy it to be rid of Thread?' F'lar asked.

'The best way to reduce the threat of Thread is to alter the orbit of the eccentric planet that brings it into Pern's system.'

'And when will you tell us how we accomplish that?'

'The research and technology required will shortly be completed.'

'Then finding the fuel makes no difference?' F'lessan slumped in disappointment, his usually merry expression glum.

'It may make a difference in another area, F'lessan. It is always good to have alternatives. You have all done exceedingly well.' That, from Aivas was praise indeed. 'Do not succumb to apathy.'

'What should I do with all these fuel sacks then?' F'lessan asked, dispiritedly.

'They should be transferred to a safe storage facility in Landing.'

'I shouldn't put them into anything else? Those sacks are old.'

'If they have lasted twenty-five hundred and twenty-eight years, they will suffice for another. Now, here is the schedule for bronze and brown dragons to jump to the cargo bays of all three ships. The latest readings exhibit sufficient oxygen levels to allow every dragon and rider some experience in free fall.'

'Why?' asked F'lar.

'So far even the smallest dragons have proved capable of learning to handle weightlessness. But it is essential that all the dragons of Pern be subjected to the experience. That will be essential for the success of the plan.'

The schedules were forwarded to the Weyrleaders of all eight Weyrs, and there was a good deal of jubilation from all but a few – and those were mainly riders of elderly dragons for whom even hunting was becoming difficult. The weyrlings were ecstatic and weyrlingmasters hard put to maintain discipline.

Each group was sent up with someone experienced in free fall, even Jancis, Piemur and Sharra were sent as monitors. There were often full fairs of fire-lizards tagging along and though that occasioned complaints, Aivas approved of their interest. A new enthusiasm swept through all the Weyrs, overcoming the mid-Pass apathy.

Three days later, fires were set among the fuel sacks but fire-lizards gave the alarm so no harm was done. On hearing of the near disaster, Aivas was unperturbed and, in an off-hand tone, informed the agitated Lytol and D'ram that this fuel was nonflammable. The relief was palpable but, when Fandarel heard, he immediately wanted to know exactly how this fuel provided the desired effect. Aivas responded with a lecture on the intricacies of seven kinds of jet engines, all different from simple reaction engines they had learned about, which made little sense even to Master Fandarel, to more complex multi-stage affairs.

That evening Master Morilton dispatched his fire-lizard with an urgent and horrified message that someone had destroyed all the lenses his Hall had ready to be installed in microscopes and telescopes, ruining months of hard and patient work. Later the next morning Master Fandarel found that the metal barrels he had been producing to house the lenses had been thrown into the forge fire and distempered overnight.

It was as well that the orientation programme for dragons was going so well or morale would have hit a new low. Then, as if the spate of bad news had ended, Oldive and Sharra were successful in penetrating the shell of the Thread egg with a black diamond cutter.

'I'm not much wiser,' Sharra told Jaxom when she returned home that evening. 'It's a complex organism and it's going to take us time to analyse it. We have to work so slowly. I think that may be why Aivas taught us how to culture bacteria. Good training for this investigation.'

'What did it look like . . . inside, I mean?'

'The most astonishing mess,' Sharra said, frowning in perplexity, then she gave a disparaging chuckle. 'I don't know what I thought it'd look like. In fact, I never thought about it at all. But, the ovoid is coated in layers of dirty, rock-hard ice, with all kinds of pebbles and grains and . . . and junk mixed up. It's sort of whiteish, yellow, black, grey . . . Is the yellow helium? Were you there for those lectures on liquefying gas? No, that was Piemur and Jancis.

'At any rate, there are rings that wrap round and round. You can separate the rings from the other material. There are tubes, and patches of bubbling stuff. Aivas said it was a very disorganized life form.'

Jaxom laughed in surprise. 'It certainly disorganizes us!'

'Silly! He doesn't mean it that way. But we couldn't do much today because we don't have the proper tools to work in 3 degree absolute temperatures.' She grinned in reminiscence. 'The tools we brought sort of went brittle and disintegrated in the cold.'

'Metal? Turned brittle?'

'Good Smithcraft steel, too. Aivas says we have to use special glass.'

'Glass, huh.' Jaxom thought of all the time Aivas had spent with Master Morilton and grinned. 'So that was why. But, how could Aivas have known then that we'd capture Thread when he didn't even know we could?'

'I'm not sure I followed all of that, Jaxom.'

'I'm not sure I did, too, lovey. I wonder who's getting the bigger surprises? Aivas? Or us?'

The next morning, Sharra asked Jaxom if he'd mind letting Ruth convey her to Master Oldive to confer on who else they would need to assist them in this study. Ruth was always glad to oblige Sharra so Jaxom needn't take her. His presence was required in Ruatha to preside with Brand over a long delayed Hold disciplinary meeting.

Jaxom was just taking his seat in the Great Hall when he caught a glimpse of Ruth departing with Sharra on his back. He bounced back to his feet in alarm.

'The harness, Ruth! Which harness did Sharra use?'

Simultaneously with Ruth's *She's safe*, her two fire-lizards screamed so loudly that Lamoth, the elderly bronze on Ruatha's heights, bugled a warning. As Jaxom watched, paralysed by shock, he saw Ruth slowly descending. Sharra clutching him tightly about the neck; Meer and Talla had hooked their talons in the shoulders of her riding jacket. The main riding strap dangled loosely between Ruth's legs.

Trembling with reaction to the near disaster to his beloved wife, Jaxom forgot dignity and duty as he tore out of the Great Hall. In his wish not to worry her with an incident he had almost forgotten, he had nearly cost her her life. As Ruth delicately landed in front of him, his hands were still shaking as he helped Sharra down from her precarious perch and embraced her tightly.

I should have asked which harness she had with her, Ruth said, his tone remorseful, his hide tinged grey with anxiety. *I could have told her where you hide the harness you're using now.*

'It's no fault of yours, Ruth. You're all right, Sharra? You didn't hurt yourself? When I saw you hanging . . .' His voice broke and he buried his face in her neck, aware that she was trembling nearly as much as he.

Sharra was quite willing to be comforted but, soon enough, she became aware of the audience and, with a weak embarrassed laugh, struggled to be free. He eased his hold further but did not relinquish the contact. If she hadn't been such a skilled rider . . . if Ruth hadn't been such a clever dragon . . .

'I thought you'd mended that harness,' she said, anxiously looking into his eyes.

'I had!' He couldn't tell her the truth, not with so many within earshot, but despite the bond between them, she did not apparently realize he was not being entirely candid.

'I've got to go, Jaxom,' Sharra said, duty warring with fright. 'Would Ruth be totally offended if I went with G'lanar on Lamoth?'

'You'll go on?' Jaxom was both amazed by and proud of his wife's courage and resilience.

'It's the best thing I can do, Jax, to get over this shock.' She leaned across him to stroke Ruth's nose. 'I know it wasn't your fault, dearest Ruth. Please relax! That shade of grey is not becoming!'

I felt the strap go as I leaped, Ruth told Jaxom. *I should have asked her which straps she used. I should have.*

'It's all right. *You saved Sharra,'* Jaxom repeated, never more grateful to his dragon than at this moment. '*She still has to get to the Healer Hall. On Lamoth with G'lanar.'*

Ruth eyed his rider, the orange of panic beginning to recede. *He's all right for an Oldtimer,* Ruth allowed grudgingly. *I wish that Dunluth and S'gar were back.*

'That pair can fly Thread. G'lanar is failing and Lamoth can barely chew his food any more, much less firestone.' Jaxom didn't think more of Ruth's comment then but tactfully asked the elderly dragon and rider to convey Sharra to the Healer Hall. He stripped off the dangling harness, rolling it up until he could examine it.

He watched the three until Lamoth went *between,* Meer and Talla following without fuss. Then he retraced his steps to the Great Hall while Brand and the understewards gestured for those attending the court to settle themselves.

'You never told her?' Brand murmured in Jaxom's ear as they sat down.

'I will now. That was too close.' Jaxom saw that his fingers were trembling as he sorted the papers he had scattered in panic.

'Indeed it was. Does this . . . obvious attempt on your life have anything to do with all the recent incidents?'

'I wish I knew.'

'You will speak to Benden now, won't you?' And Brand's look was severe and implacable.

'I will,' Jaxom agreed with a faint smile, 'because I know that you intend to.'

'So long as that's understood.' Then in a louder voice, Brand went on, 'the first case concerns the alleged misuse of Hold supplies . . .'

That evening Jaxom told Sharra every detail of the incident at Tillek Hold, and the investigations that Brand had set in motion: investigations that had produced no results at all, for Pell professed himself to be quite content working in his father's craft. And no-one had asked him about his Ruathan Bloodline. He was only a second cousin at best.

After Sharra had torn strips off him for 'sparing' her anxiety, they went over the entries in the Hold visitors' book and could find no one in the least bit suspicious. Ruth could not even be encouraging for he was not always in his weyr when Jaxom was at home. He usually joined whichever dragon was on duty on the heights.

Even old Dunluth, he added. *I scratch his itches, he scratches mine.*

Both Sharra and Jaxom were due at Landing the next day for a meeting concerning the vandalism.

'If you don't come clean about this incident, Jaxom, I will,' Sharra said, her expression fierce.

'That was about succession, Sharrie,' he objected. 'The destruction is a different matter entirely.'

'How do you know that?' she demanded, clenching her fists on the arm rest and shooting him an angry and reproachful glare. 'Especially when you're the leader for all of Aivas's plans.'

'Me? The leader?' Jaxom stared at her in complete surprise.

'Well, you are, even if you don't realize it.' Then her severe expression softened. 'You wouldn't,' and she gave him a sweetly condescending smile. 'You are, though. Take my word for it, and everyone on the planet knows it.'

'But I . . . I . . .'

'Oh, don't get fussed, Jax. It's one of your most endearing traits that you don't get puffed up with importance and irritate people with an inflated self-consequence.'

'Who does that?' Jaxom rapidly thought of all those working so diligently with him.

'No-one, but you'd have the right to.' She came to sit on his lap, coiling one arm about his neck, and stroking his frown smooth. 'That's why you might well be a target for the dissidents. You certainly can't hide from the fact that dissatisfaction about Aivas's far-too long-term project is increasing?'

Jaxom sighed, for it was but one more thing he had tried to play down. 'I'm all too aware. In fact, it's almost a relief to know they've come out in the open . . .'

'You know who they are?' Sharra stiffened in his arms.

He shook his head. 'Sebell knows who's likely to be involved but none of his harpers have been able to produce any evidence. And you can't really accuse a Lord Holder without pretty substantial proof.'

She murmured agreement to that and laid her head down on his shoulder. 'You are being careful, aren't you, Jax?' she asked in a low and anxious voice.

He hugged her to him. 'More than you are. How many times have I told you to check riding harness before you use it?' he wanted to know, grinning at her outraged reaction.

When the meeting convened the next day in Landing, Aivas took charge, first ordering the building cleared of all but those immediately involved.

'While these incidents are clearly directed at the new technology you are developing,' Aivas said, 'none, so far, threatens the success of the main drive of your efforts.'

'Not yet,' Robinton said darkly.

'I disagree,' Sharra said and fixed Jaxom with a steady

glance. When he hesitated, she added, 'Someone's trying to kill Jaxom.'

When the commotion subsided, Jaxom gave a full and concise report.

'That is disturbing,' Aivas said, raising his voice over the babel of questions. 'Is not the white dragon protection against such attempts? Can he not prevent them?'

'Don't get so upset,' Jaxom said, annoyed at the fuss, though he wanted to set his mind at rest over any further threat to Sharra. 'Ruth knew the moment the leather went and he saved Sharra's life. I left those riding straps right out in the open, and hid the set I use. It was only . . .'

'He was trying to keep me from worrying,' Sharra said in an acid tone. 'Brand is trying to find out who could have sliced the leathers. It was done very cleverly by someone who knew exactly what stress would be put on riding straps . . .'

'A dragonrider?' Lessa's voice rose to a near shriek and outside half the dragons on the heights bugled in alarm. 'There isn't a dragonrider on Pern who'd endanger Jaxom or Ruth!' And she glared at the young Lord as if he were at fault. He glared right back.

'Nor any way a dragonrider could do so without his dragon's awareness,' F'lar said emphatically.

'Nothing would be gained by . . .' and Lessa faltered, 'by disposing of Jaxom.'

'Could it have been as protest to my involvement with Thread?' Sharra asked.

Jaxom shook his head violently. 'How could it? Who would know that you'd want to have Ruth fly you to the Healer Hall?'

'Since it is usually Jaxom who flies Ruth,' Aivas's calm voice said, 'it is logical to assume that he was the target. No further attempts on his life must be permitted.'

'Meer and Talla have their orders,' Sharra said resolutely.

'What about Ruth?' Lessa demanded and was silenced by a cacophony of bugling from the massed dragons at Landing. She blinked in surprise at their belligerence. 'And, it would appear, every other dragon on Pern!' Then she leaned across to lay her hand on Sharra's arm. 'We're alert to the danger now.' She swung her glance to Jaxom and radiated rebuke. 'We should have known much earlier, young man!'

'I have not been in danger,' Jaxom protested. 'I have been very careful.'

'You would be wise to increase personal vigilance, Jaxom. Also, proper security measures must be promptly inaugurated to prevent further vandalism in every Crafthall which has undertaken to do specialized work!' Aivas said sternly. 'The recent destruction certainly delays the completion of useful equipment, but the vandals were, fortunately, not aware of the true significance of other crucial projects: the space helmets, the oxygen tanks and the additional spacesuits which are vital to the success of our endeavour.'

'All that work is divided among several Halls and different locations,' Fandarel said with an air of relief. Then he shook his head, his expression doleful. 'I find it very hard to believe that some member of my Crafthall could so wantonly destroy the hard work of his colleagues.'

'Your society is a trusting one,' Aivas said, 'and it is sad to see that trust betrayed.'

'It is indeed,' Fandarel said, his voice heavy with sadness. Then he straightened his shoulders. 'We will be vigilant. F'lar, would there be any riders available for extra guard duty?'

'Watchwhers would be more effective,' Lytol said entering the discussion for the first time. He had turned very pale, despite his southern tan, when Jaxom's peril was being discussed. 'They would be most effective and I am of the opinion that the Weyrs are stretched as far as they should be right now.'

'Watchwhers AND fire-lizards,' Fandarel said. 'Many of the Craftmasters involved have fire-lizards and once they know that they are to be vigilant, they will be.'

'My brother Toric has had good luck using some feline cubs,' Sharra put in. 'Of course, they have to be caged in the daytime for they are ferocious beasts.'

'Recruit whatever guardians are necessary but do not permit the essential manufacturing to be damaged. Tomorrow the dragons assigned to exercises in the *Yokohama* are to transport the fuel sacks. Master Fandarel, you will see that the sacks are emptied into the main tank. That will eliminate one security problem.'

'Would that we could remove all the vulnerable materials to the *Yokohama*!' F'lar said. 'Could we?' he then addressed Aivas.

'Unfortunately, that is impossible for a variety of reasons. However, as soon as items have been completed, they should indeed be transported to the safety of the *Yokohama*.'

'Is there any guarantee that they'd be safe there?' Lytol wanted to know.

He ignored those who regarded him with anger, dismay, disbelief or anxiety as he waited for Aivas's reassurance.

'This facility can efficiently and easily monitor the *Yokohama* as you cannot your individual Holds, Halls and Weyrs,' Aivas replied.

'And the guardian guards himself!' Lytol added in a low voice.

'QED'

'Cue ee dee?' Piemur asked.

'That has been demonstrated.'

Chapter Fourteen

O n the bridge of the *Yokohama* the next afternoon, Jaxom and Piemur leaned over the engineering console.

'I know we emptied all those sacks in,' Piemur said in an aggrieved tone, 'but you wouldn't know it from the gauge.'

'Big tank,' Jaxom said, giving the dial a tap. 'Drop in the bloody bucket.'

'All that work for nothing,' Piemur added, disgusted. They'd had to suit up because the fuel auxiliary intake pipe had been in a low pressure section. Piemur did not like the restrictions of a suit and the smell of tanked air. Despite weightlessness, the sacks had been awkward to manage: they could only take two at a time to the engineering level from the cargo bay where the dragons had transported them. And even more awkward to empty into the intake, following Aivas's instructions on the procedure to pour a heavy fluid like the fuel in free fall.

'Not for nothing,' Aivas replied. 'It is now safe from any tampering.'

'Then it was dangerous?' Piemur asked, shooting Jaxom an 'I told you so' look.

'The fuel was not flammable but, if spilled, there would be toxic effects. Soil impregnated with the fuel becomes sterile. It is wise to avoid any unnecessary problems.'

Jaxom rotated his shoulders, easing tense muscles. Sometimes, working in these free-fall conditions was harder than doing a similar task on Pern.

'We have quite enough trouble as it is,' Piemur said and then turned to Jaxom. '*Klah*?' and he lifted the hot bottle, one of Hamian's contraptions: a large, thick glass bottle, insulated by teased fibres of the same plant Bendarek was using to make paper and set inside a casing of Hamian's new hard plastic. It kept liquid warm or cold, though some people didn't know how the bottle knew the difference. 'Meatroll?' And he held out several wrapped rounds. They took turns sipping the *klah* from the bottle, being careful not to let droplets fall from their lips or the mouth of the flask.

Jaxom grinned. 'How is it that you always seems to have the very latest thingummies?'

Piemur rolled his eyes expressively. 'Aivas said it was a thermos and harpers traditionally try new things out! And besides, I'm resident at Landing where Hamian has his manufactory and you're just a runner-in, always missing the fun.'

Jaxom refused to rise to the jibe. 'Thanks for the food, Piemur, I'd worked up quite an appetite.'

They had taken off their helmets and gloves on entering the bridge and now made themselves comfortable in the console chairs. After the first edge of their hunger was allayed, Piemur gestured to Ruth, Farli and Meer who were plastered across the window, staring out.

'Do they see something we don't?' Piemur asked.

'I asked Ruth,' Jaxom said, leaning back as far as his oxy-unit would permit. 'He says he just likes to look at Pern, all pretty laid out like that. With the clouds and the differences in light, it never looks the same twice.'

'While you are eating,' Aivas said, 'this is an opportunity to explain another very important step in the training process.'

'Is that why we got the sack duty?' Piemur asked with a wink and a grin at Jaxom.

'You are as perceptive as ever, Piemur. It is easier to secure this channel to the bridge than any point at Landing.'

'We're all ears,' Piemur said, then added hastily. 'Figuratively speaking, naturally.'

'Accurate. It is essential to learn how much time dragons can spend in space unprotected by such suits as you are now wearing.'

'I thought you'd figured that out, Aivas,' Jaxom said. 'Ruth and Farli suffered no harm at all during the time they were on this bridge. They didn't seem to notice the cold and certainly weren't in oxygen debt.'

'They were on the bridge for about three and a half minutes. It is required that dragons function normally for a minimum of twelve minutes. Fifteen would be the upper time required.'

'For what?' Jaxom asked, leaning forward, elbows on his knees. Piemur's eyes were very bright with excitement.

'The exercise is to accustom them to being in space . . .'

'Having already become accustomed to weightlessness?' Jaxom asked.

'Exactly.'

'So we're at the walking stage?' Piemur asked.

'So to speak. The level of adaptability of your dragons is commendable. There have been no unfavourable reactions to the experience of free fall.'

'Why would there be?' Jaxom asked. 'It's on a level with hovering, or being *between*, and dragons have no problem with that. So now, they're to go extravehicular . . .'

'Wouldn't they float away?' Piemur asked, casting an anxious look at Jaxom. 'I mean, like the Thread eggs do?'

'Unless a violent movement was made, they would remain stationary,' Aivas said. 'As they will exit from the *Yokohama*, they are moving at the same speed, not at a different velocity, as the incoming Thread spheres are. However, to prevent any panic . . .'

'Dragons don't panic,' Jaxom said in flat contradiction, speaking before Piemur could utter a similar rebuke.

'Their riders might,' was Aivas's reply.

'I doubt it,' Jaxom replied.

'Perhaps dragonriders are a breed apart, Lord Jaxom,' Aivas said at his most formal, 'but records of many generations indicate that some humans, despite training and reassurance, can find themselves overwhelmed by agoraphobia. Therefore, to prevent panic, the dragon should anchor itself . . .'

'Himself . . .' Jaxom automatically corrected, for Aivas sometimes forgot the respectful pronouns.

'Or herself,' Piemur added, waggling a finger at the white rider.

'The dragon should be anchored securely to the *Yokohama*.'

'Lines? We can get rope or some of that strong fine cable Fandarel's been extruding,' Piemur suggested.

'That will not be necessary as a suitable surface is already available.'

Jaxom winked at Piemur for there was a hint in Aivas's voice that their chivvying was an annoying irrelevance.

'What?' Jaxom asked, his tone contrite. Such banter was delaying details that they had wanted to hear for Turns.

The screen in front of them lit up, showing a graphic of the *Yokohama* profile. The display altered to a close-up of the long shaft on which the engines were fitted, and the framework of spars that had once held the extra fuel tanks in place.

'Dragons can hang on the frames!' Jaxom cried. 'That would definitely offer a secure grip. And, unless I've misread the dimensions, those rails are as long as a Weyr Rim. Imagine, all the Weyrs of Pern, Piemur, out in space, along those girders! What a sight!'

'The only drawback to that,' Piemur said in a pragmatic tone, 'is that there aren't enough spacesuits for all the riders of Pern.'

'There will be sufficient spacesuits available when required,' Aivas informed them calmly, 'though not all the dragons in the Weyrs of Pern will be needed. Since you are still suited, Lord Jaxom, and have taken nourishment, perhaps you and Ruth would attempt an extravehicular activity today?'

Piemur's eyes grew wide and round, half bulging out of their sockets as he assimilated Aivas's astounding suggestion.

'By the first Egg, it's not the humans you've got to be wary of, Jaxom. It's Aivas who's trying to kill you!'

'Nonsense!' Jaxom replied hotly though, to be candid, he had felt his stomach leap almost in time to the accelerated beat of his heart at the notion of extravehicular activity. *'Ruth?'*

I'll see a lot more from there than I can from the window, was the white dragon's thoughtful response.

With a laugh that was only a trifle shaky, Jaxom told Piemur what Ruth had said.

The harper gave him a long incredulous look and sighed. 'I don't know which of you two is more outrageous. You'd dare anything, the pair of you would.' Then in a wry tone, 'And I'm supposed to be the reckless one.'

'But you aren't a dragonrider,' Jaxom said gently.

'The dragon makes the man?' Piemur shot back.

Jaxom smiled, sending a loving look at Ruth who was watching the two humans. 'With a dragon to guide and guard you, you tend to feel secure.'

'So long as your riding straps hold,' was Piemur's quick retort. Then the harper shook his head. 'Come to think on it, with Aivas as your mentor, you don't need to worry about what mere men could do to you.'

'Lord Jaxom will not be in any jeopardy, Harper Piemur,' Aivas said with customary composure.

'So you say!' Then Piemur fixed Jaxom with a fierce stare. 'So you're going to do it? Without checking with anyone?'

Jaxom glared right back, anger rising. 'I don't need to check with anyone, Piemur. I've been making my own decisions for a long time. This time I get to make it without anyone else's interference. Not yours, or F'lar's, or Lessa's or Robinton's.'

'Sharra's?' Piemur cocked his head, his eye contact unswerving.

It doesn't seem to be a hard thing Aivas asks us to do, Jaxom. It is no more dangerous than going between where we have nothing to hold on to. My talons are strong. My grip will be secure for both of us.

'Ruth sees no problems. If he did, I would certainly listen to him,' Jaxom said, very much aware that Sharra would undoubtedly share Piemur's reservations. 'I don't know why you're upset about e.v.a. I thought you'd want to be first.'

Piemur managed a flicker of a smile. 'One, I don't have a dragon to reassure me. Two, I dislike being trussed up in this thing,' and he flicked his hand at the spacesuit. Then his expression changed to a cocky grin, 'and three, it's just likely I'm one of those humans who'd panic out there with solid earth a million dragon lengths away from my feet. So,' and he got to his feet and reached for Jaxom's helmet, 'since I can't talk you out of it, go and do it. Now! Before I get myself in a knot!'

Jaxom gripped his shoulder. 'Don't forget that Aivas cannot endanger human life. And we've read, and seen tapes of spacemen doing e.v.a. drills.'

So let us go. Ruth pushed himself away from the window with just enough force to arrive by Jaxom. He peered down at Piemur's scowling face. *Tell Piemur that I won't let anything happen to you.*

'Ruth says he won't let anything happen to me,' Jaxom said.

With a roughness born of anxiety, Piemur adjusted Jaxom's helmet, securing the fastenings, checking the oxy-tank unit, gesturing for him to turn on the helmet's audio.

'Keep up a running commentary, will you, Jaxom?' he asked.

'Nod if you can hear me all right.' Jaxom still found the sound of his own voice echoing in the confines of the helmet unnatural. Piemur nodded, his expression carefully blank. 'Aivas, show us where we're going so Piemur can watch.'

Jaxom gave his friend one more buffet and then, pulling first one foot, and then the other free of the deck, floated up to Ruth. Hauling himself into position, he attached his riding straps to the toggles that had been designed to hold snap-on equipment for e.v.a.

'You wearing the right riding harness?' Piemur asked acidly.

'That's the second time you've asked me that today.'

'Bears repeating. Can you see the screen perched up there?' Piemur's tone was even more acerbic. Jaxom wished

Piemur wouldn't. But that was yet one more difference that only another rider would understand: the supreme confidence one could have in one's dragon's abilities. And Ruth had more than most.

'I can see it,' he said, his voice high and tinny to his ears. *D'you know where we're going, Ruth?'*

Certainly. Shall we go?

Jaxom was accustomed to very short passages *between* but this must have been the shortest they'd ever taken. One moment they were on the bridge, the next, they were surrounded by a different sort of darkness. For one heartbeat, Jaxom tasted as deep a fear as he had ever known. But Ruth's head, erect and swinging around as the white dragon surveyed the scene, was all the token of reassurance he needed. Then he became aware, unlike the total lack of sensation in *between*, of his legs pressing against Ruth's neck, even the tug of the straps against his belt.

I won't let go, Ruth said as calm as ever. *I could hang by my claws. The metal is so cold it feels hot.*

Jaxom peered down, over the lower edge of his helmet and saw that Ruth had, indeed, curled his talons about the spars – two different spars. Carefully extending his forepaw talons, he gripped the upper bar and had arranged his hindfeet on tiptoe, one in front of the other, for a purchase on the lower one, stretching in comfortable but not exaggerated posture between the two levels.

I'm holding my breath but I am in no discomfort, Ruth continued as he gazed alertly around. His left eye was whirling ever so gently in the blue of interest. Above them, Jaxom could see more horizontal spars, a longitudinal framework that circled the engines. Their mass was behind the grid, an immense rectangular boxlike structure in which the effect of the matter/anti-matter drive provided propulsion for interstellar travel.

'Are you all right, Jaxom?' Aivas asked.

'Perfectly,' Jaxom replied, unwilling to give any other response although, even as he spoke, he felt his muscles relax just a trifle. After all, nothing had happened.

'Ruth suffers no discomfort?'

'He says not. He's holding his breath.'

'There is nothing to breathe in space.'

'If he feels better holding his breath, that's fine by me.' Jaxom regretted that momentary flare of petulance. This manoeuvre had got to him.

I wish to climb higher, for a better view. There is nothing to be seen here but the engines. They are uninteresting.

Before Jaxom could forbid him, Ruth had reached for the spar above his head.

'*Whatever you do, Ruth, don't let go entirely,*' Jaxom said urgently.

I'd only float.

Jaxom wondered at his dragon's nonchalance in this new, and dangerous environment. But then, didn't dragons meet danger every time they flew Thread? At least there was none of that here to score a white hide or pierce a fragile wing. Or his spacesuit.

See? And Ruth did begin to float, rather than climb, upwards. Jaxom was so surprised by his dragon's initiative that he could think of nothing to say. Then he didn't wish to, for Ruth's glide had taken them above the engines and he could see, without benefit of mechanical means, the spectacular panorama of Pern stretching out behind them. *And it doesn't matter if I float because all I have to do is jump between wherever I need to go. Is it not beautiful up here?*

To that, Jaxom had to agree for he was gaining a perspective of Pern that was a far cry from the very limited view afforded by sensors, screens and windows. Ruth had them perched on the topmost rail. Pern lay stretched westward below them: he thought he recognized the Paradise River Hold estuary and, just as the horizon curved, the purple hills of Rubicon and Xanadu. Above were the stars, behind him, far too brightly, was Rukbat's blaze. He thought he caught sunlight glinting off one of the other ships: *Bahrain* was the nearest. Yes, sunlight illuminated the spheroid passenger bulk. And far, far above him, at an impossible distance, was the Red Star and the Oort Cloud that the Red Star would penetrate in another hundred or so Turns.

Abruptly Meer and Farli appeared beside Ruth, blinking out a moment later to reappear, claws hooked on the spar, daintily keeping their flesh from contact with the absolute chill of the metal. Their eyes began to whirl into excited reds.

We're not staying much longer. You'd better go in. You can't hold your breaths as long as I can, Ruth told the two fire-lizards. *They say space is much too big. It is also colder than* between. *I think we will go in now. I feel the need to breathe.*

Once again, before Jaxom could direct the proceeding, Ruth had executed his intention. Almost without any sensation of transfer, they were back on the bridge of the *Yokohama*.

That was splendid! Ruth said, chirping happily.

Piemur's complexion, Jaxom noted, was noticeably pale under his southern tan and his expression unusually grim for a man who had traversed the southern coasts for months with only a gold fire-lizard and a runt runner beast for company.

'Did you have to make Farli and Meer come?'

'They came of their own accord,' Jaxom replied. 'Ruth says they think space is too big,' and he managed a laugh at their understatement. 'Ruth thoroughly enjoyed it,' Jaxom went on, knowing that was an equally inadequate comment. 'And so did I,' he added staunchly, a vision of the grandeur and immensity indelibly scored in his brain, 'once I got used to it.' He undid his helmet and grinned down at Piemur. 'No difference really, from *between* and not really as dangerous. As Ruth pointed out, all he has to do is go *between* wherever he wants so we'd never really be in any danger in space.'

'You sound to me a bit like a man convincing himself against the evidence of his own senses,' and Piemur regarded his friend through narrowed eyes.

'Well, it does take getting used to,' Jaxom repeated, running his fingers through sweat damp hair and grinning in what he hoped was a more convincing fashion. He wouldn't admit to Piemur that he had been apprehensive, though he could now appreciate the sour smell of sweat rising from his suit – but nothing more damning.

'I wonder,' Piemur went on, 'just how Sharra, and Lytol,

and Lessa, and F'lar and Robinton will view your latest escapade.'

'Once they've tried it, they'll see that it's not really dangerous. It's just . . . a different aspect of travel on a dragon!'

Piemur let out an exaggerated sigh. 'And if you and Ruth can do it, every other dragon and rider on Pern will feel required to follow your example. Is that what you wanted, Aivas?'

'The result is inevitable, given the friendly competitiveness of dragonriders.'

Piemur raised both hands in a gesture of resigned impotence. 'As I said, with a friend like Aivas, you don't need enemies!'

Jaxom had let himself in for a series of harangues once they got back to Landing.

'True harper instincts!' he remarked acidly to Piemur who bellowed the news to Lytol on the duty desk. His old guardian turned pale and stern, and Jaxom had the satisfaction of seeing Piemur blanch at the effect of his news. 'Just let's keep this all in perspective, shall we?' he added, striding to Lytol. 'I'm all right, really I am. Ruth wouldn't put me in danger any more than Aivas would. Someone!' He raised his voice, 'I need some help here.'

Jancis came running down the hall, halted as she took in the scene and darted into a side room. She was back in a moment with a hot bottle and poured Lytol a cup of *klah*. 'Just don't stand there, Piemur, get some wine. Some of that fortified wine would be best,' she called after him as he scurried for the kitchen. 'And just what have you been up to?' she demanded of Jaxom.

'Nothing as dangerous as springing news on . . .' Jaxom caught himself before saying 'old man', 'someone with no advance warning or preparation. I gather Aivas did not mention what he had planned for us today.'

'How could emptying fuel sacks be dangerous?' Jancis wanted to know, her pretty eyes wide with astonishment.

'I'm perfectly all right,' Lytol was saying. After he had

obediently taken several sips of the hot *klah*, his colour improved.

Piemur burst back into the hall, a wineskin in one hand and several glasses in the fingers of the other. He set these down on the table with more force than was needed, but he could see that Lytol was recovering. 'I need a drink as much as anyone else,' he said, splashing wine into the first glass so sloppily that Jancis, uttering a protest, took the skin from his hand. Piemur downed the glass he had filled and held it out for a refill. 'Thanks. I needed that!'

'You wait your turn,' she scolded, frowning at his bad manners.

Jaxom gestured for her to pour wine into Lytol's cup and for him to drink again.

'Now, whatever made you attempt such a dangerous manoeuvre?' Lytol demanded of Jaxom.

Jaxom sighed. 'It wasn't dangerous, Aivas asked Ruth and me to do an e.v.a., and we did. Ruth and I were quite safe. He had his claws hooked on that framework around the engine section and I . . . I was hanging on to him.' Jaxom grinned at the consternation on Jancis' face.

'Dragonriders!' In that tone, Jancis' single word was a profound condemnation.

'Wouldn't you agree, Lytol, that a dragon won't endanger his rider? That a dragon can take himself and his rider anywhere *between* to safety?'

Jaxom realized that this was the first time in many Turns that he had asked Lytol to verify draconic abilities. He could see the muscles along his guardian's jaw clench and relax, and wondered if he had overstepped tactful bounds.

Lytol exhaled. 'On occasion I have thought that Ruth acted on impulse but you, Jaxom, have always been cautious, thus balancing each other. He would no more endanger you than you would put his life in jeopardy. But your extravehicular activity should have been discussed beforehand.'

Piemur shot Jaxom a righteous glare and Jaxom shrugged.

'We did it, and we have proved that it can be done with no harm.'

I am going to sleep in the sun. You're going to be talking for hours. I'm glad we didn't talk about doing it first. It could have taken days to arrive at permission. We might never have got to do it.

Jaxom did not repeat Ruth's less than diplomatic remarks or his appraisal of talk to come. Talk which was more harangue as Lessa, F'lar, Robinton and D'ram were informed of the e.v.a.

'One more incidence of Aivas's obsession,' Lessa said, not at all pleased to be summoned to the hastily convened meeting.

'I wish you would all address the meat of the exercise,' Jaxom said with more irritation than he had ever before betrayed in the Benden Weyrleaders' presence. 'The important fact is that it can be done, has been done, and that Aivas says that e.v.a. by dragons and riders is crucial to his plan.'

They were not in the Aivas chamber, but in the conference room.

'Why on Earth would he want dragons clinging to that bloody framework, thousands of miles above Pern?' F'lar demanded.

'To accustom dragons to being in space,' Jaxom said.

'That's not all,' Robinton said in a slow thoughtful tone.

'No,' and D'ram sat erect and alert, 'the dragons must move the *Yokohama*.'

'Why?' Lessa asked. 'What good would that do?'

'To ram it at the Red Star . . .' D'ram started.

Jaxom, Piemur and F'lar shook their heads.

'Why not?' Lessa demanded. 'That must be why he wanted the fuel in the tanks.'

Jaxom smiled wryly at her ignorance. 'That drop of fuel would not explode on impact and ramming the Red Star with the *Yokohama*, ponderous as it is, would not alter its orbit one bit. But I grant you, he needs the dragons to move something.'

'Let's ask him!' Robinton suggested, standing and starting for the door. When the others did not move, he turned back at them. 'Well, don't we *want* to know?'

'I'm not so sure I do,' Lessa murmured but she rose

and followed the others as they trooped down the hallway to Aivas.

Jaxom, Jancis and Piemur closed the doors into the various rooms occupied by students and, when all were inside Aivas's chamber, that door was closed and Piemur leaned against it.

'What do the dragons have to move and where?' F'lar asked with no preamble.

'So you have perceived part of the plan, Weyrleader.'

'You mean to use the *Yokohama* to ram the planet?' Lessa asked, still sure that she had the answer.

'That would be totally ineffectual and the *Yokohama* is needed as a vantage point.'

'Then what?' F'lar insisted.

A picture came up of the Red Star, with details gleaned from Wansor's patient study of the face the planet presented its viewers. This showed a deep chasm that ran diagonally across one hemisphere: an unusual feature caused, Aivas had said, by an earthquake of incredible force, rending the basic rock of the eccentric wanderer.

'You all see this fracture. It is entirely possible that the chasm goes deep into the planet. It is probable that an explosion of sufficient magnitude at this point would have the desired effect on the planet's orbit. Especially when the planet is already perturbed by its proximity to the fifth satellite of this system.' The visual altered to the familiar diagram of the Rukbat system. 'Ordinarily an explosion of this magnitude would be impossible to effect. Not only to amass the elements required to make such a blast but to prevent chaotic elements entering the equations of motion of the Red Star and even of the other planets.

'It is apparent from Master Wansor's investigations that the fifth planet is devoid of atmosphere and life. It is also at its furthest distance from Pern. There will be some perturbations throughout the system but these have been calculated as negligible to the desired result, the relief from any further incursions of Thread on this planet.'

For a very long moment, no-one spoke.

'We have no such exploding capability,' Jaxom said.

'You do not. The *Yokohama*, the *Bahrain* and the *Buenos Aires* do.'

'What?' F'lar demanded angrily.

'The engines,' Jaxom said. 'The bloody engines. Oh, you are devious, Aivas!'

'But the engines are dead.' 'There's not enough fuel . . .' 'How would we get them there?' Everyone tried to be heard.

'The engines are dormant,' Aivas said and Jaxom thought he sounded well pleased by the uproar. 'But it is the material in the engines that will provide the explosive power. If anti-matter is allowed to contact matter, the result will suit your needs.'

'Now wait a moment,' and Jaxom called for order over the babel of questions. 'You specifically stated in those engineering lectures to Fandarel, that the anti-matter is held out of contact with matter, buried in the densest metals Mankind has ever forged. We don't have the equipment to penetrate those casings. Or is Fandarel working on something we don't know about?'

There was a little pause and Jaxom tended to agree with Master Robinton that Aivas laughed to himself sometimes.

'It is true that the safety factors built into the great interstellar engines were immensely sophisticated, and schematics for their design are not available in the engineering data. Of course the anti-matter engines were employed for interstellar travel. Other fuel was used for the shuttles and the captain's gig, and now to allow the ships' manoeuvring thrusters to correct orbital decay. But it has long been the case that complex things can be attacked best by simple methods. This facility must also obey the stipulation that you are not to be instructed in levels of technology beyond what your ancestors had. But you already have an agent that will provide the penetration. You have used it in every Fall for many centuries.'

'HNO_3!' Piemur said in a gasp.

'Correct. The metal casings of the matter/anti-matter drives are not impervious to its erosive effect.' The visual of the *Yokohama*'s engine shaft reappeared but now there were large extraneous tanks placed on the drive cube. 'It

346

will take time, which is why there is a wide window of two weeks for this part of the activity, but the acid will penetrate the casings, and once the magnetic chamber is broached, matter and anti-matter will self-destruct, causing the cataclysmic explosion necessary to shift the Red Star's orbit. Any further questions?'

Jaxom broke the silence that time. 'So all the Weyrs of Pern will be needed to take the engines, not the ships, *between* to the Red Star. To drop them into the chasm?'

'To drop them might disarrange the HNO_3.'

'How heavy are those engines?' F'lar asked.

'Their mass has exercised this facility for it is the one weak point of the plan. However, you have constantly stated that the dragons can carry that which they think they can carry.'

'Correct, but no-one has ever asked them to carry engines!' F'lar replied, awed by the scale of these loads.

Jaxom began to chuckle and received offended stares. 'That's why the bronzes have been exercising in free fall – to get them used to things being so much lighter in space. Right, Aivas?'

'That is correct.'

'So if we don't tell them how much those bloody things weigh . . .'

'Now, really, Jaxom,' F'lar began.

'No, really, F'lar,' Jaxom replied, 'Aivas is applying a valid psychological tactic. I think it'll work. Especially if we think it can work. Right?' He gave F'lar a challenging look.

'Jaxom makes a good point,' Lytol said and, beside him, D'ram nodded accord. 'With many dragons, all working together . . . it could be done. No one dragon bearing more than his fair share of the burden, everyone believing that he can succeed. That framework is convenient. Each dragon will be able to grip.'

'With padding on their feet to reduce the effects of space-cold metal,' Aivas added.

'And take that much weight *between*?' Lessa asked, still sceptical.

'You know,' and now F'lar rubbed his jaw speculatively.

'I think they could do it. If we think they can. Tell me how Ruth reacted to being in space, Jaxom.'

'Wait a minute,' Lessa said, holding up her hand, her brow wrinkled in concentration, 'how long would such a manoeuvre take? We could get an engine *between* but to go that distance *between*, so laden . . .'

'You have frequently averred,' and Aivas' voice dominated the excited responses, 'that your dragons will take you anywhere you can clearly visualize in your minds.'

'The chasm!' Jaxom leapt to the screen and tapped it agitatedly. 'This is so clear, so large, so impossible to mistake. THAT is our guide as well as our target.'

'Correct!' said Aivas.

'Fine! You've got that problem solved,' Lessa said. 'Now, how do you solve the distance the dragons have to travel?'

'You and your queen, Ramoth, travelled backwards in time . . .'

'And nearly died,' F'lar said, his tone as bitter as the look he gave his weyrmate for the anguish he had suffered then.

'The riders will all have oxygen – which is doubtless what you lacked, Weyrwoman – to breathe, and protective suits . . .'

'There aren't that many!' D'ram protested.

'Not yet,' Piemur said, his eyes glinting, 'but Hamian's turning out the plastic-coated fabric faster than Master Nicat's men can glue them into shape.'

'From what has been said by every rider interviewed, only eight seconds elapse to reach most destinations here on Pern,' Aivas went on. 'This is clearly an instance of basic time as opposed to variable time. Of the 8 to 10 seconds seemingly required to transfer anywhere on Pern, the dragons seem to use a basic 5 or so seconds to assimilate their coordinates and the rest of the time for the actual transfer. Using this premise and adapting it to a logarithmic computation, assume that travel takes 1 second for 1,600 kilometers, 2 seconds for 10,000, 3.6 seconds for 100,000, and 4.8 for 1 million and 7 to 10 seconds for 10 million. While this method of transference is still incomprehensible to this facility, it does appear to work. Therefore, knowing the approximate distance from Pern to the Red Star, it is simple to compute an interplanetary jump. It has also been established that dragons are able to function for fifteen minutes before their systems are in oxygen debt, more than enough time to make the journey, position the engines in the chasm and return. The dragons are accurate flyers.'

'I'd want to try that journey,' F'lar said and Lessa turned on him. 'Love, if we believe in our dragons, we can believe in our own abilities as well. Before I ask the Weyrs to undertake such a trip, I must be sure it is feasible and I won't risk anyone. Not this time!' he said, and everyone knew he was alluding to F'nor's nearly fatal attempt to reach the Red Star so many Turns before. 'Is there any air to breathe on the Red Star?'

'No,' Aivas replied in an uncontradictable tone. 'Certainly not breathable atmosphere, but there is some, mostly noble gases and nitrogen. Whatever denser atmosphere it once had would have been lost when it escaped from its original system. There is no water as repeated circuits past Rukbat have boiled off much of its volatiles, too. F'nor has seen this in process. Gravity on the surface would be more than one tenth of Pern's so the atmosphere is much less dense than you are accustomed to.'

'You will not take such a perilous expedition by yourself, F'lar,' D'ram said, rising to his feet, his expression resolute.

'D'ram,' and Robinton reached for his arm to restrain him while Lytol's expression was both pitying and approving.

'D'ram, this is a young man's duty,' Lytol said, shaking his head sadly. 'You have long since done yours.'

'F'lar?' Lessa's face was screwed up in an anxious grimace, as if she couldn't deny him but wanted desperately to do so. She shook her head, her grey eyes wide with fright, as she realized that nothing she could say would dissuade him.

'I will go,' F'lar said.

'Not by yourself,' Jaxom repeated, shaking his head. 'I'll go with you.' He held up his hands against the arguments that caused. 'Ruth always knows where he is and when he is. No other dragon has that ability, and you all know it. I'll go without permission if you keep on at me like this!' He allowed his anger to be seen, glaring at Lytol, Robinton and D'ram. Lessa glared back but she didn't join in the verbal disputes.

'Jaxom, you may not come with me. You're responsibilities . . .' F'lar began.

'I'm not going to die and that's that. I trust Ruth as you trust Mnementh. Let's keep this expedition down to as few as possible. Right?'

'What happens though,' Robinton said, his composure recovered, 'if the one man,' and he gestured to F'lar, 'who can keep this planet united and the young Lord who has earned the respect of Hall, Hold and Weyr should be lost to Pern at this very critical stage?'

F'lar gave a rueful laugh. 'I don't intend to be lost and, if I will not go where I expect the Weyrs to follow, how can I ask them to go?' He took Lessa by the arms, appealing to her. 'I must go, Lessa. Surely you see that.'

'I do,' she said in snapping tones, 'but I don't have to like it. Furthermore, I'll go with you two fools!' She startled everyone but she laughed at the reaction. 'Why not? There're plenty of queens now to continue dragonkind. Ramoth's still the largest dragon on the planet and the bravest, going where no-one dared go before. I think we three deserve the right!' She lifted her chin, haughtily oblivious to persuasions. 'When do we go?'

Piemur let go a bark of laughter. 'Just like that?'

'Why not? We don't have Threadfall for another two days. Jaxom?'

Three dragons bugled from the mounds beyond the building. Lessa, F'lar and Jaxom smiled at the draconic agreement.

'I won't tell Sharra,' and he paused while Jancis savagely muttered something to the effect that Sharra wouldn't let him go. 'I wouldn't be so sure of that, Jancis,' and Jaxom gave her a quelling look, 'but there are a few things I must put in order. And to be perfectly candid, I'd like a good night's sleep. It's been a busy day!'

'Tomorrow then?' Lessa said, pinning him with a fierce stare.

'Certainly! I'll send Meer with a message that I'm staying over at Cove Hold.'

'A good idea,' F'lar said, quirking one eyebrow in amusement. 'Mnementh is pretty excited . . .'

'Ramoth, too,' Lessa said and frowned. 'We can't risk some other dragon sensing what we plan. There are fortunately no other dragons at Landing right now.'

'All to the good for our clandestine outing,' Jaxom said.

The three riders discussed every aspect of this unprecedented leap *between* with Aivas and the others. As the riders seemed more and more confident of the success, the others began to cease their opposition, lapsing into nearly morose silence.

'If we do not leave soon,' Robinton said into a pause as the three dragonriders were studying their landing site at the highest magnification Aivas could produce, 'some of our more perceptive students will start speculating about the length of this meeting.'

'A good point,' F'lar said, entirely too cheerful. 'Aivas, can you print out a copy of what's on the screen right now? We can study it further at Cove Hold.'

'I'd've thought it was burned in your brains already,' Lytol remarked caustically.

'Nearly,' Jaxom replied gaily. He was buoyed by the confidence which F'lar and Lessa exuded, not realizing that each was infecting the other. Jaxom had not missed Lytol's frequent brooding looks but, after his first protests, his old guardian had only been silently reproachful.

Aivas printed three copies.

'This facility would not recommend such an exploration if any foreseeable danger was involved,' Aivas said to reassure the sceptics.

'Foreseeable is the important word,' Lytol said and walked out.

Chapter Fifteen

'I've never seen so many fire-lizards!' Jancis exclaimed
as she helped Piemur and Jaxom wash Ruth in Cove
Hold's lagoon.

Lessa, F'lar and D'ram were similarly occupied, being
assisted by other members of the Cove Hold research staff.
Lytol and Robinton had gone to oversee the preparation
of the evening meal. Though the atmosphere was tense
with anticipation and Jaxom hoped the stress would not
be communicated to the Hold people, it was not unusual
for the Benden Weyrleaders and the Ruathan Lord to enjoy
Cove's hospitality.

'Ruth, have the fire-lizards twigged tomorrow's journey?'
Jaxom asked. He refused to think of it as an 'attempt'
which implied failure.

*They're excited because I am. Ramoth and Mnementh are,
too. Look at their eyes! But the little ones don't know why
they're excited.*

Jaxom put some extra effort into scrubbing Ruth's left
wing. There were hundreds of questions rattling about in
his brain but to settle to any one of them and find an answer
was beyond him. This wasn't at all like the day that he and
Ruth had gone hunting for Ramoth's queen egg, averting a
major confrontation between the Southern Oldtimers and
Benden Weyr. He'd been a boy then, struggling to achieve
manhood, to be both Lord Holder and dragonrider. This

also wasn't as spontaneous an acceptance of challenge as this morning's e.v.a. had been. This was planned and in the company of two of the most important people on Pern.

And the three best dragons, Ruth added, his whole being emanating satisfaction with tomorrow in prospect.

Aware that his roiling thoughts might also leak to the fire-lizards, Jaxom earnestly pulled soothing thoughts to the fore in his mind. Just then a fire-lizard arrived from *between* with the faint pop that a re-entry caused. It was Meer, and Jaxom hadn't even noticed that he'd disappeared.

So, it did not exactly surprise him when Sharra strode into the Hold while they were finishing their dinner. Meer had conveyed something to her, so he'd best play for innocence.

'Darling, what an unexpected surprise,' he said, rising to greet her with an embrace. 'There's nothing the matter at Ruatha, is there?' he added with a fair pretence of alarm. He caught Piemur, rolling his eyes at his performance.

'No, nothing's wrong at Ruatha,' Sharra said in the sort of tone that made him wary. However, if she gave him a calculating glance, she smiled with genuine warmth at the Weyrleaders and harpers, Lytol and D'ram. 'It's just that the biology team is starting the dissection tomorrow. Mirrim said she'd convey me up. G'lanar point-blank refused. I hope I'm not interrupting . . .'

She was abused of that notion by offers of *klah* from Lessa, wine from Robinton, sweet breads from Jancis while Piemur hastily drew another chair up to the table.

'G'lanar bring you?' D'ram asked.

As she nodded, Jaxom left Piemur to settle his wife and strode out to the porch to offer hospitality to the Oldtimer. But Lamoth and his rider were already airborne, circling to the east above the lagoon, disappearing into the night sky.

'I didn't catch him,' Jaxom said. 'He ought to have at least joined us for a cup.'

D'ram brushed away Jaxom's discontent. 'G'lanar was always a surly one. How does he happen to be at Ruatha these days?'

Jaxom grinned. 'The weyrling we had was judged old enough to fight and was sent to join K'van's wings. He asked us to accommodate G'lanar and Lamoth in their stead. The old bronze sleeps almost as much as G'lanar does.'

'It does them both good to feel needed,' Sharra said, her eyes glittering although her tone was social.

Jaxom wondered what on earth Meer had conveyed to her that brought her to Cove Hold. His message had been innocuous enough, and the Egg knew staying over at Cove Hold was nothing out of the ordinary. Wives! But he was glad to see her. That is, if she was really *happy* to be here.

It was also very like Sharra to say nothing to the point in company. But he began to worry about how to dissemble when they were alone in their sleeping quarters. As the dragonriders whiled away the after-dinner hours, no hint of their morning's plans was raised. Partly because the young men and women of the Archive were present but especially because Sharra was there.

'I've a new song from Menolly,' Master Robinton said, gesturing for Piemur to bring him his gitar and to get his own. He unrolled the score, passing a copy to Jancis to put on the rack for Piemur. 'An odd tune, unusual for our Masterharper Menolly. She says the words were written by young Harper Elimona,' he went on, plucking a string to tune the instrument. Piemur corrected the pitch of his and, reading the music, soundlessly fingered through the chordings. 'But a lovely haunting melody and words to lift hearts at this point in a Pass.'

Then he nodded to Piemur and they began. Having sung and played so often together, they knew each other's style so well that they interwove and harmonized as if they'd rehearsed this brand new song a hundred times already.

> A heart that's true in harper blue
> makes song from heart's own fire,
> and though betrayed, is not afraid:
> in danger, leaps up higher.

Jaxom suppressed the start of surprise the words gave him, and dared not look at either Lessa or F'lar.

> No world is free of minstrelsy
> nor noise, nor rage, nor sorrow.

> A harper must discharge his trust
> before he asks to borrow.
>
> My Harper Hall is free to all
> who serve with song and playing.
> But you who'd hide your song inside
> are very sadly straying.

At those words, Jaxom wondered what cryptic message Menolly and Elimona were giving, and to whom. The next verse was even more germane to the problem of Halls and Holds who held Aivas to be the Abomination.

> Will you withdraw beyond the law,
> lie safely in your slumber,
> while dangers shake your world awake
> and Death makes up his number.
>
> Did harper here betray those dear
> he'd feel more than my tongue.
> If place you'd earn, you'd better learn
> more music than you've sung.
>
> For if you die, while safe you lie
> halled in your selfish bone,
> no chant will come, no harper drum,
> and you'll lie long alone.

Jaxom could watch Robinton's face as he sang, and wondered if the words could possibly have been prompted by Robinton or Sebell who so often suggested themes to their harpers. But then, Menolly had such an uncanny knack of catching exactly the mood of the moment, this could have been merely serendipitous. The two harpers played a bridging passage, then their voices which had been light and almost taunting, deepened for the final verse.

> Get up, take heart – go, make a start,
> sing out the truth you came for.
> Then when you die, your heart may fly
> to Halls we have no name for.

There was a respectful silence as the last chord died away before their audience burst into loud applause and compliment. Robinton and Piemur disclaimed humbly, Robinton saying that with such music any harper found himself doing his very best.

'Who's next?' Piemur asked, strumming his gitar into a complicated alteration, minor to major.

The next hour was spent happily enough so that Jaxom relaxed, holding Sharra's hand, playing with her long fingers as he often did. He could, however, sense the distance she had put between them and tried to ignore it. Talla coiled up on her shoulder but he saw nothing of Meer.

'Ruth, did Meer tattle on us?' he asked his dragon when Sharra was occupied in singing descant for one of her favourite songs.

He has curled up on the beach and pretends to be asleep. What could he tell her? That would make sense?

'Sharra's perceptive, Ruth. She could guess.'

She knows you are always safe with me.

'But she also doesn't want me risking my neck . . . more than I already do.'

She will not refuse you. Ruth added encouragingly, though his tone held a nuance of doubt.

Lessa called an end to the evening's entertainment, murmuring something about never quite becoming accustomed to double-ended days.

Robinton acted the perfect host, making certain, with Jancis' help, that all the guests were comfortably installed – just as he had on so many other occasions. Then, when Sharra and Jaxom were in their usual corner room, she frowned in puzzlement.

'Why was Meer so agitated, Jaxom?'

'He was? Not much happened today.' He pulled his shirt off, muffling his voice and incidentally hiding his face lest his expression give him away. Sharra had become adept at reading him. It usually smoothed matters between them but he really didn't want her unnecessarily upset. He'd written notes for Brand, and one for her, and given them to Piemur. Not that he expected Piemur would have to deliver them but he had to plan for contingencies. 'Anyone at Ruatha got a randy green or gold?'

He could see her considering that possibility for it would have been reason enough for Meer to return unexpectedly to Ruatha even if she had given the bronze specific instructions to remain with Ruth and Jaxom.

'I don't think so. Are you all going up to the *Yokohama* tomorrow?'

'Yes,' and Jaxom gave her his best grin which he expanded into a yawn, gesturing for her to climb in first. She preferred the left-hand side – even if here it was the inside. But then, she wouldn't have to rise in the night here to tend to a fretful child. When she was settled, he lay down, putting his arm around her, cushioning her head on his shoulder as he so often did. Only now he did it consciously, not in response to the habits of five Turns.

'What's the schedule?'

'More of the same. Getting accustomed to free fall.'

'Why?'

'Well, Aivas let us in on that today,' Jaxom said, choosing his phrases carefully. This would account for them all staying over at Cove Hold. 'Seems like all the Weyrs of Pern are going to be needed to hoist the engine part of the ships to that big rift on the Red Star.'

'WHAT?'

He pushed her back down in the bed, grinning at her astonished expression, clearly visible in the moonlight flooding the room. 'That's what I said. He's going to call our bluff that dragons can lift anything they *think* they can.'

'But . . . but . . . why?'

'Those engines will be made to blow up, and the force of the explosion will nudge the Red Star into a new orbit.'

'Oh, my!'

Jaxom grinned. It took something as sensationally fantastic as that to reduce his beloved to an incredulous whisper. He pulled her close enough to lay a kiss on her forehead, meaning only to reassure her. But, as his lips touched her soft skin and his nostrils inhaled the spicy fragrance she used, he desired her. And, though at first her response was reflexive while she mulled over his news, he had no trouble in getting her complete attention.

He wasn't so deeply asleep that he wasn't aware of the first scratch of a fire-lizard claw on his cheek. It was Meer, for he established that identity by the individual smell of the little bronze. And a Meer who was worried and puzzled.

Jaxom! Ruth's anxious tone reinforced Meer's warning. *There is someone in the hall by your door. Meer senses danger. I'm coming!*

'For the love of the egg that hatched you, keep Meer quiet right now,' Jaxom told Ruth. 'And be as quiet as you can.'

You know how quietly I can move, Ruth replied, slightly aggrieved at the unnecessary caution.

'I want this one alive, and identifiable!'

Carefully, so as not to disturb Sharra or alert the intruder, Jaxom rolled out of the bed and went for his belt and the knife sheathed there. In the darkness, Meer blinked orangey-red eyes that were whirling in a gradually increasing speed but the little bronze made no move or sound.

An alteration in the shadows of the room told Jaxom that the door was being stealthily opened. He stayed where he was crouched, muscles relaxed but every fibre of him ready to move.

The door shadows separated into a crouching figure, knife-holding hand raised in a strike position as the intruder crept toward the bed. Then paused. Realizing that the man saw a clearly vacated space in the bed, Jaxom sprang, encircling the figure from the side.

'Oh no, you don't!' he cried in a hoarse whisper, half hoping that this incident could be resolved without waking Sharra.

But Meer, released by his action, swooped at the man's face while Jaxom struggled to hold him. And Meer bugled with no regard for sleeping folk. Outside, Ruth bellowed and half the fire-lizard population of the Cove tried to come in the open window.

Though the man struggled, breathing hoarsely in his desperation, Jaxom was the victor of far too many wrestling matches to have his hold broken easily. But he didn't quite avoid the slashing blade which scored his bare shoulder. Cursing, Jaxom grabbed the dagger hand and, twisting it in a hold F'lessan had taught him, broke the man's hand. The attacker crumpled, crying aloud in pain just as F'lar, Piemur, Lytol and D'ram came bursting into the room. Someone behind them had an open glowbasket and light spilled past the reinforcements to fall on the face of the man Jaxom had downed.

'G'lanar!' Jaxom fell back in surprise and shock.

The old bronze rider snarled up at him, batting at the shrieking fire-lizards who pursued their own attack.

'G'lanar?' D'ram grabbed the man by the arm, and as F'lar lent a hand, hauled him to his feet.

Jaxom told Ruth to call the fire-lizards off and, still screaming their challenge, the fair swooped back out the window.

Sharra stared from the bed as Jancis and Lessa crowded into the room, each holding a bright basket.

'What did you intend, G'lanar?' F'lar said, his voice coldly implacable.

'He's to blame . . .' G'lanar cried, spitting in his fury, cradling his broken wrist to his chest.

'Blame?' Jaxom stared down at the old rider.

'You! I know who it was now! It was you, and that white runt that ought to have died the moment it was born!' Outside Ruth roared exception to the insult, and thrust his head through the window. 'If it hadn't been for you, we'd've had our own fertile queen! We'd've had a chance!'

Jaxom shook his head slightly, trying to understand the accusation. So few knew that he and Ruth had recovered the abducted queen egg from Benden Weyr. How had G'lanar learned?

'So it was you who cut the riding straps?' Jaxom demanded.

'Yes, yes, I did, and I'd've got you. I'd've kept trying till I did. Nor wept if your woman'd died that morning. Save Pern from more like you and that abortion!'

'And you, a dragonrider, would seek the death of another?' D'ram's scorn and horror made G'lanar flinch.

'Yes, yes, yes!' His voice climbed in fury and frustration. 'Yes! Unnatural man, unnatural dragon! Abominations as vile as that Aivas thing you worship.' G'lanar's eyes glittered, his features contorted.

'That's enough of that,' F'lar said, stepping forward purposefully.

'It is! Enough!' Before either Jaxom who had stepped back from the man, or F'lar who was moving towards him could act, G'lanar plunged his dagger into his own breast.

His action shocked everyone to immobility.

'Oh no!' Jaxom breathed, dropping to the man's side, feeling for the throat pulse. Rider dead, the dragon would suicide. Had G'lanar's thrust been true? His heart quailed, waiting for the keen all dragonmen dreaded to hear.

Ruth had pulled his head from the window, and Jaxom could see him, rearing back on his haunches and stretching to his full height, wings spread to balance him. The sound he uttered was muted, an oddly strangled noise. There were other sounds in the night and then Ramoth and Mnementh dropped to the ground outside the room, deepening the shadows.

Lamoth dies. In shame. And Ruth sank back to the ground, wings limp against his back, his head low. *They were mistaken to steal Ramoth's egg. We only set matters right. I am not an abomination or unnatural. And you are a very natural man, Jaxom. How can Aivas be wrong when he does everything to help us?*

Lessa moved to Jaxom, lifting him up from the dead man, her eyes watering with tears, her expression dreadful but her hands were gentle. Sharra, hauling the sheet about her, put her arms around him, and draped a corner of the sheet over his nudity.

'I don't understand this,' D'ram said, running trembling fingers through his thick grey hair. 'How could he so corrupt the truth? How could he seek the life of another dragonrider?'

'There have been moments,' Lessa said in a broken voice, 'when I wonder what good I did bringing the five Weyrs forward.'

'No, Lessa,' and D'ram recovered from regret to touch her

shoulder supportively, '*you* did what was necessary. So did Jaxom, though I never realized it was he who saved that situation.' He shot a grateful and approving look at the young Lord.

'Why did no-one realize that G'lanar harboured such a grievance?' F'lar demanded. 'Who sent him to Ruatha?'

'He told me he volunteered to come when S'rond left for Southern Weyr,' Sharra said in an ironic tone. 'A fair exchange, he said. Ruatha was known to be the most hospitable of Holds to dragonkind.'

'I'm going to get to the bottom of this,' Lessa said, her tone resolute. 'I'd thought the Weyrs united in this project! Surely even Oldtimers are! They've fought two lives' worth of Thread . . .'

D'ram was scrubbing at his face, shaking his head, his shoulders hunched against this night's treachery. 'Every Oldtimer I've spoken to, and there are few enough of us old ones now, and all the younger riders are definitely in accord with Benden. Everyone sees the help, the training, the promise Aivas holds out as the culmination of the Weyr objective since the first egg hatched. The project has given us all hope at this critical point in a Pass.'

'Ramoth has started speaking to the other queens,' Lessa said, her voice strained. 'We'll know by morning if there are any other disaffected riders in any Weyr.'

'I'll take care of this,' F'lar said and gestured to Piemur and Jaxom to help him with G'lanar's body.

'No, I will,' D'ram said, stepping over the corpse to heave it over his shoulders. His face was devoid of expression but his cheeks were tear-stained. 'He was a good rider before he went south with Mardra and T'ton.'

The others stepped back so he could pass with his sad burden. Sharra handed Jaxom his long-tailed riding shirt and he slipped into it gratefully. The night breeze was chill. She had pulled on a tunic and went past Jaxom to the door.

'A cup of hot wine is indicated,' she said and Jancis followed her to the kitchen.

Sharra had added something to the wine, Jaxom decided, when he woke and found morning well started. She was

361

still asleep beside him so she'd taken her own medicine. A boon for him since he had no intention of delaying their day's plan. He eased out of the bed, scooped up his clothing and dressed in the heads. When he entered the main room, Lessa was up, cradling a cup of *klah* in her hands while F'lar, a set expression on his face, was spooning cereal into his mouth. Without a word, Lessa rose and filled a cup and a bowl for Jaxom.

'Is everyone else still asleep?'

Lessa shook her head. 'Piemur and Jancis have gone to Landing with D'ram and Lytol. Robinton's to sleep himself out.' She took another sip. 'Ramoth says the queens report no other traitors in our midst.' Her tone was as bleak as her eyes. 'She says that Southern's queen is inexperienced and Adrea too young to understand G'lanar's grievances. However the headwoman did recall that old G'lanar had begun to get quite testy, going off a lot on his own after Tillek. When S'rond was due to join the fighting wings, he begged for the duty at Ruatha. That would have made me suspicious!'

'Why?' F'lar asked. 'Ruatha's the duty everyone wants.' He gave Jaxom an encouraging smile, and spooned more sweetener over the remains of his porridge.

Noticing that, Lessa opened her mouth to scold and then shut it, looking away in her disgruntlement. F'lar winked at Jaxom, pretending relief.

'No, the Oldtimers who chose to go south with Mardra and T'ton were already antagonistic to Benden's aims,' F'lar said, 'as much because Benden suggested them. G'lanar would've brooded long enough, ripe for any scheme to support his grievances. And we already know there's a fair number who see Aivas as an Abomination.'

'There may be more after today,' Lessa muttered.

F'lar dropped his spoon with a clatter. 'No-one's going to know about today . . .'

She shook her head, surprised at his remark. 'I didn't mean what we plan to do,' she said, showing some exasperation with her weyrmate. 'I meant G'lanar's death. The Weyrs know the old fellow died but certainly not why. We can at least keep the attack quiet.'

F'lar shot an anxious look at Jaxom who shrugged acquiescence. He certainly didn't wish to have it known.

'That's what D'ram's going to ensure. That everyone thinks old G'lanar suffered a brainstorm.'

'That's lame. The dragons'll know . . .'

'Ramoth says not. Lamoth had gone to sleep in the clearing, totally unaware of what G'lanar was doing here. Of course, he knew when G'lanar died and floundered *between* somehow. To be doubly cautious, D'ram means to speak to each of the remaining Oldtimers. Tiroth may not be a queen but no dragon could hide his heart from that bronze.'

'*How*,' Jaxom wanted to know, 'did G'lanar realize that Ruth and I rescued Ramoth's egg?'

'Have you been timing it much lately?' Lessa asked bluntly.

Jaxom tried to shrug that question away. 'Not often.'

Lessa raised her eyebrows in resignation. 'I keep telling you that timing it is dangerous. It was bloody sure dangerous for you. Lamoth would have known. He would have told G'lanar. G'lanar was misguided, but not stupid. I know that all the Oldtimers at Southern have puzzled over who rescued the egg. In spite of our precautions, they all know Ruth's abilities and might have suspicions.'

'G'lanar's the only bronze rider left from that group,' Jaxom said, after a quick review of names and dragons.

'We have a more important to-do today than fret over this incident.' F'lar said, rising to clear the table of his bowl and cup. 'That is, if you feel up to it, Jaxom . . .'

Jaxom regarded F'lar scornfully to call his courage in question. 'I've been waiting on you. Let's do it.'

'From here, or the *Yokohama*?' Lessa asked.

'The *Yokohama*,' Jaxom said, grabbing his riding gear from the bench beside him. 'We don't have the spacesuits down here.'

'You're sure there's one to fit me?' Lessa asked, shrugging into her leather jacket.

Jaxom grinned. 'There're two small ones. One ought to fit even if we have to truss you up some.' As he came out on to the porch, Meer chirped at him. 'Lessa, to preserve my image in my wife's eyes, would you ask Ramoth to keep Meer from following me today? Ask her to tell him I'm safe with you two.'

Lessa quirked her eyebrow, grinning up at him. 'You're sure of that?'

Cord rucked the tucks that had to be taken in the arms and legs and waist of the smallest of the suits, causing some amusement to F'lar and Jaxom, but none to Lessa. They contacted Aivas when they were ready to proceed. He brought up their objective, the immense long scar on the Red Star, on the screen in the cargo bay.

F'lar frowned at it again, not so much imprinting the scene firmly into his mind, as rationalizing what he saw.

'When F'nor made his flight to the Red Star, he said there were roiling clouds . . .'

'There probably were,' Aivas replied easily. 'In orbiting so close to Rukbat, the planet's surface would have become heated, hot enough to melt rock and certainly causing steam from the ice that coats Thread ovoids. It can be posited that the planet itself is coated with the debris of the Oort Cloud. Steam or dust clouds of considerable density are entirely possible. That is undoubtedly what F'nor saw, not the actual surface. His memories of the event, even the abrasive injuries he and Canth sustained, bear out the supposition. Now that the surface has cooled, that phenomenon has subsided and you see a sterile planet, its surface slowly freezing again at this point in its orbit.'

'Well, let's do it!' F'lar said and vaulted to Mnementh's shoulder, grabbing the riding straps to swing himself to his customary position between neck ridges.

Despite free fall, Lessa moved more clumsily.

'How anyone can be expected to move anywhere in this sort of gear . . .' she muttered, finally settling herself in place. She had a bit of trouble snapping the riding straps on to rings lost in the folds about her middle. 'Can't see what I'm doing, trussed up like a wherry for the spit, and this helmet obscuring my sight . . .'

Jaxom grinned at her griping and looked towards F'lar.

'Are you leading this expedition?'

Something like a growl came over the helmet's com and Jaxom chuckled.

'Do our dragons know where we're going?' Lessa said. She held her suited arm up high above her head, looking first to the left at F'lar and then to the right and Jaxom who was, as all three must be doing, concentrating on that tremendous fault. 'Very well, then, let's go!' And dropped her arm.

Jaxom counted as Ruth shifted them *between*. He remembered to continue breathing, an exercise he frequently suspended on such trips. He didn't think of the blackness or the frightening cold of this familiar oblivion: he thought only of where they were going.

I know where we're going, Ruth said patiently.

And how long it was taking them. Twenty-seven slow seconds Jaxom had counted, seconds that seemed an eternity. He wondered if Lessa had counted when she'd gone back four hundred Turns to . . .

The three dragons emerged simultaneously over a chasm that made Ruth extend his wings uselessly in an attempt to slow his entry in the light gravity and thin atmosphere.

'Aivas?' Jaxom cried, though in the next second he knew that they were too far from Aivas in space for any contact.

'Shards! Jaxom, we can handle this without his supervision!' F'lar roared. He moderated his tone for the next sentence. 'There are times when I think we've got too dependent on Aivas. Slow your descent, Jaxom! We want to land on the edge, not in that bloody rift.'

Just beyond Ruth, the rift widened into a crater more immense than the Ice Lake above Ruatha Hold. Jaxom's body gave a massive shudder and he had the most incredible feeling that he had expected to see exactly that crater, though the detail hadn't been on the visuals. To centre his wandering attention, he concentrated on the rim below him and, in the next breath, Ruth obediently glided to the hard-packed surface of the planet, his wings fully extended. Mnementh and Ramoth, necks extended, eyes whirling in a brilliant rainbow expressing their consternation, landed gracefully beside him.

'Quickly, now, mark those boulders . . .' F'lar pointed

to the huge stone shafts that made a rim, like so many immense jagged teeth, across the mouth of the huge aperture.

'That crater's a fine landmark,' Jaxom said, experiencing a slighter degree of shock.

This place is strangely familiar, Ruth said, walking forward to peer over the edge.

'*Watch it!*' Jaxom said, as Ruth's feet seemed to sink into what appeared to be a mass of oval shapes. 'Look, F'lar, Thread ovoids.'

F'lar peered over Mnementh's shoulder while the big bronze dropped his head to examine the surface under his feet. He didn't appear particularly concerned.

'I don't like this place,' Lessa said.

Ramoth seemed to share her distaste for she placed her feet with extreme care, as one having to walk through putrid mud.

'And watch that edge, too, Jaxom, it might not be stable,' F'lar added.

Ramoth now looked straight ahead, trying to see to the other side of the gorge. Jaxom could not see the far side in the dim light available. When he looked over his shoulder towards Rukbat, he had no trouble looking directly at the dim sun. It did give sufficient light for Jaxom to pick out details of the terrain beyond the canyon. Not that there was much to see. The surface of the Red Star was pocked and slagged, minor fissures and fractures spreading out from the immense fault across what looked more like bare rock than sand. An appallingly sterile landscape. Jaxom could almost feel sorry for the battered planet.

It's a long way across, isn't it? Ruth remarked.

'*You can see across it?*' Jaxom asked, squinting in the dismal gloom at the shadowy far edge.

There isn't much to see but more of the same.

'See how those levels are situated?' F'lar said, peering down. 'We could settle the engines along them.'

'Are they stable enough to hold that sort of weight?' Lessa asked.

F'lar shrugged. 'I don't know why not. Look at the size of the slabs! Gigantic.'

'Like teeth. You know, this looks as if some force broke the planet's surface as you or I would open a redfruit,' Lessa said, her voice awed.

'Ruth, can you drop down to that first level of rock? Take it easy now. We want to see how stable the protrusion actually is.'

'Easy now, Jaxom!' F'lar cautioned, raising one hand as if to cancel the experiment.

There was plenty of wing space and Ruth delicately lowered himself in the thin atmosphere, past the lip of the canyon and down on to the first stone sheet. He dislodged a small boulder which continued to fall. Jaxom listened for a long moment.

'Have you got all your weight on this, Ruth?' Jaxom asked.

Jaxom could feel Ruth grunting as he bent his knees and pressed downwards.

It's not going anywhere.

'We should have brought some lights,' Jaxom told the others, peering along the stone protrusion. It was a lighter coloured material so it was visible against the darkness of the abyss below him. 'But this shelf looks plenty long enough to hold even the *Yokohama*'s engine.'

'D'you want me and Ruth to see how far down we can go before the canyon closes up?'

'Shards! No!' F'lar said. 'What you're doing is dangerous enough.'

'How much time has elapsed?' Lessa asked. 'The dragons have only so much air in their bodies.'

'We're only seven minutes here,' Jaxom said, glancing at the built-in suit chronometer. As a leader he was wearing one of the original spacesuits, not those Hamian had so cleverly contrived.

'C'mon up out of there, Jaxom,' F'lar said. 'If the jaws of that canyon should snap shut . . .'

As the bronze dragonrider had only spoken the thought in Jaxom's mind, he was quite willing to comply.

Ruth rose, beating his wings much faster than he'd need to on Pern, from the black chasm, facing the other two dragons. This immense geological feature stretched in both directions into the tenebrous distance. Much, as Lessa had said, as if the planet had been ruptured. Jaxom looked behind him. There were more jagged projections from little more than terraces to great sheets that would have taken up most of Benden's Bowl.

'This would be one likely site then,' F'lar said. 'I'll go up, you go down. Lessa, see what the other rim is like. How much time, Jaxom?'

'Five minutes! No more!'

Jaxom found it somewhat unnerving to fly over this aperture, knowing that it extended to the depths of the planet. He kept his eye open for unusual extrusions to use as landmarks, but the sides had sheared clean for almost four minutes of flight. Then a dragonlength below the lip he saw another long thick sheet of pale mottled rock. He asked Ruth to mark it in his mind.

Ramoth says we must return. They have found a third place, Ruth told Jaxom.

'Then our mission is accomplished. Let's join 'em and go back.'

Ramoth says to jump back from where we are.

'Are you all right?' Jaxom asked. 'Are they all right?'

I'm all right. They're all right. But it would be good to get back to the Yokohama *and breathe.*

'Let's go then.' And Jaxom thought with longing of his own for the safety of the cargo bay and the relief of weightlessness.

A fraction of a breath after they arrived, the two big Benden dragons arrived. Even in the dim light of the cargo bay, Jaxom could see that their colours were greyed. Apprehensively he looked down at Ruth but any fading was not visible. And saw that their journey had an elapsed time of 12.30.20 minutes.

'Are you all right?' he asked, leaning forward on Ruth's neck, aware that his mouth was wide open as he inhaled and exhaled, great deep breaths. Jaxom could feel him trembling.

'Jaxom? Lessa? F'lar?' Aivas' voice sounded very loud in the helmet.

'We're here. We're all right. We've found three points

for the engines. Well down in the chasm, wide ledges. Perfect.' He looked at his wristpiece. 'Twelve minutes, Aivas. Twelve. Strange place.' Jaxom added, as he had time now to review what he had seen of the lifeless surface, the jumbled, tortured terrain, with the vast canyon like a gaping wound that had killed the planet. Had anyone ever lived on it?

I am thirsty and I need a bath, Ruth said so plaintively that Jaxom laughed. *Ramoth and Mnementh agree.*

'I think we'll just let you get your full breath back, Ramoth dear,' Lessa said, unsnapping the riding straps. 'There wouldn't be any *klah* up here anywhere, would there, Jaxom?' she asked, almost as plaintively as Ruth had. 'I'm thirsty, cold and I feel as if I've been gone from Pern for a century.'

'Water's all we've got up here,' he told her. 'But we're not that far from hot *klah.*' He wouldn't mind a pitcherful or two. His guts felt cold from his navel to his backbone.

Jaxom let himself float, relaxing. The gravity on the Red Star had felt twice that of Pern despite Aivas's assurance that it was less. Perhaps it was the thin atmosphere . . .

The water cask was empty and he cursed under his breath. He'd have a hard word or two for whatever dimwit hadn't had the consideration to bring the onboard cask to be refilled.

Lessa was furious, too, but that made them quick to shed their suits and rack them carefully away. By then, all three dragons insisted that they were restored and wanted nothing more than a long drink and a longer swim.

'One thing,' Lessa said as she remounted Ramoth, 'this trip was much further away, but it didn't take as long as I thought it would. I wonder . . .'

'We've enough to wonder about, Lessa,' F'lar said firmly, 'and I want to get the details down as soon as possible before they fade.'

'My impressions of that sterile place won't fade,' Lessa replied emphatically. 'I could almost feel sorry for it.'

'It has been a dead planet for longer than Pern has been viable,' said Aivas.

'That doesn't make me feel any better,' Lessa said.

*

Meer was waiting at Cove Hold and he gave both Jaxom and Ruth such a scolding that Lessa and F'lar doubled up with laughter as Jaxom evaded the agitated dives and fierce shriekings.

You're wasting energy. Come, bathe me, little one. We are safely home, Ruth said and ambled down towards the beach. *You are not coming?* he added plaintively when he saw Jaxom heading towards the hold.

'Can't, dear heart. Got to put down the details while they're fresh in my mind! Be with you soon enough,' Jaxom called as he jogged up the beach with Lessa and F'lar. Fairs of fire-lizards erupted into the air, diving for the dragons. 'Not that you need us!'

The spacious living area of the Hold was empty and calls for Robinton and Sharra went unanswered.

'I wonder where Sharra's gone,' Jaxom said, remembering all too clearly that he had left her asleep, diverted Meer, and she would be worried. Or angry! And with genuine cause, he thought, wincing.

Lessa grinned at him, understandingly. 'You were with us.'

'That'll be no excuse,' Jaxom said glumly, wondering how he was going to restore himself in Sharra's eyes: especially when she found out what he'd been doing the last two days. He gave himself a mental shake and turned to immediate tasks.

As the Benden Weyrleaders collected drawing materials, Jaxom found a pitcher of cold fruit juice in the cooler. They emptied the large jug as they recorded their visit. When they compared the images, there were few deviations.

'That's done!' Lessa said, with a sigh of relief.

'You know,' Jaxom said, propping his head on one hand and grinning at the other two. 'I still don't believe we've been there and back!'

F'lar regarded him before managing a wry grin. 'I don't know what I expected – especially after F'nor's try – but it's incredible that something as dead as that has threatened us for so long.'

'Well, it has!' Lessa said, planting both hands on the table and pushing herself to her feet. She picked up the sketches and thrust them at Jaxom. 'Put them somewhere safe until you can show Aivas. Now, I'm going to swim!'

Though he wanted a swim as badly as the others, Jaxom detoured through the room he had shared with Sharra, hoping that she'd left him a message. There was none and he felt more dejected than ever. He shucked out of his clothes, thankful that he kept a spare change here at Cove Hold, and made his way down to the lagoon.

Meer and Talla separated themselves from those scrubbing Ruth and circled his head, chittering happily. Not entirely encouraged by their response, he waded out to Ruth.

Sharra's above. She wouldn't let Meer or Talla come. They'd get in the way, Ruth told him.

Jaxom slapped his forehead in dismay: she'd told him, too, and he'd forgotten about it, once again so immersed in his own business her doings hadn't quite registered in his brain. And Jaxom laughed in self-deprecation. Sometimes he *knew* he didn't deserve a woman like Sharra and this was one of them. How conceited he was! He missed her. Even if he couldn't have told her about the marvellous journey he had just taken, he missed her.

I'm here, Ruth said in subtle reproach.

'Indeed you are, my dearest friend, as you always are!' Jaxom waded out in the warm water to help the fire-lizards give his lifemate a good scrubbing.

Chapter Sixteen

When Mirrim came to collect Sharra for the trip up to the *Yokohama* to begin their own project, she found Sharra still asleep.

'Sharra? We're to start this dissection business? Remember?' Mirrim said as Sharra groggily roused, plainly disoriented.

'You know about Lamoth and G'lanar?'

Mirrim wrinkled her nose. 'I feel sorry for the dragon. Didn't know one would die of shame. You get dressed. I'll get you some *klah*.'

As Sharra quickly dressed, she hoped that Mirrim's response was shared by others, even if Mirrim was rarely in a majority. Mirrim wouldn't necessarily side with Jaxom, if she felt he was wrong, however, and that reassured his wife.

'You'd better eat, too,' Mirrim said, returning with the *klah*. 'And let's bring some food, fruit and juice. I thought I'd faint with hunger during that last session Aivas put us through. Maybe he's sophisticated, but my stomach's not. It's real primitive. It likes to be filled at regular intervals.'

Sharra smiled over her cup rim. That was Mirrim, talking up a storm to hide her real feelings. The death of any dragon for any reason upset all riders. With the *klah* stimulating her, Sharra lent Mirrim a hand to pack provisions.

'No meatrolls!' Mirrim said with a dramatic shudder as

Sharra reached into the cupboard for some. 'I'll puke if I have to eat any more. Thank goodness Master Robinton likes proper bread and sliced meats and raw vegetables.' They placed fresh fruit in the special quilted sacks that were a spin-off product from Hamian's search for spacesuit paddings and filled thermoses with cool drinks. 'There's no decent water up there and no end of *klah*,' Mirrim said in conclusion. 'All right, then, let's lift.'

'Isn't Brekke coming with us?'

'No, F'nor's to do something aboard the *Yokohama* today.' Mirrim grinned at Sharra. 'Probably the same thing Jaxom and T'gellan are doing only I'm not to ask.'

'Is it dangerous?' Sharra spoke casually, but she knew Jaxom well enough to know that he had *not* been telling her something last night: a something that had fretted Meer badly enough to send the little bronze skittering back to Ruatha in fright.

'I doubt it! Riders take good care of their dragons and the reverse is true. The dragons are all very happy with themselves. I wouldn't let *today* worry me, Sharra,' Mirrim said sympathetically.

More bolstered by Mirrim's breezy tone than her words, Sharra followed the green rider out to where Path awaited them, her green hide gleaming with undertones of deep blue, her eyes dazzling in a green that exactly matched her hide.

'Does she do that often?' Sharra asked, pointing to eye and hide.

Mirrim flushed and ran a hand over her short front locks escaping the tieback. 'Sometimes.' Though she had a slight grin on her face, she wouldn't meet Sharra's eye. T'gellan was very good for Mirrim, Sharra thought.

When the two women arrived at the *Yokohama*, Mirrim left Path to amuse herself at the big window of the bridge, an occupation which would engross the green dragon for hours on end. Hefting their provisions, they made their way to the first level of the coldsleep storage facility where they, and the others Master Oldive had inducted to assist in the project, would attempt to understand the complexities of Thread. It was a project that would take far longer than any of them had estimated. It would occasionally cause them to wonder, over the next few weeks, why they'd started such an investigation in the first place.

Whenever she could, Sharra cadged a ride back to Ruatha, to spend a few hours with her sons, whom she missed terribly – when she had time to miss anything. She was relieved that Jaxom seemed so involved in his own project that he apparently didn't notice, or mind, her preoccupation. Sometimes, when she and the others found themselves working long hours, they stayed up on *Yokohama*. Mirrim, of course, had to fly Threadfall, but the others had been released from any other duties for this important investigation.

Other times, when the team had to perform endless boring tasks, they grumbled about Aivas's obsession with the biology of the Thread organism: especially as once the primary task of shifting the Red Star's orbit was accomplished, Thread would be relegated to a menace with which to threaten disobedient children. But Aivas repeatedly insisted on the necessity of this research: how vital it was to *understand* this organism. They were all, including Oldive, so accustomed to obeying an Aivas directive that they complied.

Caselon, who now sported journeyman's knots as well as a unique pattern of tiny white scars on his tanned face, did comment about the irony of their grabbing a few hours' sleep in the very capsules which had brought their ancestors to Pern.

Skilfully guided by Aivas, they had sufficient successes to keep a high level of enthusiasm and interest, and to ignore discomforts. As Aivas often reminded them, the routines they were learning in dissecting the very complex organism that had menaced their world for centuries could be applied to other bio-organisms of their own kind. So this discipline was a useful end in itself.

Aivas did insist that they bring one ovoid up to 'normal' temperatures in an airlock on the far side from those sections of the *Yokohama* that were used. With no friction to destroy the tough outer layer, the ovoid remained inert.

374

'The friction then,' Aivas observed, 'is essential to free the organism.'

'Let's not free it!' Caselon suggested in a droll tone.

'It is as well,' Master Oldive remarked thoughtfully, 'to know that it is helpless.'

'At our mercy,' Sharra added, grinning.

'The observation will be continued,' Aivas said.

'Do let us know if its condition changes,' Sharra said.

Besides Caselon, Sharra, Mirrim and Oldive, Brekke had volunteered and brought Tumara, the unsuccessful queen candidate, for the girl didn't seem to mind monotonous tasks as much as others did. Two more Healers, Sefal and Durack, and Manotti, a Smithcraft journeyman, completed their staff. There were times when they could have used twice the number but all had been trained by Aivas and soon worked well together, often doubling up on chores to help a workmate.

Initially they had the barest essentials for the task at hand. In the laboratory there were two cubicles. On the top of the work benches were disks which lit up with various kinds of light: Sefal, a dour but diligent sort, was fascinated by the effects obtainable during initial demonstrations. Most important for their purpose was the binocular stereo microscope which each had to learn to use. The x and y dimensions caused no problem but to learn to use the z, which exaggerated that dimension, was far more difficult. To demonstrate that, Aivas had Sharra take a hair from her head and tie knots in it under the microscope – not as easy as it sounded – as each of them learned when they tried it.

To one side of the microscope was a flush drawer, with a sliding cover, in which some oddly truncated glass instruments were found. These, Aivas told them, they must learn to duplicate to do the dissection work required.

Two more work benches and stools were found and dragged into the two cubicles although that limited what free space there was.

While Sharra was tying knots in her hair using the binocular microscope, Aivas had Sefal and Manotti take apart one of the two refrigerators to obtain the parts necessary to bring the other one down to −150 degrees, the temperature they would need to work on the Thread organism. They might have to reduce its temperature to that of the Oort Cloud from which it came, −270° C or 3° Absolute, but for the present, they could be content with maintaining the Thread's temperature in Pern orbit about −150° C.

'I don't know what I'm doing,' Manotti complained at one point as he gutted the dispensable refrigerator unit.

'That is not at issue,' Aivas reassured him. 'You need only follow instructions, for there isn't time to teach you cryogenics or refrigeration engineering. Do as you are told.'

'I will, I will,' Manotti said, grimacing as he very carefully removed a coil of tubing from the back of the first refrigerator. 'Now where does this go?'

Aivas explained and encouraged, through the medium of the optic now focused on Manotti. When the transfer was completed, Manotti gave a whoop of triumph as the machinery purred into activity. Next, several of the cold capsules were altered to provide additional 3°. A temperature storage for their specimens. For they needed many more than the original Thread ovoid that Farli had caught. The ovoids, as they shortly learned, came in a variety of sizes and in many conditions and, surprisingly, temperatures.

'You'd think one would be enough,' Mirrim muttered to Sharra.

'Humans are not duplicates of each other,' Aivas replied, though she had not intended being overheard. She rolled her eyes at Sharra. 'Patently the Thread organisms will also exhibit anomalies, deviations and, quite likely, mutations. They are as much a life form as humans are, and they are in a very stressful environment so near Rukbat.'

'That puts us neatly in our place,' Oldive said with a grin.

Over the next few days, each team member had to learn to cope with the binocular microscope. Tying knots in a strand of hair gave way to carving flowers from splinters of wood and making paper flowers one millimetre across. Sharra proved the deftest of all, with Brekke and Mirrim not far behind her.

Caselon and Manotti, aided by Sefal and Durack, assembled a micro forge with a flame 2 mm long, in which they heated the special glass Aivas had had Master Morilton mix, a glass with such a high lead content that even the amenable Morilton protested. After Aivas told him that he could make knives sharp enough to cut bread out of this high-lead mix, Morilton was at least curious enough to wish to experiment. So Aivas and Caselon got the unusual material.

Working carefully, Caselon pulled glass in the tiny flame, then took the resultant tube down to 3° A in which the finished product would be used. When the first rod shattered, Caselon reflectively jumped back despite the fact that he wore protective face and body shields. He glanced around sheepishly.

'A good habit to acquire, Caselon,' Aivas remarked approvingly. 'Try again.'

When the fourth rod had shattered, Caselon was disgusted.

'The glass may not have been blended well enough, Caselon. Master Morilton supplied you with several different mixes. Use the one with the highest lead content. The instruments must be flexible, bending rather than shattering,' Aivas said, projecting such a reassurance of eventual success that Caselon took heart.

The fifth attempt bent slightly in the extreme cold but it didn't shatter or crack.

'Now, using that mix, make more rods which you will then fashion into knobs, spikes, blades. Each of you will work your own tools, with Caselon as your instructor. To further dissect Thread, you will need what are ordinary tools, hacksaw, chisel, mallet, scalpel, but in miniature. Carborundum stone will sharpen edges.'

Caselon's set were much admired by the others despite what Mirrim saw as stubby inelegant implements. Consequently, when she, on her competitive mettle, made her set longer she discovered that the flexibility of the length proved a disadvantage when the instruments were used.

'There is so much to do before we DO anything,' she complained. 'We've wasted weeks on all this!'

'And you will spend weeks on the next procedures, Mirrim,' Aivas said in a tone that chided her for impatience. 'You have worked with great diligence, and achieved feats of expertise that two Turns ago you would not have been capable of performing. Do not despair. You are about to embark on the truly interesting phase.'

'What?' Mirrim asked bluntly.

'Dissecting Thread.'

'But haven't we?' Sharra exclaimed, pointing to the cold capsule where the sectioned Threads were housed.

'You have cut the ovoids apart but you have not truly examined them as minutely as you shortly will. Now, let us see if the waldoes still operate.'

Caselon had been fascinated by these devices, which would allow them to work in a chamber maintained at the very low temperatures at which the Thread specimens were kept. He volunteered to be first. Aivas chose Sharra as she had already done more microscopic work than the journeyman. The apparatus was powered up, the specimen and the glass tools placed inside the waldo chamber and the binocular microscope swung into position.

Resolutely, Sharra put her hands into the gloves and gave a little shudder.

'Cold!!' she said by explanation and attempted to move her fingers. 'I thought you said these waldoes would follow my movements.'

'Meters show that current is being taken into the mechanism,' Caselon said, looking at the dials. 'Here, let me.'

Sharra withdrew her hands but Caselon had no more luck than she.

'All right, Aivas,' she said. 'What do we do now?'

There was one of the brief but noticeable pauses they had all come to expect when Aivas conducted an internal search.

'The mechanism has been unused for twenty-five hundred years. It is not unreasonable to assume that maintenance might be required. A lubrication of the finger joints with silicone fluid may restore mobility.'

'Silicone fluid?' Caselon asked.

Manotti raised his hand. 'I know what he means. Aivas, is there a Smith journeyman or Master available?'

'I can send Tolly down for it,' Mirrim suggested.

Manotti gave her a sardonic look. 'He'll have a day's wait.'

Mirrim groaned. 'Then I'm going down,' she said. 'I feel the need of a swim and fresh food and some time with my mate.'

'If we really are out of action until the silicone fluid is prepared, I ought to take the day off, too,' Sharra said, thinking it had been an age since she'd had any time with her sons, or Jaxom.

Caselon grinned. 'I'll stay here and manufacture some more tools. If I go down, someone's surely going to find work for me.'

Aivas gracefully gave permission for such departures but, to those who remained, he immediately assigned other tasks.

Jaxom was as absorbed in his current tasks as Sharra in hers, though he spent more time at Ruatha, with the two boys, than she was able to. He would listen to her descriptions of the failures and small successes of her project, and encourage her.

'Aivas knows what he's doing, even if he doesn't devote much time to explanations,' he told Sharra on more than one occasion. 'He's done so much for us already, we simply have to take the enigmatic on faith and follow his instructions.' Jaxom reminded himself to take his own advice.

To the chagrin of Lessa and F'lar, Aivas had insisted that Jaxom and Ruth must be involved in every aspect of training the dragons and riders in extravehicular activity. According to Aivas, Jaxom and Ruth must also guide any further excursion to the surface of the Red Star.

'Ruth is the younger dragon,' Aivas said at his most diplomatic, 'and has not suffered the strains and stresses of Threadfall . . .'

'I ride Fall with Fort Weyr all the time,' Jaxom protested, as much to soothe Lessa as because he wanted to make it clear that he and Ruth did not fail in their primary obligation.

'No offence intended,' Aivas said in a deferential tone.

'Be all as it is, it is not recommended that such a long journey be made without good reason.'

'It's certainly no Gather site,' Lessa said.

'I do propose one more investigative trip,' F'lar said, 'taking along an observer to record the abyss in a permanent form. Every dragon and rider who is to help bring those engines there must have a vivid picture in his mind of where he's going.'

'Apart from that necessary contingency,' Aivas went on smoothly, 'this undertaking should be recorded. There is nothing to match this endeavour of yours in the annals of any other world.'

'Not that any other world is interested in our feats,' Master Robinton said in a droll murmur.

'Mankind needs heroes,' Aivas replied. 'This project is of heroic stature.'

F'lar gestured in disclaimer. 'What has to be done can scarcely be termed heroic!'

Master Robinton shot the Weyrleader a long thoughtful look.

'We have three engines to place,' F'lar went on, ignoring the Harper's stare, 'so the leaders of each group need to visit the place. 'I lead one . . .'

'Jaxom leads another,' Aivas said crisply.

'All right . . .' F'lar allowed.

'And I lead the third,' Lessa said.

F'lar immediately objected. 'You've risked yourself and Ramoth enough already.'

Lessa's eyes flashed and her expression hardened. 'If you go, I go. Ramoth's scarcely the only queen on Pern these days.'

Suddenly F'lar's resistance dissolved and, if Jaxom found himself surprised, Ruth was not.

'*Why not?*' Jaxom asked his dragon very privately.

Lessa would not risk Ramoth if she is in clutch, would she?

Jaxom hurriedly covered his mouth with his hand and turned a guffaw into a cough. No wonder F'lar hadn't pressed the point of Lessa's involvement in the event, and Mnementh had cooperated by getting Ramoth in clutch. F'lar had learned subtlety in handling his Weyrmate.

'On this one admissible expedition,' Jaxom said, 'I think F'nor ought to be included.'

F'lar gave Jaxom a friendly clout, grinning more broadly than the circumstances warranted. 'I was about to insist that F'nor and Canth deserve to see the place.'

'It's only fair,' Robinton said, nodding wisely, 'and Canth won't object to taking Perschar, who's got the best eye for detail. D'ram must be allowed this opportunity. And Tiroth can easily convey me,' he added, daring protest.

'You can't be put at risk,' Lessa said, rising to the bait.

'There'd be no risk involved, would there, Aivas?' Robinton said, shamelessly appealing to the one authority that Lessa would respect.

'The Harper would not be at risk.'

'Tiroth's too old . . .' Lessa declared, glowering at Robinton.

'Tiroth is sturdier than most beasts his age and the insight of both his rider and Master Robinton might prove invaluable,' Aivas said.

It took a few moments for Lessa's irritation to subside but the matter was soon settled. One more exploratory jump would be made to the Red Star's surface. The group would include D'ram, F'nor, N'ton and Jaxom, with the dragons carrying Master Robinton, Fandarel, Perschar, and Sebell as observers. The discretion of these few was unassailable so there would be no chance of careless talk generating more rumour and misconception than already abounded.

Lord Larad of Telgar and Lord Asgenar of Lemos asked Masterharper Sebell to meet them at Telgar Hold at his convenience.

Since Sebell appreciated the diplomatic tone, he dispatched his fire-lizard, Kimi, with a message that he would attend them an hour after the evening meal at Telgar.

'What do you suppose is bothering them?' Menolly asked when Sebell told her of the meeting.

'Rumours have abounded lately, pet,' Sebell said with a sigh.

Menolly leaned back from the lectern on which she composed much of her music and, grinning slyly, cocked her head at her husband. 'You mean the ones about Sharra and Jaxom, the ones about G'lanar and Lamoth, the latest Abomination mischief or why the bronze dragons are looking so inordinately pleased with themselves?'

'I'd rather not have so much choice.' He carefully tucked a vagrant strand of her long hair back into the clasp before bending to kiss her neck. 'I hadn't heard of either Telgar or Lemos having any problems with vandalism so it can't be that.'

'Those who approve do so wholeheartedly, while those who are fearful, apprehensive, or downright sceptical scuttle around the edges and ruin what they haven't the wit to understand.'

'It's our task to see that they do understand,' Sebell said, gently remonstrating.

'But some don't *want* to,' she said in a rebellious tone, stretching both arms well above her head to ease her back. 'I know the breed. Oh, how I know the breed! It's just too bad we can't leave them alone with their closed minds, but they're standing in our way forward.'

'We are altering the fabric of their lives. That frightens people. It always has, it always will. Lytol's sent me some fascinating excerpts from Aivas' historical data. Fascinating. People don't change, love. React first, think later, regret at leisure.'

He bent to kiss her cheek. 'I've time to tell Robse and Olos a story before I go.'

Menolly snaked an arm around his neck before he could straighten. 'You are such a loving man,' she said and then kissed him again deeply before releasing her hold.

When he paused at the threshold to look back at her fondly, she was already bent to her composition. He smiled at the concentrated pose of her back, one shoulder angled up. She did love him but he accepted that fact that he would have always two rivals – music and the Master. He had the same loves and went down the corridor to sing to his sons who enjoyed such attention and to admire his daughter, Lemsia, who was too young for more than adoration.

*

Laradian, Larad's oldest son, was waiting for Sebell in the well-lit court when the obliging Fort Hold dragon deposited the harper at Telgar.

'My father and Lord Asgenar are in the small study, Masterharper,' Laradian said in a formal tone and then, relaxing, grinned a welcome at Sebell.

A fine fire was burning on the hearth angled in the corner of the pleasant room, its walls hung with rich tapestries, and framed sketches – probably by Perschar if Sebell didn't mistake the skill – of the current Lord's offspring. Several heavy, old wherry-hide chairs, sagging from the comfort they had given several generations of weary bodies, the huge desk and table where the Lords of Telgar had done their accounts for centuries, furnished the room adequately. Sebell immediately noticed the latest addition: a very good rendering, though considerably reduced in scale, of the Honshu mural.

'Hmmm yes,' Larad said, noticing his glance, 'my daughter, Bonna, went along with Perschar's group and brought that back. Of course, she was under Master Perschar's eye all the time but it's judged to be a fair representation.'

'You'd be welcome to see the original,' Sebell said, nodding to Asgenar who was ensconced in one of the armchairs.

'What?' Larad asked, his pleasant face affecting a horrified expression, 'and let rumour have it that I wanted the place for one of my sons?' He gestured for Sebell to take a chair and held up a wine bottle. 'It's Benden.' His grin was for the allusion to a harperical preference for that wine, though his reference to rumour told Sebell that rumour was indeed a concern.

'I follow many of Master Robinton's traditions,' Sebell said, accepting the generous goblet. He sipped judiciously and raised his brows in appreciation. 'A '16?'

'Indeed, and it was Master Robinton who urged me to acquire as many skins as I could wheedle.'

'So?' Sebell turned politely to the two Lords Holder. 'Rumour bites?'

'I wish it were only rumour, Sebell,' Larad said and took a small message roll from his sleeve cuff, handing it to the harper. 'This is far more serious and demands your urgent consideration. I know the sender well enough to heed his words.'

After a glance at the message, Sebell shot out of the comfortable chair, seething with anger and swearing blackly. '"I have good reason to believe that Masterharper Robinton may be abducted to force those at Landing to destroy what they call the Abomination".' Sebell was consumed with outrage. 'Hazard the Masterharper! Ransom him for the destruction of Aivas!' Outrage gave way to panic. 'Who is this Brestolli who signs the note?'

'He's a wagonmaster. We both know him,' and Larad gestured toward Asgenar who nodded earnestly. 'He wouldn't send a false alarm. Actually, it was delivered by his fire-lizard to his employer, Trader Nurevin, who's here now. Nurevin brought it straight to me, leaving his train a day's trip out. He said that he'd had to leave Brestolli at Bitra with a broken leg and cracked ribs from a wagon accident.'

'Nurevin's just outside. I'll ask him in,' Asgenar said and slipped out of the room.

Larad gave a wry smile. 'Nurevin felt you would heed this message more if we presented it to you.'

'He'd need no one vouching for him to me,' said Sebell, rereading the message. 'This has the ring of truth. Nothing Bitra initiates surprises me.'

'Then you also know that your harpers at Bitra Hold have been put in quarantine for a virulent disease?'

'The Bitran euphemism for "reporting truth"?' Sebell asked. He ran his fingers through his hair, an exasperated gesture. 'We haven't heard from them recently by the usual route. I should have sent at least one who had a fire-lizard.'

'Our Master Celewis can mount a rescue mission, if you'd like?' Larad suggested.

'If that can be done without jeopardizing Brestolli,' Sebell replied.

Larad raised his eyebrows and grinned slyly. 'Surely you know Celewis' abilities . . .'

'Indeed I do,' Sebell said with an answering grin.

'Then you may be certain that he'll be adroit in the matter.'

Nurevin came in just then, preceding Asgenar.

'I've not had occasion to pass time with you, Trader Nurevin,' Sebell said, smiling as he extended his hand and returned the strong pressure given. 'But I can tell you that the Harper Hall is more than grateful to you for passing this message.'

'Brestolli's not the sort makes things up for mischief, Masterharper,' Nurevin said, cocking his head to emphasize his opinion. He was a swart man of medium height, with grizzled hair worn in a long plait that had recently been neatly redone. His clothing was of excellent quality but road-worn. 'So I knew I'd best get it to someone who could see it was handled proper. I hated to leave him in Bitra Hold but he'd broke his leg in three places, mangled his arm and cracked some ribs when a cart overturned. Caught a wheel on uneven flags in Bitra Court. Healer said he couldn't be moved so I paid the brewer both good marks and trade goods to tend him. Brestolli's one to keep his eyes and ears open, despite he talks such a streak you wouldn't think he'd hear for the constant sound of his own voice. But if he's heard what that message says he heard, then he's heard it. Make no mistake about that. I wouldn't want it said we didn't give warning when there're them what'd harm good Master Robinton. No, I wouldn't.'

Larad offered him a goblet of Benden wine and Nurevin's eyes lit up with appreciation after his first sip.

'You honour me, Lord Larad.'

'Telgar is in your debt, Trader Nurevin.'

'Not just Telgar, Trader Nurevin,' Sebell added solemnly as he tilted his glass to him and drank ceremoniously. Nurevin flushed at such courtesy.

Sebell called Kimi to him then, for she had been visiting outside with Telgar Hold's fair. Silently, Larad proffered writing materials and a message tube.

'I'm sending this to Lytol who will take appropriate measures,' he said after penning some quick lines. Kimi extended her leg for him to attach the capsule, knowing exactly what was required of her.

'Kimi, take this to Lytol, in Cove Hold, where our Master lives! Where Zair lives. Yes?'

Kimi had listened intently, cocking her head this way and that, her eyes whirling with noticeable increase in speed. She gave one chirp and disappeared.

'Forewarned is forearmed, Trader Nurevin. Has Brestolli's fire-lizard returned to him?'

'Yes, it's only a blue but he's got it well trained. I can send my queen if you need more information. I've been keeping in touch with Brestolli to be sure he's well tended.' Nurevin winked and grinned. 'Bitrans need me more'n I need them, since they're so hard to deal with. I'm the only trader who does their route in these parlous times. So I've an edge on 'em, so to speak.' He paused, his expression grim. 'Did Lord Larad tell you about your harpers?' When Sebell nodded, he went on. 'That was done a-purpose or I'll be scored next Fall!'

'When a harper is silenced, all men should listen harder.'

Nurevin nodded solemnly. 'I heard some other stuff whilst I was at Bitra . . .' He hesitated.

'Be easy, man,' Larad encouraged him. 'There's not much a harper doesn't hear sooner or later. And, if it's along the lines of Brestolli's message, perhaps Master Sebell'd better hear it from you.'

'Well, it's them rumours,' Nurevin paused again, obviously not happy to utter them, but by gesture and expression, all three men encouraged him to speak. 'It's said that Lord Jaxom and that white dragon of his killed G'lanar and Lamoth . . . deliberate.'

'Shards! How could anyone repeat such a foul slander?' Asgenar asked, incensed.

'Oh, there've been worse,' Sebell said, but he turned to Nurevin. 'Master Robinton was there himself and told me that Jaxom was victim, not assailant, and Lamoth died of shame that his rider would turn on another rider. Any more?'

'Well, and this's stupider,' Nurevin went on, both reassured and encouraged by his audience. 'That dragonriders will take the three colony ships and disappear from Pern, leaving us with only flame-throwers to kill Thread!'

'Did you hear the one that suggests that the dragons

will take the old shuttles and throw them at the Red Star and destroy it?' When Nurevin shook his head, Sebell continued, his expression serious. 'There's one that the Masterhealer has been given medicine by Aivas that will paralyse folk so that pieces can be carved out of their bodies to repair others who have sickened?'

Nurevin snorted. 'I heard that one at Bitra. I didn't believe it then and I don't believe it now. That Aivas thing is scary, but I've not seen anything produced yet that didn't help us in some way or t'other. Best axle grease I ever had was something that Aivas gave the Smithcrafthall. And that new metal for cotter pins that don't bend or snap when the wheels are stressed.'

Kimi re-entered, chittering about the success of her trip and stroking her golden head on Sebell's cheek before she held out her message laden leg. Excusing himself, Sebell read the message.

'Late as it is there, I'm bid to Cove Hold. If you'll excuse me . . .'

He was ushered out by the two.

'You wonder sometimes, don't you, Asgenar,' Larad said sadly as they turned to re-enter the warm comfortable room, 'why people can be so ornery.'

'I think it has to do with a resistance to being done good to.'

'Not if they're putting Master Robinton at risk,' Larad said, still horrified by that possibility. 'He's never harmed anyone in his life. This world would rise up to the least child to protest such infamy.'

'Which, unfortunately, makes him the most useful hostage,' Asgenar said with a sigh of regret.

By the time Sebell reached Cove Hold, it was early morning hours. He and the brown dragon who was conveying him were immediately greeted by swarms of chittering fire-lizards, as dense in the sky as Thread. Tiroth, ensconced on the grassy sward before the Hold, blinked orange-laced eyes until he and brown Folrath identified each other. Sebell was pleased to see so many guardians already in place. Not that the would-be abductors could as yet have got so far as

Cove Hold, given the journey they'd have to make from Bitra, or even the nearest seaport.

Every glowbasket in the main room was wide open, shedding light on Robinton, D'ram, Lytol, and T'gellan who were sitting at the big round table. A collapsed wineskin indicated that much discussion had already taken place. Sebell was glad to see the Eastern Weyrleader present.

'Ah, Sebell,' Robinton cried, raising his arm in welcome, his expression so merry that Sebell thought the Harper was perversely enjoying his jeopardy, 'any more news of this scurrilous scheme?'

Sebell shook his head, grinning at such a reception although the Harper's ebullience was by no means echoed by others at the table.

'You know as much as anyone though Nurevin has assured me he'll keep in touch with Brestolli, by fire-lizard, in case the man hears more to the point.'

'I've sent Zair with a message to Master Idarolan,' Robinton said, 'in case he can intercept the conspirators.'

'We've had quite enough of petty vandalism and wanton destruction of property,' Lytol said, a deep angry scowl on his face. 'This time we must catch the scofflaws and discover everyone who has aided and abetted them. For anyone to even contemplate harming Master Robinton, a man to whom all Pern owes a very great debt . . .'

'Now, now, Lytol,' Robinton said, circling Lytol's stiff shoulders with a soothing arm, 'don't carry on so. You're embarrassing me. And this whole scheme only shows how basically stupid our detractors are. As if they had a chance of penetrating my loyal minions,' and the Harper gestured to the storm of fire-lizard fairs outside the window.

'I know they can't reach you, Robinton,' Lytol said, banging his fist on the table and making the goblets jump, 'but the fact that they would *dare* . . .'

Robinton grinned maliciously. 'Maybe I should let myself be captured? Hauled off unceremoniously . . .' Lytol stared at him, aghast. 'Taken to wherever they plan to incarcerate me, and then,' he lifted his free hand and clenched it suddenly into a fist, 'let the avenging wings swoop down on the despicable rabble and carry them off forthwith to be dropped in the deepest of Larad's mines, condemned to toil off their misspent energies in useful work.'

Lytol's expression turned to resignation and disgust. 'You should take this seriously, my friend.'

'I do. I really do!' And Robinton altered his mobile face. 'I'm deeply saddened that I, or anyone on Pern, could be victimized in this horrendous fashion. But,' he held up one finger, 'it's more ingenious than trying to burn space engine fuel or sabotage Aivas. We really ought to ask his advice, you know.'

'If it weren't for Aivas . . .' Lytol began heatedly, broke off when he realized what he'd said and when T'gellan and Sebell tried to smother their spontaneous guffaw. Lytol abruptly got to his feet and strode out of the room.

When Sebell made to go after the old Warder, Robinton held up his hand and Sebell settled back down into his chair.

'He has every right to be upset,' D'ram said in a slow, sad voice. 'It is terrible to think that there are people who oppose all the good that Aivas has done for us and would go to such great lengths to destroy him, and those of us who have the vision to appreciate the potential.'

'Look, I see no real chance of anyone reaching Master Robinton,' T'gellan said, leaning forward on his elbows across the table. 'They cannot have thought this through very carefully. They can know nothing of Cove Hold or how many people are in and out on a daily – and,' here T'gellan gave Sebell a wry grin, 'early morning basis.'

'Have you forgotten the raid on Landing?' Sebell said. 'Horses, gear, experienced mercenaries. If Aivas hadn't his own defences, that could have succeeded. We can't allow ourselves to be complacent.'

'Well said, Sebell,' D'ram replied. 'However, what Robinton suggested so glibly has merit. If we wish to find the ones behind these attempts, it would be smart of us to set no apparent,' and he held up his hand to emphasize that adjective, 'reinforcements, make no obvious alterations of our daily routines.'

'Agreed . . .'

'All the while making certain that Robinton is never left alone.'

'As if I ever am,' Robinton said, feigning an outraged glower.

'I apologize in advance,' Sebell said in a contrite tone, 'for suggesting this. But if G'lanar was disaffected . . .'

D'ram raised his hand in understanding but it was T'gellan who answered, his expression bleak.

'Ramoth herself spoke to the remaining Oldtimer dragons. Every one of them was appalled by G'lanar's action,' the bronze rider said, 'and none can dissemble before Ramoth!'

Sebell looked immensely relieved. 'Then we can rule out that possibility of abduction.'

'Somehow that doesn't greatly reassure me,' D'ram said in a lugubrious tone of voice. 'We're not dealing with fools.'

'No, we're dealing with fearful men and they're more dangerous.'

The silicone fluid, worked well into the joints of the waldo gloves, restored mobility – except in the third finger of the left hand. Since all but Caselon were right handed, this posed no great problem even to him.

'What would we have done if the silicone fluid didn't work?' Manotti asked, winking at his colleagues to indicate he was teasing their mentor.

'There is always an alternative course of action, though it may be less efficient and productive,' Aivas replied. 'Now, Sharra, be good enough to place a Thread section in the chamber and, using a blade, slice the specimen at a slant, thus exposing all layers. Now, what do you see?'

'Rings, springs and the shapes you called toruses in our biology class,' Sharra said. 'An odd goo, a yellow liquid, some strange pastes in peculiar shades of yellow, grey and white, and some other substances that seem to change colour.'

Tumara made a revolted noise deep in her throat and turned away.

'You must all realize,' Aivas began, in a stern tone, 'that

the most important piece of apparatus in the laboratory is your brain. Just as you made the micro-tools to effect this dissection, you must make your brains the right instrument for this task. The most useful thing is the moment-by-moment interaction of your brain seeing these things for the first time. Even your reaction, Tumara, has a certain validity. Now, set that reaction aside, and observe. What else do you see, Sharra?'

She tapped her micro-blade on a ring. 'This feels like metal.'

'Then excise it and any more like it that you see, and have the items sent to Master Fandarel for analysis. What else?'

'There're a lot of particles lodged in the pasty parts, and . . . and it's hollow in the centre. Could that yellow liquid be liquid helium?' Sharra went on. 'It's just like the stuff you showed us in the liquid gas experiments and it boils as soon as it's exposed to the $-150°$ atmosphere. We haven't yet tried it at $3°$ A.'

'There is no reason why it cannot be helium. Helium is liquid at the temperature which Thread inhabits. Isolate a sample and a positive identification can be made.'

'This whole thing resembles those micrographs you displayed, Aivas,' Mirrim said.

'You are quite right, Mirrim. This is the real thing though, not a slide. Continue, Sharra.'

'How?'

'Dissect another ring. Slice it so that you go through more than half the torus. That will show more of its composition.'

'That's odd,' Brekke said. 'Compare that ring with the other one. The first has all kinds of springy-like things sort of layered while in the other they're all twisted up . . . oooh, shells!'

Sharra had prodded one of the rings and suddenly it flipped away from the tool, sticking to the wall of the examination enclosure.

'This could be their method of reproduction,' Aivas said in an excited tone. 'Or it could be a parasite, escaping from the dying organism. But this is quite interesting. Try another ring to see if the reaction is the same,' Aivas said eagerly and, though Sharra's prod was more tentative, there was a second eruption.

'Now, apply your blade to the springs in the first torus. Nothing happens. Now you have seen two entirely different facets of this organism. You are investigating a wholly new creature and we must see everything that it is.'

'Why?' Mirrim asked.

'Because you must know how to destroy this organism, so that it cannot reproduce, so that it cannot multiply anywhere in your system.'

'If it doesn't fall on Pern, that's enough, isn't it?' Brekke asked.

'For you, perhaps, but the sensible thing would be to destroy it at source.'

Caselon recovered first. 'But if the Red Star is moved . . .'

'That doesn't destroy Thread. It only removes its vector. Your task is to discover how you can destroy the Thread organism itself!'

'Isn't that a bit ambitious for us?' Sharra asked.

'The means are available. Even in your very brief investigations today, you have discovered much about the organism. Each day you will discover more. You will uncover its parasites . . .'

'Parasites?' Oldive nearly laughed.

'It is possible that some of those bits are parasites, smaller entities built on the same plan. Parasites or progeny. Or predators.'

'Like those limpets on the tunnel snakes?' Oldive asked. 'The ones that would attach themselves to the snake and eat their muscle tissue and then leave when they're sated?'

'A good example. Were they predators or were they parasites?'

'I don't think we ever decided,' Oldive remarked, 'even based on your definition that a parasite does its host no harm while a predator most certainly does. As the snake limpet did not really injure its host and left when it had accomplished a meal, it was more of a parasite, not quite a predator.'

'What must be found are parasites that can be made into predators. Just as you isolated bacteria, and altered bacteriophages so that they killed their hosts, to reduce wound infection.'

'I still don't see the purpose,' Mirrim muttered.

'There is one,' Aivas said so emphatically that Mirrim made a grimace of dismay and pretended to be frightened.

'Sharra, have you isolated those parts which must be subjected to other tests?'

'I've got a lot of messy bits, and springs and metals, and lumps and bumps, if that's what you mean.'

'Good. Place them on the petri dishes and we can proceed with the investigation. You are to examine them under high pressure, with inert gas, I suggest xenon, which we have in that cylinder, to discover if those tubes are full of helium. Now that you have opened the containing tubular vessels to vacuum, you are losing all the helium, if that's what it is, very rapidly.'

When Lessa and F'lar learned of the threat against Master Robinton, they were all for sending him up to the *Yokohama*, or to Honshu, or back to the Harper Hall.

'I'm not a child,' he said, considerably incensed by such protectiveness. 'I'm a grown man and have faced down every danger that has come my way. Do not deny me that right. Besides, if these conspirators should learn that their victim has been put beyond them, they'll merely think of something else we might not learn about in time to counter. No, I'll stay here, with half the fire-lizards of Pern as my escort and whatever other,' and he held up a warning hand, 'discreet guardians you choose to appoint. Beat a cowardly retreat I will not!' With his head up, his eyes flashing, his breath rapid, no further protest was made.

If he noticed those set to guard him in the following weeks, he did not register the surveillors with so much as a flicker of his eye. Master Idarolan, as irate as everyone else, sent messages to all harbourmasters, consulted at great length with his most trusted captains and dispatched his fastest courier ship to Monaco Bay. Menolly sent Rocky, Diver and Mimic to assist his own Zair, and Swacky and two other big mercenaries were established at Cove Hold.

Master Robinton continued his duties at Landing, and on the *Yokohama*, where he nodded and pretended to be highly intrigued by the biological team's exacting work.

How Aivas learned of it no-one knew, or admitted. He gave Fandarel the schematics for a small device which Master Robinton was to wear at all times. 'A locator,' Aivas termed it. 'Wearing that, you can be traced anywhere on this planet and as far as the spaceships.'

That afforded all his friends far more relief than any would admit. With Aivas as protector, Master Robinton was surely safe.

Chapter Seventeen

B y the end of the Summer, there was still no sign of would-be abductors. Nurevin collected Brestolli from the brewer's cot in Bitra, limping but adamant about what he had overheard; a visit to Lord Sigomal by Benden Weyrleaders secured the release of the 'contagious' harpers and Master Sebell told Lord Sigomal in terms of insincere regret that he had no suitable replacements for a Hold of such stature. Several other Crafts withdrew their Masters, leaving the Bitran Halls staffed by minor journeymen and apprentices of local origin.

A similar withdrawal occurred at Nerat but not at Keroon for, despite his increasing distrust of all Abomination-originated improvements, Lord Corman did not interfere with any of his Crafts or the performance of their traditional duties to his Hold. He also made it plain that he was distancing himself from Sigomal and Begamon.

Every Weyrwoman kept her queen on her mark and every harper tracked down the faintest whisper of clandestine activities. Major Crafthalls discreetly doubled security measures. And dragonriders continued to drill outside the *Yokohama*, the *Bahrain* and *Buenos Aires*. Hamian and his crews worked overtime producing protective covering for riders and ones that fitted like gloves on dragon hindpaws to shield the flesh from the burn of dread ice-cold metal. Oldive, Sharra, Mirrim, Brekke and the others laboured under Aivas' close guidance to analyse and describe the peculiar organism that was Thread – or, rather, that *became* Thread as it met its fiery frenzied doom in the skies of Pern.

There was one untoward incident at Landing, where Sefal and Manotti were carrying on experiments involving certain metal intrusions found in Thread. Sefal was killed and Manotti badly injured, and three students in an adjoining laboratory were also hurt. Manotti couldn't tell what had gone wrong because he'd had his back turned on Sefal. They were working on separate apparatuses. The accident did serve to increase alertness.

Sharra tried to explain the task Aivas had set his investigators to Jaxom, as much to hear herself explain what she was doing as to make it clear to her mate.

'We had one marvellous day when Mirrim discovered the beads under the microscope. Aivas was excited, too, for he feels certain that the beads are the genetic information of the Thread organism.' She grinned as she remembered that moment of triumph. 'The microscope was at high magnification so we could all see these tiny, tiny beads strung along one of those long wires I told you Thread has. Not the springs, but the wires, which are coiled ever so tightly in a volume no bigger than the tip of my finger. Aivas says these ring beads use the material of the Thread ovoid to reproduce themselves.' She made a face, indicating her ignorance of how this was done. 'What he wants us to find now is a bacteriophage to infect the beads and then discover just the right one that will replicate itself fast before it uses up all the Thread material. We've done something of a similar nature, you know, when we located bacteria from wounds and then learned how to disimprove their symbiotic bacteriophages so that they could kill their hosts. Our ancestors could certainly do marvellous things biologically to heal people. I hope we can begin to do as well as they did. *This* exercise could heal our planet.'

'Then why didn't they do it?' Jaxom wanted to know. 'Why are we left with the job?'

Sharra grinned smugly. 'Because we have dragons to replace fuelless shuttles, fire-lizards who can nick Thread ovoids out of space and Aivas to tell us exactly what to do. Even if I don't always understand what we're doing or why we're doing it.'

'I thought you said it was to disimprove the Thread's symbionts. Though why that's necessary with what the dragonriders are to do, I don't know.'

Sharra was silent a moment, considering that. 'Aivas hates Thread, insofar as an inanimate machine is capable of hatred. He hates what it did to his captains and Admiral Benden. He hates what it's done to us. He wants to be sure it can never menace us again. He wants to kill it in the Oort Cloud. He calls the project Overkill.'

Jaxom regarded her in puzzled astonishment. 'He's more vindictive than F'lar!'

Sharra sighed dejectedly. 'I'm not sure that we can *do* what he wants. It's all so very complicated. And we're so limited in our understanding. He may be the machine but I feel like one, doing this and that without knowing why.'

She was more buoyant three days later when she told Jaxom that Aivas had found the appropriate parasitic vector.

'He says that similar life forms were found in micro-gravity conditions in the asteroid belts of old Terra's system. It's very like the one found in the ecology of the Pluto/Charon pair in the original Earth solar system.' Sharra frowned in perplexity. 'Well, that's what he says. He has named the springs zebedees. And zebedees are what we will now use to make our tailored parasite, like a virus, jump from one Thread ovoid to the next . . . once the parasite has disimproved itself as a symbiont and become really destructive! We've got to culture it now, though.'

Jaxom managed a suitably appreciative grin for her enthusiasm. 'Who are we to protest an Aivas pronouncement? What next?'

'Well, he's got all the fire-lizards searching the ovoid streams for the springs. Sometimes they're embedded right on the surface of an ovoid. We've had to start up nine more cold capsules to contain the things, and infect them with the zebedee makers.'

'Zebedees, the Thread fleas!' Jaxom said, teasingly.

'Well, fleas *are* parasites, but I could wish we were able to disimprove some of them quickly! As it is, the time we have available is nowhere near long enough for the work that must be done.'

She had been properly disgusted to discover canine fleas on Jarrol who was incurably attached to one of the kitchen spit animals.

'That will be my priority project to disimprove fleas,' she told her husband, 'as soon as we're finished with Aivas's.'

'Whenever that'll be,' Jaxom added. There were so many Aivas endeavours, at various stages of completion, that he wondered if any of them would get finished on time now that the deadline drew nearer.

'Would you and Ruth have time to get me back to the *Yokohama* tomorrow before you fly Fall?' Sharra asked.

Jaxom groaned. 'I thought you'd be here a few days.'

Sharra looked properly repentant. 'I've been over everything for the Gather with Brand and the other stewards and all's ready for our guests. But this is an especially critical time, Jaxom . . .' Her eyes pleaded for his understanding.

'You'll be exhausted. You won't enjoy the Gather . . .' he heard himself saying and then pulled her into his arms, savouring the feel of her body against his, the spicy fragrance of her hair. Gathers were always special times for them.

'Please, Jaxom?' her lips brushed his neck.

'I'm just griping, love. I could never keep you where you didn't wish to be.'

'Won't it be wonderful, when this is all over, to be just us again?' she said. 'I want a daughter, too, you know.'

That earnest wish elicited a response he was glad to make.

Threadfall was uneventful, though this was not one in which the spaceships' shields had carved tunnels of Thread-free air. Then Hamian sent a message that he had a new glove for Ruth to test on an e.v.a. So, after Ruth had tested it and found it comfortable as well as a good shield with an easy buckle attachment to hold it in place, Jaxom reported the success to Aivas to pass on to

Hamian. Unusually enough, Jaxom and Ruth were alone on the bridge, Ruth spread across the big window as usual, devouring his favourite view.

'Aivas, just why are you so obsessed with this zebedee project?' Jaxom asked when he had delivered his message to Hamian. 'Sharra says you call it Overkill. Why isn't blowing the Red Star out of orbit sufficient?'

'You are alone?' Aivas asked.

That was an unusual question as Aivas unerringly sensed additional presences.

'Yes. Are you going to come clean?' Jaxom said, half joking.

'This is as good a time as any,' Aivas replied, startling the young Holder.

'That doesn't sound good.'

'On the contrary, it is all to the good to know what has been expected of you since learning of Ruth's unusual abilities.'

'His knowing when and where he is?' Jaxom asked slyly.

'Precisely. An explanation is needed.'

'They usually are with you!'

'Flippancy has always covered apprehension. Candour is required. There are three engines which must be exploded to push the Red Star out of an orbit hazardous to Pern. Two of those explosions have already taken place.'

'WHAT?' Jaxom sat upright in the comfortable chair and stared at the screen in front of him.

'As you are aware, records from every Weyr, Hall and Hold were presented and analysed. Two small entries illuminate an anomaly.

'Based on the position of the Red Star when Mankind first landed on Pern, that planet is not now in the orbit it should be tracking at this point in time. Repeated calculations were made during the First Fall by Captains Keroon and Tillek. Eccentric it might be, but its current position differs from an extrapolation of those original calculations. Its path shows that it has suffered a perturbation of 9.3 degrees off its original elliptical orbit. That is not consistent with the extrapolated position. Therefore, something has already altered its path. Substantiation occurs in two minor references found in Istan and Keroonian records in the Fourth and Eighth Passes which were each prior to each Long Interval. During each Pass, bright flashes were observed when the Red Star was at the same anomaly in it's orbit. Bright enough to be remembered and noted.'

Stunned, Jaxom blinked as if that act would help him focus his thoughts on what Aivas meant.

'Those two craters?'

'Your perception is acute.'

'My fear is also, Aivas!'

'Man is wise to fear: it sharpens the sense of self-preservation.'

'But, what I felt when I saw the first crater was not fear. It was . . . it had to be . . . it was as if I knew it had to be there! I discounted such a ridiculous notion at the time. And you, Aivas, would not have me believe that I have been there before?'

'The time paradox has bewildered many. Your presentiment of involvement with the crater is unusual, but similar incidents are reported in the annals of psychic phenomenon.'

'Are they?' Jaxom asked facetiously. 'I'm not at all sure I appreciate the position you've put me in . . . That is, if I understand you correctly?'

'How do you understand what has been said?'

'That somehow I, on Ruth, with enough dragonriders to perform the task, took an engine back in time and deposited it in that rift? Where it blew up to form the crater I find on my initial trip to the Red Star some eighteen hundred Turns in the future?'

'You have done it twice. The second time was six hundred turns ago. It is the only explanation. Furthermore, *you* know that you've done it.'

'I don't want to do it,' Jaxom protested, thinking how far back he'd have to ask Ruth to take him, and the others. Yet Aivas had been accurate in so many other unlikely things. 'What if something went wrong?'

'True to the time paradox, if something had, you wouldn't

be here, and there would be some thirty or forty dragons missing from this time.'

'No, that's wrong,' Jaxom said, struggling to understand the paradox, 'we wouldn't have gone yet. So we'd still be here. We won't be here if we fail when we try it. No, no!' He waved one hand irritably at his confusion.

'You have gone. You have been successful and each of those previous explosions have caused Long Intervals – which are inexplicable by any other rationale – thus setting up the planet for the final orbital dislocation.'

'Now wait a minute,' Jaxom said, waggling his finger at the screen in an aggravated fashion, 'we've done a lot of queer things to propitiate you, Aivas, and we've done them because you've proved to be right . . .'

'This facility is correct in its findings and conclusions in this matter as well, Lord Jaxom.'

'Don't try that tack on me, friend. It doesn't work! The dragonriders are not going to go along with this. Timing it has always been extremely tricky. You know that Lessa nearly died of going back four hundred Turns. You want us to go back eighteen hundred?'

'You will be carrying your own oxygen supplies so you will not suffer from asphyxia as she did. You are aware of the sensory deprivation syndrome and will not be disturbed by the disorientation . . .'

Jaxom kept shaking his head. 'You can't ask bronzes to do that, even if they are able to. I don't think F'lar times it. In fact, the only one I do know who has is Lessa.'

'And your Ruth. Futhermore, you have been proud of the fact that the white dragon always knows where and when he is going.'

'I have, but . . .'

'If Ruth knows where and when he is going . . . and specific guides are available . . . he can supply the necessary visual coordinates.'

'But I know that the other riders won't wear this . . .'

'They will not know!'

Jaxom stared straight at the screen for another long moment.

'How,' he asked in a very patient saccharine tone, 'will they NOT know?'

'Because you will not tell them. And since you now have been to the Red Star on several occasions, and since the distance in terms of travel *between* will not be appreciably longer than what they would expect, they will not know that they have been transported back in time AND to the Red Star in the position required by the equations that cover the two disparate explosions.'

Jaxom mulled that over and, inhaling deeply, realized that, in his state of shock, he had not been breathing regularly.

I think we can do it, Ruth remarked with more confidence than Jaxom was feeling at that moment.

Jaxom turned his head towards his beloved friend.

'You may think we can but I'm going to be bloody sure we can. Now, Aivas, let's go through this again . . . The other riders are not to know the time of our destination. But there are to be three teams of us, taking the three engines . . .'

'Hamian will not have sufficient spacesuits for the three hundred beasts required to shift all three engines at the same time. You will lead two of the three groups. F'lar will, as planned, head the third. He will be the only one depositing an engine in this time. As you know,' Aivas went on, overriding Jaxom's protest, 'the locations chosen are not in sight of each other. Since F'lar will think that you are at one end of the rift, N'ton at the other, he will not know what you are doing.'

'The timing's wrong, Aivas. I cannot be in two places at once. Nor doing that kind of timing without a respite. Ruth doesn't have auxiliary oxygen.'

'You missed the point about insufficient spacesuits. Your team will have to get out of their suits and turn them over to the members of the second unit. That should allow Ruth sufficient time to regain energy. You will, of course, be certain that he eats well beforehand and can feed immediately afterwards to restore himself.'

I could do it the way Aivas suggests, Ruth said amiably.

'I haven't said I'll risk us!' Jaxom roared, bringing both

fists down on the console with such force that he bruised his hands. Rubbing them, he grumbled to himself.

'You already have or there would not be two craters on the rift and there would not have been records of bright flashes.'

'You're inveigling me, Aivas. And I'm not going to let you.'

'You already have, Lord Jaxom. You are the only one who can, could, would, has. Think this proposal over carefully and you will see that the project is not only within the capabilities of yourself and Ruth, but feasible. And essential! Three explosions at this point in time will not have the desired effect on the future path of the Red Star.'

Jaxom sighed deeply, almost as if he already felt it needful to fill his lungs for a jump timed eighteen hundred Turns away. His mind refused to settle into a logical examination of the affair.

'Since this is a confessional moment, tell me why you are so obsessed with this project you've involved Sharra in? Especially,' and he laughed ironically, 'if you say you know I've already succeeded even before I've begun it . . .'

'You do succeed and there is an easy way to prove it,' Aivas said, his tone not quite ingratiating but as close as Jaxom had ever heard.

'No, first explain to me about these zebedee things.'

'It is extrapolated by the closer examination of the Thread ovoids that there is life, not as you know it, and not even as we see it brought here by the Red Star, but a whole ecology of life forms throughout the Oort Cloud. Some of them are probably quite intelligent, judging by the complexity of their nervous systems; but when they arrive here, as a cluster around the Red Planet, they have lost most of their liquid helium so they can be termed only "rude mechanicals". It is these degenerate, warmth-tolerating forms that make it to the surface of Pern; they don't live long enough to replicate themselves there, of course, or on the Red Planet. It is only these "mechanicals" who can reproduce without helium in Pern's orbit. But if these mechanicals could be contaminated, infected with our disimproved parasite, they would carry it with them to destroy all similar life forms in the Oort Cloud itself, probably including the more intelligent ones, too. Then no matter what happens, Pern will forever be freed of this menace. That is why there were long intervals: the disimproved zebedees which you will establish – have established – on the surface of the Red Star twice in the past and once in the future will infect the Cloud when the Red Star cuts through the Cloud twice in every orbit.'

'I'm also to be a disease carrier?' Jaxom wasn't sure which he felt more keenly: indignation, fury or incredulity at the audacity of Aivas's scheme.

'You will seed the Red Star three times. That is why it is so important to breed up the disimproved zebedees. A triple thrust in two different areas.'

'But if I'm to blow the planet out of orbit . . .'

'The perturbation will be slight and you can seed the zebedees at a sufficient distance from the rift to ensure their safety. There will be plenty of host ovoids on the planet's surface as well as in orbit around it . . .'

'We saw them . . . but on the surface, not in orbit.'

'Were you looking for them?'

'Not in space. Now, tell me how you can prove to me that all these incredible designs of yours will work, have worked!'

'It is very simple. Access the file that gives you a graph of the Red Star's current orbit.'

Jaxom had no trouble doing that. The all too familiar diagram filled the screen.

'Hold that on the monitor.' Jaxom pressed out that command. 'Now, if you will mount Ruth, you can go forward in time fifty years, Turns, using the digital time piece as your reference.'

'No-one goes forward in time, that's the most dangerous . . .'

'Only if alterations will have taken place,' Aivas replied. 'There will be no changes on the bridge of the *Yokohama*. That will be your responsibility. Today, you will go forward in time, call up the orbit. Print it out. Then, with that hard copy, return here after a safe interval and compare the two graphs. The doors have been locked. No-one is likely to come to this bridge right now, or until you have returned.'

Every ounce of common sense Jaxom possessed shouted resistance to a timing forward. And yet . . . to have done so would be a feat no-one else could possibly manage successfully. For he had Ruth.

'Did you hear what Aivas said, Ruth?'

I did. Given his assurances, and I know that he would not risk you, Jaxom . . .

'Or you . . .' Jaxom put in.

I would like to see what Pern looks like in the future. I would like to know that the future is going to be a good one.

And so would I, Jaxom thought.

Then, before he could come up with too many arguments against this rash, foolhardy, reckless endeavour, he signalled for Ruth to float over to him.

'You will, of course,' said Aivas in his drollest tone, 'be very sure to keep oxygen tanks full on the bridge for fifty Turns to come.'

Jaxom gave a grim smile. 'I'm not going to take any chances, Aivas. I'll just get into my suit.' He was becoming quite adept at inserting himself into the space gear. He mounted Ruth and buckled on the riding straps, just to be very sure, in case they emerged in nothingness. He also knew that Ruth would have no trouble anywhere or anywhen finding his way back to Ruatha Hold.

He read the date exposed on the digital and added fifty to the year displayed, 2577. With that legend firmly in his mind, he told Ruth to transfer to that time.

I know when I'm going, Ruth said cheerfully and they were abruptly *between*.

Jaxom counted, counted the breaths he was taking and was rather pleased that they were slow and steady. At fifteen, they were back on the bridge. Which had not apparently altered.

The view hasn't changed, Ruth said disconsolately.

'No, it hasn't,' Jaxom said, surprised because the diagram was up on the screen. The digital clock, however, definitely registered fifty full turns past his last view of it. He unhooked his straps and floated down from Ruth's back to the screen.

'I suppose I could have put this back up in preparation

for my coming,' he told himself. 'I'll remember. I hope. Is there air up here, Ruth?'

Yes, but it's not very fresh.

Jaxom pulled off his gloves and put them down on the console. He didn't bother to unsuit since he had no intention of remaining longer than this errand required. He tapped out the appropriate code and saw the cursor outline a second orbit, deviating by several degrees from the earlier one and with the return path intersecting that of the fifth planet, and spiralling in! With trembling fingers, he pressed the print command and a sheet obediently emerged: a sheet that, to his fingers, felt subtly different to the paper he had become accustomed to. Much whiter, softer! Bendarek had really improved the quality of paper over the intervening Turns. Then he compared its diagram with the one on the screen.

'Shards! Aivas, the path of the Red Star has shifted. Aivas?' An iciness flowed across Jaxom's midsection. 'Aivas?'

How can he hear you fifty Turns into the future, Jaxom? Ruth said in some amusement.

'I suppose that's what's happened? Except that he'd know where we were going.' Jaxom was uneasy about that but there was likely a good explanation. 'I've got so that I rely on Aivas far too much. But he was right. So we're stuck with this new madness of his, aren't we, Ruth?'

I do not think it is madness to be certain we never have Thread again.

'We're not out of this Pass yet, even if it is possibly the last one we'll have,' Jaxom said, pushing himself off the deck to grab at Ruth's neck and swing his leg into the saddle. 'The old bridge hasn't changed . . . and yet, it feels awful still and unused!'

I thought the view would have changed, Ruth said, clearly disappointed.

Jaxom thought vividly of the digital in the correct present, added thirty seconds to prevent an overlap and Ruth took them *between* to that corrected time. Exactly fifteen breaths later and he was looking straight at the digital advanced only the thirty seconds.

He did, however, feel very tired and as he looked at

Ruth's neck, he noticed a definite tinge of grey exhaustion in the usually lustrous hide.

'And?' Aivas' inimitable voice queried him.

'I must have put the graph up because it was there when I arrived.'

'And?'

Jaxom undid his helmet, determined to spin this scene out.

'Well, I must have remembered to keep oxygen tanks topped up for there was air, even if Ruth said it wasn't fresh . . . Shards!' He looked down at his bare hands. 'I left my gloves there.'

'Then. You will have left your gloves then.' Aivas could play the same game.

Jaxom grinned. 'I think I'll just wait and retrieve them . . . later. Here's what came up in the future. Is the variation sufficient for you, lord and master?' He placed the graph from fifty Turns in the future in front of a sensor so that Aivas could see and compare.

'Yes,' Aivas said, unperturbed, 'that will be sufficient. The explosions have exactly accomplished the desired dislocation. Project Velikovski will be a success. Jaxom, your vital signs show a depletion. You must eat carbohydrates.'

'Ruth's a bit grey, too. He needs to eat more than I do.'

You should have told me we'd be doing this today, Jaxom. We have flown Fall and I haven't eaten since those wherries last week.

'As soon as you're feeling able, dear heart, you shall have as many fat bucks and wherries as you can stuff down your maw.'

Then let us go now. I really feel very hungry.

'Jaxom?' Aivas said as the white rider started peeling off his spacesuit.

'Yes?'

'Will you comply?'

'With your mad scheme? It appears I must because I have. Haven't I?'

Ruatha Hold was gay with banners in the bright autumnal air and folk had been flowing down all the roads to the immense camping grounds near the racing course. One of the first tasks Jaxom had undertaken upon being confirmed as Lord of his Hold was to revive Ruatha's breeding of runners. The animals he had produced had won significant races from time to time at other Gathers, but he hoped that on home ground they would perform even more prestigiously.

He and Ruth had transferred from the *Yokohama* immediately to an upland meadow where Ruth had replenished his energies on three bucks and two does. He had then glided home, emitting an occasional satisfied burp, so that Jaxom could eat a more substantial meal than the handsful of berries he had found in the bushes surrounding the field. Jaxom had seen his white dragon comfortably curled up on his weyr couch, given orders to the first steward he saw that he was not to be disturbed even if Thread fell out of phase, grabbed some bread and cheese from the kitchen and consumed it on his way to his quarters where, somewhat sated, he removed only his boots and riding belt and crawled under the sleeping furs to sleep himself out.

Sometime during that exhausted rest, Sharra joined him for he awoke just as the sky was lightening to find her nestled against him. What had roused him were unmistakable greetings of Gatherers, arriving after an overnight journey. His nose told him that the spits were already turning over open flames in the roasting pits and his stomach told him that he needed to fill it. He must have slept an entire day.

'Mmmm, Jax?' murmured Sharra, sleepily reaching for him.

'Yes, love, who else were you expecting?' He leaned over and kissed her. 'You let me sleep?'

'Hmmm. Ruth said you were very tired. Meer wouldn't let anyone in the room but me.'

He angled himself up to a sitting position, scrubbing at his tousled hair, running his tongue around his teeth and hoping that his breath hadn't been too rank. Meer appeared, Talla right behind him, chirping a gentle inquiry.

'We're up, we're up!' Jaxom assured them although

Sharra hauled her pillow under her head, her eyes determinedly shut.

The two disappeared and very shortly there was a timid scratch at the door of their bedroom.

'Come!' He could smell the aroma of *klah* as soon as the door opened and a drudge who looked freshly scrubbed and attired entered with a well-stocked tray.

Once he had some *klah*, and had cajoled Sharra into waking up enough to join him, he revived sufficiently to bathe and dress in new Gather finery.

'Whatever were you doing that exhausted you and Ruth so much?' Sharra asked as she let him fasten her new Gather gown, a splendid affair in golds and rusts that so suited her.

'Well, there was Fall, and then Ruth and I had to test those new gloves Hamian's produced and . . .' he waved his hand airily. 'I guess things just mounted up. Did you get enough rest?' he asked solicitously, dropping a kiss on her bare neck before he fastened the topaz necklace which had been his nameday present to her.

'Well,' she began in the tone he knew was to make him feel guilty, but she turned in his arms, her face alight with love and mischief, 'I did the honours of the Hold for our guests from Cove Hold, and Lord Groghe and those from Fort Hold and . . .' she grinned up at him. '*They* said I'd better get an early night and they'd make themselves comfortable. Master Robinton was well on the way through the first wineskin but he was so pleased that you had some of the '16 for him.'

A loud halloo from the dawn-lit road brought them to the window and they saw a huge contingent of riders, bearing Tillek's banners.

'Come, we must greet Ranrel,' Sharra said, grabbing him by the hand. 'And it's high time the Lord of Ruatha Hold showed himself to his diligent stewards and staff.'

The Gather attracted hordes from every Hold, Hall and Weyr. This was one of those few days when there was no Fall to be met and it would be one of the last of the Northern Gathers before winter weather made roads impassable. Jaxom and Sharra, accompanied by Jarrol and Shawan, now a sturdy toddler, walked the long line of booths until Shawan had to be carried and Jarrol revived by one of the first bubbly pies out of the oven. There was an exuberance and buoyancy to the day that affected everyone, and was mirrored in the gay new clothing and in high spirits. Harpers strolled up and down the Gather line, playing and singing; children congregated in knots to play their favourite games; adults settled in their own groupings or at tables around the huge dancing square where brewers and wine sellers were doing a brisk business.

Jaxom and Sharra hosted a midday meal in the Hold at which those Lords Holder, Weyrleaders and Craftmasters gracing the day were entertained. Robinton, Menolly and Sebell gave a special performance of the latest ballads and airs with a full orchestral accompaniment, conducted by Master Domick. It was a leisurely meal though Jaxom noted that Lords Sigomal, Begamon and Corman were conspicuous by their absence – which caused Jaxom to recall the abduction plot.

The racing went very well, with one Ruathan sprinter winning its first race, and their other runners taking placings in almost every one of the eight starts. Jaxom and Sharra also found a well-trained little runner to start Jarrol riding for they had nothing in the beasthold suitable for a beginner. Saddlery then had to be arranged with the Tanner Hall. In between these chores, Jaxom and Sharra circulated among the guests, speaking to all the small holders that looked to Ruatha.

About midafternoon, young Pell brought his intended to meet his Lord and Lady and Sharra was warm in her responses to the pretty dark girl, daughter of a hill holder from Fort. There was nothing in Pell's manner to suggest he was not totally engrossed in his future as a joiner, especially after his lady showed Jaxom and Sharra the beautiful little coffer Pell had made her.

Ruth, his white hide radiant after a restoring sleep, had emerged sometime in the morning and was on the fire-heights, sunning himself with the other dragons. Hundreds

410

of fairs swarmed about the Hold, their cheerful voices a descant to whatever music harpers were making.

Whether it was the long sleep or the stimulation of the day, Jaxom found himself well able for Gather exertions. He and Sharra led several of the energetic dance figures, and then he allowed Sharra to be swirled away by N'ton, then F'lar while he partnered Lessa. They sat at the harpers' table, to one side and back away from the dais, with Robinton, D'ram and Lytol during one song break, Jaxom making certain that the Masterharper had sufficient wine. A dark-haired young drudge whom Jaxom did not recognize – but so many were hired in to assist during a Gather – kept the Harper supplied with food, even bringing some tidbits for Zair.

It was no wonder then that Robinton would need a short nap and because Jaxom was busy doing his duty dances with Lady Holders, he only noticed as he danced past that Robinton was alone at his table, alone and asleep, Zair curled up beside him.

It was Piemur who discovered that it was not Robinton asleep at the table, but a man dressed in clothing similar to Robinton's Gather suit – a dead man. It was Piemur who realized that Zair was barely breathing, his colour dangerously dull and what breath he had tainted with a sickly odour. Piemur had the good sense not to alarm anyone, sending Farli to summon Jaxom and Sharra, then D'ram, Lytol and the Benden Weyrleaders.

'This man's been dead a long time,' Sharra said, putting her hand on a cold cheek, and testing the muscular resistance. She shuddered. 'This is too macabre!'

'Robinton's ill?' Lessa asked in a hoarse whisper as she and F'lar arrived. 'That isn't Robinton!' First relief and then fury distorted her features. 'They did abduct him. Right out of a Gather.'

She called Ramoth, Jaxom had already called Ruth, as F'lar and D'ram alerted their beasts.

'Don't just jump about in panic,' Lytol said, even as the big dragons landed quietly in the shadows beyond the dancing square. 'Let us decide what to do and who is to search where. There're enough dragons here to cover every

411

possibility. Why did it have to be here where that device of Aivas's won't reach to Landing?'

Sharra was now bending over the limp Zair. 'He'd find Robinton no matter where he is. C'mon, Zair.'

'D'you need your medical kit?' Jaxom asked.

'I've already sent for it,' but her face as she turned it to Jaxom was anxious. 'Lessa, is your Healer here? She knows more about dragon and fire-lizard care than I do. Zair's been poisoned but I don't know what was used . . .'

Jaxom picked up a half-eaten piece of meat from the table and sniffed cautiously at it, and promptly sneezed vociferously. Sharra took it from him and smelled more daintily.

'Fellis all right but mixed with something else to disguise taste and smell. Poor Zair. He doesn't look good. How wicked!'

F'lar picked up the wine goblet Robinton had been using and carefully sipped. He spat it out immediately. 'Fellis in the wine, too. I should have known Robinton wouldn't pass out from mere wine.' F'lar was disgusted with himself.

Jaxom groaned. 'I saw him, sleeping, and I ought to have known he never sleeps at a Gather . . .'

'Many's the night he's outlasted everyone else at a Gather,' Lessa said, 'but how much of a head start do these miserable fiends have? Which way would they go?'

Jaxom snapped his fingers. 'There are marshals on every road. They would have seen who left and in which direction.'

'We'll each take a different road,' F'lar said, gesturing for all the riders to mount their beasts and check with the marshals. 'You stay here as if there was nothing amiss,' he told Lytol, Piemur and Sharra.

But each rider returned. No-one, the marshals assured them, had been seen leaving the Gather, not riders or wagons on any road.

Tell the fire-lizards to search, Ruth said to Jaxom.

'Ruth says to tell all the fire-lizards to hunt for Robinton,' Jaxom said aloud.

'That's exactly what Ramoth just said,' Lessa said. There was such a noise of winged exodus that it could be heard

412

above the rollicking dance tune that was encouraging the dancers to outdo themselves.

'If we announce this to the Gather,' Lytol suggested, 'we'd have sufficient people to search the entire Hold from border to border.'

'No,' Jaxom said, 'there'd be a panic! You know how well loved Robinton is. It can't be more than an hour, at the most. That's not enough time to get to the coast . . .'

'Up into the hills?' Lytol suggested. 'There are so many caves up there we'd never be able to search them all.'

'The fire-lizards can, and will,' Piemur said.

'There are only so many tracks to the hills,' Jaxom said. 'Ruth and I will start the search. Lytol . . .' and then Jaxom hesitated.

Lytol clutched his arm. 'D'ram and Tiroth will take me. I know Ruatha as well as you do, lad.'

'So do I,' Lessa said roughly.

'I'll go north east to the Nabol Pass,' F'lar said.

'We'll need some Fort riders,' Lessa said.

'And some to follow the river to the sea,' Lytol added.

'We'll stay here for the fire-lizards,' Piemur said, nodding to Sharra. There were tears dripping down his cheeks. 'Just find him!' Then abruptly he sat down, where the shadow of his body fell across the dead man dressed in harper blue.

Dawn was breaking by the time the dragonriders, augmented by Fort Weyr riders, admitted defeat and returned to Ruatha. There were a few folk preparing to return home but most of the Gather area was populated by those sleeping off the night's excesses.

'Not a single wagon is leaving here without being searched,' Sharra told Jaxom when he got back. 'That was Piemur's notion.'

'And a good one,' Jaxom said, gratefully taking the cup of *klah* she handed him. 'For there was nothing moving on the tracks and I went as far as the Ice Lake and Ruth was particularly vigilant over the wooded areas.'

He saw then that someone had thrown a blanket across the dead man's shoulders. Piemur and Jancis sat nearby as if guarding their Master's sleep.

'We thought it wiser to pretend it's Master Robinton,'

Sharra murmured. 'Sebell and Menolly know, of course, and her ten have been out searching all night. Sebell's gone back to the Harper Hall to alert everyone. You heard the drums?'

'You can't miss them.' She grimaced. 'Asgenar and Larad know harper codes and they were talking of mounting an attack on Bitra . . .'

'They'd never be fool enough to imprison the Harper there? Sigomal's not stupid. He'd know it would be the first place we'd look.'

'That's what Lytol told them, but they feel badly because they heard of the abduction first. Larad says that he ought to have confronted Sigomal immediately and demanded that he forget such a heinous scheme.'

'That would have done no good,' Jaxom said wearily.

'And it had been such a lovely Gather . . .' Sharra said, turning into his shoulder and softly weeping.

Jaxom put his arms about her, soothing her rumpled hair back from her forehead, wanting very much to give way to the tears that burned his eyes.

'Zair?' he asked, suddenly remembering the little creature.

'Oh! Yes,' and Sharra pulled herself from his arms, mopping her eyes and sniffing, 'he'll recover, Campila says. She purged him and,' she managed a little smile, 'he looked so embarrassed. I've never seen that particular shade in fire-lizard eyes before.'

'When will he be able to help us find Master Robinton?'

Sharra bit her under lip. 'He's terribly weak and awfully confused. I didn't ask her that because if they've drugged Master Robinton, not even Zair could find him in a comatose condition.'

Suddenly the air was full of agitated fire-lizards, shrieking and bugling.

They've found him! Ruth cried and, in three mighty hops, landed at Jaxom's side.

Jaxom was astride the white dragon before he realized his own intention. Ruth was aloft with such speed that Jaxom was nearly unseated. Other dragons were airborne, and why there were no collisions was a minor wonder. Like an arrow composed of many bodies, flying so closely together, many must have been winglocked, the fire-lizards pointed to the south-eastern direction.

'*Can you understand who or where from them?*' Jaxom asked Ruth.

It is not far and they picture a wagon. You can see the tracks plainly.

And Jaxom could for the marks were visible over the headlands of fields recently ploughed under. The abductors had been clever, taking to the fields not the roads, in a line as straight as the terrain permitted. It had to be a small cart to manoeuvre over muddy field and rocky terrain once the ploughed fields were past. They were not airborne long before they saw the first of the foundered runners, splay-legged and gasping, its feet bound in thick rags to muffle its passage. Ten minutes onwards and another exhausted beast lay, breathing its last, bloody welts indicating how it had been driven.

'*Tell the others, Ruth, that they must be heading to the sea. Have some riders go on ahead . . .*'

They go, Ruth replied and Jaxom looked about him as spaces opened up all around him from dragons going *between*.

But dragon wings were quicker than the fleetest of runners, even with a headstart of six hours. With some satisfaction, Jaxom saw the bouncing cart just before the final slope down to the sea and the small ship waiting for its clandestine cargo. Dragons encircled the ship and, from his vantage point, Jaxom could also see men diving from it, vainly attempting to evade capture.

Then Ruth and the Benden contingent swooped down to halt the cart.

There was a brief attempt at innocence by the three men: two on the driving seat of the unusually designed vehicle, and one inside, lying on a thick mattress and pretending to be ill.

The fire-lizards however were far more interested in the dropped load bed, swarming over it, crooning encouragement, bugling triumph. Man and mattress were turfed out of the way and the boards of the false bottom pulled free.

There they discovered the Masterharper, looking ashen and almost wizened.

Carefully they lifted him out, rearranging the mattress for his comfort.

'He may just need air,' F'lar said, 'stuffed in that pit and jostled like a package . . .'

He glared at the three who were held in no gentle grip by angry riders. Overhead, fire-lizards made as if to bombard them, claws and beaks held in attack readiness.

'We need Sharra,' Lessa told Jaxom urgently. 'Unless Oldive is still at the Gather . . .'

Jaxom vaulted to Ruth's back . . .

'Don't meet yourself coming, Jaxom . . .' Lessa shrieked at him.

Despite his anxiety and fury, Jaxom recognized the sense of that warning but he didn't waste any time returning, for Sharra had had her medical case to hand.

'I think they gave him too much,' she said, her face paler than the Harper's. 'We must get him back to Ruatha where I can treat him properly.'

It was easier to hand the limp figure up to Jaxom astride Ruth, with Sharra to help hold the Harper between them. When they arrived back at Ruatha, N'ton was already in the courtyard with Oldive so Jaxom knew that the Fort Weyrleader had timed his errand.

'Hold on, Sharra,' Jaxom told her. 'Ruth's going to take us straight to our room.'

'Will he fit . . .' Sharra did not quite complete her question when they reappeared in the large living room, although Ruth knocked over a few pieces of furniture in doing so.

Jaxom and Sharra had the Harper in their bed, his clothing removed by the time N'ton and Oldive reached them.

Master Oldive was already fumbling to open a vial and, with Sharra holding the Harper's head, poured the potion down his throat. Then he examined the Harper's eyes and listened to his heart.

'We must get him warm,' Oldive said, but Sharra was already tucking furs about the lax body. 'His body has had a dreadful shock. Who did this?'

'We'll find out who's behind all this. The abductors were

almost to the beach,' Jaxom said, 'a ship waiting to take him who knows where.'

'We'll have the answer to that, too,' N'ton said in a grating tone. 'Master Robinton will recover, won't he, Oldive?'

'He must,' Sharra said, fervently, kneeling beside the bed. 'He must!'

Chapter Eighteen

It was fortunate for the conspirators that Master Robinton recovered from the overdose of fellis and suffered only bruises from that wild cross country journey. Until he was certain that Zair, too, would recover, he was not disposed to charity. Then he started murmuring about no real harm having been done.

'They have been grossly misguided,' he began.

'MISGUIDED!' Lytol, D'ram, F'lar, Jaxom, Piemur, Menolly and Sebell chorused in outrage.

'The very idea that they intended to abduct YOU,' and Lessa's expression was so fierce that Robinton regarded her with widened eyes and open mouth, 'to force US to destroy Aivas . . . bloody nearly *killing* you, and Zair! And you call them misguided?'

'I've another name for it entirely,' Lord Groghe said, his face flushed with anger. 'I'm certain that almost every other Lord Holder will come to the same conclusion. Norist has never made any bones about his disagreement but for Sigomal to actively assist him! Norist may call Aivas an abomination, but it is *he* and Sigomal who has acted abominably!'

'The Masters will deal with Norist now,' Sebell said implacably. Master Oldive was in complete agreement.

A special convocation of both the Lords Holder and the Mastercraftsmen was hastily called for that next evening.

The two groups would hear the evidence against the scofflaws although they would deliberate on their verdict separately, meting out justice as each group saw fit.

'These sessions are rare in Pernese records,' Lytol said, trying to find precedents in the now legible Ruatha Hold records.

'They've rarely been required,' Lord Groghe remarked, snorting in displeasure. 'By and large, Hold, Hall and Weyr have regulated their own members with few grievances spilling over. Everyone knows what is expected of them, what rights, privileges and responsibilities are due or required.'

'It is such a pity,' Robinton said, his voice reflecting the exhaustion of the ordeal, 'that they should take such a perverse view.'

'Especially when they've had no scruples about using the things which Aivas helps us produce,' Lytol said, outrage sparkling in his eyes.

'There may be some justification for their attitude . . .' Robinton began again, trying to lighten the severity of their attitude.

'There's no talking to the man,' Menolly said, disgusted. 'He must still be tired to come out with twaddle like that!' She gestured for Robinton's visitors to leave.

'It's not twaddle, Menolly,' Robinton replied testily, restlessly thrashing about in the bed where Oldive had insisted he remain. Zair, looking considerably more bronze than tan today, chirped a protest for he had made himself a very comfortable nest in the furs by the Harper's feet. 'We harpers failed somehow . . .'

'Failed nothing!' Menolly said, furious. 'Those misbegotten idiots nearly killed you . . . and Zair . . .' She caught Robinton's scowl. 'Hah! At least you care about him, even if you don't give two hoots and a holler about your own skin. Out, everyone. Robinton must rest if he's to be fit for the council.'

With so much excitement charging the air, few had left Ruatha's Gather site when the dragonriders returned with Robinton and his captors. The riders had then been forced to protect the nine men from being torn to pieces by a crowd incensed by their terrible deed. Jaxom had them interned separately in some of the small dark inner rooms of the Hold, supplying them with only water and dim glowbaskets. The little drudge who had served the Harper drugged food was found and, although she was plainly of very limited understanding, she was also placed in confinement.

As the ship's captain was one of Sigomal's sons, the Bitran Lord was doubtless involved. The dragonriders had not been particularly gentle with their charges on the way back from the coast. Not that physical harm had been needed for it was remarkable, N'ton said, how willing a man became to talk after he'd been dangled in mid-air from a dragon's forearm.

When a wing of Benden dragonriders appeared at Bitra Hold, Sigomal loudly and indignantly denied any involvement with such a dreadful, contemptible business: bitterly denouncing a son who would bring so much dishonour to his sire and his Hold.

F'lar admitted later that he had come very close to smashing Sigomal's lying mouth: only Mnementh had saved him. The big bronze dragon was so incensed by his rider's anger that a little curl of flame had escaped his lips. That had the immediate effect of silencing Sigomal.

G'narish of Igen Weyr and his bronze riders took into custody Master Norist, five of his Masters and nine journeymen, who had all been implicated.

By then the abduction cart, and the abused runners, had been brought back to Ruatha. Two would have to be put down. To compound the offence, they had been stolen out of a Ruathan paddock. While the Ruathan beastmaster attended to the poor creatures, the Woodsmith and Master Fandarel inspected the vehicle used to carry Robinton away. Bendarek found the maker's name on the footrest: one Tosikin, a journeyman joiner in Bitra.

'Purpose made,' Master Fandarel murmured to Bendarek as he scrutinized the vehicle.

'No question of it,' Bendarek replied, 'with this sunken load bed, padded, and long enough to accommodate a tall man like Master Robinton. Look at this lock top, these extra springs, heavy duty axle and larger, reinforced wheels. It was made to be used for fast hard going.' Then Bendarek scowled, noticing a poorly mitred edge and nails which had been badly sunk. 'And for the one use. Man shouldn't have put his name to such a shoddily made contraption.'

'Shall we have him here to speak his piece?' Fandarel asked, his dark eyes sparking as he rubbed his big hands together.

'Might as well. I wouldn't trust Sigomal not to slip out of this if he possibly can.'

'I doubt he will this time,' Fandarel said, sombre-faced.

The original intention was to hold the extraordinary convocation in the Great Hall. So many people flocked to Ruatha Hold, increasing the numbers of Gatherers who stayed over, that Jaxom, after conferring with Groghe, Lytol, D'ram and F'lar, transferred the proceedings to the outside court. The weather, while crisp with autumn, remained clear and, by using the dance square light standards, the court would be brilliantly illuminated if the matter took time. Massed dragons on the fire-heights, their eyes glowing with vivid whirling colour, added a bizarre display while fire-lizards whipped restlessly about. Folk who had fire-lizards were asked to control them but many were seen to be wild ones, unbanded, and agitated by the unusual circumstances.

When Lord Begamon sent word that he could not attend, F'lar dispatched F'nor and two wings to see that he did, for the Neratian was also implicated.

The drudge, however, was excused. Sharra, Lessa and Menolly had talked with her, kindly enough when they realized how simple she was. She had been told by a man in 'beautiful new clothes' to be sure to feed the Masterharper well from special provisions that were brought a great distance, just for him. She was shown the wineskins which were reserved only for Master Robinton and she was also to feed the fire-lizard only meat from a special bowl.

'Clearly she didn't know she was doing wrong,' Lessa said after the interview. Then her expression hardened. 'Appalling of them to use a simple child like that.'

'Clever, too,' Menolly said, with a grim twitch of her lips.

'Zair would have sensed an open threat to Robinton, so they *had* to use an innocent pawn.'

'Clever, but not clever enough, Menolly,' Jaxom said. 'Where does she come from?'

'A hold,' Sharra said, sighing, 'near a big mountain, and she was so excited to be allowed to come to a Gather and serve someone as pleasant as the man in blue. I'll keep her here. She'll be safe from misuse at Ruatha. The cook says she's very good with the spit animals.'

As soon as Lord Corman arrived that evening, he stomped up to Jaxom who was standing with Groghe, Ranrel, Asgenar and Larad.

'I don't agree with what you are doing to Pern. I don't like to see so many of our traditional ways and values flouted by what that . . . that machine is teaching you, but what you others do, is your business. What I refuse to do is mine!'

Larad nodded solemnly. 'Which is your prerogative.'

'Just so that my position is understood,' Corman said, his brows running together in a fierce scowl.

'No one doubts your integrity, Lord Corman,' Jaxom said.

Corman raised his eyebrows, seemed about to take umbrage at the youngest Lord's comment, then reconsidered and, scowling once more, allowed Brand to lead him to a chair on the dais.

This had been hastily constructed, with a centre and two wings, slanting outward: one side provided for the Lords Holder and the other for the Craftmasters. In the centre, as resident Lord Holder, Jaxom would be seated, with Lytol on one side, D'ram on the other. The accused would be accommodated on benches in the space between the wings. Lytol had tried to find an impartial spokesman to represent the accused, following the legal practices about which he had been reading in Aivas' historical files. Harpers generally performed such a service in those instances but as no harper could be truthfully called 'impartial' in this case and no-one else could be found to perform that function, it was decided that the accused would have to speak for themselves – that is, Piemur had remarked, if there could be anything that would mitigate their offence since guilt, itself, was already proved.

Promptly at the appointed hour, the accused were brought to the court, jeered at and reviled by the huge throng, comprising representatives from all parts of the planet. It took some time to restore order when the accused were seated. At which point the Lords Holder and the Mastercraftsmen took their places. Then Jaxom, D'ram and Lytol settled themselves and Master Robinton, as the victim, seated himself just below them, facing his abductors.

Jaxom rose, holding up his arms for silence.

'Last evening Master Robinton was drugged and taken from the Gather without his consent and knowledge. A dead man who has not been identified was left in his place, wearing similar clothing. So there are two crimes which must be answered tonight: abduction and murder.

'These three men,' and Jaxom pointed to each of them, holding his hand up to still the angry murmur from the crowd, 'drove the vehicle which transported Master Robinton without his knowledge or consent. These six men,' and again Jaxom pointed at each, 'were aboard the ship awaiting them, to take Master Robinton to a place of concealment without his knowledge or consent. I now read their statements, taken in the presence of a harper, myself as Lord Holder, and Master Fandarel, representing the Crafthalls.'

The statements, though brief, began with the name and origin of the man involved, and summarized the job they had been hired to do. Lord Sigomal and Master Norist were named as those who had given orders and supplied both marks and equipment. The Glasscraft masters and journeymen also assembled had delivered messages to those involved and passed over payments. Master Idarolan produced a bill of sale for the ship, signed by one Federen, Masterglass-smith, now seated among the accused. He had also led the initial attack on the batteries supplying Aivas and he was the older brother of one of the men involved in the assault which Aivas had foiled. He was very bitter about his brother's punishment and deafness. Lord Begamon was implicated because he had supplied marks, the horses used on the abortive assault on Aivas and a safe harbour for the ship.

Journeyman Tosikin, a meek and obsequious fellow plainly awed and terrified by this experience, did point to Gomalsi, Lord Sigomal's son and the captain of the ship, as the man who had commissioned the strange cart. He had had no idea of its purpose and had tried to argue them into a different sort of vehicle to carry a 'delicate cargo'. No, he had not known that a man was to be the cargo.

Brestolli had asked to be allowed to speak of what he had overheard. He further provided a positive identification of three of the Bitrans from the ship as those he had overheard in the brewer's. That caused a surge of consternation and recriminations among the accused.

'You will each be allowed to speak in your own defence and inform this panel of any mitigating circumstances.'

Jaxom pointed first to the three men who had absconded with Robinton but before any of them could speak, Lord Sigomal got to his feet, suddenly rousing from his apathy.

'I am innocent, innocent, I tell you! My son has been misguided, led astray by bad companions whom I pleaded with him to give up, little knowing what they were involved in . . .'

'I protest,' Gomalsi shouted, jumping to his feet, eyes blazing at his father. 'You *told* me to do what I could to discredit that machine. You *told* me to destroy the batteries . . . and where to look for them. You *gave* me money to hire men . . .'

'You fool! You imbecile!' Sigomal shrieked back, stepping forward and clouting Gomalsi so hard across the face that the young man fell backwards over the bench.

Immediately Jaxom signalled for guards to force Sigomal back to his place and to help Gomalsi.

'Any more outbursts and Lord Holder or not, you'll be gagged,' Jaxom said sternly to Sigomal. He motioned for the guards to remain behind the two. Then he pointed at the first of the three actual abductors. 'You may speak in your defence. First tell your name and your rank.'

There was a soundless conference and the oldest of the three stood.

'My name is Halefor. I have no rank, nor hold, nor craft. I hire my services to whoever pays enough. This time it was Lord Sigomal. The three of us struck a price with him and were paid half in advance to take the Harper in the cart to the ship. That was all we was hired to do. Not to kill. That was an accident. Biswy had to drink some of the wine, so the fumes would be on him. But he was not meant to die from it. Nor did we wish any harm to Master Robinton. I didn't much like that part but Lord Sigomal said it had to be him because he was so well liked. They'd smash the machine to get Master Robinton back.'

He looked about him, first at the Lords Holder and then at the Mastercraftsmen, gave a sharp nod of his head and sat down.

From the men who were Gomalsi's crew came much the same story: they had been hired to do a job, to man a ship from Ruatha waters to an island off the eastern shore of Nerat. Lord Begamon groaned at that and hid his head in his hands. He continued to moan off and on through the rest of the proceedings. When asked harshly by Master Idarolan if any of them were either apprentices or journeymen, two replied that they had sailed a few seasons in fishing fleets but hadn't much cared for the long hours. Master Idarolan looked relieved that no craftsman of his had been involved.

Jaxom could understand Master Idarolan's desire to settle that point in the hearing of his peers and the Lords. In many seacoast holds, boys and girls grew up able to handle a small skiff adequately. Knowing one end of a ship from the other was no crime. What offended Idarolan was the audacity of Gomalsi, who was not trained in seamanship and had thought that he could sail that small craft safely from Ruatha to the eastern coast of Nerat, across the Currents and into some of the trickiest waters of the planet, risking Robinton's safety every wave of the way.

Master Norist, however, was made from a different mould and stood proud and defiant.

'I did what my conscience dictated, to rid this world of that Abomination and all its evil works. It encourages sloth and dalliance among our young, distracting them from traditional duties. I see it destroying the very structure of our Halls and our Holds. Contaminating our Pern with vicious complexities that deprive honest men of work and their pride in workmanship, turning whole families away from what has been proved good and wholesome for twenty-five hundred Turns. I would do it again. I will do all in my power to destroy the spell this Abomination has placed on you!' He extended his arm and swept his pointing finger at every one of the Masters who sat in judgment on him. 'You have been deluded. You will suffer. And all Pern will suffer because of your blindness, your lapse from the purity of our culture and knowledge.'

Two of his masters and five of his journeymen cheered their Master.

Jaxom could see the shocked expressions of other Craftmasters: Nicat, Belesden, Briaret and Sograny who, it was true, had not benefited quite as much from the stored knowledge of Aivas as other Crafts had. But there was no hint of pardon in the expressionless faces of Masters Fandarel, Zurg, Morilton, Idarolan, Bendarek and Andemon.

The Lords Holder were solemn to a man. Toric was plainly scornful whenever he looked towards either Sigomal or Begamon. Corman was disgusted and didn't try to hide that any more than he had equivocated about his distrust of Aivas.

The Neratian Lord did not choose to say anything in his defence. When Jaxom asked him again, he just kept on shaking his head and moaning, and refused, even at Jaxom's third time of asking, to speak.

'Lord Jaxom,' Master Oldive said, rising to his feet, 'my colleagues have just handed me their opinion concerning the cause of the dead man's state.'

'And?'

'There is sufficient bodily evidence to suggest that his end was due to natural causes. There were no visible wounds, nor damage to his skull. His lips and nails, however, were blue, a common indication of heart failure.' Oldive cleared his throat. 'His stomach contained a great deal of fellis which possibly caused his heart to stop.'

'Under these circumstances, it would seem that the deceased met his death by misadventure rather than the design of the defendants, so the charge of murder is no longer applicable,' and Jaxom noticed the palpable relief of Halefor.

'Has the matter of the premeditated abduction of Masterharper Robinton been established?' Jaxom asked.

He ignored the vehement affirmatives shouted, almost in chorus, from the audience. The Lords Holder duly raised hands, even Corman. Brand wrote down the count. Then Jaxom repeated the question to the Craftmasters. Every hand was raised, Idarolan's as high as he could push his clenched fist in the air. 'Then you may retire to the Great Hall to consider your verdicts . . .'

Master Robinton suddenly put his hand up and, surprised, Jaxom allowed him to speak. As the victim, he had the right to be heard as he had the right to face his assailants. Jaxom worried that Robinton might plead for leniency and that would only exacerbate the problem: especially with a man as narrow-minded and vindictive as Norist had proved to be.

'For those of you who witness this,' Robinton began, speaking not to the Lords Holder or the Craftmasters, but to the people outside the court, lining the walls, the ramp, the roofs of the nearer cots. His voice was weak but true. He cleared his throat and started again, this time his voice was a bit stronger, and all sound ceased to hear the Harper's words. 'For those of you here, let me say that Aivas has taught us nothing that our ancestors did not know. He has given us no machines and tools and conveniences that they did not have and use when they first came to Pern. He restored to all crafts the knowledge which time had blurred or eradicated in records. So, if that knowledge is evil, then we all are. But I do not think any of us here believe that we are intrinsically evil, or work evil in our Crafthalls. For the Holds he also filled in the gaps in their separate histories so that all know of their past and which of those who travelled to start a new life on Pern started each Hold. And they do not consider themselves evil, or spawned by evil men and women.'

Master Robinton stared at Norist who refused to make eye contact.

'For our Weyrs, he gave the promise of deliverance from a long long struggle, a deliverance made possible by the abilities of our dragons, who were created by our ancestors and the courage of their riders. They are not evil or they would have turned the power of the dragons upon us and enslaved us all. But they have not.

'The evil that was done to me by these men was brought on me for the worst of reasons: to force others to destroy our link with our past, our chance of making this world what our ancestors hoped it would become: peaceful, prosperous, pleasant. I have done none of these men harm,' and Robinton's hand indicated Sigomal, Begamon and Norist, 'nor wished them harm, nor *wish* them harm now. I pity them for fear of the unknown, of the unusual, for their violence and unthinking narrowness of vision and spirit.'

Now Master Robinton looked at the three abductors. 'I forgive you for myself; but you took marks to do evil, which is a great wrong. And you were ready to silence a harper and that is a greater wrong, for when speech is restricted, all men suffer. Not just I.'

He sat down, almost as if he could not stand any longer but when Menolly would have gone to his side, he shook his head.

Groghe bent across Warbret beside him, whispering, to Bargen; and Toric, who couldn't hear, stepped around the table to be where he could. Ranrel, Deckter, Bargen and Laudey followed his example. Nessel looked exceedingly uncomfortable with Asgenar on one side and Larad on the other while Sangel and Toronas disputed a point.

The Craftmasters, with Fandarel in the centre, his voice lowered to a harsh rumble, also huddled close together. Morilton spoke only once and then was silent though he listened intently to the others. He was sitting on that tribunal as the Glasscraft had to be represented and none of the other Glassmasters would accept the onus.

'My Lords and Masters, you may retire if you choose,' Jaxom repeated.

'We're well enough here,' Groghe said in a loud voice.

Jaxom thought that Robinton might be the better for a glass of wine which a recess permitted. He sipped it first before passing Robinton the glass, with a reassuring grin. Master Robinton made a little show of distrust but then, after raising it to Jaxom, drank eagerly and smiled approval: a little byplay which sent a ripple of applause and laughter through the waiting crowd. It was a deft way of reducing the tension that had been building.

'I find what I resent the most,' Robinton said in a guarded aside to Jaxom, 'is that people might think that I could no longer handle my wine, to see me sprawled asleep like that so early in a Gather.'

'We have come to a decision, Lord Jaxom,' Groghe announced and the Lords Holder resumed their seats.

'And we,' said Master Idarolan, standing up.

'What is your decision, Lord Holder Groghe?' Jaxom asked.

'Sigomal and Begamon have proved themselves totally unacceptable to this Council; they must not govern their Holds. They are dishonoured. In the first part, to plot and carry out a punitive action in another Hold or common property, which is the designation of Landing, and in the second part, to abduct a person against his will for purposes of extortion against the best interests of the planet, and of all of us.'

Sigomal took his censure with some dignity but Begamon began to sob, falling from the bench to his knees.

'Sigomal's third son, Sousmal, is known to most of us and it is our decision that he should temporarily manage Bitra Hold until further notice by the Council of Lords Holder. As Begamon has no children old enough to hold in his stead, we appoint his brother, Ciparis, as temporary Lord Holder, also until further notice. Gomalsi is to be exiled with his father for his part in the first attack on the Aivas installation, for his part in the abduction, and because, by setting himself up as a captain of a sea-going ship without qualifications, he has offended all members of the Fishercrafthalls. We suggest that one of the islands in the Eastern Ring be designated the place of exile.'

Sigomal groaned and Gomalsi bit back a cry of protest.

'Master Norist is also stripped of his rank, as are the other Craft members of this conspiracy. All are to be exiled. The same place would doubtless give them the company of like minds,' Idarolan said. Then he turned toward the crowd and where the other Glasscraftsmen were standing. 'It is the decision of this body that you must accept Master Morilton as your Craftmaster until such time as we, your peers, decide that you can choose, without prejudice, a man with a more open mind and forward vision than Norist.'

Lytol nodded at Jaxom whose task it was to pass judgment on the other scofflaws. Jaxom had never had to discipline a man for the rest of his natural life but he thought again of the anguish which he had felt on that wild ride to rescue Master Robinton.

'Exile!' Most of the men accepted that though two of the younger ones looked so desperate, Jaxom added. 'Your families may accompany you into exile if they so choose.'

He saw Sharra's slight smile and noticed Lessa nod approvingly at that addition.

'The convicted will be returned to their quarters and tomorrow will be taken to their place of exile. From this time onward, they are holdless, craftless men and no longer protected by the Weyrs.' Jaxom raised his voice over Begamon's frightened babble. 'This court is adjourned.'

Guards closed in around the condemned and judges and jury filed into the Hold.

Somehow food had been prepared to serve the unexpected numbers who had come to Ruatha. Sharra told him in the few moments they had for private conversation that everyone had been exceedingly helpful, Hold, Hall and Weyr, in accumulating enough provisions to send none away hungry.

'You were, by the way, my love, magnificent,' she added. 'It was a terrible case to have to judge but, given the evidence and the admissions, no-one can fault your decision. The sentence was fairer than they deserved.' Her face set in angry lines, and she clenched her fists. 'When I saw the bruising Master Robinton sustained . . .'

'He'll be all right?' Jaxom wondered if maybe he had been too forbearing, though he could not have ordered a death sentence. Had Master Robinton died . . . or had Biswy not died of a heart failure, he would have had to decide other.

Lord Groghe sought him out then, to reassure Jaxom that he himself, had the offences happened in his Hold, would have done exactly the same. To Jaxom's surprise and a certain sad gratification, Lord Corman also approached him later in the evening.

'Well handled, Jaxom. Only thing you could have done under the circumstances.'

The Keroonian Lord did not remain for the evening meal nor did he ever visit Landing again. But he did not prevent his holders from using any new products, or even object when young folk asked to go south to study. Of Aivas developed items, Lord Corman purchased only paper, remarking once in his harper's hearing that Bendarek had discovered a form of paper on his own before 'the machine' awakened.

The next morning three wings of Fort Weyr arrived at Ruatha to convey the convicted to their place of exile. Delivery of the letters the men had written to their families was promised. Those wishing to join their menfolk would be brought to the island as soon as they were ready.

Master Idarolan had chosen the exile site. 'Not too large, not too small, with good fishing, some game, though wherry makes a dull diet. Plenty of fruit and root vegetables. They'll have to work to survive but that's no more than we must do.'

'Threadfall?' Jaxom asked.

Master Idarolan shrugged. 'There're a few caves, and you're taking care of the future of that problem. They can endure it or not as they choose. There's also an old volcano and evidence that the island has been inhabited before. It's far more hospitable than Far West Continent where they'd have only sand and snakes.'

When the men were mounted on the dragons, they were handed sacks with basic tools and a few supplies. Then the wings took off and, reaching height and an eastern direction, they went *between*.

Jaxom felt enervated as never before, his spirits sunk to a bleak nadir. But he was Ruatha's Lord Holder and was forced to respond with courtesy and civility to others who were acrimonious in their opinions and harboured considerable rancour for the guilty. Those he admired most among the Lords Holder said little or nothing.

Asgenar and Toronas departed to assist young Sousmal at Bitra. On their way back to Cove Hold, D'ram and Robinton would drop Lytol off at Nerat Hold as Lytol had been appointed to apprise Ciparis of his new status. Ciparis was thought to be a capable man, having acted as Begamon's steward.

Brand and his understewards were busy arranging for transportation for the many visitors, seeing to travel supplies for those who had exhausted their own, and directing the drudges to clear up the debris and repair the damage inevitably caused by any large crowd.

Jaxom was even perversely grateful when Sharra, looking extremely torn between her responsibilities, asked him if she was needed to help.

'You're wanted back at the laboratory on the *Yokohama*?'

'Oldive and I both.'

He gave her a brief hug and a kiss and nodded. In a way it would be a relief to be able to sort out his thoughts without infecting her with his dejection.

'I'll spend some time with the boys. I'm not needed right now for anything at the *Yokohama* or Landing.'

That was not essentially true and Sharra knew it, giving him a quick stare but then she smiled sadly, kissed his cheek, and left him in their quarters.

From his window, he saw her and Oldive mount on the young blue who was now on duty at Ruatha and that unfortunately reminded him of G'lanar.

I am here, Ruth said softly from his weyr in the Hold.

'*You always are here for me, dear friend*,' Jaxom said, intolerably weary.

You did as you had to, as you ought to. No blame is yours.

'But I am left to deal with its aftermath.'

You have acted with honour. Others did not. Can you do more than act with honour?

'A good question, Ruth, a very good question,' and Jaxom stretched out on his bed, hands clasped behind his head. 'Could I have avoided this outcome?'

How? By not helping Piemur and Jancis to uncover Aivas that day? The machine would have been found by someone. More good has come of that day's work we did than any other . . . except, of course, and Jaxom, hearing the odd satisfied chirp in Ruth's tone, smiled faintly, *the day we brought the queen egg back to Ramoth. And today, when we went forward and assured our success.*

Jaxom's smile deepened in spite of his disconsolate state, as he envisioned Ruth's eyes twirling with blue mischief.

Men think differently than dragons do, Ruth went on in a thoughtful tone. *Most of the time dragons understand their mates. Sometimes, like now, I cannot quite understand why you are troubled. You allow people to think as they wish so long as they do not impose their thoughts on you. You are good about listening to both sides of a problem. I've heard you. You allow people to do as they wish, so long as they do not injure anybody, especially someone you love and admire.*

'Ah but when we knew that Sigomal was plotting against Robinton, we should have confronted him then.'

Were the plans known?

'No, not exactly.'

And you took measures to protect the Harper.

'Which didn't work, did they?'

Not your fault. Who could have thought that they would try something at a Gather? With so many other people about. You must put aside such useless thoughts, Jaxom. You only make yourself miserable. WE have much to look forward to . . .

'Don't we!' Jaxom grimaced as he flopped over on to his stomach, burying his face in the pillow, knowing as he did so that he was merely evading that issue. He made himself think of it: would he and Ruth tackle the problem Aivas posed them?

It is not a problem, Jaxom. For it has been solved. Aivas has told you so. He has shown you so.

'And you agree with him? You'll risk it?'

We went forward to see if it worked. It had. Therefore we will do it because we have done it. It will be quite a feat. Ruth sounded eager and elated. Surprised by those feelings in his dragon, Jaxom pushed himself up to his elbows. *It will be even more challenging than saving Ramoth's egg. And even more important for the future of this world. That is what you must think of, not these sad and useless pasts. What has been done, has been done and cannot be undone.*

'Did Sharra have a word with you before she left?' Jaxom wouldn't have put it past his wife to enlist the aid of his dragon.

She did not need to. Am I not always close to your heart and your mind?

'Always, dear heart. Always!' And Jaxom swung his legs over the edge of the bed. There was still a lot to be done here at Ruatha before he could return with a clear conscience to Aivas and Landing.

Chapter Nineteen

Aivas had explained to Fandarel and Bendarek exactly how to alter and reinforce the HNO_3 tanks that were to corrode the metal casing of the anti-matter engines. Fandarel followed his instructions though the tolerance needed on the alloy of the tanks as well as the padding seemed redundant. He did enjoy contrapting the gauges and the nozzles which would let the agenothree drop on the engine casing.

'A slow process, to be sure, but the rate of penetration can be measured and monitored,' Aivas told the Craftmaster. 'The safety factors built into the great star-crossing engines were immensely sophisticated. The construction data are not available to discover a more efficient way of broaching the anti-matter suspension so this crude method is the only option. Sometimes, the simple solutions are best. Therefore, it is prudent to allow a wide window, which has been calculated as two weeks, give or take a few days. By the time the dragonriders transfer the engines to their positions, the corrosion will be close to the anti-matter capsule.'

'Now, look here, Aivas,' Fandarel began. 'I know the rate at which agenothree corrodes metal . . .'

'Not metal such as the builders of this ship used, Master Fandarel.'

'That's so,' and Fandarel scrubbed at his close-cropped

scalp. 'What puzzles me is the amount of agenothree required to reach the anti-matter material.'

'As has been explained,' and one of Aivas's diagrams appeared on the monitor in the engineering section: a massive block surrounding a ridiculously small cube in a slightly larger sphere, 'the anti-matter material is not a large mass, approximately 200 grams. Even the suspension unit only masses about 1,500 kilograms.'

'Frankly, Aivas, that's what perplexes me. How could 200 grams of anything power a ship the size of the *Yokohama* through space?'

'Do you not appreciate efficiency, Master Fandarel?' Aivas asked in reply, in a tone which could be interpreted as amused. Fandarel often had the feeling that the machine *was* amused. 'The matter/anti-matter engine is the quintessence of efficiency. Only a small amount is ever required.'

'With 200 grams of black powder or even nitro, one cannot explode very much,' Fandarel replied.

'Do not equate black powder or nitro, or anything which is used in mining operations, with anti-matter on any count. There is no comparison to the explosive energy released. Despite the distance involved, you will be able to see the flash of the explosion with an ordinary telescope when the anti-matter explodes on the Red Star. You would see no trace of an explosion using 200 grams of black powder, or even nitro. You must be assured that this facility does comprehend the power that is to be discharged.'

Fandarel continued to scratch his pate in wonderment, nodding his head as he tried to accept what Aivas said. Fandarel always considered concise and complete explanations as another indication of efficiency.

'You are an excellent craftsman, Master Fandarel, and have advanced at an astonishing pace in the past four years and nine months. Since anti-matter, unlike the atom which you have recently been investigating, cannot be studied in laboratory situations, you must rely on explanations. It cannot be exposed to matter as you know it – ore, earth, gases, water. Anti-matter can be contained, as it is in the ship's engine, and, with control, become the most efficient source of power Mankind has at its disposal. At this point in your study of physics, you cannot understand these concepts. But you can use them to your advantage; with proper guidance, techniques known to this facility, and the safeguards which have already been explained to you. As you pursue your studies, you will come to understand even the anomalies of anti-matter. But not now. Time becomes a critical factor. The Red Planet must be jarred out of its current orbit just where it will later approach the fifth planet of your system.

'Do you have the couplings to attach the HNO_3 tanks to the engine blocks?'

'Yes,' Fandarel said with a sigh and indicated the metal braces and T junction which he and his best Smiths had contrapted to hold the tanks tightly against the engines so that the corrosive material would leak in a regulated flow against the metal.

'Then you should proceed to install the tanks as indicated.' The screen altered to show that diagram.

'I could do it in my sleep,' Bendarek muttered.

'It would be unwise to fall asleep in space, Journeyman Bendarek,' Aivas replied immediately.

Bendarek grimaced and shot Fandarel an apologetic glance. He didn't think that Aivas's hearing would be quite as keen here in the engineering section of the *Yokohama* as it was in Landing.

'You will remember to use tether lines while you are e.v.a. F'lessan and his bronze dragon are in the cargo bay in case of an emergency.'

Gathering up their bundles, more awkward in size than heavy in weightlessness, Fandarel and Bendarek made their way to Airlock E-7, nearest the engine shaft. The bulky agenothree tanks, the largest that Fandarel had ever manufactured, ringed the wall of the lock where the rest of the work detail awaited them, suited up except for helmets. These were donned and secured, each member of the six-man team checking his mate's tank, fastenings and safety lines.

Bendarek took Fandarel's nod to cycle the airlock closed, and then to open the outer door. Evan and Belterac took one tank while Silton and Fosdak took the second. Bendarek handed out the couplers to the other journeyman, checking that each had the tools that would be required. Fandarel swung himself out on to the catwalk that led from the hatch to the great engine shaft.

Big as the Mastersmith was, he was dwarfed to insignificance by the immensity of the metal mass that contained the so-efficient 200 grams of anti-matter. For once in his life, Fandarel felt inadequate as he made his lumbering way: a grain of sand beside a dune. However there was work to be done, for which he was quite capable, so he suppressed this comparison and, without looking back, gestured for Evan and Belterac to follow him. Below them, Pern spread out and, with an accustomed glance, he located the odd pimples that were the Landing volcanoes. It comforted him in the grandeur of space to be able to identify something he knew. He proceeded, feeling the vibration in the walkway as others set foot upon it.

They all had e.v.a. time, were accustomed to moving in free fall, aware of, yet fascinated by, the inherent dangers of this new environment. To his surprise, Terry who had been his second hand for so long, could not handle the vastness of space, nor even the lack of gravity. Yet Terry never minded going a-dragonback. Still, Master Fandarel thought, this was a different medium altogether than *between* and just as hostile as Aivas told them. There had been those one or two – well, actually five – mishaps, Fandarel had to be candid. Fortunately there had been dragons about and the men, who had inadvertently loosened their safety-lines, had been hauled back to the *Yokohama*. Belterac was the only one who overcame fear of a repetition and continued that exercise. But Belterac was phlegmatic by nature.

Fandarel's gloved right hand touched the access ladder, crafted as a recess into the metal side of the engine shaft, complete with safety-line rail. Beyond his reach, by half a length, were the long rounded spars to which cargo pods had been attached during the *Yokohama*'s fifteen Turn journey from Earth to Pern. When it was time to move the engines to the Red Star, the dragons, wearing special gloves to protect their flesh from the lacerating cold of the metal, would grip these spars and carry the engine *between*. Aivas, Fandarel knew, still entertained doubts that the dragons, even in their hundreds, could move such a mass. Fandarel thought that if they must have faith that what Aivas told them was true, he should return the compliment. Fandarel caught a glimpse of Evan and Belterac behind him and, clipping his line to the safety rail and placing his hands on the rungs, he pulled himself up.

It was a long way up. When he reached the top of the engine block, it was wide enough for five dragons to stand tail to nose. The length of it was four times its width. Fandarel was still not accustomed to thinking in such colossal measurements.

With Aivas' diagram firmly in mind, he stepped carefully to where the tanks should be positioned, nozzles end to end and joined by the junction that would permit their contents to drip-drip relentlessly into the metal without evaporation into space. The waste of all this incredible metal distressed Fandarel, especially after Aivas insisted that they did not have some of the basic raw materials on Pern to reproduce such an alloy. He contented himself with the knowledge that he had seen it, felt it, and, yes, even destroyed it. There was nearly as much destruction in smithing as there was creation.

Bendarek and Fosdak had stayed below, to attach the hoist cables to the tanks. When those on top had adjusted their lines, they were secure enough to haul the tanks up without drifting off in the effort. The team had been well drilled and soon the tanks were up, then pressed down so that the ingenious suction cuppings would keep the tanks firmly in place until the special glue set. The couplings attached, and the junction installed. Finally the black solar panels were clipped on, so that the agenothree would not freeze or boil, during the operation. Then Bendarek ceremoniously handed Master Fandarel the spanner to open the plastic nozzles to release the corrosive agenothree.

'One down, two to go,' Fosdak said in his usual impudent manner.

'And we will all be careful going down that ladder,'

Fandarel said, relieved that there had been no mishap Efficiency was safety.

He motioned for the others to precede him and checked the gauges that would indicate the amount of agenothree in each. There was of course no change of the amount yet but it was second nature for Fandarel to check.

'I know, I know,' Hamian said irritably, using both hands to push sweaty hair off his face. He regarded F'lar levelly. Hamian was stripped to work pants in the heat which was part of his discomfort. The major dissatisfaction was the plastic material which he, Zurg, Jancis and a half hundred other journeymen and masters of a variety of crafts were trying to produce in sufficient quantities, and quality, to protect the dragonriders in their epic endeavour.

While the plastic he had produced, using Aivas' formula, was pliable and tough as an outside layer, the filling and cotton lining made assembly difficult. Since the plastic outer skin of these spacesuits must be airtight, it could not be sewn. Hamian had been experimenting with glues of every sort, trying to find one that would not become brittle in space and that bonded all three layers. He could not recall now how many suits he had sent up to the *Yokohama* to be tested.

The dragon gloves had been relatively easy in comparison, even if dragon feet differed in length and width as much as humans' did. Still the production of over three hundred pairs had taken some of his work force several months.

'Yes, I know that time is catching up with us, F'lar, but we're working flat out. We've got one hundred and seventy-two finished and tested.' He held his hands in a gesture of resignation.

'No-one can fault you for trying,' F'lar said.

'Look,' Jaxom said in a placatory manner, 'if worse comes to worst, we can send the engines in three sections. There should be enough variety of sizes so that they can be swapped over.'

F'lar frowned, not liking that alternative.

'Well, it's a suggestion,' Jaxom said. 'It would take the pressure off Hamian.'

'But this was to be a joint effort . . .'

'You know as well as I do, F'lar, that there's a wide window available,' Jaxom said, arguing as subtly as he could so that F'lar would not realize that Aivas would ensure that there would be only two hundred suits. Jaxom had hated the necessity of manipulating his best friends but it was essential if he was to bring off Aivas' plan. He didn't like it any better. But he had come to realize that Aivas was not all that confident about the dragons' abilities. The zebedees were a slower way of destroying Thread. But it did give them two options. 'It isn't as if the engines have to be deposited at the same instant.'

'No, that's true,' F'lar said, absently blotting the sweat off his forehead. He didn't like this alteration.

'How long does it take us to shuck spacesuits now? Half an hour at most between the two lifts. Hamian needs only to get another twenty, more if at all possible of course, Hamian, but we've almost enough as it is.'

'And time's running out,' Hamian said, some of the tension easing from his face and body. He hadn't liked to fail in this project but so much time had been spent in little details that no-one had considered when they'd blithely started. 'Everything takes longer and costs more. Shells! but I hate to fall down on you.'

'Who said you had?' Jaxom demanded. 'You've got enough kits to do the job right now.'

F'lar regarded Jaxom with faint surprise. Jaxom knew that he had usurped some of F'lar's prerogative here but he smiled as ingratiatingly as he could, giving a slight shrug.

'Yes, as you say, Jaxom, there are enough suits to do the job right now if riders trade off.'

'Well, then,' Hamian said, radiating relief, 'I can take time for a bite to eat. Join me?' He gestured towards the trestle table set under an awning. Some of his large teams were already serving themselves for meals were taken whenever there was time for them in Hamian's all-out effort. 'There's always enough in the pot for dragonriders.'

Although Jaxom knew that F'lar scrutinized him all during the meal, he pretended not to notice, teasing Jancis who had joined them. Jaxom intended to have a few private words with Aivas about easing up on Hamian. The man *was* trying. He had no idea that Aivas was deliberately rejecting spacegear that was probably suitable in all respects. Two hundred finished and acceptable units – and no more – would solve Jaxom's travel problems.

Landing might bear the brunt of the preparations for this final assault on Thread, but there was excitement throughout the planet as the days of the last month were ticked off.

Oldive and Sharra had drafted in as many Healers as possible, and then at Master Nicat's suggestion, some of the gem cutters who were accustomed to the use of magnifying glass and small tools. To the relief of everyone, eight of the twelve recommended accepted the unusual assignment. Efforts to find the most effective 'disimprover' for the Thread spring were redoubled. Many parasites of the Thread ovoids had been found, and many had been infected with a variety of 'viruses'. While some of the 'disimproved' forms had adverse affects on the Thread, none had produced virulent enough reactions, according to Aivas. Massive reproduction must take place, with the chosen virus – changed towards a more parasitic mode – able to replicate itself using the material within the ovoid.

Everyone in the laboratory on the *Yokohama*, or in the schoolrooms at Landing, worked long, hard, tedious hours, suffering eyestrain, headache and back cramps.

Aivas consoled them. 'Thread is a very disorganized life form, not even as organized as the indigenous bacteria you were isolating in biological studies. You cannot be expected to understand reproduction of such a life form.'

'We don't have time!' Mirrim said, speaking through clenched teeth. It was her offering which Aivas was rejecting. 'Of course,' and she brightened, 'we could keep some around to study and learn from, couldn't we?' She saw the horror and disgust of some of her colleagues. 'No, I guess we couldn't. Ah, well, back to microscope. My 98th batch of trials today. Maybe we luck out at 100!'

'Twenty-two more days!' Oldive said with a massive sigh as he, too, turned back to his station.

*

Afterwards when Lytol wrote up the history of these Aivas years, he would remember the results, not the frenzy that accompanied them, though he gave full credit to everyone involved in the different projects.

Then all the preparations had been completed. Two days *before* the date Aivas had set them.

Two hundred suited riders on two hundred gloved dragons awaited the signal in their Weyrs. Another nine suited riders were ready to do their part in this great enterprise, scattering the 'disimproved' ovoids. The three leaders, F'lar, N'ton and Jaxom, were in the *Yokohama* cargo bay. Lessa was there, with Ramoth who was breeding, and Jaxom did not dare ask how F'lar and Mnementh had timed that so precisely. She had accepted the fact that she would not take part in this venture but she didn't like her exclusion one bit.

Master Fandarel and Belterac were about to proceed with the separation of *Yokohama*'s engine shaft from the main sphere. Bendarek was aboard the *Bahrain* and Evan on the *Buenos Aires* to perform the same operation. Once that was done, the dragons would be called up to take their places.

Aivas had appointed F'lar to take the *Yokohama*'s unit and deposit it in the approximate centre of the great rift on the Red Planet. Jaxom was to take his group to one end of the rift, while N'ton was to take his to the other, more or less, close to the immense craters. Only Jaxom knew how those craters had occurred and *when* those craters had been made. The trick would be to keep N'ton from guessing.

Each section would be accompanied by three brown, blue and green dragons, Mirrim included, who would scatter the sacks of Thread toroids carrying disimproved parasites in a low altitude flight across the bleak Red Planet's surface and across the flat orbiting ring of ovoids above the planet's equator. Oldive and Sharra had just barely accomplished their part of the undertaking. Mirrim's 100th attempt was indeed the crucial one.

With careful fingers and a frown of concentration, Master Fandarel pressed in the code-words that would permit the appropriate sequence of separation to be activated. Aivas had had to delve deeply to find the secret ciphers in the captains' private files.

'There,' the Mastersmith said with an air of triumph.

The monitor displayed lights and then a message lit up, but not the one that Fandarel expected.

'There is a problem,' he said. 'The computer refuses to activate.'

'The appropriate code-word was given, the necessary sequence was provided. Separation should be initiated,' Aivas said in a crisp tone.

'The screen says "Unable to activate".'

'Unable to activate?' There was genuine surprise in Aivas' voice.

'Unable to activate,' Fandarel repeated, wondering what the problem could possibly be. The *Yokohama*'s machinery, though it had lain dormant for many centuries, had always complied with the proper action for every operation requested. 'I will try again . . .'

'A scan is being run to ascertain if there is any computer malfunction,' Aivas replied.

'Master Fandarel?' queried Bendarek from the *Bahrain* on the ship linkup, 'shall I proceed now?'

'We do not have separation here yet,' Fandarel said, keenly feeling this failure and hoping it would be momentary.

'Should I not see if the *Bahrain* is more responsive?' Bendarek could not quite suppress his eagerness to begin.

'Aivas?' Fandarel was always a generous man. If Bendarek could proceed, it would be as well.

'No malfunction in the program can be discovered,' Aivas said. 'It is recommended that the *Bahrain* proceed with separation.'

Bendarek had a little more luck than Fandarel. 'My screen says "dysfunction discovered". Dysfunction of what?'

Evan, on the *Buenos Aires*, initiated the program in his turn and received 'mechanical malfunction' as his message.

'Which one is correct?' Fandarel asked, somewhat vindicated by the failure of all attempts.

'They may all be correct,' Aivas replied. 'Reviewing.'

Fandarel felt that in order, for himself as well, and rehearsed the sequence he had inserted.

'It is a mechanical malfunction,' Aivas announced.

'Of course,' Fandarel said, bellowing as he realized what it had to be. 'These ships have been in space for over twenty-five hundred years. The mechanical parts have had no maintenance.'

'You are correct, Master Fandarel,' Aivas replied. 'That is the obvious malfunction.'

'What's the delay up there?' F'lar asked from the cargo bay.

'A minor one,' Fandarel answered. Then paused. 'Where?' he asked Aivas.

'The clamps have locked due to cessation of timely servicing.'

'It's not just frozen, is it?' Fandarel asked.

'You have learned much, Master Fandarel. Fortunately the clamps can be lubricated on the inside, through an access, a narrow one,' and the screen lit up with the schematic of the area between the skins of the *Yokohama*. 'It will however be necessary to use a special lubricant for there is little heat in that area and the oils you ordinarily use will be ineffective. A mixture of liquid neon, liquid hydrogen and liquid helium must be made with a tiny amount of silicone fluid. That is the equivalent of penetrating oils for use in these very cold conditions. The very low molecular weight of gases evaporate first but their viscosity is very low and carries the heavier silicone oil into very thin spaces. That should effect the solution to this minor problem.'

'Minor problem?' For once, Fandarel lost his patience. 'We do not have those liquids.'

'You have the means to produce them if you remember the liquid helium experiments.'

Fandarel did. 'That will take time.'

'There is time,' Aivas said. 'A wide window was allowed for this transfer. There *is* time.'

The dragonriders would be not pleased with the delay for they had built themselves and their dragons up to this incredible effort and were impatient to go.

'If it isn't one thing, it's another, isn't it?' N'ton said, with a wry grin.

'Tomorrow?' Jaxom asked, grinning to allay F'lar's irritated frown, 'same time, same stations?' In his mind, he wondered if the star patterns that he and Ruth were using to guide themselves back eighteen hundred Turns would alter much in one day. But he couldn't ask Aivas right now.

F'lar pushed back the lock of hair that never seemed to stay in place but he acknowledged the unanticipated delay with a flick of his finger.

'We'll speak to the riders, Aivas.'

Despite his light-heartedness, Jaxom had experienced an incredible letdown to have the expedition postponed. More than anyone else, he had had to fortify himself for the tremendous effort required of him and Ruth.

A day makes little difference to me, Jaxom, Ruth said encouragingly. *The meal I had yesterday will last long past tomorrow.*

'That's good,' Jaxom replied, more grimly than the circumstances warranted – but he was primed for action today! *'Well, let's get back to Eastern, and tell my wings to relax.'*

It was in fact several days before the penetrating oil could be manufactured. Jaxom had Ruth eat at least one small wherry each evening. Ruth complained that he'd be so full he wouldn't be able to complete one jump, let alone two.

'That's preferable to having you fade out on me when we're stuck between times.'

Jaxom waited out the delay at Cove Hold with Sharra who was recovering from intensive hours in the laboratory. She'd lost weight and had deep circles under her eyes. At least he could occupy himself with seeing to her needs. And his. And Robinton's.

Jaxom was distressed to see the change in the Masterharper: a subtle one, but he could tell that Lytol and D'ram were also aware of it. Robinton had recovered from the physical shock but not from the mental one. He 'seemed' himself when in company but, too often, Jaxom would catch him deep in thoughts, disturbing and unhappy ones, from the sadness in the Harper's eyes and mouth. Also, he seemed to drink less, and with less relish. He was a man going through the motions of living.

Zair is worried, Ruth told Jaxom when the white dragon caught him worrying about the Harper.

'It may just take a little more time for Master Robinton to recuperate,' Jaxom said, trying to reassure himself. 'He's not as young as he was, less resilient. And it was a ghastly experience. When this is over, we'll think of something to rouse him from his apathy. Sharra's noticed it, too. She'll talk it over with Oldive. You know how testy he gets when he thinks you're fussing over him. We'll do something. Tell Zair. Now, just once more, let's go through the star pattern for our first timing.'

We both know them better than the ones above us now, Ruth said but dutifully did as Jaxom asked.

The call to assemble came in late afternoon. Fosdak, the slimmest of the Smith journeymen, had squeezed his suited self into the interstices and pumped the penetrating liquid and oil into the fine crack of each of the huge clamps that held the engine shaft on to the main ship segment. By the time he had done the *Buenos Aires* and returned to the *Yokohama* to see if the application had dispersed, he was reasonably confident of success.

Once again Fandarel used code-word and key sequence, punched 'enter' and waited. This time the computer acknowledged the commands and printed 'ready to execute'.

'I am ready to execute the order,' Fandarel said.

'Go, man, go,' F'lar cried.

Fandarel activated the program. He didn't know if anyone else heard the metallic squealings and clangings, or the final 'clunk' as the clamps let go. The noise was loud enough in the engineering section.

'We have separation,' he said, and then remembered to activate the exterior optics to view the effect.

'Weyr, alert!' F'lar called and Fandarel had a fine view of the sudden appearance of the massed dragons, each dropping to prearranged positions along the upper spars. 'Magnificent!'

'The *Bahrain* has separation!' cried Bendarek.

Fandarel could not see the *Bahrain*.

Jaxom could, for this was his responsibility. When F'lar had alerted the wings under his command, from Benden, Igen, and Telgar Weyrs, Jaxom had called up his from Eastern, Southern, and Ista. The assembly that answered him was the most impressive he had ever seen in all his Turns. They had drilled, it was true, but each arrived in place at the same moment. Dragon claws gripped the long spars and every face plate was turned in his direction where he and Ruth perched on the tail section.

'Ruth, give the dragons their direction to the Red Star in star-pattern. Remember, there will be no crater at that end of the rift.'

I do, because we will put it there! Ruth sounded elated at the prospect.

There would be no confusion over that formality: the dragons expected to receive their destination from Ruth. None of them had been to the Red Star. All the riders had been told that it would appear to be a longer jump than they were accustomed to making and to remember to breathe regularly in the interval.

They understand and are ready.

Jaxom took in a deep breath, resting one gloved hand on Ruth's shoulder before he raised it high. '*Then we must go*,' he said, before I lose my nerve. And dropped his arm.

It was a long jump, even if it was expected. Jaxom counted thirty carefully inhaled and exhaled breaths. Too bad that Lessa hadn't remembered how long it had taken her to go back four hundred Turns. That knowledge would have been reassuring. On thirty-two breaths, Jaxom's anxiety began to ooze out of his control.

HERE! Ruth said in a great echoing shout in Jaxom's mind.

And they were hovering inches above one end of the great rift. The stars were in the correct pattern in the sky. The desolate landscape at this edge of the rift was just as bleak at this time of its life as it was in Jaxom's Turn.

Jaxom hauled his mind back to the business at hand. They had ten minutes to let the massive engine down into the rift.

Those who sow the ovoids are proceeding, Ruth told him.

Jaxom then relayed the order for dragons to lower their burden. And then grinned broadly. The dragons HAD accomplished this incredible journey. The weight of the engine had been as nothing . . . because they had not thought of it as anything out of the ordinary. A surge of elation buoyed his spirits immeasurably.

'We did it, Ruth! We did it!'

Of course we did it. Easy now, keep that thing level, Ruth added and Jaxom gestured to the rear dragons who were dropping faster than the forward ones. *T'gellan asks how far down are we to go with this?*

'Tell him, as far down as we can lower without the dragons scraping their wings. There should be some rocky protrusions that'll hold it in place long enough. Steady now, keep a regular rate of descent.'

They were well below the rim of the rift when Jaxom felt the whole structure jar.

'Can we drop down, Ruth, and see if this will do?'

Ruth's eyes gleamed off the strata of rock, feldspar, granite and darker stone mixtures. Then he was below the bulk of the engine which decreased the sparse light that reached this level.

It will slant a bit if they release it, Ruth said, his sight more acute than Jaxom's.

'Who's on the bow end?'

Heth, Clarinath, Silvrath, Jarlath . . .

'Please ask them to lower as far as they can.'

They have.

'Ask them to release their grip but be ready to grab again. We can't have the thing slipping down into the abyss.'

Heth says if the stern will move forward half a length, there is a good shelf of rock for the bow end.

'Give Lioth that message.'

I have.

Jaxom could see the slight movement as the engine mass settled.

'All right,' and Jaxom gestured to the riders facing him to release their end carefully.

That accomplished, with tension obvious as talons hovered inches above the spars, the massive engine seemed secure. Jaxom glanced at the time piece strapped to his wrist. Eight minutes had elapsed. There was nothing more to be done here.

As he signalled for the wings to rise out of the rift, he asked Ruth to tell the dragons to land on the rim.

'*Are the sowers all right, Ruth?*'

They are, the white dragon said equably. *Mirrim landed Path once to look at the ovoids in the dust. There are many many more than she thought there would be.*

'Tell Path that Mirrim is NOT to bring a sample back. We have enough of them,' Jaxom said firmly. The last thing they needed was an artefact from eighteen hundred Turns ago.

Path says a lot of them are rotten.

'All the more reason to leave them where they are!

Path will not bring one.

Jaxom glanced at his watch. Another minute had ticked by. He looked around him, the dragons and riders were glancing curiously about them.

Lioth says T'gellan says Threads are welcome to this planet, Ruth remarked. *The engine will not explode yet, will it?*

'No, not according to the way Bendarek read the gauge when he checked this one over. I wonder how F'lar's doing.'

The small hand had circled once again.

'*Call the others in, Ruth. We'd better get back.*'

In eight seconds the green, blue and brown riders reappeared.

Now came the dangerous part, the one Jaxom had fretted over since Aivas had informed him of this manoeuvre: getting all the dragons and riders safely back to their own time.

'Impress on every dragon, Ruth, that he is to return to his own Weyr. We will have been gone fourteen minutes so there is really no chance that they will collide with themselves on the way back. Is there?'

I have told you many times, Jaxom, that I do not think they will become lost. Every dragon knows his way back to his own Weyr.

'Every dragon is to impress on his rider that there are to be no exceptions to this order.'

I will tell them that they are too far away from Pern to disobey. They will not. The dragons certainly will not. Ruth paused briefly. *I have told them. I may not be a queen but dragons trust me.*

Still apprehensive, Jaxom asked Ruth to raise up over the surface, so that every dragon could see him.

'Back at their Weyrs, they are to get out of the suits immediately so they can be collected by browns and brought to Fort Weyr.'

For our next trip. Jaxom couldn't believe the smug satisfaction in Ruth's tone. So much for worrying if this double time jumping would affect the resilient white dragon. He saw that face plates were turned in his direction and he raised his arm, making the hand gesture to go *between*. A second later, he asked Ruth to take him back to *Yokohama*.

Curiously time seemed to go more slowly on the return. Yet Jaxom reached his thirtieth exhalation just as they emerged in the cargo bay of the *Yokohama*. The first dragon he saw was Ramoth, Lessa beside her, and to one side, F'lar appeared. Jaxom glanced down at his wrist watch: F'lar's trip had lasted the full fifteen minutes that dragons could endure without oxygen. The cargo bay was lit, but not well enough for Jaxom to tell if Mnementh was off colour. Looking down at Ruth, he saw no alteration in the lustrous coat.

'We've done it. Every one safely back below?'

Lioth tells me so. Heth . . . Jaxom felt part of him shrivel in fear. *Heth says they are all back but several dragons are in bad colour.*

'If that's all, it's nothing a good meal won't cure. And you?'

I'm fine. We have done very well. So far.

'Now if I can only think of some pretext for the *Buenos Aires*,' Jaxom said as he removed his helmet.

You will.

'Yeeeeow!'

Jaxom was so startled by the loud cheer from F'lar that he nearly lifted himself from Ruth's back. The white dragon, eyes whirling in amazement, also turned his head to see F'lar propel himself off Mnementh, floating at a good rate towards Lessa. His momentum spun them off in a lazy twirl

451

until they careened into Ramoth who arched her neck to look down at the extraordinary behaviour of the Benden Weyrleaders.

'We did it! The dragons of Pern did it! Aivas'll have to eat sand on this one! He never thought we could do it!' F'lar was yelling at the top of his voice, laughing when echoes bounced back at him.

'Really, F'lar . . .' Lessa regained her balance but Jaxom could see that she was smiling. 'Yes, it is a splendid moment for the Weyrs! A splendid one! You've kept your promise. Indeed you have. That'll show the Holds and Halls!'

Still grinning fatuously, F'lar leaned back against Ramoth, pushing back his wayward lock.

'In point of fact, Lessa,' and F'lar's expression turned wry, 'we haven't quite done it. There's N'ton's wings to lift the third engine and then we have to wait. First for the explosion and then to see if it had the proper effect.'

Jaxom rubbed his hand across his lips. Knowledge of the future was a parlous asset. It was enough that Jaxom *knew* this great enterprise would work.

'All safely down with your wings, Jaxom?' F'lar inquired as Jaxom floated to the deck.

'A few dragons off colour . . .'

'Ruth's not,' Lessa said, scrutinizing the white dragon and smiling approval at Jaxom.

'He says I've been stuffing him. Which of us gets to tell Aivas?' Jaxom asked, broadly grinning.

'We both do,' F'lar said, and clapping an arm across Jaxom's shoulders, they bounced across the deck to the cargo bay console. 'You know, I didn't see your wing.'

'Nor I yours,' Jaxom said, chuckling. 'Us poor soil bound Pernese have no appreciation of real size . . .' and he spread his arms wide. 'That rift is mammoth. We planted our engine really well down in the rift on a wide stone ledge.'

'Aivas already knows,' Lessa said. 'I told him you'd all gone and that Ramoth was in touch with Mnementh. Oddly enough,' and now she peered at Jaxom, 'she couldn't hear Ruth.'

'That is odd,' Jaxom said, appearing puzzled. 'Ramoth

hears him quite well. But you both forget how far that rift stretches and we were at the far northern tip of it.'

They were at the console now.

'Aivas?' F'lar said.

'You have succeeded. Are all safely returned?'

'Yes! Now do you doubt draconic abilities?' F'lar asked, vindication mixed with the triumph in his laugh. He pulled Jaxom over in a comradely fashion. 'You didn't want to believe that dragons could do what we said they could.'

'We were right on schedule, too,' Jaxom said, allowing himself to chuckle. 'My team set that engine down right where you wanted it. No problem!'

'You are both to be complimented on your courage and daring.'

'Don't lay it on too thick, Aivas,' F'lar said.

'You deserve every credit that will accrue to your valorous deed. You have performed an incredible feat, Weyrleader F'lar. There is no doubt of that. Or that you have achieved your personal goal – the end of Thread to this planet.'

Jaxom grinned at F'lar, pleased by Aivas' unusual rhetoric.

'Your achievement is historically equivalent to that of the first dragonriders to fight Thread. Your name will be remembered with Sean O'Connor's, Sorka Hanrahan's . . .'

'That *is* laying it on too thick,' Jaxom said, 'for only you remembered who were first to fight.'

'Actually, Jaxom,' F'lar said, grinning broadly, 'Sebell showed me the corrected Harper Hall records and the eighteen riders who participated in that Fall were honoured in their Turn. No-one ran afoul of any of those dangers you warned us about,' F'lar added, savouring this auspicious moment.

'It is wise to prepare for unusual contingencies,' Aivas said.

'Well, we've done it.'

'And you deserve this,' Lessa said, joining them with a wineskin in her hands. 'Best Benden.'

'The '16?' Jaxom asked, craning his head for a look at the label.

'What else?' Lessa said, with a coquettish smile, before she put the skin to her lips.

Jaxom blinked and, recovering, grinned back. It was about time that she treated him as an adult. Then he turned serious when it was his turn to drink from the skin, which he first raised to the Weyrleaders. 'To all the Weyrs of Pern!'

'To us for this triumphant day!'

Jaxom took a long swig before he passed the wineskin back to Lessa. As she drank, F'lar turned to Jaxom. 'You did tell 'em all to shuck those suits for the next round?'

'As planned, brown riders'll bring them to N'ton at Fort Weyr.'

'Did your team scatter those treated ovoids as Aivas wanted?'

Jaxom winked at Lessa. 'Mirrim wanted to bring back some examples of empty ones she found lying about.' Lessa looked outraged but Jaxom waved a reassurance. 'I recommended that she didn't.'

'How long before the explosion, Aivas?' F'lar asked.

'The HNO_3 gauge readings reassure that there is no stoppage. The corrosion continues.'

'That's no answer,' F'lar said, frowning.

Jaxom grinned. 'That's all you're going to get right now. And we've still the third one to go.' Which constituted a major problem for him. He desperately needed a few private words with Aivas, to see if he had come up with any ideas on how Jaxom could insinuate himself into N'ton's flight and get the dragons to take Ruth's coordinates for the second time leap of a mere five hundred Turns. Somehow he had accomplished it for the other crater was there on the southern tip of the rift. Jaxom had wracked his brains and, whenever he was private with Aivas over the past few days, had tried to figure out any way that didn't involve explaining to N'ton. Not that N'ton wouldn't believe Jaxom, and wasn't discreet, but the fewer who knew about this time-travelling the better. Lessa would be infuriated!

So now he looked around him. 'Are you the only ones up here, Lessa?'

'Oh no,' and she grinned. 'Everyone else is on the bridge, peering through the telescope, hoping to see the explosion. Oh, I told them it wouldn't happen soon. They were confident that they'd see the wings . . .' Jaxom's breath caught. 'Of course, they couldn't. Sometimes, even Fandarel doesn't comprehend vast distances. But today's excitement is being shared.'

'How long has it been since we got back?' F'lar asked Jaxom.

'About twenty minutes,' Jaxom replied. 'N'ton's wings won't be ready yet, F'lar. Does anyone need your suit?'

'I shouldn't think so, but to be on the safe side, I'll shuck out of it. Could you bring it over to the *Buenos Aires* if it is needed?' F'lar handed Jaxom the helmet and, with Lessa's help, started removing the bulky suit. As he laid it over Jaxom's arm, he added: 'I think we'll join those on the bridge, and the telescope, and watch N'ton work.'

As soon as the lift doors closed on them, Jaxom returned to the console. 'All right, Aivas, just how do I get to go with N'ton?'

'That is being arranged,' Aivas surprised him with his reply.

'HOW is it being arranged?' Jaxom demanded, wanting concise instructions.

'You are quick and clever. You already have a reason to be on the *Buenos Aires*. You will know what to do when the time comes. Transfer now to the other ship.'

'I'll know when the time comes, will I?' Jaxom muttered to himself as he threw the extra suit over his shoulder, his hands full of helmet. He made his way over to Ruth. 'Hand this one up to me, will you?' he said, giving the white dragon one of the two helmets so he'd have a free hand to mount. 'How's N'ton doing? Has he got all the suits yet?'

As he arranged F'lar's in front of him he caught a whiff of sweat. Well, he didn't smell that sweet himself after his exertions.

N'ton says that some suits have to be sponged, and helmets have to match the suits.

'Washed? Dragonriders tended to be fastidious in their personal habits and dressing in a sweaty suit might be distasteful to many. *Oh, yes, perhaps they might at that. I don't understand about the helmets.*

There was a pause while Ruth inquired of Lioth, N'ton's bronze.

They forgot to put the suits back together, and Ruth was obviously repeating something he didn't quite understand, *and the helmets got mixed up.*

'How long is sorting going to take?' And suddenly Jaxom had a glimmer of an idea. He hoped it would take a long time. With nearly a hundred suits to match to helmets, it could take several hours.

Lioth didn't know. N'ton is not happy.

'Reassure Lioth and N'ton, would you please, Ruth? Because this is going to work for our benefit. I think we can now put in an appearance on the *Buenos Aires.*'

There were three blues and two greens waiting there, all from Eastern Weyr, and Ruth was greeted with considerable awe by the young dragons. Knowing that the white dragon would enjoy their deference, Jaxom took the lift up to the smaller bridge of the *Buenos Aires.*

'What's holding up N'ton's wings?' Fandarel asked, relieved to see Jaxom. 'That was a splendid sight, Jaxom, watching all those dragons lifting the engines like they were so many firestone sacks. Aivas has informed us that all went well.' Fandarel looked concerned. 'Why isn't N'ton here?'

'Because no-one thought to keep helmet and body suit together,' Jaxom said. Then realized that he should also appear concerned and managed a frown. 'I don't think it's going to matter in the long run,' he added thoughtfully, as he made his way to the nearest console. 'Aivas, there is going to be a delay. Helmets weren't kept with suits, and they've got to match.'

'That could be inconvenient if the delay is prolonged,' Aivas said.

'It's three quarters of an hour since we went off. How long before N'ton has to have different star pattern references? It would be disastrous if he arrived at the wrong time and his engine went off either prematurely or too late.' If Aivas expected Jaxom to use his wits, he hoped Aivas saw what he was aiming at.

'A consideration to be sure. Reprogramming contingency.' The screen altered from the current view of the *Buenos Aires* to rapid shifts of star configurations. 'With any lengthy delay, the star picture would be slightly different.'

'Is there going to be a problem?' Fandarel asked.

Jaxom smiled reassuringly at the Mastersmith and the others on the bridge, Masterminer Nicat, Master Idarolan, Jancis and Piemur. Jaxom would rather not have Piemur about: they knew each other far too well. 'I don't think it's insurmountable. As you heard, Aivas is already programming contingency plans. I'd better inform Lessa and F'lar of the delay.'

When he had, a call came through from Evan in engineering where he was patiently waiting to complete the separation. Jaxom was glad it was he, rather than Fosdak, in charge of that task. Fosdak had no patience.

Of all on the three bridges, Jaxom was the only one delighted that it took N'ton and his wings nearly four hours to get suited up. Usually a calm, easy-going and relaxed Weyrleader, his patience had been sorely tried by the delays.

Lioth says they're ready. Ramoth says they must get the new configurations from you. Aivas has told Lessa it is nearly night on the Red Star. He is giving you the new star patterns to memorize and give Lioth. Ruth delivered the various messages just as the new configurations came up on the monitor. They were, as Jaxom knew, those for the five hundred-Turn jump with the Red Star in the same relation to Rukbat at the Eighth Pass. Aivas had made a slight time alteration on those original coordinates, to judge by the position of the Wheel and the Plough constellations on the horizon.

'Lessa,' Jaxom said, toggling the ship-to-ship link, 'I've got the visuals here. I'll give them to N'ton. Can Ramoth tell them to transfer in five more minutes? I have to get Ruth from the cargo bay.'

'Just give N'ton the coordinates, Jaxom,' Lessa said.

'That's what I intend doing,' Jaxom replied mendaciously. 'Fandarel, five minute warning for Evan?'

The Smith nodded enthusiastically for the waiting made

everyone edgy. Waiting, in the Smith's lexicon, was ineffic-
ient. As Jaxom took the lift to the cargo bay, he wondered
if Fandarel ever rested. Here he had completed the most
complex and exhausting work of a lifetime and he fretted
over inactivity.

We go? Ruth asked Jaxom, his eyes whirling with
excitement.

'*We don't really have to go, you know, Ruth*, Jaxom said.
'*Lessa said we only have to give N'ton the new coordinates . . .*'
Jaxom chuckled as he saw the disappointment in Ruth's
eyes. He mounted him and, crowning his head with the
helmet, twisted it shut. '*That will get them there safely enough
but . . . I think you'll make an error and go, too. You feel all right
about that?*'

I have rested and this is the shorter trip, isn't it?

'*I hope so.*' Between the first jump, fretting over how to
join N'ton's wings, and the long wait, Jaxom was feeling
slightly frayed. He took care not to let Ruth sense that.

Monarth comes! Excitement coloured Ruth's tone.

'Fandarel, do you see them?' Jaxom asked through his
helmet link.

'Yes, magnificent. I have given Evan the order to
separate.'

'*Let's get to the stern, Ruth.*'

Jaxom took a deep breath, they flashed *between* so fast
he hadn't quite completed the inhalation when Ruth was
gripping the stern. Monarth and N'ton were beside them
and below, the bronze dragons of Fort, High Reaches, Telgar
and Ista ranged along the top spars.

Jaxom held the image of where they were going vivid in
his mind. '*Give Monarth and N'ton my compliments and ask
Monarth to take our destination from you.*'

N'ton threw Jaxom a salute but Jaxom couldn't see the
Fort Weyrleader's expression, obscured by the face plate.
He gave a deferential salute.

Monarth says we go!

They went. The cold of *between*, the depth of its black
cold, seemed to penetrate Jaxom's spacesuit and he could
hear his breath coming raggedly. He forced himself to
slow down.

I'm here, was Ruth's encouragement.

'*As always*,' Jaxom replied and continued to count his inhalations. Eighteen, nineteen, twenty, twenty-one, twenty-two.

They were hovering inches above the southern tip of the rift.

Monarth says where's the crater?

'*Tell him that Aivas picked this spot so here's where we'd better deposit the engine. We don't have time to find that bloody crater!*'

Jaxom turned toward N'ton who was looking at him, arms raised in query. Jaxom gave him an exasperated shrug in reply.

Monarth says N'ton understands. They proceed.

N'ton was signalling to the auxiliary dragons to begin their task of sowing the zebedees. Then he turned all his attention to lowering the massive engine into the rift. The manoeuvre went well, even better than Jaxom's, in just ten minutes. Practice makes perfect.

N'ton waited another few moments, allowing the dragons a chance to rest. Then he called in the auxiliaries.

I have told Monarth that everyone must return to their own Weyrs. But to keep the right helmets with the right suits this time.

'*We're not likely to need two hundred slightly used spacesuits again*,' Jaxom said, trying to contain his elation until they were safely back. '*We must go back to the* Yokohama.'

I have told Monarth. N'ton says he is grateful and apologizes for the delay.

'Tell him that it all worked out well in the end.'

It did, didn't it? Ruth added. *Shall we return now?*

Once again, the return seemed longer than the outgoing journey but it wasn't. The comforting dimness of the big cargo bay of the *Yokohama* surrounded them. And they were immediately attacked by Ramoth and Mnementh.

Where have I been? Ruth exclaimed, rearing back away from Ramoth's savage expression, and dodging Mnementh's massive wings. *I'm fine. I'm fine. So is Jaxom. He didn't tell me not to go!*

'JAXOM!' F'lar was bellowing the moment he stepped out of the lift, with Lessa on his heels.

Jaxom loosened his helmet. 'So we went, too,' he said, raising his voice to top the angry ones of the Benden Weyrleaders. 'Ruth's not even a trifle off colour. Not his fault. I forgot to tell him not to follow Lioth. But the job is now completely done!' He glared back at F'lar and Lessa, and slid down Ruth's side, patting his foreleg. 'I could certainly use another pull at that wineskin, Lessa, if you wouldn't mind . . .'

He spoke with no trace of regret or apology, and he felt rather too battered to bother with the deference the Weyrleaders deserved from him. He undid the first of the suit's fastenings, knowing that they were still angry with him and hoping they'd give it over.

'Here, I'll help,' F'lar said unexpectedly. 'Lessa, this Lord Holder deserves another swallow of that '16!'

Jaxom gave F'lar a sharp look and then grinned back. By the first Egg, so he had finally come into his own in the cargo bay of the *Yokohama*.

Chapter Twenty

There were a few riders in the third group who suffered some physical attrition which Jaxom thought very odd, until he talked with them.

M'rand, one of the older bronze riders of High Reaches, returned long after the rest of the Weyr and in terrible condition. He was tormented by bad dreams, insisting that he'd returned to his Weyr but it had not been *his* Weyr. Tileth had been frantic for he recognized none of the dragons and there was a strange bronze asleep on the ledge of his weyr. M'rand couldn't understand at first but he'd heard that bronzes could slip through time. He kept his wits and, giving Tileth the most vivid images of their favourite view of High Reaches, with the blue M'rand knew was that day's watchdragon, had tried to get home again. This time they had emerged in the right place and the right time.

'Sloppy visualization,' Lessa said when she and F'lar had also spoken with M'rand, and the others: two in Fort Weyr and another in Igen. 'And they're all older riders, leaving more up to their dragons than they ought.'

Jaxom noticed that N'ton was regarding him with a quizzical expression and he responded with a perplexed grin. He had felt woefully tired after the exertions of that momentous day, pausing only long enough to let Ruth feed on a juicy buck before returning home. If he slept nearly a day, no-one thought that odd. Sharra was equally exhausted by her last few days in the laboratory, churning out zebedees.

Despite the fact that Aivas had repeatedly told everyone that the explosion would not take place for several more days, and then would not be immediately visible due to light speed – which he had to explain again to some – a twenty-four hour vigil was kept on the *Yokohama*. Every screen in the various areas on the ships where air was available was permanently adjusted to the ships' main screens and the big telescope which was aimed at the Red Star.

'Jaxom, aren't you going to watch?' Sharra asked. 'You of all people ought to have the right!' She was baffled by his apparent indifference to the event.

'Frankly,' he said, 'I have a lot of more important things to do here in Ruatha than floating about on the bridge, waiting for the thing to blow. Unless, of course,' he added considerately, 'you really want to see it.'

'Well,' and Sharra paused, then smiled at him, 'I've got those cultures going right now and . . .'

Jaxom grinned at her: 'If there's enough warning, Ruth'll get us there in time.'

Sharra gave him a startled sideways glance.

'All in a good cause,' he said, trying for nonchalance, 'and a minute or two isn't going to disrupt the universe. I'll ask Ruth to keep an ear open, if you like. There's always some fire-lizards or a dragon or two up at the *Yokohama* these days. Easy enough.'

'If he can stay awake long enough to listen,' Sharra replied, having noticed that Ruth seemed to be taking an unusual amount of sleep.

'He can sleep with one ear open,' Jaxom said and then they each went about the concerns of the day.

Brand had also observed Ruth's somnolence and, while Jaxom and he were checking the brood mares, he mentioned it.

'I don't think it's so very unusual, Brand,' Jaxom said easily. 'N'ton said that all the bronzes who went with us are also sleeping a good deal. I suspect none of the dragons care to admit that they had to work pretty hard to transfer those engines.' Then Jaxom noticed his steward's hesitation. 'Why? What's wrong?'

'It's just that there have been some complaints about Fort Weyr.'

'What do you mean, Brand?' Jaxom and Ruth had not flown the most recent Fall with the Fort wings but N'ton was a conscientious Weyrleader. 'Have I missed out on something?'

Brand shrugged expressively. 'Well, because the bronzes are a bit logey, they haven't been as – well, diligent in chasing airborne Thread. There have been a lot of unhappy groundcrews. And that's the other problem . . .'

'Tell me.'

'Somehow,' and Brand paused to frame his explanation, 'a lot of people thought that there'd be no more Thread *now*. That once the dragonriders had done this explosion thing, Thread wouldn't fall again.'

'Oh!' Jaxom made a face. 'Bloody shards, Brand. Don't they ever listen? Harpers have been explaining for the last four Turns that we can't stem this Fall, but there won't be any more!'

'They don't see it that way, I'm afraid, from the accounts I've heard. And Holder Grevil isn't a stupid man, as you know, but *he* hadn't understood and feels aggrieved, especially when a clump of Thread came down on his best field.'

'I can appreciate his annoyance. Did you manage to soothe him?'

'I did, but he's sure to approach you on the matter the next time he can. I thought I'd warn you. And you should know that he blames Aivas.'

Jaxom compressed his lips against rash words, momentarily defeated by this news: especially coming from Grevil who was a moderate man. 'I thought we'd straightened all that out at the trial.'

Brand shrugged, holding his hands up in an impotent gesture. 'People will hear what they wish to hear, and believe what they want to. If they put the blame on Aivas, however, that absolves you, Jaxom, and even the Weyrs to a certain extent.'

'I can't really count that as an advantage,' Jaxom replied. 'Why should Aivas bear any blame after all he's done to help Pern.'

'Ah, but the help is not so visible to some,' Brand said. 'It'll all sort itself out, Jaxom. But I did feel you should know current opinion.'

'Hmmmm, yes, I should. How many has that new stallion covered of this lot?' he asked, welcoming the chance to change to matters less complicated.

The more he thought about it, the more he felt obliged to let the Harper Hall know, and those at Cove Hold. He hated to disrupt the mood of euphoria and triumph they would be feeling. Robinton would take it badly, too, but he'd also better know. Meer was still his constant shadow when Ruth slept, and he sent a message by him to Lytol who could mention the report at an appropriate moment.

'What I don't understand,' Sharra said when he mentioned the matter to her over their midday meal, 'is that with all that has been explained so carefully to everyone who would listen, how they can possibly misconstrue what you and the Weyrs were doing, and its immediate consequences.'

Jaxom grinned. 'They probably stopped listening after the words "Thread will be for ever destroyed."' He sipped his *klah* pensively.

F'lar and Lessa are up on the Yokohama, said Ruth in a sleepy voice. *Ramoth says Aivas thinks the explosion will be any time now.*

Sharra politely cocked her head at him, knowing that Ruth had spoken to him. 'What woke him up?'

'It should be any moment now. The explosion. Want to go?'

'Do *you* want to?'

'Let's not play the you-first, no you-first game. Do you want to go?'

She blinked rapidly, considering, and looking so like Jarrol, that he grinned. 'No,' she said with a sigh, 'I think I've seen quite enough of the insides of the *Yokohama* to last me the rest of my life. And everyone will be crowding about up there. But if you want to go . . .'

He laughed, reaching for her hand and bringing it to his lips. 'I think I won't. This moment should be F'lar's.'

Sharra eyed him long and thoughtfully, her eyes beginning to sparkle. 'You're a good man but I do not concede that it is ALL F'lar's triumph.'

'Don't be silly,' he replied, 'it took all the Weyrs of Pern to do it.'

'And a white dragon!'

As she turned back to her soup, Jaxom wondered exactly what she meant by that. Could Sharra have guessed Ruth's unusual role?

After so many long days, and hours, of watching the round ball that was the Red Star, the explosion when it became visible was definitely an anticlimax. An orangey-red fireball blossomed on the side of the wanderer planet. The spectacle was also being seen on Aivas's screen in Landing though the best view to be had was, of course, on the bridge of the *Yokohama*.

'Only one?' F'lar exclaimed, feeling a certain chagrin that half the planet had not exploded, too, after all Aivas had told them about the awesome power of the antimatter.

'That is how it would appear at this distance,' Aivas replied.

'It *is* rather spectacular,' Robinton murmured.

'Then all three engines went off at the same time?' Fandarel asked.

'It would seem so,' Aivas replied in a tone which Robinton interpreted as demur.

'Well done, Aivas, well done.' Fandarel beamed, evidently not bothered by a tinge of disappointment. 'That junction was successful.'

'And efficient,' D'ram said, unable to resist the opportunity.

'It's odd, you know,' Piemur began, more to Jancis beside him than all those watching, 'you work your butt off to achieve an end, and suddenly you've done it! And all the excitement, frustration, sleepless nights and involvement are over! Gone!' He snapped his fingers, 'In one large and impressive fireball! So what do we do with all that extra time we have on our hands now?'

'You,' and Robinton pointed a stern finger at his journeyman, 'will now have the unenviable task as a harper of explaining the true facts of the achievement to those who didn't understand that this effort would not alter the path of Thread during the remainder of this Pass.'

To Lytol's surprise, Robinton had not been at all dismayed by Jaxom's report. The Harper had seemed to expect such disgruntlements.

'Menolly's already composed one ballad,' Robinton went on, 'with a chorus to hammer home the point that this is the Last Pass for Thread, that Pern will be for ever free from the end of this Pass.'

'A point!' Piemur said. 'Is that certain, Aivas?'

'That is now guaranteed, Piemur. You must realize, of course, that an immediate alteration of the Red Star's orbit will not be perceived,' Aivas said, 'for some decades.'

'Decades?' F'lar exclaimed, surprised.

'Naturally. If you consider the size of the object you were trying to move,' Fandarel said, 'and the scale of this solar system, there is no such thing as sudden change. Even chaos takes time to develop. But in several decades, that alteration will be measurable.'

'Rest assured of that, Weyrleader,' Aivas added in a tone so laden with certainty that F'lar's consternation eased.

'It's too bad Jaxom and Sharra didn't come,' Lessa said, slightly irritated by their absence. 'I knew that Ruth would strain himself, taking part in the second lift.'

'Jaxom is quite capable of making his own decisions now, my dear,' F'lar said, amused at her proprietary concern for the Ruathan Holder.

'There is one more minor adjustment to make, however,' Aivas said, 'which it is recommended to be undertaken by the lesser colours.'

'Oh? What?' Lessa and F'lar were very much aware that the brown, blue and green riders were somewhat aggrieved by their exclusion from the project. 'All the Weyrs of Pern' had been limited to most of the bronze dragons and only a few of the other colours, even if it had

466

been obvious that there wasn't space enough on the spars to accommodate every dragon who wished to take part – much less spacesuits to protect their riders in space.

'The matter of the *Buenos Aires* and the *Bahrain*.'

'What about them?' F'lar asked just as Fandarel emitted an 'ah' of comprehension.

'Readings on the orbits of the two smaller ships have shown a marked increase of frequency of adjustments. The adjustments take more and more power and the prognosis is that their orbits are likely to decay over the next decades to the critical point. The *Yokohama*, of course, has the fuel to remain in a stable orbit. It must also be maintained as long as possible since its telescope will be used to track the Red Star. But the other ships ought to be moved.'

'Moved?' F'lar asked. 'Where?'

'A slight alteration in their speed and altitude will send them harmlessly off into space.'

'Eventually to be captured by the sun's gravity and pulled into it,' Fandarel added.

'Burned up?' Lytol asked.

'A heroic end for such valiant ships,' Robinton murmured.

'You mentioned nothing of this before,' F'lar said.

'There were more urgent priorities,' Aivas replied. 'It is certainly a task that must be accomplished sooner rather than later when the orbits have decayed, and while the skills your riders have learned for the more essential task are still fresh in their minds.'

'It would certainly ease the tension in the Weyr,' Lessa said. 'We hadn't anticipated that.'

'What exactly does this entail, Aivas?' F'lar asked.

'As stated, the dragons are to alter the direction of the two ships and give a "push". There are many handholds on the exterior of the ships to give dragons a grip to transport the ship *between*, all moving at the same moment. From what you were able to accomplish in transferring the engines, such a manoeuvre is well within the scope of your smaller creatures.'

'You're no longer sceptical about them?' F'lar grinned at Aivas' capitulation on that count.

'In no way, Weyrleader.'

'What is the time frame on this?' Fandarel asked.

'Preferably within the next few weeks. There is no immediate danger but do not let the dragons and riders lose the edge.'

'I think that will be good news,' F'lar said, nodding acceptance.

'Then you will set a time for this manoeuvre?'

'As soon as I can discuss it with the other Weyrleaders.' Oddly enough, F'lar's spirits rose with the thought of another project. Flying Threadfall had become less exciting after the momentous event.

'It seems ungrateful to condemn those ships to death,' Lessa murmured.

'It's a crime to waste all the material,' Fandarel added.

'These ships were never designed for planetary landings, Master Fandarel.'

'In one piece, that is,' Piemur said.

'Yes, Piemur, the pieces could have lethal consequences if they entered the atmosphere and did not disintegrate entirely. Even so, a hot rain of metal fragments could occur and should be avoided.'

'I'll let you know,' F'lar said. 'Shall we go, Lessa?'

Watching the fireball soon lost its appeal for many on the *Yokohama* bridge that day. Shortly thereafter, when D'ram and the Eastern Weyr rider were ready to take the last watchers back to the Landing, Fandarel and Piemur cycled the life support systems down to the holding mode.

'I'm glad we're able to keep the *Yokohama*,' Piemur said. 'I've got rather fond of this old girl.' He let his fingers trail along the console.

'She has served long and well,' Robinton said, sighing deeply.

'Why don't you write a ballad about her, Piemur?' Jancis suggested.

'You know, I think I will!'

As the last one entering the lift, Piemur palmed off the bridge lights.

Jaxom heard about the second expedition from N'ton who

dropped in to Ruatha Hall two days after the Red Star explosion. N'ton had been on the *Buenos Aires* with half a dozen of his wingleaders.

'I feel an affinity to that little ship,' N'ton said, with a wry smile. 'I'll be sorry to see her go.'

'I wonder why she needs to,' Jaxom said, 'surely the solar panels . . .'

'Aivas said that there have been too many corrections and the panels can't handle them.'

'Hmm, that's quite possible.'

'He also recommended doing it while we're still accustomed to working in weightlessness. There is, I might add,' and his grin was broader, 'great rejoicing among the riders of browns, blues and greens. At that, they know that there are only two hundred and some suits available so they'll have to draw lots. But that's fair enough.'

'Let's hope the helmets are with the right suits, this time.'

'Oh we made sure of that,' N'ton said, rolling his eyes. 'What a mess that was! I tried on twenty helmets before I found one that would attach snugly to the collar. Then I had to get the wingleaders to check every rider to be sure all the bloody things fitted properly. Some riders were just cramming helmets on any old way.'

'The important thing is that everyone did get rigged out and we got where we were supposed to go.'

N'ton regarded him for such a long moment that Jaxom wondered if the Fort Weyrleader had somehow guessed what had happened. Considering his disoriented bronze riders, a man as intelligent as N'ton might extrapolate the truth. As long as Jaxom didn't admit it, N'ton would be kept guessing.

'Maybe that's what happened to those disoriented riders,' Jaxom went on as if the thought had just occurred to him. 'They did have badly fitting helmets and lost air.'

'I hadn't thought of that,' N'ton replied. 'You know, that would certainly explain a lot.'

Jaxom nodded in agreement, saying nothing more.

'F'lar's not best pleased to have to wait, yet again, to be sure that the blastings did the trick,' N'ton went on.

'Aivas was evidently satisfied.'

'Yes, but he always sounds certain.'

'Everything he's sounded certain about has worked just as he said. He's never prevaricated. I don't think an a.i. facility can.'

'You'd know better than I.' N'ton grinned at Jaxom over his wine glass. 'We certainly can't fault Hold and Hall for disbelief then if the Benden Weyrleader is still sceptical.'

'Again, Aivas has been right so often we have to trust him this time.' Jaxom had a whimsical desire to confide in N'ton that he knew, incontrovertibly, that Aivas's great plan had worked. At least as far as the orbit of the Red Star was concerned. That he had seen it with his own eyes – fifty Turns on.

'As he trusted our dragons?'

'Well, he did, in the end, didn't he?' Jaxom replied. 'No, N'ton, don't fret. It'll be as Aivas has predicted. You wait, you'll see.'

'Ah, but F'lar might not. And he's the one who wants to know for certain, or he will not have kept that promise!'

Maybe, Jaxom thought, he could just reassure F'lar.

I wouldn't, Ruth said. *You'd have to explain everything to him then.*

'*Not necessarily*,' Jaxom replied.

Ruth's silence indicated complete disagreement.

'So,' N'ton went on, 'now that we've solved the world's problems, what do you intend doing with all that spare time you've got?'

'What spare time, N'ton? I've only just scraped the surface of the information in Aivas's files. I'm in the process of organizing Hold affairs before I resume my studies . . . at an easier pace, now that the urgency is over.'

'We've Threadfall in two days. Are you and Ruth rested enough to join us?'

'I'd better, what with all these misconceptions about the end of Thread.'

'Indeed!' From that succinct but heartfelt comment, Jaxom knew that N'ton had been heavily criticized for letting Thread get through the Fort Weyr wings.

'I'll be there!'

*

'Master Robinton, it is good to see you,' Aivas said as the Harper entered.

'I've been meaning to come for the last week,' Robinton remarked with a droll smile. Even that short walk down the corridor took more breath than he had in his body.

'You are well?'

Robinton laughed softly and eased himself into the chair he had occupied for so many hours in the recent past. 'Can't fool you, can I?'

'No.'

Robinton sighed and stroked Zair, curled asleep on his shoulder. 'I did forgive them, then, you know,' he began slowly so his words wouldn't come out at the end of a gasp, 'at the trial. I'm not so sure now that I would.'

'The effects of inappropriate fellis administration?'

'Yes, I must assume so.'

'You have not consulted Master Oldive?' Aivas's tone was sharp.

Robinton waved one hand, dismissing the advice. 'He has enough to do, teaching his Healers all the new techniques he learned while doing your work. That will take him the rest of his life.'

'You must consult . . .'

'Why? You can produce no cures for worn-out human parts, can you, Aivas?' When there was silence, Robinton went on, still stroking Zair's soft body. 'Neither Zair nor I will recover from that abduction. Sometimes, I think he stays out of spite . . .'

'Or love of you, Master Robinton?'

The Harper had never heard that particular tone from Aivas.

'Quite likely, for they can be exceedingly loyal, these fire-lizards.'

Robinton had his breath back now, and being in this room brought back some of the excitement of those early discovery days. He felt at ease here, in the Aivas room, as he did not at Cove Hold, especially when Lytol and D'ram kept treating him like an invalid. Which, he had to admit, he was. He heard the chatter of students changing classes in the hall.

'The classes continue?' he asked, well pleased that they did.

'The classes continue,' Aivas said, using that soft almost rueful tone that had surprised the Harper before. 'The machines now harbour all the information this world will need to build a better future.'

'The future which you have given them.'

'The priorities for this facility have now been met.'

'That's true enough,' Robinton said, smiling.

'This facility now has no further function.'

'Don't be ridiculous, Aivas,' Robinton said somewhat sharply for the sentence had an ominous undertone. 'You've just got your students to the point where they know enough to argue with you . . .'

'And to resent the superiority of this facility. No, Master Robinton, the task is done. Now it is wise to let them seek their own way forward. They have the intelligence and a great spirit. Their ancestors can rightfully be proud of them.'

'Are you?'

'They have worked hard and well. That is in itself a reward and an end.'

'You know, I believe you're right.'

'To every thing there is a season, and a time to every purpose under the heaven, Master Robinton . . .'

'That is poetic, Aivas.'

There was one of those pauses that Robinton always thought was the Aivas equivalent of a smile.

'From the greatest book ever written by Mankind, Master Robinton. You may find the entire quotation in the files. The time has been accomplished. This system is going down. Farewell, Masterharper of Pern. Amen.'

Robinton sat straight up in his chair, fingers to the pressure plates, though how he could possibly avert what Aivas was about to do, he hadn't a single positive thought. He half turned to the hall, to call for help, but no-one who could, Jaxom, Piemur, Jancis, Fandarel, D'ram, or Lytol was near enough at hand.

The screen which had paraded so much knowledge, issued so many commands and diagrams and plans, was suddenly blank, lifeless. In the right-hand corner, a single line blinked.

'And a time to every purpose under the heaven,' Robinton murmured, his throat almost too tight for him to speak. He felt incredibly tired, overwhelmingly sleepy. 'Yes, how very true. How splendidly true. And what a wonderful time it has been!'

Unable to resist the lethargy that spread from his extremities, he laid his head down on the inactive pressure plate, one hand holding Zair in the curve of his neck, and closed his eyes, his long season over, his purpose, too, accomplished.

D'ram found them there, for Zair had breathed his last as well, following the Harper as selflessly as any dragon followed his rider into death.

Tiroth lifted his head, his keening alerting Landing, and indeed, broadcast to every Weyr, every dragon, and every rider on Pern, and throughout the Halls and Holds, from mountain to plain, from sea to sea on both continents.

D'ram was so tear-blinded that he did not notice the opacity of the screen, nor read the blinking message.

In Ruatha Hold, Ruth gave out a bellow of anguish that had everyone in the Great Hall rushing to the door.

The Harper! The Harper!

Jaxom didn't think. He grabbed Sharra by the hand and propelled her down the steps to where Ruth had reared, head back, wings extended.

'Jaxom!'

'The Harper! Something's happened to the Harper!'

She needed no more urging. They scrambled astride the white dragon.

'We need Oldive for this, Ruth. Take us first to the Healer Hall.'

As they emerged in the central court of the Hall, Ruth managed to avoid setting down on anyone. Oldive, jacket flapping from one hand, his medical case in the other, was limping down the stairs.

I told him! Ruth said.

Just then the Fort Hold dragons began to keen and swirling storms of fire-lizards, ululating in weird descant, flashed in and out of the court.

'What has happened to the Harper?' Oldive demanded, handing his case up to Sharra and struggling into his jacket. 'Neither of you has a jacket!'

'Don't worry about us,' Jaxom sat, leaning down to grab Oldive's arm and haul him up. '*Is it Landing? Or Cove Hold?*'

Landing!

'*Take us there! We must be in time!*'

Neither Jaxom or Sharra even noticed the dread chill of *between* in that anxious trip. Dragons were arriving from all directions so Ruth, ducking low, skimmed the tops of the houses and landed in front of the Aivas building, once again missing collisions with those on the ground rushing in response to the emergency.

It is too late! Ruth said, and folded his wings over his head.

'It can't be too late! Move aside, let us through. Let Oldive through!' Jaxom pushed people aside, one hand hauling the Masterhealer along beside him, the limping Oldive somehow keeping up with him. 'Make way here. Make way!'

At the doorway, he came to an abrupt stop. Piemur, Jancis, D'ram and Lytol stood around the chair, the Harper's silver-haired pate visible where it rested against the back. Choking back the sobs that threatened to overwhelm him, Jaxom slowly approached, moving to one side so that he could see. The Harper looked as if he were merely sleeping. Zair, grey with death, curled against his neck.

'He just . . . went . . . to . . . sleep,' Piemur said in a broken voice. 'He's not even warm anymore.'

'I thought he was just asleep,' D'ram said, 'the last time I looked in. I never thought . . .' Hand to his face, he turned away.

'AIVAS!' Jaxom roared. 'Aivas, why didn't you call someone? You must have been aware . . .'

'Look,' Sharra said, touching his arm and then pointing to the screen, and the blinking message.

'"And a time for every purpose under the heaven?" What is that supposed to mean, Aivas? Aivas!'

Only then did Jaxom realize the difference in the screen, as lifeless as it had been the first time he had entered this room. 'AIVAS?'

He pressed a restore sequence. Then, cursing at fingers that fumbled, he tried other codes with no response.

'Piemur? Jancis? What do we do?'

Sharra grabbed his trembling hands and held them, her tearing eyes bright with the knowledge he could not accept.

'Aivas has gone, too,' she said, her voice rough. 'See the smile on Master Robinton's face? Just as you and I have seen him smile so many times. The message was for him as it is there for us.'

'We'll go back, we'll go back to when he was still alive . . .' Jaxom began, reaching for Master Oldive, heading towards the door. If he and Ruth could time it . . . F'lar and Lessa stood in the doorway. He didn't care if they knew he meant to time it.

Oldive grabbed his arm, shaking his head, his eyes blurred with tears. 'We could do nothing for him, Jaxom. "A time for every purpose under the heaven," Jaxom. And it was time for the Harper.'

'He wouldn't let us tell anyone,' Sharra said to Jaxom, 'how serious his condition was.'

'It was only a matter of time,' Oldive murmured, peering up at him, his long face grooved with sorrow. 'His heart was badly strained by the abduction. This was a kind ending, Jaxom, no matter how abrupt and unexpected.'

'I know Robinton wasn't well,' Jaxom went on, shaking his head, tears coursing down his cheeks. 'But I don't understand about Aivas, too.'

'He tells us plainly enough,' D'ram said, having recovered his composure. He pointed to the message. 'He has served his purpose in helping us destroy Thread. You will come to realize just how wise Aivas was in this. We were beginning to count on him too heavily.'

'Machines can't die!' Jaxom chewed the words out resentfully.

'The knowledge he gave us will not,' F'lar said and stood aside to let Menolly and Sebell enter the room. 'Now let us all honour Masterharper Robinton.'

The day was inappropriately beautiful when the Masterharper, wrapped in a harper-blue shroud, was laid to rest in the beautiful blue-green waters of Cove Hold which he had come to love. Master Idarolan had dispatched his fastest ship and came a-dragonback to captain it himself. Master Alemi with his sloop from Paradise River and the small ketches who fished in Monaco Bay assembled to accommodate the many people who would escort Master Robinton to his resting place.

All the Weyrs of Pern hovered in the sky, and fire-lizards made sad swirls around them as the ship sailed out of Cove Hold. Lords Holder and Craftmasters lined the decks amid harpers of every degree.

Sebell and Menolly sang all the songs that had made the Masterharper so beloved by everyone, Menolly remembering the day that she had sung farewell to his father, Petiron, the day that had begun the major change in her own life.

And as the ship moved into the current, scores of shipfish led the way, slipping, diving, gliding, weaving among the ships' bow waves.

When his body was consigned to the sea, the dragons bugled one last note for Masterharper Robinton.

Jaxom, aloft on Ruth, watched the ripples spread and then meld into the waves. After a bitter night, he had come to terms with his grief for Master Robinton and his wild notion that he and Ruth could or should have forestalled that peaceful death.

But he could find no surcease yet for the bitter blow of losing Aivas. He felt that he had been abandoned just when he had the most grievous need of Aivas's wisdom and support. Had he not done everything Aivas wished? Put himself and Ruth in danger to fulfil those bleeding priorities of the ungrateful machine?

I understand your grief, Jaxom, Ruth said quietly, his head, like that of every other dragon, watching the scene below as the ships tacked about for their return to Cove Hold. *Why do you harbour such anger and resentment?*

'He left us, and with Master Robinton gone, we need him now more than ever.'

Not we, you. But that is the wrong way to think about this. Aivas left behind all the information you need – and you have only to access it to solve problems now.

For the first time in their long association, Jaxom resented Ruth's words.

Probably, Ruth said at his drollest, *you know I'm right. I think that Aivas was as tired as the Harper, having waited all those long Turns to complete his tasks and keep faith with his makers.*

Though Jaxom fought against the idea, the words of Aivas' last message reverberated in his head. How much Robinton had enjoyed Aivas! Had Aivas ended his existence before, or after, Master Robinton had fallen into his last sleep? Surely if Aivas had been aware of Robinton's condition, he would have summoned help? Those options had exercised everyone yesterday. But everyone had agreed with D'ram that Aivas had achieved those ancient priorities. With great honour.

Then give Aivas the honour that is due him, Jaxom. Anger and resentment cloud your mind and heart.

Jaxom sighed, accepting the gentle reproach of his white dragon.

'I haven't been thinking straight, have I?'

Think of what we have done together, you and I, to show Aivas that we could. We did the impossible because I knew where and when to do it. It's as well you cracked my shell that Hatching Day, Jaxom, or where would Pern be now?

Laughter burst from Jaxom, provoked by the dragon's sly cajolery. But draconic logic lifted him out of his depression.

'And a time for every purpose under the heaven!' he cried into the air about them. What Ruth said was true: only he, Jaxom, Lord of Ruatha Hold, and Ruth, the white dragon, could have done what had to be done to free Pern for ever from Thread, serving their world as only dragon and rider could, united in mind and heart to their purpose.

Jaxom and Ruth turned back to Cove Hold, ready to delve into the legacy of knowledge which Aivas had left for them.

THE END

THE ROWAN
BY ANNE MCCAFFREY

The Talents were the élite of the Nine Star League. Their gifts were many and varied, ranging from the gently telepathic, to the rare and extremely valued Primes. On the Primes rested the entire economic wealth and communications systems of the civilised worlds. But Primes were scarce – only very rarely was a new one born.

And now, on the planet Altair, in a small mining colony on the western mountain range, a new Prime existed, a three-year-old girl – trapped in a giant mud slide that had wiped out the rest of the Rowan mining community. Every Altarian who was even mildly talented could 'hear' the child crying for help, but no one knew exactly where she was buried.

Every resource on the planet was centred into finding 'The Rowan' – the new Prime, the first ever to be born on Altair, an exceptionally unique Prime, more talented, more powerful, more agoraphobic, more lonely, than any other Prime yet known in the Nine Star League.

The Rowan – a new concept, a new legend, from the creator of the Dragons of Pern.

0 552 13763 4

OTHER TITLES BY ANNE McCAFFREY
AVAILABLE FROM CORGI BOOKS

THE PRICES SHOWN BELOW WERE CORRECT AT THE TIME OF GOING
TO PRESS. HOWEVER TRANSWORLD PUBLISHERS RESERVE THE
RIGHT TO SHOW NEW RETAIL PRICES ON COVERS WHICH MAY
DIFFER FROM THOSE PREVIOUSLY ADVERTISED IN THE TEXT OR
ELSEWHERE.

☐	08453 0	**Dragonflight**	£3.99
☐	10661 5	**Dragonsong**	£3.99
☐	11635 1	**Dragonquest**	£3.99
☐	10881 2	**Dragonsinger: Harper of Pern**	£3.99
☐	11313 1	**The White Dragon**	£4.99
☐	11804 4	**Dragondrums**	£3.99
☐	12499 0	**Moreta: Dragonlady of Pern**	£4.99
☐	12817 1	**Nerilka's Story & The Coelura**	£3.99
☐	13098 2	**Dragonsdawn**	£4.99
☐	13099 0	**Renegades of Pern**	£3.99
☐	08344 5	**Restoree**	£3.99
☐	13728 6	**Pegasus in Flight**	£3.99
☐	09115 4	**The Ship Who Sang**	£3.99
☐	12497 4	**Stitch in Snow**	£1.75
☐	08661 4	**Decision at Doona**	£3.99
☐	10965 7	**Get Off the Unicorn**	£4.99
☐	12097 9	**The Crystal Singer**	£3.99
☐	12556 3	**Killashandra**	£4.99
☐	13763 4	**The Rowan**	£3.99
☐	13729 4	**All the Weyrs of Pern**	£4.99

All Corgi/Bantam Books are available at your bookshop or newsagent, or can be
ordered from the following address:
Corgi/Bantam Books,
Cash Sales Department,
P.O. Box 11, Falmouth, Cornwall TR10 9EN

UK and B.F.P.O. customers please send a cheque or postal order (no currency)
and allow £1.00 for postage and packing for the first book plus 50p for the
second book and 30p for each additional book to a maximum charge of £3.00 (7
books plus).

Overseas customers, including Eire, please allow £2.00 for postage and packing
for the first book plus £1.00 for the second book and 50p for each subsequent
title ordered.

NAME (Block Letters) ....

ADDRESS ....

....